FURY

of

FIRE

Text copyright ©2011 Coreene Callahan
Printed in the United States of America

Published by Montlake Romance
P.O. Box 400818
Las Vegas, NV 89140

ISBN-13: 9781612182728
ISBN-10: 1612182720

FURY
of
FIRE

COREENE CALLAHAN

Montlake
Romance

For my fearless front man, Alain.
This one's for you, babe.

Acknowledgements:

Every once in a while, I get something right. Coming back to writing was one of those things. Thanks Mom and Dad for believing, supporting, and cheering me on. And to both my brothers (and their wicked computer skills) for being the great guys you are, and answering every question I throw your way.

Thanks to Alain, the man who makes all things better simply by being, and my beautiful girls, the Triple As. You light up my life every day.

Special thanks to Kallie Lane—friend, fellow writer, and critique partner. Your awesomeness knows no bounds.

To Christine Whitthohn, literary agent extraordinaire, all-around amazing person, and teammate. Your generosity and wisdom blows me away. I could never have done it without you. You are, quite simply, the best!

Thanks to my fabulous editor, Eleni Caminis, for taking a chance on me and believing in this book as much as I do. And to the entire team at Amazon Publishing, whose hard work and dedication is nothing short of inspiring.

To Steve Wiebe and Joanna Scott—without whom I would be lost under a mountain of medical information. As always, thank you. You saved my skin on this one!

Last but not least, thanks to the BC Babes, who make me laugh every day and teach me bucketfuls along the way. To Lucy, Debbie, the MTL gang, and ORWA, thank you for your unfailing support and encouragement.

I raise a glass to all of you.

Chapter One

The flash of strobe lights struck with the force of a hammer. Bastian squinted against the glare and scanned the dance floor, taking in the exposed skin and barely there skirts writhing to the rhythm of hard-core techno. His practiced eye picked up all kinds of trace, the faint glow of female energy swirling in dark corners. He downed another shot of Blue Label.

The whiskey went down smooth. His mood headed in the other direction.

"Anything?" Rikar slid into the booth across from him.

"Did you expect there to be?" He glanced at his friend, registering the shimmer in Rikar's pale eyes. The iridescent glow meant one thing. His friend had fed, taken his ease in an obscure corner of the club with a willing human female. No surprise there. Dragonkind appealed to women, and his first in command never wanted for company.

Rikar palmed his microbrew and took a pull from the bottle. "Pick one and be done with it, for fuck's sake."

If only it were that simple. In the quiet of their lair, his decision—and the rationale behind it—had made perfect sense. Now, surrounded by thumping bass and the swell of perfumed female flesh, Bastian wondered what had possessed him. It wasn't that he didn't want a woman. Hell, he enjoyed them as much or more than his brothers-in-arms

1

did, but the thought of taking one to mate made his blood run cold. "I still have time."

His friend threw him an amused look. "You've less than a week."

"Lay off, Rikar."

"Hey, it's your crazy-ass plan, not mine."

Yeah, crazy. That pretty much summed it up. But it didn't matter. His hands were tied. The war had gone on for so long that Bastian had lost count of the casualties. Centuries of fallen comrades, of hunting and being hunted. It would never stop. A clean victory was an impossibility for either side now. With only a handful of warrior dragons left, little choice remained but to replenish their numbers…and that meant breeding the next generation.

The idea sat like a stone in his stomach. He wanted a mate like another hole in his head, but he must lead by example: be the first to commit, to have a son, to lose his female in childbirth.

Bastian swirled the ice in his glass. Christ. He didn't even know what she looked like and yet, he mourned her. Already felt sorry for the life he would take. It wasn't murder. Not really. He would never willingly hurt a woman, but that didn't change what he must do. To save his kind he must breed, and females never survived birthing Dragonkind.

"You take too much on yourself, B. Dragonkind is healthy enough." Glacial eyes flicked over the scene before returning to him. Bastian read the censure in his friend's gaze as well as the truth. Rikar knew, just as he did, there was no other way. "You should feed. It'll improve your mood."

No doubt, but the suggestion left a bad taste in Bastian's mouth. He only indulged when forced by hunger and desperate need. Foolish, maybe, but despite his nature he disliked taking what didn't belong to him. Women deserved better than to be used and have their memories wiped. Besides, the low-level energy in the club wasn't enough. One of the oldest of his kind, he required a female capable of drawing pure power from the Meridian to feed him.

The electrostatic current nurtured Dragonkind, an all-male race born of human females. Without the energy exchange, his kind would starve to death. And the only way to draw from the source was to get close to a female. So close that bodies clashed and skin met skin. Not that any ever complained. Begged for the pleasure he gave? Always. Never once in all his years had one objected. Even now, the women closest to him watched, waiting for the slightest encouragement.

Normally, he took what they offered, but not tonight.

Tonight was about leadership. About showing the warriors under his command that sacrifices needed to be made for the greater good of the race.

Bastian scanned the club again. Dancers were getting animated, pairing off in twos and threes, female skirts rising, male hands roaming whatever real estate they could reach. Tipping his head back, he swallowed the last of his Blue Label and found the waitress in the crowd. A redhead, pretty enough, but too Goth for him. He liked his females fresh-faced, without the layers of makeup the women in clubs always favored.

He issued a mental command anyway.

Her kohl-lined eyes blinked once before she spun on spiked heels and headed for the bar. He cleared a path, tapping into the collective psyche, warning the crowd out of her way. They parted like the Red Sea, opening a wide swath as she approached the stainless steel counter and high-backed stools. In under a minute, she returned, fingers curled around the neck of a bottle, hips swaying in a low-slung micromini.

Crystal clinked as she set a matched pair of VIP tumblers in front of them. "Want me to pour?"

Her voice was little more than a sensual purr, a hum of invitation a human male would never have heard over the throb of bass pounding through the club. But Bastian was only half-human. Like all of his kind, his senses were keen, alive with the hunt, eager for the chase. He considered her a moment. She had adequate energy, better than most. It wasn't enough to truly feed him, but enough to take the edge off his appetite. The beginnings of hunger gnawed at the pit of his stomach.

"I'm on break in five." She leaned toward him, flashing cleavage as she placed the bottle of whiskey on the tabletop. "Meet me out back?"

Wild heat and sexual inexperience rolled in her scent. The fragrance was one of youth, beautiful in its own way, but she didn't appeal to him. He'd lived too long to be interested in the unproven. "Another time."

Rouged lips pursed into a pout. "You sure?"

"I'm good," he said, releasing a soothing spell to soften his rejection. "Leave the bottle and go."

With a sigh, she retreated, turning her attention to customers at the next table.

"Can't do it, can you?"

Bastian's eyes narrowed on his friend. "The Meridian won't realign—"

"For another five days. Yeah, I know, but a female with the kind of energy you need isn't going to be a pushover. She won't fall into bed with you...not like these ones." Rikar tipped the mouth of his bottle toward the dance floor, pointing to the women. "You're going to need every second you can get to seduce her."

Fuck. Like he needed the reminder.

Bastian grabbed his friend Johnnie Walker by the neck, wishing it was Rikar's instead. He needed some air, had to get out of the heat and the noise and the smell of the club before he exploded. "I'm going rooftop."

"Suit yourself."

He always did.

Without a backward glance, JW in hand, Bastian headed for the red glow of the exit sign to the right of the bar. His long leather trench fanned out behind him, an unnecessary addition to his already unusual size. The human males recognized him for the predator he was and shied away, giving him a wide berth. Just as well. He was in the mood for a fight and, given his proclivities, a little encouragement in the wrong direction would send his fists flying.

Halfway to his destination, a shimmer of sensation ghosted over the back of his neck. His stride slowed to a stop as he looked over his shoulder. Rikar was already on his feet, moving toward him, microbrew left wobbling on the tabletop.

"*Bastian.*" The voice whispered through his mind, through the mental link he shared with all the warriors who fought by his side—the cosmic equivalent of a cell phone for his kind.

He completed the link, his gaze trained on Rikar's. *"Sloan, what's up?"*

"*Shit loads.*" Even through mind-speak, he heard the fast click of computer keys. Sloan, their resident cyber cop, was never far from the system. Some nights, Bastian suspected he slept in front of the bank of monitors. *"Haul your ass outta there. The female's out of pocket and in trouble."*

"Shit. Lay it out."

"A nine-one-one call. The ambulance is rolling...headed for Route Eighteen."

"ETA?" He set the whiskey on a table as he passed.

"Thirty minutes."

"We're on it."

Bastian was out the back door and up the first flight of stairs before the last word left his mouth. He took the treads three at a time, cold resolve settling like ice in his veins. The steel door blew off its hinges an instant before he strode over the threshold and onto the rooftop.

Gravel crunching beneath his metal-tipped boots, he took a deep breath. Crisp autumn air and the scent of newly turned leaves registered an instant before he leapt skyward. Shifting without thought, he transformed; skin turning to blue-black scales, hands and feet to claws, wings extended in full flight. Cloaked by magic, hidden from human eyes, he banked east, soaring over skyscrapers and Seattle suburbs until civilization turned to forest.

Slashing through wispy clouds and cool mountain air, he settled into a fast glide over Route 18. The blacktop rolled between hills and around S-curves, winding its way through ancient white pines and Western red cedar. Red lights flashed in the distance. Twin beamed headlights ate through the gloom, reaching forward only to be swallowed up from behind as the ambulance sped ahead.

A firm fix on their target, he mind-spoke to Rikar. *"Get in front. Slow them to a stop."*

Rikar came out of the cloud cover on a slow roll, rising like a wreath of mist in the darkness. Almost pure white, his friend was a rarity among their kind; a frost dragon that not only preferred the brutal cold of his arctic home, but could also command the weather at will. *I'll ice 'em up. You got the driver?*

"*Yeah. Go, ice cube.*"

"*Fuck off, fire breath.*"

With a grin, Bastian banked left, sailing in over the treetops. The long glide put him even with the ambulance's back end as Rikar dipped low. Directly above the speeding vehicle now, emergency lights clashed with white scales, bathing his first in command in bursts of red flash. Rikar inhaled hard and exhaled smooth. Twin tendrils rose from his nostrils as frost rolled out in front of him and hit the blacktop, leaving a wide track of thick ice on the asphalt. The humans inside the vehicle cursed as they lost visibility. The ambulance swerved and the driver over-corrected into a fifty-mile-an-hour, three-hundred-and-sixty-degree spin.

Another full revolution. More yelling from inside the ambulance cockpit.

Bastian landed on the shoulder of the road. Claws spread, gravel flying, he slid sideways into the middle of the highway. His razor-sharp talons bit into the tarmac. Friction burned the pads of his paws as he raised his horned head and waited for the out-of-control ambulance to reach him. The hood swung around, headlights painting the trees in amber-white glow. He saw horror flash across the EMTs' faces—put there by the wild spin or the sight him, he didn't know. A second before the grill smashed into him, he grabbed the front end and stopped it mid-slide.

Metal groaned and the back tires bounced, giving the human males another jolt.

"Show-off," Rikar said, tone filled with disgust as he touched down on the passenger side.

He raised a brow. "Jealous?"

"Christ." With an exaggerated eye roll, his friend shifted to human form.

Bastian tucked his wings and, unable to resist, snarled at the idiots gawking at his dragon form in open-mouthed astonishment. Both had probably wet their pants and still, they sat there, glued to the seats. He snorted. So much for the critically acclaimed intelligence of human males.

Self-preservation finally kicked in, and the men screamed, scrambling to unclip their seatbelts. Following Rikar's example, Bastian shifted, conjuring his clothes as he stepped around the curved front of the bumper. As his shit-kickers settled on his feet, he drew even with the driver's side window. Brown eyes the size of shot glasses met his own an instant before he yanked the door open. Burying his hand in the EMT's shirtfront, Bastian dragged him out and held him high, boots dangling a good foot off the ground. Incoherent with fear, the male babbled, chin trembling, knees knocking, arms hanging limp at his sides.

Bastian took pity and, delving deep into the man's mind, seized control, calming him while he wiped his memory clean. As the paramedic quieted, Bastian studied his clothes, picking out the details he needed to replicate when they reached the house and the female who called it home. Arriving in leather wasn't a good idea. He wanted her moving and cooperative, not terrified.

Finishing his inspection, Bastian set the man down and told him to start walking. A gas station sat no more than a mile away. The EMTs would make it that far, though they would have no recollection of how they'd lost their ride.

With one last look at the two men ambling down the shoulder of the road, he turned to the ambulance. Rikar was already sitting inside, playing with the knobs on the radio.

The sound of static filled the air, and his friend threw him a worried look. The crackle told him all he needed to know. The equipment was reacting to the electrical charge in the air. More Dragonkind were headed their way, none of them friendlies.

Hopping into the cab, Bastian slammed the door behind him, wishing he didn't need the ambulance. Flying would be better—faster—than driving. But carrying a pregnant female in his talons wasn't a good idea. He might squeeze too hard, hurt her or the baby.

With a curse, he threw the vehicle into gear and stomped on the gas pedal. The engine roared and the back tires spun, burning through ice to grip asphalt, rocketing them down the deserted highway.

He must reach the female first. Before the enemy tore her apart and stole the precious life she carried.

Chapter Two

Myst Munroe was so tired her left leg could have fallen off and she wouldn't have noticed. All right, so maybe not a leg, but really, the fourteen-hour days were getting ridiculous. Clichéd in a nasty sort of way. Long hours were part of the job, what she'd signed on for when she'd become a nurse practitioner. But the neat little letters after her name at the bottom of her business card read "DNP," not "slave."

Though, come to think of it, she might have to check. The last batch of black and white cards had only arrived yesterday.

In a small cardboard box: no embossing, no fancy lettering, nothing exciting.

Just like her life.

Not that she was complaining. She got to help people every day, and there wasn't much more fulfilling than that. But some mornings she wished for something beyond 5 a.m. wake-up calls. Like cuddling and kisses and the warm male body required for both.

Myst popped the latch on her hatchback, wondering what she'd been drinking when she scheduled house calls two straight days in a row. Something strong, with high alcohol content...doubles, maybe, with colorful little umbrellas in them. Yeah, definitely plural, as in many over the course of a very few hours.

One of those fruity concoctions would taste good right about now. She settled for coffee instead, taking a sip from her oversized travel mug. A nutty favor spiked with cream coasted down her throat as she stared into her trunk. The dome light cast a yellowy glow over boxes filled with medical supplies. She frowned at them, trying to get her brain to work.

What did she need again?

She rubbed the grit from her eyes. "Oh, yeah, extra gloves."

Taking another sip of her café au lait, she rattled off the rest of the list in her head. Her medical bag needed restocking in a bad way. Two days on the road, visiting patients had taken its toll on the duffle's tidy interior. Myst set her mug down on the only available patch of trunk floor uncluttered by the jumbled assortment of what constituted her office when she wasn't working out of Seattle Medical Center. Flipping cardboard box tops, she grabbed what she needed, tucking supplies into compartmentalized sections and nifty pockets, pausing now and then to nurse her addiction... caffeine.

Some might not have enjoyed living out of their trunks. Myst didn't mind. No matter how exhausting, she enjoyed her home visits, liked driving the rural routes.

Washington State was more than scenic. It was beautiful, with its mountains, Douglas fir forests, and panoramic ocean views. She loved the coast best, though: the rugged cliffs and sandy beaches and fresh salty smell. Something about it called to her, made her yearn for something more. Maybe it was the wildness, the unpredictability and unbridled strength of nature's force...and the possibilities inherent in it.

Then again, maybe it wasn't any of those things. Maybe the restlessness her hippie mother had always accused her of was finally catching up.

Heaving the duffle, Myst slammed the hatchback closed. She didn't want to think about her mom. The pain of losing her was still too much. She missed the long bohemian skirts, bead-strung doorways, and tarot card readings. The smell of jasmine incense, homemade cookies, and...

God, she needed to get moving.

Night had arrived, bringing with it the kind of darkness never seen in the city. The skyscape was absolute, nothing to disturb the wispy clouds as they swirled beneath a blanket of pinpoint stars. The lights from Sal's highway restaurant, fluorescents flickering in protest behind the S, barely touched the gloom.

With a shiver, she tossed the bag onto the passenger seat. Just as she slammed her door closed, her cell phone rang, Mariah Carey's "Touch My Body" rolling with the beat of her heart. Myst sighed. If only.

She glanced at the caller ID, flipped the phone open and said, "I think my brain is hemorrhaging."

"That bad, huh?" Her best friend's laugh came over the line. "Headed home?"

"One more stop."

"Jeez, Myst, it's almost nine o'clock. Can you say workaholic?"

"Right...and where are you calling from?"

"Okay, busted," Tania said, an eye roll in her voice. "Big contract, you know. Gotta get the specs in."

"What does your boss do again?" she asked, knowing her friend's job was as heavy as hers was. A landscape architect, Tania was working her way up from the bottom of the totem pole, putting in long hours, hoping to impress the suits and ties to land that elusive promotion.

"This is my baby. I'm on point."

"Good luck with that. Woolsey is going to stick his nose in for sure."

"Got him handled," Tania paused, her worry echoing all the way from Seattle. "You're going to try again, aren't you?"

Myst bit her bottom lip, wondering how much to tell her friend. She appreciated the concern—she really did—but Tania was a worrywart. She'd stay up all night, agonizing over the fact that Myst's late-night mission might land her in trouble.

Silence swelled on the line.

Tania sighed. The sound was like the ocean tide, sucking at Myst's will to resist. "You shouldn't be out there alone."

"I can't let it go, T. She's missed three appointments. Something's wrong."

"What if he comes back?"

"All the more reason to go…Caroline can't hold her own against that guy." Just thinking about it made her mad. The abusive jerk. Okay, so he'd never actually hit her patient, but she'd heard him talk to her—belittle her—and it wasn't pretty.

"You've got the local cops on speed dial, right?"

"The paramedics, too."

"Crap, I hate it when you do this," her friend said, anxiety making her tone short.

Myst didn't answer. What could she say? That she would turn around and come home? That Tania's worry was more important than a patient in trouble?

"God, I'm sorry. You know I'm a worrier and—"

"A pain in the butt," Myst said, tone teasing to lighten the mood.

"Right back at ya, hotshot." Tania huffed, the beginnings of laughter coming through the line. "Okay, look, call me when you get out of there. And take care of you."

"I will...promise." Myst hit the end button and threw her car into gear.

As she drove out of Sal's lot, headlights shining on the blacktop, her mind stayed on Caroline Van Owen. Eighteen and pregnant. Man, the girl didn't stand a chance. Not with a less-than-average education and an unsupportive partner. Myst saw so many like that. It broke her heart every time.

Her colleagues would say it was none of her business, that she should do her job and stay out of the personal stuff. But no matter how hard she tried, she took it personally when one of her own got hurt. Stupid, maybe, but her clients were more than just patients. They were people she cared about. She'd sat in their kitchens, shared coffee over croissants, listened and talked and advised about more than just their medical concerns.

The hospital liked to think she provided a service. And she did, for the most part. But what had started out as a way to keep foot traffic in the facility down and the administration's bottom line trimmer had become so much more.

Way more than she ever expected.

She pulled into the Van Owens' driveway. More road than entrance, the long lane twisted through huge red cedars and white pines. Tufts of grass grew in the middle, snaking between the rutted tire tracks. As her headlights swung around the last bend, she leaned over the steering wheel and peered ahead. She breathed a sigh of relief even as apprehension knotted her stomach.

Someone was home. The kitchen light was on.

The question now? Was it the jerk? Or Caroline?

Myst hoped it was the latter. She needed to see the girl for herself. To make sure everything was okay and get her back on track. Eight months along and dancing with gestational diabetes, Caroline couldn't afford to fool around. She'd missed her recent blood tests, and her last one hadn't come out clean.

The anomaly with her blood platelets wasn't one Myst had seen before. The lab was working on it, but so far, the techies didn't have a clue.

Parking next to an old tractor with flat tires, she tossed her keys into the cup holder and, grabbing her bag, headed for the front porch. The old Cape Cod looked strange sitting in the middle of a West Coast forest: faded yellow paint peeling, eaves sagging, sad-looking couch on display beneath the glow of lights on either side of the scarred cedar door.

Duffle bag bumping against the side of her leg, she climbed the crooked porch steps and knocked on the cedar panel. She waited a minute, ears tuned and listening hard.

Nothing. No squeak of wood floors. Not a glimmer of movement from inside.

Myst rapped harder, the contact making her knuckles ache as she peered through one of the narrow windows flanking the door. Unobstructed by curtains, the view gave her a straight shot down the corridor into the kitchen. On the floor, flowing out from behind the island, a dark pool spilled over light tile.

Her heart jumped like a jackrabbit.

From this distance, she couldn't be sure, but...

"Goddamn it." Myst dropped her bag and yanked her phone out of her jacket pocket. She dialed nine-one-one and banged on the door with the heel of her hand. "Caroline!"

No answer.

She twisted the door handle. Locked.

"Shit."

Scanning the porch, she looked for something heavy. She needed to get in there. Maybe the dark stain was spaghetti sauce. Maybe she was losing her ever-loving mind. But she didn't think so. She'd had a bad feeling all day... one of the those ride-your-ass-and-won't-let-you-go kind of things.

A spade-shaped shovel caught her eye. Running past the ratty couch, she grabbed hold of the wooden shaft, jerking the tool away from its lean against the wall. The phone still ringing in her ear, she returned to the front door. Turning her face away, she wound up with one arm and set metal to glass. The window exploded inward, shooting shards into the entryway.

Not wasting a second, she reached through the opening and flipped the deadbolt. An instant later, she was through the door with her bag, sprinting down the hallway and into the kitchen.

"Nine-one-one. What's your emergency?"

"Oh, God."

"Ma'am?"

Myst stood frozen, phone to her ear, paralyzing shock pumping through her veins. Caroline lay sprawled on the floor between the island and the sink in a pool of her own blood. The horror of it registered, sent her spinning back to another scene. One in which her mother lay instead.

"Ma'am? Ma'am?" The voice broke through, firm tone commanding her attention. "Talk to me. Tell me what's going on."

Her medical training kicked in. "Myst Munroe, DNP out of Seattle. Send an ambulance. I've got a pregnant woman down. Eight months along. She's...God, there's so much blood."

She snapped on her gloves and, shoes sliding, waded into the bloodbath. Needing both hands free, she hit speakerphone and tossed the phone onto a clean patch of tile.

"Where are you?"

Checking the girl's vitals, she rattled off the address.

"Get here. Get here fast. She's nonresponsive."

"Myst, stay on the line with me. I'm connecting to dispatch."

It wasn't going to be fast enough. The EMTs wouldn't reach them in time. Caroline was bleeding from the inside out. And an internal bleed was nothing she could stop, not without an operating room and a damned good surgeon.

Myst dragged her bag over. She must find a way to—

Caroline grabbed hold of her wrist. Her dark eyelashes flickered against her pale cheeks.

"Caroline, honey. Stay with me." Two fingertips pressed to the girl's carotid, Myst checked her pupils for dilation and counted off the seconds. "Stay with me. Come on, darling. Help is on the way."

Her lips moved. No sound came out. She tried again and whispered, "Save him."

"Who, honey?"

"My baby," she breathed, more wheeze than words. "Save...my baby."

"I will. I promise. The ambulance is coming. We'll get you to the hospital."

A lie. Point-blank and terrible.

Myst felt it like a knife to the chest. Neither one of them was going to make it out of the situation unscathed. She swallowed the tears working their way up the back of her throat. God, if only she'd insisted Caroline see her. If only she'd come sooner. She could've skipped supper, could've driven faster, could've—

"Myst?" The nine-one-one responder came back on the line. "An ambulance is rolling to you. ETA thirty minutes."

Caroline's pulse fluttered as her breath slowed to a rattle inside her chest.

"That's too long."

"Hang in there. Help's coming."

Static interrupting her words, the woman kept talking. Myst stopped listening, grim reality hitting her hard as Caroline flatlined. She started CPR, blowing air into the girl's lungs between palm presses to her chest. But it was no use. The girl she'd tried so hard to help was gone.

Save my baby.

The whispered words rolled through her head. An urgent plea from a dying mother.

Bile trapped in the back of her throat, heart pumping like a freight train, Myst ransacked her bag. She came away with a fetal heart rate monitor. The handheld unit clicked on with a twist of a button. Wrenching the cotton shirt out of her way, she squirted ultrasound gel onto the skin, set the wand to Caroline's rounded stomach and searched, rolling right then left.

A faint thump came through the speaker.

Her hands shook as she tossed the monitor aside and reached back into her bag. She must have something sharp. Anything that might...

Goddamn it! She didn't carry scalpels. Had never needed any.

Lunging toward the island, she wrenched open the nearest drawer. Nothing but butter knives. She pulled open the next. Black-handled carving blades, some narrow, some thick, stared back at her. Steel clanged against steel as Myst grabbed a fillet knife and turned back to Caroline.

There was no choice. She could do it. Obstetrics was her specialty. She'd assisted in more C-sections than she could count. It didn't matter that she could lose her job and go to jail. The baby mattered more than all that.

"Dear God in heaven, forgive me," she whispered, losing a piece of her soul as she put blade to flesh and made the incision.

———

The smell of fresh blood propelled Bastian up the porch steps and through the open door. Broken glass crunched beneath the soles of his boots as he crossed over the threshold into the small house.

He was too late.

The Razorbacks, the rogue band of dragons that hated humankind and their dependence on females, had beaten him to the mother and child. He didn't care that the infant had been sired by one of them. None of the bastards deserved to be fathers. To leave the female defenseless and alone— without any understanding of what was to come—then take the baby a month early? Christ, it was beyond unthinkable.

The enormity of his failure hit him like a body shot.

He should have come sooner. Two days ago when the results of her blood work popped up on Sloan's system. Tentacles deeply embedded in human databases, his comrade could find anything, from medical records to homicide reports.

Fuck. It was Bastian's fault.

Not her death—that had been inevitable the moment one of his kind impregnated her—but the manner of it.

The violence in it. The needless suffering. Had he done his duty, the female would have been comfortable in the end.

With grim resolve, Bastian followed the scent of death down the narrow corridor. He inhaled deep and listened hard, sifting to find any trace of the enemy's trail. He would honor the woman and then hunt the rogues down; take the child back before he became polluted by hatred. The last thing he and his warriors needed was another soldier in the Razorbacks' ranks.

He spotted the blood pool on the tile floor from the kitchen doorway and—

"I'm so sorry...so sorry," a female said, an agonized hitch in her voice. "Look how beautiful he is, Caro. All ten fingers and toes. Look how beautiful."

The sound of an infant's cry answered her, rising from behind the island.

Sucking in a quick breath, Bastian stepped around the edge of the gold-flecked countertop. He stopped cold, boots rooted to the floor, gaze riveted to the light-haired female. Pale green hospital scrubs covered in blood, she sat in devastation, a dead body next to her, a small, coat-wrapped bundle in her arms. Medical supplies lay scattered around her, the black bag by her side overflowing with gauze, rubber gloves, and plastic-wrapped packages. But it was the butcher knife that made him ache for her.

She'd saved the baby, knowing she couldn't save the mother. Remarkable. She was undeniably remarkable. A female with the heart of a warrior.

Bastian swallowed past the lump in his throat and ditched his leathers, conjuring an EMT's uniform. As a nurse, she would respond better to a paramedic, someone of common skill and experience. He didn't want her to freak out, but time wasn't on his side. The Razorbacks would track them quickly, and he needed her in the ambulance and rolling before that happened.

He watched her rock for a moment, head bent over the infant, wondering how best to approach her. Crouching to camouflage his size, he settled on, "Hey."

She started at the sound of his voice, nearly coming out of her skin as she tucked the baby in close and swung to face him. Huge blue eyes met his, the deep hue almost the color of violets.

Bruised. She looked bruised, battered by shock...and something more.

Even exhausted and beat up by circumstance, she possessed the most powerful energy he'd ever seen. Pure white, it pulsed in her aura, lighting her up from the inside out, nearly knocking him on his ass.

God, she was practically plugged into the Meridian.

Hers wasn't a slow draw or gentle siphoning of the electrostatic current that fed Dragonkind. Hers was so intense it would make males fight to possess her. The rawness of it seduced him, urged him to get closer, to touch her, to see what all that energy would feel like against his skin.

Bastian forgot where he was for a second, a terrible hunger rising in his gut.

No doubt sensing the sudden danger, she gasped and shuffled sideways. As the distance between them grew, he clamped down on his reaction to her, wiping his expression clean.

"Easy." He extended his arms, hands up in a gesture meant to reassure. "The ambulance, remember? I'm here to help."

A single tear rolled over her bottom lashes, running through the blood smear on her cheek. "I c-couldn't stop the b-bleeding and...I just..."

"I know." He really did. Understood exactly what she'd walked into when she entered the house.

"He would have d-died, too. I couldn't...I had to..." Her bottom lip trembled as she squeezed her eyes shut. More tears fell. "Oh, God."

A surge of protectiveness rolled through him. Fierce pride followed: for her strength and intelligence, her steadfastness in the face of overwhelming odds.

His gaze dropped to the tag visible on her bag. Picking up her name and address, he murmured, "Myst, it's all right. Open your eyes and look at me."

She exhaled a long, shuddering breath, but obeyed.

The second her gaze met his, he held out his hand. "Come, *bellmia*. Let's get you out of here."

"But, Caroline, she—"

"You can't do anything for her now. The ME will care for her," he said. "Your job is the baby. Think, Myst. What do you need to do for him?"

She blinked, and Bastian saw the moment her mind left the horror and came back online. He almost smiled. Good girl, he wanted to say. The need to praise her surprised him a little, as did his need to go gently. He should be wiping her memory and hauling her into the ambulance. But he couldn't do it. He didn't want her to forget him.

And Bastian hated himself for it—and for what he was about to do. He'd known the instant she'd turned her violet eyes on him that he wasn't going to let her go. Five days. He had five days until the Meridian's axis realigned. The biannual occurrence was the only time his kind could sire a child with a human female, and he needed to meet the deadline. He'd made a promise to himself, was bound by duty and honor to protect the race, and like it or not, Myst was coming with him.

Rikar crossed over the threshold. "Holy shit."

"Back off," he said, knowing his friend was responding more to Myst's energy than the bloody scene.

"Understood." Rikar looked away from her. The move was pure instinct, one male backing away from another staking his claim. "We need to move. Company's coming."

"How soon?"

His first in command gave him a meaningful look.

They'd run out of time. Bastian reached for Myst. Patience was no longer an option. Not if he wanted to get her out in one piece.

Chapter Three

His voice drew Myst through the fog, out of blind panic and back into Caroline's kitchen. The sight of her patient's body almost made her lose it again. She could handle blood in normal amounts. Had even worked a stint in the ER, but this?

Myst shuddered. Trauma wasn't her thing. But, babies…

Her gaze dropped to the bundle in her arms. Wrapped in her fleece-lined rain jacket, the newborn stared up at her, more alert than she would have expected for the difficulty of his birth. Myst studied him a little more closely. Tiny fists tucked beneath his chin, he yawned. Her eyes burned as she watched him. Yeah, babies were her thing.

She blew out a shaky breath and glanced at the paramedic. Calm in the face of tragedy, he crouched a few feet away, no doubt wondering whether he needed to call the mental health unit. That wasn't far from the truth. She'd held it together long enough to do her job, to save the baby only to fall apart like a freak show the second she held him in her arms.

"Myst," he said, tone soft, but somehow urgent. "Can you walk? We need to go."

Go? Yes, of course, they did.

In theory, the idea made perfect sense, but she couldn't move. She was numb all over, inside and out, unable to string much of anything together.

Gentle pressure brought her chin up. Steady green eyes met hers and she jolted, more aware of his hand on her skin than the two attached to her own body. Focused on him, she grounded herself in the inherent strength of his features. Dark hair clipped military short, his face was hard planes and elegant angles, handsome with a harshness that reminded her of the coastline. Her favorite place in the world. The thought helped to even her out. He was solid and safe, exactly what she needed to grasp the trailing ends of control.

Shifting the newborn to her shoulder, Myst kept hold of the paramedic's gaze and stripped off her rubber gloves. He was right. They had to get the baby to the nearest hospital. The ambulance would have some of the supplies she needed to check him out, but a pediatrician would be better. And a second opinion would be helpful. Her synapses weren't exactly firing on all the necessary cylinders right now.

She reached for the EMT just as he reached for her. Her palm connected with his, and she got zapped with static electricity. More startled than hurt, she flinched. He shuddered hard as though the contact pained him.

Myst let go. He held on, grip gentle but firm as he pulled her off the floor and onto her feet.

Numb from sitting on ceramic tile, she wobbled. Strong hands steadied her, settling on the bare skin of her upper arms. A prickly sensation swept the nape of her neck and spiraled out, working down her spine in a long, soothing swirl. Tense muscles relaxed and, unable to help herself, she leaned into him, touching her shoulder to the wall of his chest. He twitched, muttered something under his breath Myst didn't catch.

God, he was so warm.

Heat rolled off him in waves, attacking her bone-deep chill as he stroked his thumbs along her biceps. Myst drifted closer to him. All she wanted was the fear to go away, for the lump of ice sitting in the middle of her chest to thaw and—

It was crazy. She shouldn't be relying on him, but couldn't stop herself. Something about him calmed her, helped her let go of the horror and settle into sanity. As anxiety drained, her mind sharpened, laying out a clear action plan.

"I need an incubator," she said, the nurse in her charging back onto the battlefield.

His brows collided. "What?"

"For the baby," she said, wondering what was wrong with him. A minute ago, he'd been Mr. Calm-cool-and-collected. Now, color rode his cheekbones and he looked distracted, a breath away from true discomfort. "Do you have one in the ambulance?"

He pulled in a long breath, then let it go. "Let's find out."

Good idea. They'd just...what? That didn't make any sense. The guy should know exactly what kind of equipment he towed around with him. Most paramedics were fanatical about that, checking and rechecking their gear before they went on shift. Myst frowned at him, confusion doing a dance inside her head. Something was wrong...well, besides the obvious. Caroline's death was an awful reminder of that terrible fact. But this guy didn't seem right. He wasn't doing the usual things, and she couldn't see his medical bag anywhere. What kind of paramedic came onto a scene without his kit?

Her gaze dropped to the right side of his chest, looking for a name tag. She stared at the empty space on his shirt, wondering—

"Bastian."

She blinked. "Pardon?"

"My name," he said, picking her question out of the air before she could ask. Her mouth worked wordlessly as he tipped his chin toward the door. "That's Rikar. Now, hang onto the infant. We're out of here."

Myst barely had time to register the huge, blond man standing just inside the door before Bastian shifted his grip on her. A heartbeat later, she was in his arms, against his chest, and he was out of the kitchen, into the corridor, headed for the front porch.

"Wait…I can walk…put me…" she trailed off as the baby started to fuss, protesting Bastian's rhythmic strides and the sudden rush of cold air. Adjusting the fleece-lined folds, she wrapped the raincoat she'd swaddled the infant in a little tighter, keeping him warm while struggling to read the man carrying her off like a bag full of contraband. "Hold up a minute, my cell phone. We have to call the police…let them know—"

"They don't need to know. Whatever happens, *bellmia*, keep him with you. I'll protect you both. Got it?"

No, she didn't get it. What the heck was he talking about? Of course, the police needed to know. There were protocols that must be followed, as much for Caroline as for her. If they left now without bringing the proper departments on board, she could kiss her job—and maybe her freedom—good-bye.

And after the hell she'd just been through, prison wasn't something Myst wanted to think about, never mind go to.

"Look, Bastian, maybe—"

"Rikar?"

"Yeah, I'm on it," the blond said, skirting by them in the narrow hallway as he headed toward the front door. "Northwest quadrant. They're coming in low."

"Wha...who?"

Bastian didn't answer. He glanced down at her instead. It was like getting zapped with electricity. God, she couldn't breathe. His eyes. The green was...she didn't know exactly. Shimmering or something.

"I'm going airborne. Use the cloud cover to come in from above." Rikar paused on the lip of the porch steps to look at them over his shoulder. Glacial blue eyes glowed like twin spotlights, the aggression in them undeniable.

"I'll hold the ground," Bastian said. "Hammer a few before they reach us."

The blond flashed a grin and leapt toward the ground. Except, he didn't reach it. White and gold flashed in the low light, and Myst saw the impossible: razor-sharp claws, a curve of wing, the glimmer of scales as he took flight.

"Oh, my God. Oh, shit...let go of me!" Her scream echoed through the foyer. Panic pumped adrenaline through her system, putting her internal engine into overdrive. Myst reared, newborn wailing and tucked to her chest, legs kicking to break Bastian's hold. "Let go! My God...oh—"

"Fuck." The growl in his voice was unmistakable. She twisted, trying to protect the precious bundle in her arms and get away at the same time. Bastian tightened his grip, locking her against him. "Don't fight me. Not now."

Myst heard the warning loud and clear, but couldn't obey. Her brain was already headed south, trying to under-stand...to tell her she was imagining things. The problem? She couldn't get the picture out of her mind. The blond guy...he...Oh shit. He wasn't normal. He wasn't...God help her...

She started to shake an instant before her lungs seized. Struggling for each breath, she choked out, "P-please... please just let us go. I won't say anything. I p-promise. I'll take the b-baby and...I won't—"

Bastian leapt over the porch rail, cutting her off as he landed in the flower bed. The scent of crushed chrysanthemums spiked, surrounding them in a sweet cloud. And wasn't that stupid? Locked against a...God, she didn't know what Bastian was, but considering that he was kidnapping her she shouldn't be worried about flowers, never mind stopping to smell them.

"What are you?"

"Dragonkind." Eyes now glowing as fiercely as Rikar's had, he sprinted toward an old car abandoned in the long grass beside the garage. "Don't be afraid of me. I won't hurt you."

She almost believed him. But that was before she saw the fireball.

Like an inbound missile, it came over treetops, trailing an orange and blue-flamed tail behind it. Bastian spun into a crouch and wrapped himself around her, using his body to shield her and the baby an instant before the ambulance blew sky high. Metal groaned and the acrid smell of burning rubber billowed on a wave of black smoke. Wide-eyed, Myst watched the vehicle sail twenty feet in the air, flipping end over end before landing in a twisted heap in the driveway.

With a sob, Myst drew her knees up, curled herself around the baby and into Bastian. All of a sudden, prison seemed like a safer alternative.

Chapter Four

Bastian smelled the Razorback before he saw him. But seeing was believing, so he stayed low, eyes glued to the edge of the tree line. He didn't wait long. The rogue came in on a slow glide, wings spread, iridescent brown scales flashing in the moonlight. Caught by the sudden rush of air, black smoke swirled, touching the dragon's underbelly as he circled the debris field, looking for bodies in twisted metal and burning medical supplies.

Crouched between a rusted-out car and the garage wall, arms locked around Myst, Bastian stayed perfectly still. The big male circled again, giving Bastian a clear shot from his vantage point on the ground.

He didn't take it. The approach was all wrong, the sight line way too easy.

Hovering above the crumpled ambulance, eyes glowing like beacons in the night sky, the Razorback waited. Bastian counted to seven before the rogue gave up and banked left, dipping low over the sad-looking house. As the tip of his brown tail disappeared behind the peak of the roof, Bastian shifted right, keeping them hidden behind the Buick while he improved his view.

The jack-offs were getting smarter.

Usually the Razorbacks attacked en masse, without care for the consequences. Sending in a lone soldier to draw him out was new for them. Smart as far as strategy went; dumb-ass stupid in terms of outcome. Did the idiots really think he would take the bait?

Probably. He sometimes did—just to keep things inter-esting—but couldn't now.

Not tonight.

Tonight the battle strategy revolved around one thing... protecting Myst and the precious bundle sleeping in her arms. He sure as hell wasn't going to risk them. And the idea of Myst's death? Yeah, no way he would go there.

Bastian pulled Myst a little closer. She'd stopped fighting him—thank Jesus. But, shock had set in and she shivered, air coming in raw rasps as she struggled for each breath. He wanted to apologize for that: for her fear and what she was about to witness. She deserved better, had been through hell already, and didn't need the added trouble of discover-ing dragon-shifters in her tidy little world.

It couldn't be helped. Circumstance had dealt her a bad hand. All he could do now was make sure she lived to see another sunrise.

Sheltering her, Bastian drew the edges of his leather trench coat around her. Curled into a ball between the spread of his thighs, she turned her face into his chest. With gentle hands, he tucked her head beneath his chin, lending his heat, absorbing her chill while he scanned the perimeter and listened hard. Fire licked towards the night sky and long grass rustled as enemy claws touched down in the backyard.

The sound carried on the damp wind, the infinitesimal snick louder than a gun being cocked at close range. Battle-lust roared through Bastian, tightening muscle over bone, urging him to shift, to make the rogue pay for coming near

Myst and the baby. He locked himself down. Patience was the priority, caution an absolute must. The cloaking spell was doing its job, hiding them from enemy eyes—making the pack improvise and change tactics.

Bastian understood the Razorbacks' strategy. They couldn't attack what they couldn't find. Shit-for-brains in the backyard was a smoke screen, a decoy sent to draw him into the open for the others to tear apart.

And yeah, there were others.

Five, counting the one sniffing around the dilapidated shed.

On a normal night, the small pack wouldn't have presented much of a challenge. Not when he and Rikar closed ranks. But with a female and child to protect? The sliding scale went from mildly irritating to FUBARed in a hurry.

Rikar pinged him from outside the fighting triangle— a three-mile separation that prevented the enemy from detecting him. *"Bastian…what the fuck are you doing?"*

"Waiting."

"For what?"

"The decoy to move."

"Hell, they're getting smarter," Rikar said, soft growl tinged with amusement.

"Not exactly what we need tonight," he said, not liking the odds.

Bloodthirsty to the point of obsession, the Razorbacks were goal-oriented and single-minded—Bastian gave them full marks for that—but they fell short in other areas. Intelligence, for one.

Made his job easier most nights, if not entirely interesting.

Opening his senses wide, Bastian mapped the imprint of each, measuring the electrostatic signature all of his kind carried. Like a fingerprint, the impression was unique to the individual, a code written in his DNA. The ability to dissect a dragon's strengths and weaknesses from a distance was an unusual talent. Most never acquired the skill. Bastian excelled at it. He knew to the degree how powerful each male was, down to the color of his scales and the poison he exhaled.

The group hunting him was young, more ballsy than experienced. Good in some respects, terrible in others.

Seasoned fighters would see Myst as a trophy and keep the fighting away from her. Inexperienced ones would set the trap and attack without care for collateral damage.

"How is she?" Rikar asked, concern edging out impatience.

He cupped the nape of Myst's neck, praying his touch soothed her. She was throwing off too much energy, levels that drew dangerously close to breaking through the invisibility cloak he'd thrown around them. *"Petrified."*

"Shit."

No kidding. He needed her to calm down, to level out before enemy eyes turned in their direction.

"Figure it out, man," his friend said, ready to break cover. *"You've got about thirty seconds before I break cover and the fuckers sense me coming."*

"Give me a couple of minutes. Let me get a handle on her first."

His first in command grunted, but held course, flirting with the edge of the fighting triangle and detection.

Bastian lowered his head until his mouth brushed Myst's ear. He kept his voice low, more vibration than actual sound, and said, "Relax, Myst…you're safe with me. Take a deep breath."

Air caught, hitching in the back of her throat as she tried to do as he asked. It didn't go well. She was strung too tight, panic locking her lungs into spasm.

"In through your nose, out through your mouth…come on, baby. Listen to my voice, feel the release." Keeping his tone soft and steady, Bastian kept talking as he found the pressure point at the base of her skull. He rotated his thumb, massaged in gentle circles, hesitating, not wanting to do it. He shouldn't be touching her, not like this, without her understanding or consent.

In the kitchen, he'd been unable to help himself, had taken a sip and sampled her energy…and God. She was delicious, so sweet that arousal hit him like a brick house. The head below his waist had a mind of its own, was still complaining, wanting inside her with an insistence the circumstances didn't warrant.

Jesus, he was sick. She was scared out of her mind, and he was turned on.

What did that say about him? That he was a deranged fuck? Or that he hadn't fed in far too long?

Probably a little of both, but he couldn't worry about either now. Rikar wouldn't wait much longer.

Myst took another choppy breath and, with a silent curse, Bastian slipped his free hand under the hem of her green hospital scrubs. His palm settled on the small of her back. He spread his fingers wide, touching as much of her as he could reach, and nearly came in his leathers.

Oh, man, she was good, her skin the softest he'd ever touched.

Shifting her so he wouldn't crush the infant, he set his mouth to her temple, breathed her in, losing himself in her scent. Connected at three junctions—nape, lower back and temple—he tapped into Meridian. White hot, potent, energy surged, flowing through her into him. Bastian bit down on a groan. God, that was unbelievable. Delicious in a way that defied description.

He only meant to soothe her: to drain the excess, bank her energy to keep her hidden, ensure her safety, but... Jesus. He was starving, so empty inside he couldn't control the hunger. It was too powerful, and Myst was too good. He needed more than just another sip.

With a growl, Bastian let his baser needs take over. Guilt was nothing but an echo now—something to endure later when compulsion subsided and reason returned. Hunger overwhelmed him and, senses wide open, he pulled the white-hot energy she possessed out of her body and into his own. She hummed, the sound one of pleasure and relief as Bastian drank, mouth traveling across her cheek to her neck. Flicking his tongue across her pulse point, he took her in, damning himself with the incredible taste of her skin.

When she sagged, he capped the flow and lifted his head, so full his fingertips tingled. A violent shudder rolled through him and, dipping his chin again, he brushed the corner of her mouth with his own. The kiss could barely be called one; the simple touch nothing more than a gentle pass, a small thank you for what she had unknowingly given him.

She sighed. "I feel better now."

"Good," he murmured, forcing his hand from beneath her shirt. Continuing to touch her wasn't doing him any favors. It made him want to strip her down and take the sex he craved. The thought made Bastian back the hell up, putting space between them as he helped her sit up. She swayed. He steadied her, gripping her elbows, supporting her until she gained her balance. "Do something for me?"

Myst blinked, coming out of the feeding-induced fog a little at a time. As her vision cleared, her pupils contracted, and he felt her mind sharpen. She looked right through him, reading his intent. "D-don't go."

Her entreaty turned him inside out.

Holy shit. How did she do that? Two words—simple, non-threatening, and under different circumstances? Crazy appealing. Two words, that's all. And now, he was waffling, ready to wrap her hard against him and retreat to some place private…somewhere safe where he could lay her down.

Exhaling hard, Bastian forced his lungs to unlock. He needed to keep her the hell out of his head and stay in the game. Not wanting to leave her didn't mean he could stay. "Myst, I need you to stay here. I won't be gone long."

Balling her hand in his leather coat, she shook her head. The movement was small, tight…still desperate despite the energy drain. The new spike in her anxiety moved through him until he tasted it on the back of his tongue.

Swallowing the bitter tang, he murmured, "Myst—"

"I saw that t-thing. Don't leave us alone."

Bastian almost growled. Thing. She'd called his race a "thing." Like he and his kind were no better than the monsters children feared lived under their beds or the nasty predators humans recoiled from in movie theaters. It shouldn't bother him—her reaction was a natural one—but it did. More than he wanted to admit.

"*Bellmia,* listen to me."

Myst held his gaze. The desperation in her eyes almost killed him. "I'll go with you…follow behind. I can—"

He cupped her cheek, cutting her off. "No. I need to draw them away from you and the baby. Do as I say. Dig in. Stay here. They can't see you…won't be able to track you. The cloaking spell will hold as long as you don't move. Understand?"

"No."

Well, at least she was honest. He couldn't fault her for that. Was too taken with her to be anything but proud. Tracing her cheekbone with the pad of his thumb, he whispered, "Hang tough, baby. I'll come back for you."

"Bastian..." she trailed off as he shuffled backward, taking his hands from her. She clutched at him. "No."

"You'll be all right." With a gentle twist, he broke her hold and shifted out of range. If she grabbed him again, he wouldn't be able to leave. "Stay here. Trust me to keep you safe."

Without a backward glance, he shut out the hitch of her breath, the sound and smell of her fear, and keeping low, moved around the Buick's rusted-out rear bumper. *"Rikar... I'm on the move."*

"About fucking time."

"I'm going in hot. Deal with the back end."

Rikar hoorahed as he broke through the three-mile barrier, allowing the Razorbacks to detect him. The enemy's focus spilt, half on his first in command, half on him, as Bastian shifted into dragon form. Baring his fangs, he roared and, ignoring Myst's cry of "Oh, God," he hammered Shit-for-brains in the backyard with an electro-pulse. As much as Rikar liked to razz him about it, Bastian didn't breathe fire. His magic was more lethal than that, a wicked blue ball of energy combined with poisonous gas—more lightning strike with the added flare of a psychochemical agent.

Yeah, he was a one-man/dragon show. A regular chemical warfare specialist.

Shit-for-brains sucked wind as the blast picked him up and threw him backward into the forest. Tree trunks gave way like toothpicks, the crack of wood deafening as the enemy dragon smashed through them, traveling thirty feet into the underbrush. His eyes on the target, Bastian waited for the rogue to get up. He hoped he did, wanted to deliver another nasty exhale for the idiot to choke on. Instead, the rogue turned belly-up. Paws in the air, the dragon twitched into a full body spasm as Bastian's brand of poison went to work on his central nervous system.

Bastian snorted. So much for bright and shiny hope, never mind the satisfaction of a good fight.

Cold air stirred above him.

Rolling right, Bastian ducked under another set of enemy claws. His razor-sharp tail collided with the Cape Cod, slicing through the two columns supporting the front porch. With a groan, the narrow strip of roof slumped, collapsing over the cedar door. The new threat swung around, purple scales flashing, keen for another go at him. The dumb ass. What did he think? That an aerial assault gave him the advantage in a firefight?

Bastian almost shook his head. He bared his teeth instead, shifting to face the dragon head-on.

Warrior-honed patience kicked in and, crouched like a cat, he waited for the rogue to reach him. A split second before the enemy struck, Bastian leapt skyward, twisting in midair. His talons caught and held as he grabbed Dumb-ass's spade-shaped tail. Muscles along his side pulled, protesting the stretch as he yanked, dragging the Razorback out of the air. Bastian's paws hit the ground with a thump. Dumb-ass went down hard, wings tangled, horned head buried beneath a pile of earth.

Not wasting a second, Bastian spun and brought his spiked tail down, thumping the rogue's skull. A sickening crack went off like a bomb, shredding the air. Yeah, Dumbass was down for the count—a healthy helping of skull fracture with a side order of brain hemorrhaging.

All right. Two down, three to go, though, Shit-for-brains was on the move again, tossing enormous pine trees like pick-up sticks as he struggled to get up.

Rikar came in like a viper, hot on the tail of another Razorback. Red scales flashing in the low light, the enemy dragon was in full panic mode. Bastian didn't blame him. He wouldn't want Rikar on his ass, either.

Breathing out, his friend iced up the younger dragon's wings, sending him into free fall. The rogue collided with the ground like a derailing freight train, ripping up the front lawn as he left a huge trench behind him. Bastian jumped back to avoid getting hit as he skidded by, jostling the beat-up Buick with his hind leg.

Movement flashed in his periphery. Blond hair and green scrubs came into focus seconds later. Bastian growled and shifted, shielding Myst as she made a mad dash toward the hatchback sitting undamaged beside an old tractor.

The cloaking spell gave way, dispersing like vapor into thin air.

Fantastic. Just what he needed: a renegade female who couldn't follow orders.

Bastian killed the urge to pick her up and paddle her behind. Teaching her a lesson would have to wait. He didn't have time now. Shit-for-brains was back on all four paws, his gaze narrowed and locked on Myst.

Chapter Five

Myst took off as though she'd been shot from a cannon: the newborn a warm weight in her arms, the Lord's Prayer on her lips. The baby hampered her, messing with her speed, but she refused to leave him behind. No matter what happened, she would protect the precious bundle she carried.

At all costs.

Caroline had died so he could live. And dragons or no dragons, the vow she'd made to her dying patient stood for something. Meant more to her than self-preservation.

That left one choice. Run and pray.

Air rasping in her chest, the words fell in a messy tumble. "Our Lord who art in heaven, hallowed be thy name..."

She mouthed the rest, knowing God would understand.

Head low, knees pumping, arms sheltering her angel, she kept her eyes on the prize. Her keys were in the center console of her car. All she needed to do was reach them. She visualized her escape...imagined sliding the key into the ignition and her smooth getaway. Time slowed down, the scene coming to her in distorted waves, like sound through water: the black smoke, the chill tinged with the scent of burning rubber, the slide of grass underneath her shoes.

Fifteen more feet. Now ten. *Please God, let me make it. Help me keep him safe.*

"Fuck." The growl came from behind her, a little off to one side.

Oh, no. No. No. No. Bastian had spotted her and locked on like a laser beam.

A sob caught in the back of her throat. She pushed herself harder, held the baby with one arm and pumped the other to help her run faster. Air sawed in and out of her chest. The relentless burn hurt like hell but she didn't stop. No way would she make it easy for him. If he thought that she would turtle, roll up and die, then he was in for a nasty surprise.

He'd betrayed her. Had told her to trust him, but...

He wasn't trustworthy. Bastian was one of *them*. A monster with claws and fangs, the stuff of nightmares.

Myst skidded around the end of her car. Both feet churning up gravel, she grabbed the back bumper and pulled, helping herself change direction as she zeroed in on the driver's side door. Just another few feet and—

An ominous hiss snaked through the air, turning into an unnatural roar. Her hand clamped on the door handle. She looked up into yellow eyes with narrowed pupils. Brown with a single jagged horn in the center of its forehead, the dragon snarled at her and drew a lungful of air past razor-sharp teeth. Struck stupid, Myst froze and watched as a glowing orange ball gathered at the back of his throat.

Oh, God. Fire.

"Myst, run!" Bastian's voice came through loud and clear, but Myst couldn't move. She was locked into yellow eyes, her legs the consistency of Jell-O. "Shit! Rikar!"

A cold wind blew in. The autumn air went murky, a cloud of frost and mist on the verge of snow. The icy fog billowed over the hood of her car, settling around her like an

Arctic blanket, but it was too late. She could already feel the heat and hear the hungry roar of the inferno as the fireball gathered speed. It was going to eat her alive, leave nothing but ash in its wake, and there was nothing she could do to stop it.

Despite her promise, she turtled, curling herself around the newborn. The broken "Sorry" she whispered to him wasn't enough, but somehow needed to be. She'd tried so hard to save him, and now they were both going to die.

Painfully. Horribly. Without a lick of—

A wall of ice exploded around her, rising in a U-shaped barrier in front of her car. Thick and unbelievably tall, the barricade shuddered as the fireball hit with a boom, throwing her backward. Steam blew sky-high, raining ice chips in a spectacular fountain of cold water. The hiss and crackle clawed at the ice, digging to reach her.

Distorted by melting glacier, she watched Bastian take off. A streak of midnight blue, he tackled the fire-breathing dragon. Two shadows rolled end over end, almost indistinguishable from one another in the moonlight. Dark blue landed on top, claws embedded in brown scales.

His green eyes flashed, reaching her through the darkness. "Myst, get out of here!"

She followed the command without question: no hesitation, no "oh, my God" ringing inside her head. She was blank, rung out, too scared to do anything but listen.

Frost scraped the skin off her palm as she yanked the car door open. Not feeling the pain, she grabbed her keys, jammed the correct one home, and threw her car into gear. Without looking back—without hearing the roars and rip of claws—she put the gas pedal to the floor and, pulling a

Mario Andretti, sped down the driveway, the back end of her car leading the way.

———

The pine trees at the edge of the forest were on fire, throwing billows of smoke into the night sky. Bastian raised his head and stepped off Shit-for-brains's chest. Torn wide open, the enemy's throat was a twisted tangle of flesh, carotid artery exposed and gushing red-black blood. The rogue wouldn't live much longer. Like all of Dragonkind, he would check out in a pile of ash the second his heart stopped beating.

It was now or never.

Ignoring the injury, Bastian angled his horned head, getting up close and personal to make eye contact. "Where is Ivar hiding?"

Leader of the Razorbacks, Ivar was as ruthless as he was cunning. A treacherous opponent. One Bastian wanted to kill so badly the taste sat like rotten meat on the back of his tongue. Nothing washed the brutal tang away: not food nor drink nor sex. The thirst to spill Ivar's blood tainted everything he did.

Slippery as an eel, Ivar evaded death like a suicidal maniac avoided life. After a century of fighting, Bastian still hadn't managed to destroy him, to cut the head off the rogue organization. It didn't help that Ivar orchestrated from the sidelines. This time, though, was different. The asshole was doing more than playing armchair quarterback. He'd deliberately gone underground. Not a good sign. The enemy leader was up to something...with potentially catastrophic consequences.

"Fuck...you...Bastard," the Razorback gasped, pain in his slitted yellow gaze.

"Clever." Bastian wanted to roll his eyes at the play on his name. He pressed down on the dying Razorback's broken leg instead, using pain as incentive to make him talk. "Where is he?"

"Pretty...female, you got...there." Coughing up more blood, he wheezed, "Do you...think...Ivar will enjoy...fucking her?"

"Wrong answer," Bastian said, the threat to Myst making his voice almost melodic. Anyone who knew him well knew the soft tone was a dangerous one. When he got angry, he got quiet. And when he got quiet, things died.

With a snarl, he took hold of the Razorback's skull and twisted. Bones snapped. Between one heartbeat and the next, Shit-for-brains ashed, burnt scales and dragon blood turning to dust.

"Effective, if less than smart," Rikar murmured, landing behind him. His friend stumbled a little on impact, hopping to keep his weight off his front leg. "He might have told us something."

"Unlikely." Bastian eyed the gash on his friend's right forepaw. The wound ran in a diagonal, up his leg, oozing blood on white scales. "You all right?"

"Peachy."

"Body count?"

Rikar's gaze flickered before straying to the wall of ice still standing in the front yard. Bastian knew what he was thinking. If not for the barrier, Myst would be among the dead.

A tight knot tied itself in the center of Bastian's chest. "Rikar, man, thank—"

"Forget it," his friend said, shutting down his appreciation. The brush-off didn't bother Bastian. He knew his first in command well. Rikar wasn't comfortable with recognition...of any kind.

"Let's have it, then."

His gaze still on the fire-blackened hole in his wall, Rikar's magic rose as he drew the glacial cold back into himself. Like steam in dry air, the ice wall dissolved, leaving nothing but a U-shaped impression in the dirt. "Four dead. One flew the coop."

Shit. He'd hoped to avoid that. The retreating Razorback would run straight to Ivar and give his report. The first thing on that list would be Myst. Bastian clenched his teeth, grinding upper fangs against lower. He'd just put a huge bull's eye on her back. Not that it was the end of the world. She would, after all, be coming with him to Black Diamond. His lair was now her home.

"You need my help going after her?"

Bastian shook his head. He would track her alone. She'd feed him from the Meridian. Like DNA, the unique energy imprint she left in her wake was all her own, and now he would be able to find her anywhere. "Go home. Get stitched up."

With a murmur, Rikar unfolded his wings and leapt skyward. Bastian followed, pinpoint stars above his head as he watched his friend bank north toward their lair. He went east, drawn to Myst like a thirsty man to water. He needed to get her back. She was his responsibility...his female now. The sooner he retrieved her, the safer she would be.

———

Driving a car while holding a screaming baby was harder than juggling live hand grenades. Somehow, Myst managed. But her arms ached, one from cradling the newborn, the other from her white-knuckled grip on the steering wheel. The hatchback's headlights ate at the night-slick blacktop, but didn't reach far enough into the gloom. Still, she drove on, gas pedal to the floor, kamikaze speed breaking every law in the book.

She was one giant moving violation. And holy crap. Where were the police when she needed them? Certainly not anywhere near Route 18. The useless jack-offs.

Swallowing another sob, Myst forced herself to breathe. Unconscious from lack of oxygen was the last place she needed to end up. A close second? Wrapped around a hundred-year-old white pine. There were, of course, no guarantees, but she was pretty sure the tree would win in a game of Chicken.

And speaking of chicken, she was so cooked.

Bastian wouldn't let her go...not now. Not after seeing what she'd seen. Myst knew it with a certainty that terrified her.

She was going to have to run and hide. Create her own kind of witness protection program and disappear. Tania was going to freak out.

Not that she would tell her best friend. No way. Not a chance. The less Tania knew, the safer her friend would be. But, man. She didn't want to just disappear without an explanation. Knowing Tania, she would jump to all kinds of insane assumptions—like the truth wasn't crazy enough— and blame Caroline's jerk boyfriend for murdering and burying her under that pitiful shed in the backyard.

Myst could just see her: hard hat on, backhoes up and running, bulldozers razing the area while Tania directed the search for her body.

And God...there was something seriously wrong with her. She found the mental snapshot almost funny. In a sick, polluted kind of way.

"Okay, darling. It's all right. We're okay." Eyes glued to the road, she rocked the baby with a gentle but steady rhythm. "Please stop crying, angel. Please stop. It's going to be okay."

She kept her voice low, soothing, praying he responded to her tone. The soft cadence was the exact opposite of what she was feeling. If forced to slap a name on it, she would call it chaos squared. The height of panic coupled with full-on desperation. And the screaming wasn't helping.

"Please, angel...I need you to settle down. Please, baby." The begging came with tears. Myst sang through them, each note of the lullaby strained, the words hiccupping on each breath. Small face red with anger, he paused. She shifted him a little, patted his bottom, started the chorus of "Rock-a-bye Baby" over again. The new motion moved his wail from ear piercing to pitiful whimper. "There's my good boy. You're all right. We're fine."

He seemed to accept that—thank God. She couldn't have handled much more of his crying without pulling over. And on the side of the road wasn't the place she wanted to be. Not right now. Not when she was so close to Sal's. Five more minutes and she'd be around the bend and on the straightaway.

The restaurant sat at the end of that stretch. Much like mushrooms in the middle of a forest, nothing could kill it. Although Sal was long dead, the place was third-generation. A greasy spoon with deep roots; a hanger-on that clung to the little patch of dirt beside the narrow, two-lane highway. Cops liked it there, stopping for coffee and artery-clogging takeout while on patrol. Though what needed patrolling out here, Myst didn't know. At least, she hadn't known. Until tonight.

"Please let one of them be there." She sang the words, interjecting them into the lullaby. Her angel didn't mind the change in lyrics. With one last snuffle, he tucked his fists beneath his chin and nestled in, her heartbeat a throbbing mess against his cheek.

The road dipped and swung right. Myst slowed down to make sure she stayed on the road. The S-curve wasn't called "Dead Man's Gully" for nothing. The locals called it "unfriendly." Myst didn't think that was quite the right adjective to describe it.

Metal guardrails hugging the asphalt, the shoulder of the road took a nosedive on the left, sloping into a ravine. Worse than that? The sheer cliff on the right-hand side. The rock monstrosity walled her in, moonlight gleaming off its face, casting shadows, making Myst search for hidden monsters waiting in ambush.

Man, she hated driving this stretch. There was something creepy about it, even in daylight.

Coming out of the first curve and into the second, she forced herself to breathe. Just a bit further. Thirty seconds, maybe forty, and she'd be out the other end, Sal's exterior lights flickering in the distance. She flexed her fingers around the steering wheel. God, her hand hurt. But then, so did everything else. Her back muscles were in knots. Her legs were cramping. And her head? The ache was so bad her entire skull throbbed.

The headlights flashed off the rail, reaching out into the valley beyond the thin, metal barrier. Myst wanted the railing to hurry up, to slingshot her out the other end and let her go. The pressure inside her head was building, the buzz between her ears growing louder with each relentless turn of the tires. And the vibration—

Myst sat up a little straighter and listened hard. With the radio off, she could hear the rasp of her own breathing. The tires hummed on the asphalt as a strange stillness descended, surrounding her until she floated inside it. Her stomach dipped as a sinking feeling took over.

Oh, man. She hadn't outrun them at all. Bastian was out there...somewhere.

But...where?

She wasn't sure exactly. Her newfound dragon radar might be up and running, but the thing wasn't doing more than raising the fine hairs on the nape of her neck. Too bad. She could have used the accuracy. Knowing which way to go—how to react—would have been a godsend.

Without turning her head, Myst glanced toward the driver-side window. She didn't want to tip Bastian off if he was watching her. All she needed was another ten seconds to clear the last curve and gun it for Sal's. If she played her hand now—let him know she knew he was there—he might knock her off the road and into the ravine before she hit the straightaway.

A death grip on the wheel, she stared out the windshield into the darkness, but kept her peripheral vision sharp. If he surfaced, made his move, she would—

Something scraped the roof of her car. A second later, the tip of a dark wing came into view, dipping low over the driver's side. Metal groaned, then buckled, giving way beneath razor-sharp claws. With an "Oh shit," Myst ducked and, doing her best imitation of a pretzel, watched eight individual talons—four on the right, four on the left—punch through steel into her car. Horror ran hand in hand with astonishment, sucking her lungs dry an instant before her tires lost contact with the pavement.

"Hang on, baby." The growl was deep and sure, without a hint of exertion as he lifted her car clean over the guardrail.

Seated in her car and dangling in midair. Two very different activities, ones Myst would never have put together in the same sentence. Yet, here she was, a hundred feet in the air, over a very deep gorge…flying like the enchanted car in *Harry Potter*.

Had she described the situation as surreal earlier? Well, she'd meant certifiable, loony with a capital L. The man—dragon…whatever!—was a complete whack job. What the hell did he think he was doing?

Sucking air back into her lungs, she screamed at him, "You maniac!"

Name calling probably wasn't the best idea considering he was a dragon and she…well, wasn't. But God help her, the baby was wailing again and she'd had enough. He'd stolen her car…with her in it! "Put us down!"

"Later."

Bastian's baritone rolled over her: so calm, so in control, so beautifully deep. But who the hell cared what he sounded like? All that mattered was the word. "Later" was a good sign, wasn't it? Maybe his plan didn't include dropping her into the gorge, hood first. Which meant she would live a little longer. "Bastian! I mean it. Put us—"

He tucked his horned head under, looking at her upside down. "Try to relax, *bellmia*. Twenty minutes…half an hour tops and we'll be there."

"Where?" she asked, holding his gaze while wondering why the hell she was talking to him.

"Home."

Curled up in a ball in her front seat, Myst squeezed her eyes shut. Home. Yeah, that would be nice. Except there were all kinds of problems with that scenario. Number one, she was at a dragon's mercy. Number two? Something told her the home he referred to wasn't going to be her own.

Chapter Six

Ivar, leader of the Razorback nation, popped the black wraparounds off the bridge of his nose and rubbed the inside
corners of his eyes. Man, he was tired. Sleep-deprived with
a slap-happy helping of discouraged. Maybe PO'd was a better word. Either way, he was dead in the water...grounded
until the construction site progressed enough for him to set
his plan in motion.

Dropping his hand, the Oakleys settled back into place,
shielding his eyes. Damn delays were costing him. More
than he could afford. Though, he didn't care about the
money. Green was easy to come by...time, on the other
hand, wasn't.

Seven days behind schedule. Jesus, he had a headache.

And no wonder. Despite his best efforts to ignore the
sting, he was hungry again.

He'd last fed, what?...two weeks ago? No, not even.
Eleven days. He'd only made it eleven fucking days.

The short span between feedings worried him. Then
again, he'd been burning fuel like charcoal bricks in a bar-
becue. More waking hours meant little sleep. And not getting enough Zs made him drag-his-ass logy. He needed to
hit the streets and go hunting again, corner a female fast.
One with good energy. Ivar snorted. Screw that. He'd settle

for subpar—short, fat, and ugly—as long as the bone-deep ache went away.

Hitting the elevator button, he waited for the double doors to open. Installed just days ago, the pair of reinforced steel sliders retreated with soundless precision. Well, at least they worked right. Thank Christ.

Ivar rolled his shoulders, fighting muscle tension as he abandoned the deserted, concrete corridor. In less than five hours, the subterranean labyrinth would be buzzing again: a symphony of jackhammers, welding equipment, and the scraping turn of cement mixers playing a happy tune as his worker bees went back to work.

Right. Worker bees. A misnomer, for sure. Slave had a nicer ring to it—was more accurate, too.

Man, he hated humans. Filthy creatures, lowest of the low. But he needed them to build his facility. Each man had been selected and then taken for his proficiency—the skill he brought to his trade. Ivar would have preferred to leave the humans out of it, but his soldiers were warriors, not construction workers. And though each could have learned the necessary trades to complete the project, he didn't have time to dick around. The laboratory—and the framework of tunnels, bedroom suites, and cellblocks attached to it—needed to be finished five minutes ago.

At least, the humans had one thing going for them. They took direction well...with the right incentive. Leverage. Ivar's mouth tipped up at the corners. God, he L-O-V-E-D leverage. It never failed. The little bastards responded so well to arm twisting—literal and otherwise. Most begged for their lives, their freedom, or his personal favorite: to see their families.

Too bad Ivar wasn't into making promises. He only provided what they required to keep working: food, water, a bunk, and their lives. The last he dangled like a carrot, the proverbial golden pledge—do what I ask and you'll make it out alive. Jesus, he was a dog; the dictionary's definition of deceitful.

But, hey, the end justified the means. Didn't it?

Yeah, a big thumbs-up on that one.

War wasn't a word with any candy coating. It was a brutal contest of wills. A fuck you to the world and the enemy. May the best dragon win.

Ivar pressed the main-floor button on the face of the electrical panel. The elevator's ascent was smooth, a silent climb made possible by a series of huge magnets. He hummed his approval and glanced around the steel cage. It was a thing of beauty; the best technology had to offer.

The modern marvel slowed, coming to a bump-free landing on the top floor of 28 Walton Street. One hundred and fifty feet above his subterranean home, the red-brick, three-story walk-up wasn't much to look at from the outside. Surrounded by a quiet neighborhood filled with crooked A-frames, the abandoned fire station made the ultimate HQ. A dragon lair hiding in plain sight. It was perfect: cover and proximity to prey rolled into one.

The only problem? The building. It was long on character and short on comfort. Ivar liked it anyway. The wide-open spaces worked for him and—despite the rotten stair treads and holes in the wooden floor—the structure was solid. The roof needed patching when he'd first moved in, but he hadn't bought the place for its 1950s charm.

He'd dropped $3.6 million on the rat hole for the land. Thirteen beautiful acres of trees, tall grass, and beat-to-shit oil tanks, cars, and forgotten construction machinery. It was a graveyard, a wasteland where shit came to die. The sinkhole of Seattle.

Disgusting, just like the race responsible for it.

Without making a sound, the elevator's double doors slid wide. Ivar stepped out into what would become the Razorbacks' common room—into decay, dust, and moonlight. Into his XO's (aka executive officer's) presence.

Arms crossed, lean frame propped against the pitted brick wall at his back, Lothair's black gaze landed on him. "We have a problem."

The muscles bracketing Ivar's spine tightened. Great. Just what he needed…another screwup to toss on the ever-growing pile. Taking a calming breath, he threw out his best guess. "The female escaped."

"Not exactly."

"What then?"

Lothair shifted, leather jacket rasping against brick. The movement was small, barely a fidget at all, but Ivar knew his XO well. The male didn't like what he was about to admit. "Bastian beat us to her."

"Jesus Christ." Ivar grabbed hold of his temper before it slipped. Attacking Lothair wouldn't get either of them anywhere but bruised. And wouldn't that be the cake topper on an already shitty day?

Suppressing a growl, he crossed the large, rectangular room, skirting a jagged hole in the floorboards. He stopped at the floor-to-ceiling windows, looking out over his new backyard. Moonlight streamed in white-blue waves, casting shadows as he stared through cracked windowpanes, his gaze moving over the twisted steel shells that littered his property.

The God-awful mess was an environmental nightmare, a slap in the face to all Dragonkind. How could the humans walk by the eyesore every day? Ignore the mess while leaking oil tanks contaminated their neighborhoods and poisoned the planet? Jesus, it baffled and angered him every time he saw the same travesty repeated in different countries all over the world.

The entire human race needed to be put down. Eradicated before the damage became irreversible and every species on Earth died a horrible death. Phase two of his plan would take care of them...wipe out the apathetic beasts in one fell swoop.

But first things first.

Ignoring the smell of stale beer and rotting wood, he glanced over his shoulder at Lothair. "Where is the female now?"

"Dead. Was when we got there."

Ivar raised both brows, surprised by the new twist. Bastian didn't usually kill females, pregnant or otherwise. The male wasn't hard-hearted enough. A failing if ever there was one. "He took the child?"

Lothair nodded. "Forge is going to flip out. We need to get the infant back."

No shit, Sherlock. The conclusion was a no-brainer. Not if they wanted to keep Forge in check. Even as young as he was, the massive male was an asset to the Razorback crew: powerful, focused, with a whole lot of brutality to spare. Well, at least, he had been before meeting Caroline what's-her-face. The little bitch had sent the normally unshakable Forge sideways. In an unprecedented move, the male had bought a cell phone to keep in touch with her.

Love. A total frickin' catastrophe.

Ivar rubbed the back of his neck. What a mess. Precisely the one he'd hoped to avoid when he sent his warriors after the female to take the baby a month early. Kill her now. Give Forge his child. Sidestep disaster. All logical moves, but for one thing. Bastian had mucked it up...again.

The Nightfury commander was like a cat...all nine lives intact as he landed on his feet. Just once, Ivar wanted to see the male go splat. Once would be all it'd take—after which, he'd scoop up Bastian's ashes like dog shit, put them in an ugly urn, and set it on his soon-to-be-completed mantle. The trophy of all trophies.

"How do you want it handled?" His boots scraped the floor as Lothair pushed away from the wall. "You want me to tell him?"

"Nah. I'll deal with Forge," he said and heard Lothair exhale in relief. Ivar almost smiled. It wasn't that his XO was a coward, but only a maniac would go toe-to-toe with Forge when delivering that kind of news. A female taken too soon and a child lost to the enemy.

Yeah, the male was going to lose it.

Good thing crazy fit Ivar like a glove. He enjoyed living on the edge, and besides, who else would be able to control Forge—to channel all that rage in the right direction?

A little manipulation on Ivar's part—maybe even a lie or two—and Forge would no longer be sitting on the fence, wondering if he wanted to join the Razorbacks' ranks. He'd be gunning for Bastian and those who followed him. With the male 100 percent in his corner, Ivar would get what he wanted—his laboratory staffed and the vacancies in cell-block A filled, all while another powerful male went after his nemesis.

Man, life was sweet.

"One other thing, boss."

Ivar glanced away from his backyard, returning his attention to his XO.

As soon as he made eye contact, Lothair said, "There was another female at the scene...one with kick-ass energy."

"Is she Bastian's?"

"No clue, but he and Rikar protected her."

Well, well, well. The dynamic duo, together again. Lightning and ice. Those two were a deadly combination, one Ivar needed to do something about. He was losing too many warriors to them. "Any specifics?"

"He called her Myst. She had on scrubs."

"Check it out. Hospitals, medical centers, dentists, the whole works. I want to know everything...family, friends, financials, the places she goes, where she sleeps, what she likes to eat."

"No problem," Lothair said, ground-eating strides taking him to the elevator doors.

The brainstem of the facility, the new computer room sat in the center of the underground labyrinth. It was a great addition to their organization, a necessity in a world gone computer mad. He might not like the human race, but they'd invented some interesting gadgets. And the Internet was as good a place as any to start searching for the mysterious Myst.

"Good energy, huh?" His shoulder propped against the window frame, Ivar watched Lothair, the tidbit of information circling his mind. It didn't help that his hunger was off the charts. Just the thought of female energy had him salivating. But powerful energy? Jesus, he wanted a taste of that.

His XO hit the down button. "Most powerful I've ever seen."

Ivar's heart thumped a little harder. A female like that was valuable. Could be the first resident in the almost finished cellblock A. Hell, if she was as good as Lothair said, he would make an exception and set her up as his personal pet. "I want her."

"I'll get her for you, boss." The elevator sliders opened. Lothair stepped inside, his vow ringing as the cage closed, taking him into the bowels of the earth.

Ivar stayed unmoving a moment, absorbing the quiet before heading for the set of French doors in the middle of the bank of windows. Palming the handle, he flipped one open and stepped out onto the narrow balcony. Three stories above the ground, rotten wood cracking beneath his boots, he breathed in the chill, listening to city noise clash with cricket song.

With a sharp inhale, Ivar leapt over the railing, transforming in mid-plummet to dragon form. Red scales etched with black flashed as he banked left, heading west into the city center. His hunger couldn't wait, and downtown Seattle offered the best prey. Females came out to play on Thursday nights, decked out in short skirts and little else.

Hmm, such an excellent night to hunt.

Chapter Seven

Jesus, he was an idiot. The problem? Bastian didn't know how to change that fact. Caught between a rock and hard place, he'd done what he needed to do and retrieved Myst. But, well...hell. He'd managed to freak her out in the process. He snorted. A total understatement.

His pick-up-and-go method of transportation hadn't gone over well. But with no time to waste, grabbing her on the fly had seemed the best option—the least aggressive in his playbook.

Number one on his list of favorites would have gotten the job done, but setting down in the middle of the highway like he'd done with the ambulance? Not a great idea. The last thing she needed was another look at him in dragon form. Bastian snorted. Yeah, and wasn't that the understatement of the millennium?

All his scaliness would send her over the edge into Screamsville. And, honestly? He could do without the whole mental-meltdown thing. As far as he knew, a female going apocalyptic didn't appear anywhere on his agenda—the one entitled, "The Fastest Way to Get Myst Naked and Into Bed."

Man, he couldn't wait for it to happen.

Bastian banked north toward Black Diamond as he stuffed the fantasy beneath a pile of mental debris. He wanted it buried, gone before he went nuclear. All of that forced abstinence made him needy. Just the thought of her beneath him, of touching all that warm, soft skin?

Distracting as hell.

Bastian shook his head. Him. Distracted. That was a first. Not a particularly good one, either.

Thank God, Rikar wasn't around to witness his slide from cool commander to overheated lust boy. His friend would razz him about it, and Bastian had already given him enough ammunition for one night. Man, he was in for a roasting when he got back to the lair. He'd lost his calm, cool, and collected out there when Myst had sprinted into the open.

Rikar might not think less of him for losing his cool. It happened to the best of them. But that didn't mean the SOB would keep his trap shut. His first in command liked to tease too much to ever miss an opportunity. Bastian could see it already: Rikar gathering the other warriors around— like a bunch of pain-in-the-ass Boy Scouts around a camp-fire—hitting full story mode as he regaled them with the details.

A small price to pay, because...Jesus. He'd almost lost her. Had Rikar reacted one second later, Myst would be...

Dead.

Incinerated.

An ash pile.

The thought made his stomach roll. Which pissed him off. No way he should care so much. The attraction he felt for Myst was dangerous, not within normal boundaries for his kind. Then again, what did he know? None of the males he knew hooked up with a female for any length of time. Even if they had, none talked about it. Sure, some shot the shit about one-nighters—the fuckfests that overloaded them with pleasure—but even that kind of talk didn't happen often.

Thank God.

The last thing he needed was constant talk of sex. He thought about it often enough as it was, waking up hard and wanting most evenings. The problem? He hardly ever indulged. Couldn't bring himself to hunt females purely for release, like the others. Okay, so no one got hurt. The females were always willing and the energy exchange pleasurable, but all the deception didn't feel right.

Feeling that way was stupid.

He couldn't change what he was and yet, he yearned for more. Craved companionship without the remorse that always came after he took what he needed; after he'd fed and left the female sated on tangled sheets, all without a word or backward glance.

Bastian closed his eyes, let himself glide a moment, enjoying the rush of cold air against his scales. He wanted more from life, just...more. If only for a little while. Even if it couldn't last.

Myst's car heavy in his talons, he increased his wing speed, flying through dark skies and pine-scented air. Pinpoint stars winked, then hid behind wispy clouds, taunting him with the promise of moonlight. But light wasn't something he needed. Bastian knew the way home by heart. He recognized the forest below: the sway of crooked tree branches, the gradual roll of hills and higher altitude as he moved toward the mountains.

So quiet.

So peaceful.

So fucking ridiculous.

Normally, he loved flying on a night like tonight, with nothing but the chilly autumn air and black skies to keep him company. But fast was the only thing he wanted now. Not that the Razorbacks would follow. He was well cloaked, wrapped in a thick spell that kept both him and the car he carried from view. Still, he felt close to bursting, the pleasant hum beneath his scales pushing toward pain.

The reason? Myst.

He was trying to ignore her, but it wasn't going well.

Her energy and scent drove him crazy. He was hooked in, could feel the power and abundance that was all her. Combine that with a boatload of lust and he couldn't stop remembering how good she tasted. How well she fit against him. How much he wanted to touch her soft skin again. Sex with her would be amazing. Life altering. A hot, sweaty, gorgeously intense mating.

Jesus. He was in serious trouble here.

He was jonesing for serious bed play, and Myst wasn't even in the arena. She didn't want him anywhere near her right now. What had she called him? Oh, right. A maniac. Add that to her other descriptor of Dragonkind—*thing*—and they were a match made in heaven.

Bastian ground his fangs together, welcomed the sting against his lower lip, trying to block out her voice. It didn't work. Her fear as she'd clutched him at the house came through loud and clear.

Shit on a stick. Forget his reaction to her; *her* reaction to *him* pissed him off more. Even though it shouldn't.

She should be afraid of him.

Any human with half a brain would be scared. He was, after all, the quintessential boogeyman for her kind. Did it matter that he wasn't the bad guy? That he fought the

Razorbacks to keep both Dragonkind and the humans safe, to save them from the mass genocide Ivar wanted? No, of course not. Like all things in human society, appearances mattered more than the truth. Vanity reigned supreme. And a monster was a monster, pure motives or not.

Bastian soared over a rise of trees on a smooth glide. An earthy smell mixed with the scent of water rose from the river below. He kept his wings level, muscles stretching, following the tumbling rush of blue ribbon, working hard not to jostle Myst.

And wasn't he considerate?

She name-called while he twisted himself into knots, desperate to protect her, more concerned for her comfort than his own. His reaction was so totally screwed up Bastian had no idea how to unravel it. Hell, he didn't even know if he wanted to open that can of worms, but suspected it had as much to do with wanting Myst on her back as it did with his guilt for taking her.

Okay, so the sleeping with her part was pretty clear-cut. The guilt, though, nailed him—hit him entirely too hard in uncomfortable places. The ferocity of it made him squirm, but not enough to let her go. As much as he didn't want to admit it, he'd been waiting for a female like Myst all his life. No matter how much he scared her, the fear wasn't insurmountable. He could get around it, make her want him— like him even—if he put in enough effort.

Bastian's lips twitched. Okay, arrogant much? Well, maybe, but he believed in his ability to seduce. Myst didn't stand a chance if he applied himself, which he would, not only for himself, but for his race.

Ah, and wasn't he a prince? Sacrificing himself on the altar of Myst's desire for the good of Dragonkind?

What a crock of shit.

He wanted her for himself, to appease his own needs. The least he could do was be honest about it. Myst deserved more than a pack of lies, and as he peeked through the hatchback's window—saw her sitting so still, curled up in the front seat humming a broken lullaby to comfort the baby, to calm herself—he couldn't shake the truth.

He was going to get bloody on this one.

His chosen female was more than just appealing, she was warrior strong. Not that she knew it. She was probably sitting there beating herself up, replaying the scenario, all of the "what ifs," in an attempt to understand where she'd gone wrong.

The courageous ones did that, wanting to improve, to do better next time. He should know. He'd done the "what if" bullshit too many times to count. Knew what it felt like to second-guess every decision in the aftermath. Too bad that strategy wouldn't help either of them this time. His decision couldn't be undone. Myst belonged to him now, and he couldn't make himself regret it. He wanted her that badly. Enough to screw up her life. Enough to take what little time he had with her. Enough to raise their child alone.

"Don't think about it," he murmured, keeping his voice low so Myst wouldn't hear him. "What's done is done."

Banking right, Bastian swung around a bend in the river, hearing the rush, feeling the spray before he spotted the waterfall. The cascade tumbled from three hundred feet up, the soft rumble thundering into a roar the closer he flew. Drizzle gleamed on his scales, rolling off his wing tips as he lined up his approach. His built-in sonar pinged, finding the narrow opening behind the wall of moving water.

Mad scrambling—shoes sliding on upholstery, finger-nails scraping the dashboard—sounded from inside the car.

"It's all right, Myst," he said, smelling her fear.

Wings angled on the vertical line, he sliced through the falling water into the darkness beyond. Jagged rocks jutted out at odd angles, some coming dangerously close as he navigated the twisting tunnel.

"Bastian…I can't see anything! I can't—"

"Easy, *bellmia*." He kept his voice low, hoping to soothe her. "Hang tight. We're almost there."

It was a no-go.

She whimpered as the darkness became absolute. The small sound of distress cranked him tight, but he couldn't stop…and didn't blame her for panicking.

The first time he'd entered the cave had been a little eerie for him, too; the scent of damp earth and musty air almost suffocating. But, he'd chosen to enter the under-ground passage instead of setting her down in the driveway for a reason. He wanted her to rely on him to keep her safe. And trust wasn't something a male demanded. It was some-thing he showed his female, taught her with actions, not words. Yeah, she might not be able to see, but he could. His night vision was perfect, and the more he showed her how trustworthy he was, the faster she would accept him.

He navigated another corner. Myst's breath hitched, and he murmured, "I can see, baby. The darkness will not last."

Right on cue, light reached through the blackness. The soft glow was fuzzy at first, a mere echo of yellow illu-minating slick rock and narrow ledges along the tunnel sides. Bastian searched the craggy wall face, looking for his brothers-in-arms. Sometimes, when the pressure got to be too much, his warriors took dragon form and slipped into the passageway to rest. A bed wasn't always the answer to a good night's sleep for his kind. At times, the only thing that helped was to turn inward, to acknowledge their difference—the side that made them unique and set them apart from other living creatures. Their very dragonness.

Tonight, though, the many ledges were empty.

Thank God.

The last thing he wanted was an audience. Bringing Myst around—hell, getting her out of the car—was going to take some finessing, and a pack of Dragonkind...

Yeah, *so* not what he needed right now.

Rounding the last bend, Bastian stretched his wings wide, slowing his flight as he entered the enormous cave. Powered by magic, a thousand floating globes hung like strings of LEDs, hugging the domed ceiling, illuminating smooth sides. Beneath the glow, the LZ—landing zone— ran from wall to wall, taking up one-third of the cavern's interior. Flat, wide, and deep, the plateau counted as one of nature's more masterful miracles.

Bastian loved the LZ all the more for it. It was damned practical, big enough to land or launch four dragons at a time. A definite plus, considering the constant state of war he and his warriors suffered through day after day, decade after decade. And yeah, if war wasn't reason enough to get with the program, the LZ was a sign—yet another reminder why Dragonkind needed to sire sons.

They needed to increase their numbers. Be ready to launch a whole platoon on a moment's notice.

Bastian sighed. Hell, he was really working hard to convince himself of the rightness of his decision, wasn't he? Looking for excuses...seeing the LZ as a good reason for taking Myst. Jesus. He was beyond deranged if he believed that load of crap.

Careful to keep the car steady, Bastian landed on his back paws. His claws scraped the black- and silver-speckled granite, echoing in the vastness as he set Myst's hatchback down with a gentle bump. Time stood still for a second, the silence absolute before he uncurled his front talons. A soft screech—steel against razor-sharp claws—sounded as he released his grip on the car's frame. Bastian heard Myst suck in a quick breath as he stepped away from the car and shifted, moving from dragon to man in the space of a heartbeat.

Planted six feet from the front bumper, he gathered his clothes, drew his leather trench coat around him, and turned to look at his female. She met his stare through the windshield. Her eyes were wide. His gaze was steady, commanding her attention, willing her to trust him. She'd done it before with the baby in her arms and the dead mother on the floor beside her. He wanted her to do it again. To suspend the belief that the boogeyman came complete with scales and remember the gentleness he'd shown her.

But as the silence stretched, Bastian called himself a fool. Not much in life was easy. And Myst wouldn't surrender without a fight.

She was too smart to relinquish her power easily. His female needed the kind of attention most males didn't have enough patience to deliver. But Bastian wasn't like most males, and despite the desperate nature of his need, he appreciated her even more for the challenge she presented.

Pride for her spirit tipped his lips up at the corners.

Goddamn, but she was beautiful.

Even frightened she took his breath away, and as their gazes locked, his eyes stung a little, the tears he refused to show making his throat ache. No, it wasn't fair. At least, not to her. Yeah, he might hate the end game, but to hell with regrets and future pain, because...

Holy shit, he was glad she was here.

Chapter Eight

Myst wanted to be anywhere but sitting curled up in her car, having a staring contest with Bastian. Not that it was much of a contest.

She was losing.

He was winning. Hands down.

Which was so unfair. All she needed was a break, but she couldn't catch one. Luck wasn't in the cards.

Bastian had dealt her a crappy hand, and now? He held her in place, paralyzed. All without lifting a finger. The power was in the intensity of his gaze. The way he watched her. Waited. Gauging her response so he knew which way to jump. Or pounce.

Myst swallowed. She didn't like the analogy. It made her feel like prey to his predator.

Her mind went in circles as she stared at him, connecting the dots, trying to understand. To feel less afraid and more empowered, but...

He'd changed so quickly. Had gone from scales and fangs to, well...*that.*

Six and a half feet of WOW. Dressed in leather. Oozing raw sex appeal. And the OMG factor didn't stop there, either. She swore she could smell him. The scent drifted, claiming her attention and, unable to help herself, she breathed deep. Yeah, that was definitely him. Yummy clean male with a hit of knee-weakening cologne.

Unnatural.

Unreal.

Unbelievably hot.

With a slap, Myst hit the reverse button on her brain. No way. She refused to go there...into hotsville with a guy she'd just seen transform from a dragon.

Think scales...think scales...think scales.

The instruction stomped across her cerebral cortex, but didn't make much of an impression. How could it with him standing there looking like a freaking cover model? If only he would move...start acting big, bad, and scary. She needed to stay afraid of him, but his stillness had the opposite effect. For some reason, it calmed her, slowing her heartbeat one thump at a time. What was he doing? Giving her time to adjust to his transformation...hoping she'd forget what she'd seen?

She chewed on the inside of her lip. No chance of that. She couldn't shake the mental image of dark blue scales, a spiked tail, and razor-sharp fangs.

He was a walking, talking nightmare. A fascinating one, but...

Mesmerizing or not, Bastian was still scary. His intensity added that extra special something—sort of like the special sauce on a Big Mac—to the OMG factor.

Fighting the cold sweats, the old Mickey D's song streamed into Myst's head. She latched onto it, clinging to the familiar, and strained to remember the words. She could hear the music: the cheery jingle, the people singing along as they double-fisted their hamburgers.

Pickles.

Yes, it had something to do with pickles and onions. Lettuce and tomatoes were in there somewhere, too. Okay. All right. She was getting it, the tune and lyrics were melding, helping to slow the rush of adrenaline.

Lettuce, pickles, onions on a sesame seed bun.

Yeehaw. She had it, along with the ability to breathe again.

Way to go, McDonald's. No wonder they sold so many Happy Meals.

Held prisoner by Bastian's gaze, she shifted in her seat, hoping movement would help her break away. She didn't *have* to look at him. Eye contact, after all, was a choice, wasn't it? All she needed to do was find another focal point, one that didn't make her heart do the slam-out-of-her-ribcage thing.

Her angel squirmed in her arms, making an adorable baby sound. Myst blinked, glanced down—breaking the spell that was Bastian. Still fast asleep, the newborn stretched, then frowned, his soft, arching brows drawn into a tiny pucker. The sight evened Myst out, reminded her of Caroline. She'd made a promise to her friend to keep her beautiful baby boy safe.

Nothing Bastian planned trumped that.

A crunching sound cut through the quiet. Black leather flashed in her periphery. Bastian was on the move, long legs taking him around the front bumper of her car. Myst tensed in her seat, taking in the width of his shoulders, the muscles roping his arms, the flex and release of his long muscular legs. The word *invincible* came to mind—echoing inside her head in all CAPS—but as he got closer, she realized something important. His approach was cautious, almost gentle...as if he was trying not to overwhelm her.

At any other time, she would've approved. Appreciated the generosity. But not tonight. Trust wasn't on the table. She'd tried that once—back at Caroline's house—and he'd pulled a nasty surprise out of his hat. She refused to go for round two in the Ways-to-Scare-the-Crap-out-of-Myst Department.

Bastian paused beside the driver's side door. In slow motion, she released her white-knuckled grip on the steering wheel. She didn't want to startle her kidnapper into pouncing...or make him come after her before she was ready. Curling both arms around the baby, she secured her hold. Tiny fists tucked beneath his chin, he snuffled, but accepted the shift. Thank God. The last thing she wanted to do was bobble him when she scrambled over the middle console toward the passenger seat. But if Bastian tried to touch her, flight would become her only option.

The muscles in Bastian's forearm flexed as he grabbed the door handle. Myst slammed the fleshy part of her fist against a black button. The locks engaged, the *snick* sounding loud in the silence.

His eyes crinkled at the corners. A second later and, all by themselves, the locks flipped back to the open position. With a quick tug, he pulled the car door open.

The interior light went on, glowing yellow as musty air rushed in. With a yelp, she planted her heels on the seat and scrambled to the other side of her Honda.

"Myst..." Coming down to her level, he crouched in the space between the door and the car frame. As he met her gaze, he held his hands out, palms up in a gesture meant to reassure. "I won't hurt you."

Uh-huh. Right. Like she believed that.

Bastian wasn't some fairy tale knight in shining armor. He was a kidnapper: the one who'd taken her freedom and might even now take her life. Only a fool would give him a clear shot by allowing him too close.

Her chest heaved as she fumbled at the door behind her. He shook his head, murmured something, but she couldn't hear him. Her heart was pounding too hard, taking up all the space inside her head. Only one thing registered. She needed to get herself and the baby away from him...to some place that was truly safe. Like a US military base manned by big strong marines with submachine guns.

Maybe one of the Few and the Proud could get the freaking door open for her. Her hand was slick with sweat, and the handle wasn't cooperating. Stiff from disuse, the thing kept jamming, making her lose her grip and—

Her fingers slid off the curved plastic for a second time.

Close to tears, Myst juggled the baby, shifting him to the crook of her other arm. She found the latch and yanked hard. The lock popped. Putting herself in reverse, she pushed against the armrest, away from Bastian. God, he was still talking, his eyes so full of concern Myst almost believed he meant it. Almost. But she wasn't that naive.

The hinges creaked, and the door swung wide. Momentum thrust her backward. She hit the ground hard, tailbone connecting with stone. With a grimace, she shoved the pain aside and put her legs in gear. Bastian growled. Her breath hitched and not wasting a moment, she pushed to her feet. Without warning, the head rush hit. She stumbled sideways as her knees took a bow and nausea turned her stomach inside out.

Tasting bile, she grabbed for the car roof. Her palm slid and, grasping for purchase, she tried to pull back. Too late.

Metal scraped the inside of her forearm as her hand disappeared into a hole left by the dragon's talons, locking her arm inside a jagged steel trap.

She sucked in a quick breath, tried to adjust, protecting the newborn as she slid sideways into the door. Razor-sharp metal sliced her skin. "Oh...ouch!"

"Myst...baby, don't move." She flinched as Bastian vaulted over the roof of the car, leather coat flaring like bat wings behind him. So fast. He was too fast, and before she could react, he landed beside her—hardcore male loaded with just-kill-me-now aggression wrapped up in a pretty package. He moved in tight, getting up close and personal. "Easy...let's get you free."

God. He smelled fantastic...like Lanvin cologne mixed up with gorgeous male. She sagged a little, going soft inside. Which just pissed her off. She didn't like reacting to him on a woman-to-man level. It was insane. Kidnappers should be mean and nasty...should smell like dirt and grease and BO, nowhere near this good.

In full retreat mode, Myst pulled up on her arm. Sharp steel bit, cutting the inside of her forearm. Not that it mattered. She had one goal here. Get her arm back and her feet moving, but...ow! That hurt.

"Be still," Bastian growled, his mouth next to her ear, his chest a breath away from her shoulder.

Myst froze. "I can do it, just...don't touch me."

"As soon as I get you free, I'll let you go...all right?"

No, not *all right*. "Get away from me!"

"Shh...relax. It'll go easier that way."

Easier for whom? Not her. Bastian was too big, too strong... and entirely too close now. She was a heartbeat away from a full-blown panic attack. Myst could feel it gathering in her lungs, throbbing in her veins, tunneling her vision. Her teeth started to chatter. She couldn't breathe. There wasn't enough oxygen in the room—cave...whatever!—and she...oh, God...

"Myst...*bellmia*." Bastian's hand found the nape of her neck. His palm settled gently, cupping overly sensitive skin. She shivered as a zing of sensation moved down her spine in a sensual swirl.

"I c-can't b-breathe." Her muscles shook, loosening her grip on the baby. "I'm going to d-drop him. I'm going—"

"No, you're not. He's fine with you...*safe*...just like you are with me."

The bass of Bastian's voice came from far away, like radio waves. She tuned in, holding on to the fragile connection. It was stupid, but she needed his calming touch. Clung to each of his murmurs like a lifeline, soaking in his care as he cupped her elbow. His palm was calloused, rough in all the right places...like a man's should be. Somehow, the flaw made him seem safe, putting him on par with human men.

Not good at all. She didn't want him anywhere near her comfort zone. And comparing him to the men she knew? Yeah, that landed him somewhere north of normal, smack-dab in the middle of her I-want-to-get-to-know-you radar.

"Hold tight, baby." With care, he guided her wrist past a jagged piece of metal. "Almost there. Rotate your arm just a little...yeah, like that."

She nodded, following his instruction. When her hand slid free of the hole, he aligned their palms, her right with his left. His fingers brushed hers, slipped between, laced them together, protecting her skin every step of the way. With gentle pressure, he turned her forearm toward the ceiling to examine her skin.

"You cut yourself."

Making a fist, she tugged on her hand. "Let go."

He glanced away from the thin trickle of blood on her inner arm. As his gaze met hers, his grip on her hand tightened. Not a lot, but enough for Myst's panic parade to start beating the crap out of her mental drum kit. *Boom, boom, boom.* There went her heart again.

"Please."

"Promise not to run?"

"Yes," she said a little too quickly. His eyes narrowed as he picked up on her lie, and she babbled, "I promise…cross my heart and hope to die…" she trailed off as he raised both brows. She scrambled in full reverse. "Okay…not hope to *die*, but you get my point, so—"

"Look, I know you're dealing with some heavy shit here. I get it. I really do." One hand still cupping her nape, the other imprisoning her hand, it was as if they were slow dancing, without the body sway or willingness on her part. He sighed, as though tired. "But, here's the thing. You run. I give chase. In the end, we're right back where we started…me touching you. So, let's save ourselves the trip. You can't win this one, Myst. You're here. I am, too. Accept it so we can move on."

"I want to go home." *Crap.* Not exactly a convincing argument. She sounded like a spoiled six-year-old. Taking a deep breath, she forced herself to meet his gaze. "I won't tell anyone, Bastian. I'll keep my mouth shut. I'm an excellent secret keeper…the very best. It'll be like it never happened. I'll go home. You'll—"

"Maybe I believe you…" His pause gave her hope. He killed it with one quick slice. "Maybe I don't. But that's not the real problem."

The real problem? Bigger than the fact that she'd been kidnapped? "It can't be that bad. Not enough to take away my freedom."

His hand flexed around hers. "You remember the brown dragon you saw tonight?"

She nodded. "The fire breather."

"He was part of an elite group of warriors...my enemies...and one of his comrades escaped during the fight." He shifted, slipping his hand from her nape to her cheek. He cupped her face gently, and Myst flinched as the pad of his thumb brushed over her temple. "Do you know what he's doing right now?"

"No."

"He's telling his commander about you. About the baby. That Rikar and I protected you. You know what conclusion he'll draw?" She shook her head. Bastian continued, "He'll think you're important to me, and that makes finding you a priority. Myst, you can't go home. It's no longer safe for you in the human world. Like it or not, you are now a part of mine."

Tears stung her eyes. "No...no way. I have friends, a job...a life I love."

"I'm sorry."

Sorry. Yeah, right. He looked devastated. Completely ruined standing there, his green eyes steady...and not a bit sorry. God help her. It wasn't fair. Not Caroline's death, and her angel's sad start in the world. Nor the fact she was trapped in Bastian's stupid, upside-down war.

As he released her and stepped back—leaving her wrung out—she closed her eyes and let the tears fall. She was more than a prisoner now. She was lost. Spiraling out of control in a place she didn't understand or want to be.

And wasn't that the perfect nightcap to an already gut-wrenching day.

Chapter Nine

Calamity erupted from the bedside table, guitars riffs screaming heavy metal. Detective Angela Keen burrowed a little deeper into her pillow, trying to tune out the screech of AC/DC. It didn't work. Brian Johnson just kept singing.

Holy hell. "Thunderstruck" was fast becoming her least favorite song.

But then, that was the point. The whole reason she'd chosen death rock in the first place. She needed a good kick to jar her awake, and the ringtone was the only one that ever managed it.

Cracking an eyelid, she stared at the digital alarm clock. The red lines stayed blurry for a moment, then jumped into focus. Three forty-two a.m. Great. She'd only climbed into bed four hours ago.

Angela reached for her cell phone, fumbled a second before getting a hold of it and flipped the top open. "Yeah?"

"Wakey-wakey, Ange." The gruff male voice came through the line loud and clear. "I need you on site A-SAP. We've got another vic."

Her brows drawn tight, she pushed up onto one elbow. "Are you sure?"

"Same MO," her partner said, his East Coast accent clipped.

Not a good sign. The intensity of Mac's voice always indicated his level of pissed off. And a tight tone on Ian MacCord meant one thing...another girl had turned up dead.

A sick feeling settled in the pit of her stomach and, fighting clingy sheets, Angela shoved her duvet aside. She loved her job—she really did—even though someone had to die for her to go work. The problem here? Young women were the ones doing the dying, and she didn't have a lead. Not one. A big, fat goose egg of an information string.

Liberated from the cotton cling, Angela swung her legs over the side of the bed. "Ash pile?"

"Haven't found one...yet."

"Where are you?"

"Corner of Yesler and First," Mac said, sirens wailing in the background. "Follow the circus...reporters are already here."

Lovely. Just what they needed. Sharks already circling in the tank.

"Keep it tight, Mac." She ran her hand over the top of her head, ruffling her short hair. "See you in twenty."

"Uh-huh."

The snap of Mac's phone sounded as she flipped her own closed. Setting the Motorola Razr on the bedside table, Angela reached for the civvies folded on the bench at the end of her bed. Force of habit. She couldn't sleep unless her clothes were laid out, ready to go...just in case. Well, "just in case" had come about three hours too early. Not that it mattered. The investigation she and Mac had caught wasn't a nine-to-fiver.

Army-style chinos went on first. The plain white tee and button-down shirt got pulled over her head next before she reached for her Roots boots. The footwear was a thing of beauty, a rare budgetary splurge: heavy on comfort with gobs of style to spare.

Stomping her right foot into her boot, she tucked her shirttails in, grabbed her holstered Glock 23 along with her badge from the drawer in her nightstand. After adding her Razr to the melee, she headed for the door. As she stepped out into the corridor and reengaged her condo's double deadbolts, Angela ran her tongue over her teeth. Ugh. She really should brush—Mac would no doubt thank her for it—but with another crime scene on the go, getting there took precedence over fresh breath. Her partner would have to deal, and the Lifesavers in the glove box of her Jeep would have to do.

In less time than it would have taken to find the Colgate, she was out of the underground garage and rolling down the deserted boulevard. Streetlights cast murky shadows, LEDs barely bleeding through the haze of night fog. Typical of Seattle, but Angela thanked God it wasn't raining. The mist might be a pain, but reduced visibility was better than losing the integrity of her crime scene to weather.

Ten minutes and two Lifesavers later, she hung a left onto Yesler Way. Her hand tightened on the steering wheel as she spotted the police cruisers. Lights flashing off gray brick, three patrol vehicles angled out from the curb, establishing the outer perimeter, keeping the growing crowd at bay.

Yeah, the Thursday night club scene was a real Cirque du Soleil. And the biggest clown of all had come out to play.

Even from half a block away, Angela could see Miss Thing powering up her microphone, cameraman following behind like a whipped dog. Clarissa Newton—pain-in-the-butt reporter with air in place of a brain.

Angela shook her head, pulled up to the curb behind the cruisers. It was sad, really. The woman was a throwback, a bleached-out blonde who thought looks mattered more than intelligence. Had Clarissa used mental acuity instead of push-up bras and blow jobs to land her stories, Angela would've thrown her a bone and traded a little information. But the whole "I'm-beautiful-help-me-out" attitude annoyed the hell out of her. So, Miss Thing was on her own.

"Yeah, definitely," Angela murmured, watching Clarissa cozy up to a rookie uniform guarding a perimeter cordoned off by yellow police tape.

Slamming the Jeep door behind her, she clipped her badge on her belt and made tracks, moving down the sidewalk at a fast clip. Dressed in club wear, the crowd stood three deep, college-age looky-loos jockeying for a sneak peek. Same story, different night. Except with Mac's radar up and running, Angela knew this scene *was* different. Murdered girls, same MO, dead within days of each other. Nothing run-of-the-mill about that.

With an "excuse me" or two, the gang of coeds parted and she slipped through, flashing her creds as she ducked beneath the crime scene tape.

Miss Thing didn't miss a beat. Waving her microphone like a cheerleading baton, she went from batting her eyelashes to the flapping red-lacquered lips in a heartbeat. "Detective Keen...Detective Keen! What can you tell me about the—"

"Nothing." A warning in her gaze, Angela made eye contact with the rookie patrol officer. Her focus slid from him to the reporter then back again. "Watch out, man. She's got teeth."

One corner of his mouth quirked up. "Roger that, Red."

Angela wanted to grimace. She nodded instead and, brushing by him, quashed any outward sign of discomfort. *Red.* The nickname from hell. One she'd tried to murder when she moved from Vice to Homicide. No such luck. The guys in her squad had picked it up quick. Even after she whacked off her hair—going from ponytail to pixie— the God-awful name stuck like gum on the bottom of a shoe.

The only saving grace? Her partner never called her that, knowing she didn't like it. Not that she'd ever told him. But Mac was scary like that—so perceptive that it sometimes bordered on eerie.

"Hey, Ange...over here."

Speak of the devil.

Ignoring the smell of week-old garbage, Angela stepped into the mouth of the alley, toward six and a half feet of ripped Irish-American. Harvard-smart with a whole lot of street savvy, Mac was a man women loved to look at...eye candy without the inferred sweetness.

Most cops didn't want to work with him. He was too aggressive, too hot-tempered, too, well, *everything.* Angela had heard the stories, been warned six ways to Sunday that Mac rode the razor edge and was on his way out, but a fluke in scheduling had thrown them together. Now, almost two years later, she couldn't imagine working with anyone else.

But the biggest bonus? No sexual spark to screw it up.

Most women would have mourned that fact—done back-flips to catch Mac's eye. Not her. She liked the big brother vibe, thank you very much. And so did he. It was the perfect scenario in an imperfect job...great chemistry without the mind fuck of physical attraction. Outstanding.

Boots traveling over cracked asphalt, Angela stepped over a crumpled soda can, coming up alongside her partner. "Don't you sleep, Irish?"

Mac flashed his pearly whites, the grin half-angel, half-devil. "Not much and never alone."

Angela rolled her eyes, but let his evasion slide. She didn't need to ride him about his insomnia or taking better care of himself. No matter how subtle, he'd gotten the message. "You're a sick puppy, you know that?"

He shrugged and, tapping his pen against his notebook, returned his attention to the CSIs on the other side of the beat-up Dumpster. Silver crime-scene cases open and tools in use, the two techs were working the scene like pros: cameras flashing, markers out, gathering evidence before the ME came to take the body away.

"Less than twenty, Ange. You're getting faster." Restlessness getting the better of him, Mac walked to one of the small orange cones set out on the pavement. Crouching to examine the evidence beside it, he glanced at her over his shoulder. "Didn't take the time to brush your teeth, did ya?"

Lifesaver in her mouth, Angela drilled him with a glare. "Shut up and fill me in."

"Dead girl...name's Hannah Gains." Fighting a smile over the big cop attitude she was throwing his way, he pushed to his feet. "Nineteen, five foot five, brown hair, blue eyes. A freshman at Seattle U."

"Crap."

"I used something a bit stronger."

"I'm sure," she said, aware Mac's vocabulary rivaled a gang banger's. "Anything else?"

"Big-ass boot print...military issue." A muscle twitched along her partner's jaw as he pointed his pen toward the girl splayed like a broken doll on damp pavement. "My guess? About a size fourteen."

Saying a soft "hey" to the CSI scraping under the victim's fingernails, Angela circled around behind Mac to where the dead girl lay, eyes wide open, staring up at a starless sky. The sight made Angela's chest go tight. The sick bastard. Look what he had done...how he'd left her: half dressed, lying in the worst filth the city had to offer.

Balanced on the balls of her feet, Angela crouched a few feet away. Her heart sank as she got her first glimpse of her victim's face. Yeah, she fit the profile: young, pretty, a leggy brunette in a halter top and micromini. Just like the other two. Mac was right. It was the same guy, and he had a type.

She glanced over, catching Mac's gaze. "Military? How do you know for sure?"

"I used to wear something similar."

In the SEAL teams. Angela didn't need him to say it to know he was thinking it. She knew about his military background. Had snuck into records to read through his file before taking a second shift with him—even though IA would have her ass if they knew.

Chewing on the inside of her bottom lip, she propped her elbows on her knees and forced herself to look at the woman again...to put her anger at the senseless murder aside and do her job.

Like the others, there were no outward signs of struggle. But something told her Hannah Gains's autopsy report would read like the other two on her desk: sexual penetration but no sperm, so no viable DNA; bruises on the lower back and nape of the neck; marks on her throat. And the kicker? The COD was catastrophic organ failure, a systematic shutdown of everything...heart, lungs, liver, kidneys, and finally, brain function.

So far, the only thing different about Hannah's murder was absence of an ash pile. The other two girls had been practically laid out beside one. The lab work wasn't back yet, but the ME had given them his best guess...cremated human remains.

Angela looked down the length of the alleyway, staring into shadows and fog, wondering if they'd find the ashes at the other end. Holy hell. What kind of sicko were they dealing with here? Murder a girl...leave a cremated body behind to keep her company? It didn't make any sense, but neither did killing innocent women. So, what the hell did she know?

Wiping her hands on her thighs, she said, "Our boy's stepping up his game...escalating. It's only been eleven days since his last strike."

Her partner nodded as his cell phone went off, screaming "Highway to Hell." Unclipping it from his belt, he cut off the music by flipping it open. "MacCord."

Angela returned her attention to the body, thinking about the boot print. Maybe it was the break they needed. Not many guys wore size fourteens, and if the body dumps were any indication, he liked the club scene, so—

"Jesus fucking Christ. Where?"

Mac's snarl raised the hair on the nape of her neck. Pushing to her feet, she zeroed in on his face and caught the anger in his eyes. Crap. That look coupled with his tone said it all. Something nasty had gone down.

Expression grim, Mac held her gaze and listened hard to the rapid string of words she could hear coming through the cell phone's earpiece. She tipped her chin as she came up beside him and mouthed, "What?"

He shook his head, listened some more, and then said, "Don't touch a fucking thing. Our CSI Unit will handle it. We'll be there in forty minutes."

As soon as he snapped his phone closed, Angela said, "Tell me."

"Dead girl. Missing baby. Two ash piles off Route Eighteen. Captain fielded the call...figured the case is linked to ours and told the locals out there to contact me." Digging into the front pocket of his jeans, Mac tossed her the keys to his X-Trail. "You drive."

Quick reflexes helped her catch the Harley-Davidson keychain on the down arc before she put her boots into motion and followed Mac out of the alley. Yeah, no doubt about it. Her driving was a good idea. They were heading into a shit storm, and her partner was already pissed off.

Chapter Ten

The glowing globes hugged the cave's dome ceiling, putting on a light show. Her backside still glued to the car—with Bastian looming like the Unmasked Avenger—Myst glanced up to watch the lanterns for a second. Some big, some small, the lights bobbed like a swarm of jellyfish, paper-thin bodies suspended by, ah…

Yup. Just as she thought. Nothing. Not a cable or safely net in sight.

Too bad, really. She could have used one.

Not that she thought the globes would fall or anything. It was magic up there, a swaying extravaganza of glory, glory, hallelujah without end. So the net she needed was all about her…to catch her sorry butt when she took a header and fell into the bottomless pit called Trouble. With one foot already planted in the abyss, she could've thought of a way to pull herself out…if she'd been alone. But she couldn't run with a baby. Not without a circus-size safety net, which meant she was pretty much screwed.

Bastian knew it. She did, too.

So…one way to go, then.

Done with the pity party—and the crying—her priorities realigned. The newborn needed attention. The medical kind that included a neonatal incubator, diapers, clothes, and infant formula. He'd been born in less than ideal circumstances. Okay, now whom was she kidding? The environment had been nightmarish: unsanitary, stress-filled, and bloody. The fact he was so quiet—sleeping so soundly after all that—worried her. He wasn't injured, at least, not on the outside. But inside? Many things could be wrong: brain injury, internal bleeding, any number of preemie malformations.

Myst's throat went tight. She threw another prayer into the universe. *Please, God...don't let it be anything like that.*

Losing Caroline had been torture enough. She couldn't lose the baby, too.

Kicking her nurse back into gear, she pushed the terrible memory away and dragged her attention from the tufts of curling dark hair on her angel's head to look at Bastian. "I need something from my trunk."

His eyes narrowed a fraction.

That was all it took. She started babbling, "A bag...with baby stuff. Medical stuff. You know, a stethoscope and ah... formula, diapers, and—"

"We have all you need inside the lair." He slid left, powerful body keeping pace with her as she inched toward the back end of her car.

"I want my own equipment."

He hesitated, his gaze not only locked on her, but loaded with warning.

"Please," she whispered, unwilling to waste anymore time. What did he think she had back there? A sawed-off shotgun? Well, that was definitely going on her wish list when she got out of this mess. But here and now? It was all about the newborn...about getting him what he needed. Bastian and his mistrust could go to hell. "I need my own stuff. I trust it."

He nodded, the movement tight. "Fair enough."

Myst exhaled long and slow, a thank you on the tip of her tongue. She swallowed it. Reasonable or not, Bastian didn't deserve her gratitude. Heading around the back bumper, she almost lost control and snorted. Yeah, right. What he deserved was a boot to the gonads...a swift, hard, very accurate dropkick.

"I wouldn't advise it," he said, beating her to the back of the car. With a flick, he popped the trunk latch. A ssssssss sounded as the air hinges did their job, raising the hatch while her mouth hung open. She snapped it closed so hard her teeth clicked together.

What the heck had just happened? Had he—

"A word to the wise, *bellmia*. I'm well aware of what you think of me."

A horrible thought took hold. Was it possible...could he...

"Are you reading my mind?"

He shrugged.

And well, wasn't that a big, fat yes. Somehow, his ability to read minds didn't surprise her...which surprised her. She must be getting used to all his hocus-pocus. Being airlifted while in a car by a dragon could do that to a girl. Still, it didn't mean she liked it.

"Stop it." She glared at him, her snarl factor hitting double digits. "My thoughts are private...not for you or anyone else."

"As you wish," he murmured, all *Princess Bride*, as he took inventory of her trunk. "Which one?"

What? Oh, right. The bag. "The small blue one. And I mean it, Bastian. It's an unfair advantage. Don't even try to—"

"You want ground rules?" His big hand curled around the bag's straps, lifting it out on an arcing swing.

"No. I want my freedom back."

"Too late for that." The bag slung over his shoulder, he strode past her, heading for who-knew-where. His scent followed, all the gorgeousness of Lanvin cologne enveloping her with an erotic twist. "Come. We've wasted enough time here."

With a grumble, she followed, trailing in his wake, calling him every nasty name she could think of, hoping like hell he was reading her mind. And that his ears were burning. Maybe if she tried hard enough, all the cerebral screaming would make him deaf—or drive him insane—without her uttering a single word.

Would serve him right.

On so many levels.

All because she was trapped.

As Bastian's heavy boots echoed across the vastness—walking her closer to prison and further from independence—Myst struggled to keep herself together. The life she knew was over. He was taking away everything she loved: her friends, her job, her life.

None of it was fair. Not much of it made sense. At least, not yet. This world—the one Bastian and his friends occupied—was not, and never would be, hers.

The urge to let loose and scream almost overwhelmed her. But hysterics wouldn't get her anywhere but teary-eyed. And honestly? Becoming an emotional mess over her loss was about as productive as having a stroke. Not the best if she wanted to keep her brain in the ON position.

Halfway across the cavern, Myst checked the baby again. Looked at his small face, made sure...

Her heart skipped a beat. Was he even breathing?

Her pace slowed to a shuffle as she slid her hand past the fleece lining to touch his chest. He was warm and… thank God! His little ribcage expanded. Myst inhaled hard, more gasp than actual breath, and turned her attention to finding his pulse. The fast, steady beat reassured her. Okay, no need to lose it. He was still—

"He's all right, Myst."

Her throat so tight she could hardly breathe, she glanced up to find Bastian watching her. "I'm so afraid for him."

"He's healthy."

"How do you know?"

"Trust me."

And there it was again—the appeal—and despite everything, she wanted to trust him. Under normal circumstances, she would've given what he asked. But tonight wasn't normal. And no matter how trustworthy he acted, she knew he could turn on her in an instant.

So…no. Trusting him wasn't on her to-do list.

She forced herself to nod anyway—to play submissive to his dominant—and made herself follow him. Their footfalls echoed in the cavern, taking up space inside her head. Adjusting her raincoat around the baby, she studied her surroundings, paying close attention to the details…all the small things that might make a big difference later on. Things like the width of the cave, the number of stalagmites near the back, and the almost hidden ledge that hugged the side wall and met the landing platform. She measured its narrowness, followed its line as it disappeared into the tunnel leading toward the river. That could be a way out, but…

She'd need a few things before attempting it. A flashlight, for one. A baby carrier, for another. Having her hands free would become a necessity among jagged outcroppings and slick rocks. What else? A waterproof jacket would be good: sturdy boots, warm clothes for both her and the baby. A compass, maybe. A few power bars for her, bottles and formula for him. Add some extra diapers and she'd be set.

Yeah, that was definitely doable.

Hope picked up her heart, lifting her mood. She chanced a quick peek at Bastian. About five feet in front of her, he stared at her over his shoulder: eyes narrowed, brows drawn tight, an unhappy expression on his face.

Oh, crap. Had he read her mind on that one, too?

Leather creaked as he rolled his shoulders. As far as statements went, it was an excellent one. It showcased his strength, put it up front along with the unholy light in his eyes. "Stop planning your escape. Once inside, there is no way out of Black Diamond."

Okay, so that answered the whole thought-poaching thing. "I asked you not to do that."

He raised a brow. "I'll stop...when you start to behave."

"I am behaving."

He snorted.

She huffed. "I'm following you, aren't I?"

He uh-hummed, and she wished she had something to throw at him. Like a crowbar.

Stopping in front of a solid wall, he held out his hands. "Give me the infant."

"No." The *he's mine* went unspoken as she hugged the baby closer to her chest.

"I'll give him right back, *bellmia*." The soles of his boots scraping against the granite floor, he pivoted to face her, expression full of understanding. "He *is* yours, but he will not survive the portal without protection. Look behind me."

Myst retreated another step as the wall behind Bastian became a wavy, indistinct blur. She swallowed. "We have to..."

"Walk through it," he said, finishing her sentence. "It will be hard enough on you, but the infant will not survive unless I am holding him."

"H-how—"

"Magic...I'll cocoon him in the equivalent of a human air lock."

"He'll be protected?"

"One hundred percent." Stepping toward her, he held out his arms. "I'll be gentle, Myst. He's not the first infant I've had the privilege of holding."

The privilege. She bit her bottom lip, vacillating. As much as she hated to admit it, his sincerity convinced her. Still, as she handed over her angel—as she gave up his warmth— her heart beat triple time, fear and loss moving through her like poison.

True to his word, Bastian handled the newborn with care, supporting his head, settling him gently in the crook of his arm. "Come, *bellmia.* Take my hand."

Taking a deep breath, she slipped her hand into his much larger one, flinching at the contact. Palm to palm wasn't something she wanted to do with him. Touching Bastian was simply too intense...way beyond her comfort zone. And more than she could handle.

"Take a deep breath." He glanced over his shoulder, his gaze locking onto hers over the wide expanse of black leather. "In through your nose, out through your mouth. We'll pass through quick, but..."

"But?"

"It won't be pleasant for you."

Terrific. Just what she needed...more pain. "Bastian, why don't we just go another way? I don't think I can—"

He squeezed her hand. "You can take it."

Without giving her a chance to protest, he tightened his grip on her and tugged. She sucked in a quick breath, holding on tight as he drew her toward the wall. Rippling like water, the stone hissed, humming like an electrical station...reminding her of chain-link fences and big signs that read "High Voltage. Keep Out."

Bastian gave her another squeeze. She muttered a curse as the first wave of static electricity hit. The current arced, raising the hair on her forearms, attacking her spine as it went head to head with her central nervous system. As the spasm hit, muscles tightened over her bones. Gasping, she clung to Bastian, double fisting his hand, stumbling behind him, hopping back on the name-calling train—big jerk, bonehead, Neanderthal dragon-man all took a turn on her mental wheel. God, she sucked at this...needed a whole lot of practice in the insult arena. Maybe an urban dictionary—the one rappers used—would help with that shortcoming. Maybe—

An electro-pulse zapped the air out of her lungs. A howling burst of frigid wind followed, tearing at her already mangled braid. As the tendrils flew around her head, the terrible prickling sensation showed no mercy. Her muscles cramped, shooting pain from the soles of her feet, up her spine, to the back of her head.

Holy crap. This was...so not...normal.

She choked on empty lungs. Her vision shorted out, going dark and then light, flickering like a schizophrenic lightbulb. She blinked fast, then gave up and squeezed her eyes shut, forcing one foot in front of the other.

Dear God, when would the nastiness end?

The smell of stagnant water in the cave faded. Something pungent and clean stepped into the void. Heavy on the antiseptic, the scent reminded Myst of the hospital...of pine floor cleaner and surgical soap.

"All right?"

She shook her head as Bastian slid his arm around her. Leaning into his heat, she settled her cheek against his shoulder, feeling sick to her stomach and blank in the head. *Breathe.* In. Out. In. Out. She followed the pattern, curling her hands in Bastian's coat, unlocking her lungs one gasp at a time. Little by little, the pinwheeling stopped and the kaleidoscoping color faded into dark spots.

"Bastian?" His name came out on a weak exhalation, raspy and unhinged.

"Yeah."

"I can't see."

"Give it a minute." His voice came soft, and his breath warm against her ear. "The doorway is a little intense if you're not used to it. Keep your eyes closed. Concentrate on breathing instead of seeing. It'll come."

"Is he all right?" she asked, tasting the bile poised at the back of her throat.

"Came through like a champ."

Relief rolled through her as she listened to his voice and took his direction...even though she wanted to punch him instead. *Just breathe.* What kind of advice was that anyway? The stupid kind, and nowhere near sufficient for what she'd just stepped through. Score another point on the jerk-o-meter for Bastian. He was up to two million, and the number just kept climbing. Especially when he was playing the whole savior angle...*playing* being the operative word.

"You know, the whole nice routine?" Pressed up against him, her voice came out muffled, but at least she sounded better, more steady, less shaken. Thank God. "You might as well drop it. I'm not going to forgive you for kidnapping me...ever."

"Forever is a long time, *bellmia*."

"Jerk."

He chuckled. "Probably."

"Undeniably," she countered, pushing against his chest, her let-me-go message clear.

He released her slowly, but didn't back away. Instead, he locked her in place, spreading his big hand across the small of her back. Dipping his head, he placed his mouth next to her ear. She shivered as his lips brushed her.

He nipped her gently, showing her a little teeth. "Be very careful, Myst. I love a good challenge...and it sounds like you just threw one into the open."

Goosebumps spiked on her skin. "I wasn't—"

"I think you were and...I'll see your bet and raise you." His fingers slid along her spine. The gentle caress soothed, yet somehow stimulated at the same time. "What do you think about that?"

Every one of her muscles went tense as she fought to hide her reaction. He didn't need to know she was attracted to him. Good God, *she* didn't even want to know that, so she put on her big girl panties and said, "This isn't a game, Bastian. This is my life, so screw you and your stupid challenges. You can't keep me here if I don't want to stay."

"Hmm...I guess that leaves me only one option, doesn't it?" He shifted his hold on her, slid the tips of his fingers up the back of her arm, killing her with the purr in his voice and the heat in his hands. "I'm going to make you want to stay."

"It won't happen." Okay, time to open her eyes and escape. But, man, her focus was shot. She couldn't see a thing but indistinct blobs.

"We'll see. Now, how are the eyes. Better?" Releasing her, he stepped back, taking his warmth with him, leaving her standing unprotected in the cold.

Myst rubbed her eyes with her fingertips, mangling her eyelashes.

"Well?"

"Well, what?" she snapped, sick to death of him and his niceness.

"Vision clearing?"

Done with the rubbing routine, Myst opened her eyes again and realized two things at once. Bastian was still standing way too close. She took two steps back, correcting the oversight. And the second? She stood at the end of a long corridor. A wide one—maybe eight feet across—with polished concrete floors and whitewashed stone walls...the old kind with chisel marks on them, ones medieval builders might have used to construct cathedrals and archways.

Embedded in the floor, round lights ran like twin runways, lining the hallway's outer edges, providing the only source of illumination. She glanced at the ceiling. At least twelve feet high, the smooth plaster glowed in the low light, an expanse of white that went on forever.

"Where are we?"

"The underground lair of Black Diamond...my home."

Brushing the hair out of her face, her focus shifted to the baby. Myst held out her arms. "Give him back."

Without hesitation, Bastian handed him over, making the transfer both gentle and seamless. As the baby settled—small and soft in her arms—she breathed easier and checked him again, searching for problems. Everything looked good: the newborn's chest rose and fell in a steady rhythm, the color of his skin was a healthy pink, and his heartbeat was still strong.

She nodded at Bastian.

He tipped his chin—acknowledging the thank you she refused to say out loud—and watched her tuck the baby against her shoulder before starting up the slight incline of corridor. After a few strides, he pivoted to walk backwards, his gaze glued to her, his heavy-soled boots landing softly on the hard floor.

"One way in. One way out of Black Diamond, Myst." He pointed at the now solid wall behind her. "Through that doorway."

Resisting the urge to look over her shoulder, she suppressed a shiver. No way she wanted to pass through that God-awful thing again. She wasn't certain she would survive it. Not without Bastian's hand to hold.

His mouth curving up at the corners, he gave her a knowing look. "If you think you're going to get past me here...think again."

The words echoed, the inherent threat bouncing off concrete as Myst followed Bastian's retreat, keeping pace in the deserted corridor. He was right. The portal wasn't her way out, but that didn't mean his home was inescapable. Bastian might want her to believe it, but that didn't make it true. A problem, after all, could be solved many different ways.

Sight-stealing portal be damned.

Bastian and Black Diamond had a weakness. All she needed to do was find it.

Chapter Eleven

Rikar hated the in-house clinic at Black Diamond. The overhead lights were too bright, the smell too clean, the walls too white. Like a human doctor's office, everything belonged somewhere: in a drawer, a cabinet, a fucking rollaway cart. The place was a clean freak's wet dream. Clutter-frickin'-free, Peter Walsh approved.

All right, so the neatness served a purpose. Was no doubt a welcome quality in the whole treat-the-patient thing, but man, that didn't mean he liked the clinical vibe.

Or the fact his friend had ass-planted him in the room.

On an examination table with crinkly, white paper.

Oh, happy-happy-joy-joy. Someone just shoot him now. *Please.*

Legs dangling off the side of the table, shitkickers swinging in midair, he eyed his friend—resident computer genius cum occasional medic—as he approached with one of those carts. Rikar watched the right front wheel flap, the wobble laying down an audio track of flutter-flutter-squeak-squeak as though the thing had a bad case of performance anxiety.

Well, all right. At least something in the place wasn't perfect. For some reason, the idea made Rikar ease up and unclench the fist attached to his uninjured arm...even though he knew what was coming.

"What the hell are you grinning about?" Shaved chrome dome and mocha-colored skin gleaming under the fluorescents, Sloan slowed his roll, bringing the supplies alongside the examination table. The cart was loaded with gauze at one end; medical instruments that looked more like torture tools were laid out with surgical precision on the other. The collection of stainless steel flashed on the blue cloth. "You think it's funny I gotta reattach your arm?"

Rikar glanced at the gash bisecting his forearm. Blood welled, his heart providing a steady pump of plasma. Okay, so the rogue had gone Freddy Krueger on his ass and spilt him wide open, but a full-on reattach? "A little over the top, don't ya think?"

Sloan shrugged. "I watched *The Terminator* tonight."

"The first one?" He hoped so...Arnold rocked in that one.

"Uh-huh."

"That explains the overkill."

Picking up something pointy and sharp, Sloan asked, "Ready?"

"Go for—ow! Jesus, Sloan..." Rikar jerked as his friend went postal on his arm, prodding deep into the wound. "Watch what you're—fuck!"

"Stop being such a pansy." Done torturing him with tweezers, Sloan got busy with saline solution. As the cold spray washed into the cut, barbs of pain spiraled up his arm, and Rikar gave his colorful vocabulary another workout.

Goddamn it, the brother was a straight-up masochist.

Unfazed, Sloan shook his head, but didn't let up. "Man up, my brother."

"Man up, my dick." Grinding his back molars, Rikar tried not to twitch as the saline made another pass, but...

Jesus, that hurt. And the blood…goddamn, he was bleeding all over the place now. He could feel it, dripping over the side of his arm, falling from the tip of his middle finger to go splat on the floor.

"Shit, Rikar."

"Yeah, I know."

And he did know that he was in trouble. No way he should still be leaking like a sieve. His kind didn't bleed out from a wound like his. Their dragon DNA went to work too quickly for that, closing the wound fast and neat.

Yeah, so the nasty gash cut through muscle to reach bone. But that was nothing new. Injuries happened. Arteries sometimes got sliced. All of the warriors came home dinged up from time to time; the slice and dice with the Razorbacks the rule, not the exception.

Current plasma loss aside, however, tonight was unusual in another way. Rikar frequently got within range of rogue claws, but he always took care of himself in the icy cold of his suite. The drill went something like…clean it up, throw some stitches along with Polysporin at it, and, voilá, problem solved.

This one, though, was a bitch. With a crazy kick.

Rikar grabbed for the edge of the table as his vision tunneled. "Sloan…"

"Lie down." One big mitt planted on Rikar's shoulder, Sloan helped him shift his legs up onto the table. Rikar wanted to protest, but with his head gone topsy-turvy, pain nailed him with a great, big body slam. As his back touched down on crinkly paper, his friend murmured, "Breathe through it…and give me a sec. I'll get it ready."

"No…problem." Rikar closed his eyes.

Holy shit, he thought the mental mind spin was bad enough, but now his stomach was sloshing around, making all kinds of noise. And...where the hell were his legs? He couldn't feel them anymore.

A faucet got cranked across the room. Water started running, and a second later, he heard a door open and close. Plastic rustled and then God, yes...something hard fell, bouncing like marbles against steel. The sound was music to Rikar's ears. *Hurry,* he wanted to say, *hurry.* He needed it...needed—

Sloan came back, leaning into his visual field. "Come on, buddy. Up and at 'em."

With a groan, Rikar rolled, helping his friend get his two-hundred-and-fifty-pound, six-foot-six frame vertical. The trip across the room wasn't a picnic. Yeah, not a red-and-white-checkered cloth in sight, just blurry blobs and a boatload of nausea as they shuffled across the hospital-grade floor.

Not bothering to undress him, Sloan lifted Rikar's sorry ass over the lip of the tub and set him down—leathers and all—into the ice bath.

Fuuuuck, yeaaaaaah.

"Good?"

"More..." Sore all over, Rikar sank chin deep in the arctic chill. "More."

Something went click—a cell phone, maybe—as Sloan left the side of the tub, heavy footfalls bouncing around the quiet room. The freezer door opened with a suctioning hiss. Another round of plastic crinkled, telling him more ice was on its way. Thank Christ. He craved the cold, needed to get his core temperature down. If he lost consciousness before that happened, he would overheat—coma territory for a frost dragon.

The first round of ice chips hit him just where Rikar wanted it, up around his shoulders and the back of his neck. Sloan packed him in well, pouring bag after bag of cubes into the cold water and on top of him.

His eyes drifted closed. He burrowed in, nestled his too-warm cheek against the chips, listened to the fast click of fingers on a phone keypad as he drifted on a sick wave of Deepshitsville.

Sloan's baritone broke through, sounding clipped as someone answered the call, "Ven, where's Daimler?" A pause. Another male's voice on the line then, "Shit. We got problems down here. No...it's Rikar...uh-huh...yeah, exactly. Just get through them and get your ass down here... yeah...quick as you can. We're losing our boy."

Fighting the need for a puke bucket, Rikar cracked his eyelids. "New shipment?"

"Yeah. The anti-venom's buried ass-deep in boxes. Daimler's out running errands, but Venom's digging for it."

Poison. Yup, that explained his spectacular ass-plant.

Anyone else would've gotten the chills as the toxin went to work on his central nervous system. But, oh no, not him. Color him lucky. He got the opposite effect, a well of heat that his frosty side couldn't handle. And at the worse time... when their miracle man was out buying coffee at Starbucks or some shit.

Figured, didn't it? The second he needed the guy, he got good and ghost...poof gone, nowhere to be found. Although, that wasn't exactly fair. As a Numbai—a member of a special species born into Dragonkind's care—Daimler couldn't be blamed for his absence. It was his job to keep the lair organized and well stocked, to caretake like you read about. The TLC routine had been bred into Daimler from birth, his sole purpose and pleasure to look after those he served.

Still, Rikar wished the male's special brand of I-got-you-covered hadn't included leaving the lair tonight. Cuz, if the guy were here? The anti-venom would already be in his veins.

"Hang in there, buddy...help's coming."

The baritone sounded close, almost as though Sloan was kneeling right next to the tub. The gentle touch came next, against his temple before brushing over his hair, unsticking the strands from the side of his face.

And wasn't that a total turnaround? Was he really feeling that?

Rikar tried to open his eyes, but his eyelids weighed five hundred pounds...each. His mouth wasn't faring much better. He couldn't get his tongue to work right.

Another pass. Another soft stroke over the top of his head.

Yeah, he felt that, but man, it didn't compute. Sloan was the only one here, and the warrior was a standoffish SOB who rarely touched anyone. Bastian called him a "long-time loner," so used to his own company and his computers he existed in a world of his own making. The fact that the male might care about them—about his fellow Nightfury brothers—had never entered Rikar's mind.

Swallowing past his dry throat, Rikar worked some saliva into his mouth. He had to tell Sloan...needed to—

"Is the ice helping?"

"No. Whatever the bastard hit me with is...fuck. I need. More. Ice," he said, or at least, Rikar thought that was his voice, slurring all over the place as cold water sloshed and more of the chipped-and-chilly got packed around his head.

The frosty side of him sighed, loving the arctic blast, but the relief didn't last. The heat pushed it aside, shredding him from the inside out. As he rode the pain train, he concentrated on breathing: in, out…in, out. The oxygen infuse didn't help. The pain was too intense, making his legs churn beneath the water, the soles of his shitkickers slipping against the bottom of the stainless steel tub.

God, the enemy was getting smarter, using their brains for a change.

Hurrah for them…the rogue jerk-offs.

Moisture beaded on his skin. Rikar swiped at it, annoyed by the drip-drip-drip in his eyes, wondering what…

Christ, the droplets weren't from the water. It was sweat.

Bigger alarm bells rang inside his head, taking him into apocalyptic territory. A fever…the only thing guaranteed to kill a frost dragon. And he was sliding fast. He never perspired. Ever. He was too cold-blooded for that.

Rikar shifted around in the tub, the agony worsening with each breath. "The…anti…venom?"

"Coming. Ven's gonna—"

The airlock hissed as the clinic's glass-paneled door slid open.

"What the fuck?"

The question cracked the quiet wide open, coming at Rikar like a short burst of automatic gunfire. He recognized that deep voice. Bastian. Thank God. His best friend was here. He would—

"Oh, my God!" Female voice…short pause…a bit of a shuffle, and then, "Here, Bastian…take him. And you…"

Another pause. Light footsteps coming closer and, "Status report. Right now."

"Ahh…he's…shit, I'm…" Sloan's stuttering pierced through the mind fog that imprisoned Rikar. Wow. That was new. The male sounded shell-shocked, shaken out of his normal calm.

But why?

Rikar concentrated hard, fought through all the thick-white-and-fluffy mucking up his head, searching for the answer.

Someone cleared his throat. "Slashed right forearm. Poison's gone deep. Anti-venom's coming."

"Are you IV-equipped?"

"I…we—"

"If you are, I need a bag…stat."

Small hands touched his face, then slid away; one landed on his throat and found his pulse while the other moved around to cup the nape of his neck. Oh, man, that felt good. The touched eased him, took some of the pain, scrambling his molecules in a reenergized frenzy. Hmm yeah, that was better. He wasn't tumbling down the rabbit hole anymore… he was floating, buoyant instead of sinking inside his own skull.

The voice came again: soft, lyrical, and steady as hell. Female and Bastian…here together. Rikar's brain kicked over. Not good…so not good. Bastian's female—the one named…something…what was it?…hell, he couldn't remember—was touching him. And he was taking from her, his body drawing on her energy to fight the infection now streaming through his blood.

A nasty snarl rolled through the clinic.

Oh, Christ. Bastian was going to rip him a new body orifice...the stem-to-stern kind. Once he claimed her, a male never shared his female. Ever. Her hands on him was a bad idea, tantamount to suicide.

But, God, he needed the white-hot energy she was feeding him.

Still, Rikar made the effort, jerked in the water, squirming to get away from her. She held firm, moving his arm from under the ice. With a gentle touch that made him groan, the female checked his injury, soothing him with soft words before turning to bark orders at the others.

Unable to stop himself, Rikar slipped beneath her spell even as he marveled at the unfairness. Sure, she of the glorious energy would probably save him, but it wouldn't matter. The game would end the same way, because the instant the healing sleep let him go, Bastian would hand him his balls on the end of a blade.

Chapter Twelve

One, Mississippi. Two, Mississippi. Three, Mississippi. Four—
"Breathe," Bastian growled at himself because, God knew, the rolling count—all those stupid Mississippis— weren't doing a thing to calm him.

Shit. Shit. Shit.

Myst. Oh, God, she had her hands on Rikar. *His* female was touching another male...*feeding—*

Another snarl rolled out of him. He couldn't help it. The possessive part of him—the one ruled by his dragon— was taking over, amping up territorial instinct until Bastian didn't know which part of him would explode first; his head, his heart, or motherfucking lungs. All were getting a work-out, and not in a good way.

Yeah, no Nautilus here. Just pure animal rage. The kind that kept a male jacked to maximum velocity when another got in between him and his female.

God. He was losing his mind...with an infant in his arms.

Not that he could feel him. The warm weight in the crook of his arm barely registered on his psycho scale. He was too fixated on Myst, which was not good news...not for him or the little guy. If he lost control and attacked Rikar, the baby would get hurt...so *not* what he wanted to do.

Breathing like a wounded racehorse, Bastian hammered his internal gearshift and put himself in reverse. Careening backward, he led with his shoulders, slamming into the wall beside the clinic door. The concrete cracked, fissures spreading like a spiderweb on the cinder blocks. He planted his feet, desperate to stay away from the stainless tub.

Jesus, he was in real trouble here.

Rikar was his best friend...his buddy, and yet in the heat of his fixation, it didn't matter. He wanted to rip the warrior's head off his shoulders...fracture his skull for feeding from the female he'd claimed as his own.

And man, that scared him, because the bond he and Rikar shared ran bone deep, right to his marrow. The fact Myst overrode that connection just hours after meeting her shook the hell out of him.

He needed a bailout...fast. Someone to knock him into concussion land before shit got critical, before he couldn't control it anymore. But Sloan was busy jumping when Myst said jump, scrambling for the supplies she needed.

And holy shit. How amazing was she? Barking out instructions, controlling the situation, helping his friend, soothing him with her words. God, he loved her voice, its calm, confident lilt as she calmed Rikar while telling Sloan how she wanted things done.

"Myst...baby..." His voice came out on a groan as Myst laid her palm against Rikar's forehead. "Don't..."

She brushed his friend's hair back, stroking his skin with her elegant fingers. Rikar moaned, turning into her touch. And Bastian's body went ape shit, twitching as sweat ran in rivulets down his spine. Gritting his teeth on another snarl, Bastian locked his knees, reminding himself who he held in his arms. He needed to get out of the clinic, but... his dragon refused to leave. Had nailed his feet to the floor in the mental sphere. No matter how much he wanted to haul ass—to protect the baby and Rikar—Bastian couldn't move.

And wasn't that fantastic? Un-huh, right...the territorial bullshit was a freaking peach.

After handing Myst an IV bag, Sloan glanced over at him. And did a double take. "Oh, fuck."

Bang on, Columbo. They were in Deepshitsville, and the male was only just now noticing? Great detective work there, buddy.

"Ah, Myst," Sloan said, voice soft, trying to keep it casual. "We got a problem."

"I know." All business, Myst cracked the plastic pack on the IV needle, getting ready to nail Rikar in the arm and get fluids flowing. "His blood pressure's dropping. Where the heck is your—"

The glass door slid open with a hiss, hammering Bastian in the shoulder. As he got knocked sideways, Bastian grunted. Good. More pain. Enough to dislodge need and predatory instinct. As Bastian threw a collar on his inner beast, Venom sprinted over the threshold, his hands loaded with white boxes. Juggling the anti-venom, the warrior skidded to a halt in the middle of the clinic, picking up the vibe with one shrewd sweep of his ruby gaze.

Good boy. At least someone was paying attention.

Tossing the entire load at Sloan, Venom spun and nailed him right between the eyes with a whole lot of you-keep-your-shit-together-brother.

Shaking all over now, Bastian shook his head. "I can't... you need...to...take him."

"Nah, you're cool, Commander." Ven rolled his shoulders and got up close, blocking Bastian's view of Myst, his physique on display in a black muscle shirt. The male was huge, taller and wider than Bastian. Not that size mattered. The ruby-eyed warrior didn't stand a chance against him, and that was on a good day. "Besides, if I take the infant, you're gonna download the launch code and go nuclear on Rikar. Can't have that, my man. So, hang tight. The female's almost done with our boy."

A simple "no" would've gotten the job done, but Venom was a talker. Much to everyone's consternation, the charismatic SOB gum-flapped more than any male he knew.

"Then hit me...knock me out," Bastian rasped, the *mine-mine-mine* getting louder inside his head. The refrain downloaded into a humming chant, stomping its foot like an irate three-year-old. And yeah, that sounded about right. His dragon was nowhere near mature when it came to Myst. "I'm not going to make it. I'll kill him. Just—"

"Bastian?" Myst's voice—that beautiful, soft lilt—cut through the noise inside his skull. "I think I've got him stabilized, but..." Blue eyes the color of violets peeked around Venom's shoulder. "Holy crap. Are you all right?"

"No."

Short. Sweet. To the point. And just like that, his internal chains snapped, setting his beast free.

He needed to touch her, to wipe Rikar's scent from her skin, and...oh, fuck, this wasn't going to be pretty. She didn't know what was coming, couldn't hear the rumble deep inside him. But he couldn't stop it. The need to dominate, to show the males in this room to whom she belonged, was a force he couldn't fight.

"Forgive me." All his focus riveted on her, he played hot potato with the infant, handing him to Venom.

The handoff was quick and smooth. But as Venom took the baby and spun toward the door, the abrupt shift startled him. He woke up angry, small hands flailing, the wail so piercing that Myst broke eye contact with him to reach for the newborn.

But it was too late. Bastian was already moving.

—

Myst blinked as Bastian passed the baby to Big-Dark-and-Scary like a baton. Okay, so the transfer was steady, and the huge guy's hands gentle, but holy Hannah on a swizzle stick. What the heck did they think they were doing?

She wanted to check the baby...here in the clinic.

Everything she needed was in her bag. Well, most of it, anyway. Some of her stuff had landed on the floor in her rush to treat Rikar, but whatever she couldn't find, the clinic would provide. From what Myst could see, the place was hospital-grade, right down to the neonatal bed sitting in one corner. With that in her favor, getting her angel's APGAR score would be the work of minutes.

Her only requirement? The newborn.

Big-Dark-and-Scary, however, had other ideas. Beating feet in the wrong direction, he held the screaming infant to one broad shoulder and hightailed it over the threshold. And Sloan? The African-American guy was right behind him; wheels on the tub squeaking as he made like a NASCAR driver and pushed Rikar—IV pole, ice, and all—out of the clinic and into the corridor.

Red flags went flying inside her head. "Hey! Hang on a min—"

The snarl cut her off. She whipped her head around, looking for the threat. God, that sounded like a wild animal and...

Her gaze swept past Bastian and then jerked right back. He was the one growling. That pumping purr rolled across the clinic with the force of a hurricane as, chest heaving and green eyes glowing, he came at her from the other side of the room. Myst yelped and—in the spirit of stay-alive-first, ask-questions-later—leapt sideways, out of his path. If she got out of his way fast enough, maybe...

Oh, crap. This wasn't going to work. The instant she shifted, he did, too; zeroing in on her like a freaking pit bull. Good God, what...why...had he gone completely nuts?

Okay, no time for that. Twenty questions would have to wait. She'd figure out his malfunction later.

Right now, she needed to react. First priority? Getting something big between him (the snarling, crazy guy) and her (the sane, scared-out-of-her-mind girl). One of those rollaway carts, maybe, or...no, she needed that neonatal bed. No sense destroying a precious piece of equipment. The examination table.

Galvanized by a hit of adrenaline, Myst scrambled up and over, ignoring the waxy paper crinkling beneath her. Just as her feet touched down on the other side, Bastian fisted his hand in her shirt. She gasped as he yanked and she went airborne for a second. Oh, God, this was going to hurt and—

Except it didn't.

Bastian caught her on the downswing and, cushioning her fall, set her down. Both knees landed on the vinyl table-top. He pulled. She cursed, fighting the slide. Grabbing his wrists, she twisted, trying to break his hold. His nostrils flared and, eyes glowing with single-minded intensity, he reeled her in.

"Oh, my God!" A shriek lodged in her throat, she flailed. He retaliated by wrapping his arms around her, trapping her against his chest. Holy crap, he was solid, long-limbed and hard-muscled. "Bastian...stop it. What are you—"

He growled something—a word that sounded an awful lot like "mine"—as his hands traveled up beneath the hem of her shirt. His palms connected, skin on skin, a second before his mouth found the side of her throat. She sucked in a breath, lungs seizing while he purred. Purred!

The erotic sound sent her sideways into confusion and white-hot desire.

Like an inferno, she ignited, the push-pull of attraction reaching deep. As she tripped and got tangled in desire's deadly thread, he stroked her, each caress gentle. Soft. Enticing as hell.

Oh, man. How was she supposed to resist, well...*that*?

He felt so good. And his scent? The heated male spice surged, enlivening her senses until her need for him deepened. She moaned. He was unbelievable. A wide-shouldered, strong-bodied wet dream in black leather and—

Wait a minute. Hold on a second.

Giving her head a shake, she hit the pause button. Bastian nipped at her, overriding her moment of sanity. Damn pheromones. Stupid abstinence. God help her, but it had been so long since anyone had touched her. Years and...had she ever really known pleasure? Seemed like a good bet to say no, because Bastian hadn't even kissed her yet and she was already in orbit.

And part of her—the irresponsible half—yearned to surrender and let him do whatever he wanted. How bad could it be...really?

Except, wasn't she supposed to be doing something? Weren't there tests she should be...something about an angel? God, her brain was fried. She couldn't remember. Not with him this close...

He flicked her, tasting her skin as his hand slid over her ribcage.

Fighting for breath, she grabbed his hands. If he went any further—touched her breasts—she'd be done. She was too sensitive there and...

Holy crap. She'd just met this guy, and what she knew of Bastian scared her. Yeah, the whole *dragon* thing was a definite sticking point. All right, so he looked human—felt like a man and acted like sex on a stick—but no way could she sleep with him.

Yeah, wrapping her legs around him? Not a good idea.

Pushing his hands away, Myst leaned left, going for separation. She needed distance; couldn't think when he was...

"Oooh, G-god." She moaned as he attacked her pulse point and shook loose, sliding one big hand up her ribcage.

She shoved his shoulders. He growled, changed direction, stroking her back, over her hip to pay special attention to her bottom. As she shivered, his other hand traveled, moving up to tangle in her hair. Threading her blonde waves through his fingers, he kept her close as he sucked on her skin. Heat skittered down her spine and, instead of backing him the heck off, she lost ground, pulling him closer.

Oh, man, he was delicious. Decadent. Dangerous. Yeah, every word that started with a D.

Myst shook her head, trying to pull herself together enough to resist...enough to want to. "Bastian...hmmm, that's...oh, God. But...but, you need to...to—"

"*Bellmia*...my female...so beautiful."

Stop. Yes, that's what she meant to say, but man, oh, man, she loved the way he sounded: how his voice deepened when he talked to her like that. Darkly erotic, each word acted on her like a caress. Each touch aroused, encouraging surrender.

Still, some part of her—the annoyingly sensible side— clung to the certainty that making love to him was a bad idea.

Hmm...a very bad one that felt way too good.

Myst arched back and away, needing space to tell him, but the second she moved, he raised his head and invaded her mouth.

The kiss happened so fast that Myst didn't resist. Instead, she reacted like an idiot and opened, inviting his possession. And oh, hell...beautiful catastrophe. She knew it the second she let him in, the moment she slid her hands into his hair and pressed her body to his.

She'd expected spectacular. What she got was earth-shattering.

He tasted too good. Beyond fantastic, and oh, so crazy right it made her head spin.

And as he groaned and got busy tangling their tongues and touching her skin, Myst knew she'd made a huge mistake.

One kiss would never be enough.

———

Overhead, the fluorescents flickered, reacting to the energy surge in the room. The delicious swirl was electric, all around him, so beautifully magnetic that Bastian craved more. Ah hell, wasn't that a kicker. He'd already fed tonight—wasn't even hungry—but the taste of her...shit, he couldn't resist. Myst was better than his wildest dream.

And he'd dreamt some doozies in his time. Almost two centuries spent in the dreamscape while he slept and... *umm, yeah.*

But, who the hell cared about that? Not him. Not right now. His female was in his arms and...

Huh. Wasn't he supposed to be taking her somewhere?

Deep in Myst's mouth, Bastian reveled in her sweetness while he thought about that. Yeah, he definitely wanted to go somewhere with her, but—

Myst moaned. The desire-filled sound shorted out his brain, hauling him back into pleasure. God, she was delicious...and powerful. The energy she shared was gorgeous, so full-bodied it made Bastian groan. It was more than just her connection to the Meridian, though. It was chemistry; a human-to-human, male-to-female vibe he'd never felt before. She made him want on so many levels, almost as though she'd been created—born, designed...whatever— just for him.

And man, that pleased him so much it scared him.

The last thing he needed was to become bound to a female. Relationships were a minefield, not meant to be a part of his world. All he needed to do was ask Sloan to know that—the poor guy. Pitfalls aside, however, he didn't want to feel anything for anyone other than his warriors, the brothers who fought beside him night after night. He and his pack shared a necessary bond, one that made them stronger and crazy lethal in the field.

But he and Myst? Their mating was meant to be physical, not emotional: a straightforward, no-strings-attached kind of thing. Yeah, and look how well that was turning out. In less than a day, the whole "absence of emotion" plan he set in motion was shot to hell.

Witness the fact he was a second away from getting her naked and—

Oh, right. That's where he wanted to take her. To the recovery room, the one that boasted a big bed where he could lay her down and do her hard...do her right. But as much as his body liked the plan, Bastian knew it was a bad idea.

She was too tired, on the edge of exhaustion.

Plugged into her energy field, Bastian could feel her fatigue. She'd had a hell of a night, and with her energy ebbing, sleep was close. Just minutes away for her.

On the heels of the thought, she swayed, her grip on him loosening. Bastian slowed the pace, let their kiss become lazy, a decadent brush of mouths...more of the kind he indulged in post-sex, after he'd come inside whatever female he was with. And wonder of wonders, his dragon—the same territorial SOB that had turned him into a human torpedo to get to Myst—recognized her state and pulled back, insisting he stop.

Fantastic. His beast was now AWOL, a deserter...no longer on board with the plan. Great. So much for not caring.

Bastian forced himself away from her mouth. Eyes closed, halfway to dreamland already, she protested, making a sexy little sound that made him go back and kiss her again. This time, though, it was without passion, a mere brush of lips.

"Myst?"

"Hmm?"

"Time for bed." Holding her close, he kept her upright as she went boneless.

"Okay." Her eyes drifted open and then closed again on a lazy downward sweep.

Bastian smiled and hugged her, giving her a gentle squeeze. God, he couldn't help himself. She was so goddamn adorable.

Cupping her cheek, he tucked her against his chest before gathering her up. Carrying her like precious cargo, he headed for the exit. The quiet hiss of the airlock sounded as the motion detectors went active, opening the clinic door.

Out in the corridor now, Bastian turned right toward the stairs that would take him to the house and their living quarters. Seven stories above the underground lair, a whole wing of guest rooms waited. Bastian knew which one he wanted for Myst: the lavender one that matched her eyes.

Man, he could already see her there: relaxed, ready, her thick, wavy hair spread out on the pillows as she waited for him to come to her. For him to love her. For the pleasure he would give them both.

Bastian swallowed past the knot in his throat. He needed to stop thinking about sex with her. What was happening below his waist was already painful enough.

Strides even to keep from jostling her, he walked by the weight room and PT suites. All was quiet. No clink of metal on metal. None of the treadmills hummed, either. Nor was there a sharp, scathing sound of claws being sharpened.

Huh. Maybe everyone was already in bed, getting some much-needed shut-eye.

With the sun coming up, it was a good guess. UV rays and Dragonkind didn't mix. Their eyes got the worst of it, though. Prolonged exposure resulted in burned retinas and eventual blindness. Not something any dragon wanted... unless he was gunning to die.

He passed the computer room next—Sloan's domain— then a series of holding pens and interrogation rooms before coming out into a wide, open foyer. The vaulted ceiling curved upward, trapping the sound of his heavy footfalls, ping-ponging the echo as he walked by the Otis.

Newly installed by Venom, the elevator was a thing of beauty. A real stunner of modern efficiency. And Bastian hated the reinforced steel box. Enclosed spaces made him twitchy...violent, even. No way would he willingly put himself in that cage.

Shifting his female a little, he punched in a code, waited for the go-ahead beep and then popped the security door open to reach the double-wide staircase. Taking the steps two at a time, he kept his ascent smooth and his rhythm steady. Myst was REMed out now, sleeping so soundly it seemed a shame to wake her.

Bastian told himself he was being considerate, that she needed her rest. The truth, though, was much more damning. The second she woke, he'd be all over her. One kiss would lead to another, and then? He'd be finished: roasted, parboiled, cooked with a capital C. And for some reason, he wanted to do the right thing...whatever that was. But it sure as shit didn't mean taking advantage of her in a weakened state.

Four days.

Ninety-six hours.

Five thousand, seven hundred and sixty minutes.

Before the Meridian realigned.

Then he would have Myst beneath him, be inside of her…make her scream with crazy, orgasmic pleasure. Until then, he would bide his time, get to know her better. As far as plans went, it wasn't a bad one. Well, at least until he thought about the consequences. Then it became terrible because he knew it would get messy, and yeah, no way he would come out of it unscathed.

And wasn't that a tragedy.

Uh-huh. Huge. Gigantic. Colossal.

And man, were there any more synonyms for "big"?

No doubt, but as Bastian pushed the door open at the top of the stairs and turned toward his suite, his mind blanked out. As priceless paintings flashed by—done by guys like Jackson Pollock, Picasso, and van Gogh—it took all he had to walk past his door and continue down the hall. The lavender bedroom was just up on the left, close to his, yet not close enough. Down the hall from Myst just wasn't good enough. Instinct told him nothing would be until she slept in his bed.

He wanted her with him, if only just to spoon up against her. Holding her while she slept would be heaven. Bastian knew it with a certainty that made his heart ache. The need defied everything he'd been told. Everything he'd been taught by his father and the males who had taken charge of him after his sire's murder. The painful memory set him straight, reminding him of his goal, but didn't focus him like it normally did.

The female in his arms overrode the system, tugged at the deepest part of him, and he faltered, nearly doing a one-eighty to hotfoot it back to his room.

Standing motionless in the deserted corridor, with a Rembrandt landscape eyeballing him, Bastian debated. No...no, no, no. Myst wouldn't appreciate waking up with him. She wasn't ready for that yet, so he forced his feet to move. Made his hand grip and turn the knob to her bedroom. Compelled himself across the plush carpet to reach the bathroom on the far side of the space. Only then did he glance down at the precious gift the fates had set down in his lap.

Drained of energy from the feedings, she curled like a kitten in his arms: eyes closed, cheek against his chest, a relaxed, warm bundle against him. Bastian felt the heavy load weighing on him lighten a little. The contrast she presented amused him. Awake, she was fierce, direct in a take-no-prisoners kind of way. Asleep, she was vulnerable; so sweet he wanted to keep her close and protect her always.

Bastian sighed. He was so screwed.

Juggling her in his arms, he reached into the glassed-in shower stall to turn on the water. He shouldn't be doing this, but...

Man, he couldn't put her to bed like this...with the strain of the night and blood of another female on her skin.

"Myst." Kissing her temple, he nudged her. "Wake up for me, baby."

A furrow appeared between her brows. Unhappy with the interruption, she grumbled and snuggled closer. His chest went tight, enjoying her dependence as he jostled her again.

"Just a little. Enough to stand." The softness of his voice roused her, and the second her eyelashes flickered, he lowered her feet to the floor. More asleep than awake, she whispered something. He murmured back, holding her close as she swayed in his arms. "That's it, *bellmia*...lean against me. I'm going to..."

He kept up the chit-chat and, with gentle hands, stripped her out of the stained hospital scrubs. He tried not to look, but...wow. She was so beautifully made: all smooth skin and gentle curves. And her hair. The blonde waves were so thick, a luxurious tangle he wanted across his chest and wrapped around his—

Jesus. He needed to flambé those thoughts. ASAP.

This was about her, not him. About respect and caring, not sex. About giving Myst what she needed when she couldn't do it for herself.

On a rough exhale, Bastian shrugged out of his leather duster, ditching it on the limestone floor. The rest of his clothes, he kept on. He didn't trust himself. Couldn't get naked with her if he had any hope of maintaining control.

Sticking his hand under the spray, he checked the water, then adjusted the temperature, wanting it just right for her. When he was satisfied, he picked her up and stepped under the warm stream: letting the water hit his back first, double-checking to make sure it was warm enough before turning to let it touch her.

With stark efficiency, Bastian washed and rinsed her. When he got the shampoo out, however, he slowed down. He couldn't help himself, and as he ran his fingers through her hair, testing its texture and weight, he heard himself purr. Man, he loved her thick waves, the softness of each lock, the sheer quantity of it.

Shaking his head, he rinsed the last of the suds away. He was a walking, talking cliché. A male having a thing for his female's hair...duh, a total no-brainer.

Another one was getting them out of the shower and himself the hell away from her. If he didn't, he would do something stupid, like ditch his clothes and join her in bed.

And wasn't he a freaking hero? Myst was asleep on her feet, and what was he thinking about? Hot, sweaty, mind-bending sex.

Disgusting. End of story.

With a vicious pull, Bastian cranked the faucet, cutting off the warm rush from the rainforest showerhead. After grabbing a towel off the overhead rack, he wrapped Myst up to keep her warm, then snagged another thick-white-and-fluffy and went to work on her hair.

As he patted water droplets from her shoulders and neck, her cheeks and mouth, Bastian's chest grew tight. He was taking care of his female, looking after her when she needed him most and...

He loved it. Loved being the one to bring her comfort and protect her from harm. And as he gathered her up—towels and all—and headed into the lavender room to tuck her in, Bastian felt torn: ripped wide open by obligation and circumstance. Worse than that? The condition of his conscience.

But right or wrong, duty would win in the end. The future of his kind depended on it.

Chapter Thirteen

The human police were at the scene, circling the house like a bunch of...okay, not vultures. He was the one doing that. Ivar hadn't been able to help himself. After Lothair had dropped the bomb about the infant, he'd tried to distract himself, gone downtown to find what he needed.

The dark-haired female seemed like an excellent idea at the time, but...Jesus.

Ivar should have known better.

He'd been too jazzed to enjoy her. A shame, really. She'd been pretty, leggy, a tight squeeze inside...just the way he liked his females. Too bad he'd lost control. It was happening a little too often lately...not that he regretted taking her life.

Nah, no time for that. Her energy—subpar quality not withstanding—had revived him. Umm, umm good. Yeah, to the last drop.

Huh, where had he heard that before? Oh, right, the Maxwell House coffee slogan. Not that he ever drank the shit, but Denzeil—his second in command—loved TV. Especially the commercials. The male even DVR'd the damn things.

Ivar shook his head, laughing at himself as the last of the female's energy kicked in. Thank God. His headache was finally fading, moving from behind his eyes to the back of his head. Now the pain was just a blip, a backseat driver to the frustration shifting his gears.

Wings spread wide, Ivar circled above the house again, night vision sharp as he watched another SUV roll in.

Idiot humans. Cattle, every one of them. So clueless they didn't know he was here, one hundred feet above their heads. All right, so he was cloaked, deep in the invisibility spell that allowed him to rule the skies. Still, he couldn't keep his hatred of their species under wraps. He wanted to breathe in and let loose, burn them to cinders. But that wasn't why he'd made the flight.

The ashes. He wanted the remains of his fallen comrades.

Maybe that made him a sentimental fool, but he didn't care. Those males had fought hard for him, deserved a proper burial in the Cave of Memories. And wasn't he an altruistic gem? Yeah, those whom Ivar commanded would say he was a real stand-up guy, but what they didn't know wouldn't hurt them.

He wanted the ashes for another reason, too. They were a message...to Bastian and the Nightfury dragons that served him.

The ash piles combined with all the female lives he took were a big fuck you. A statement that said, "You can't protect them all."

The first time had been an accident. Not the death, but the ash pile left beside her body. He'd been carrying Thor's remains home after a vicious night of fighting and had needed a pick-me-up. As he'd fed and banged the nameless female against the alley wall, the bag had ripped, spilling Thor's ashes onto the pavement.

Serendipitous? Yeah, absolutely. A real-life lesson in how to upend the enemy.

Now, he possessed what the idiot police called "a signature." Every time he took a life, he left a little of his fallen comrades behind.

And the police? Useless twits. They would never figure it out, didn't possess equipment powerful enough to find the truth. Even if they tested the remains, all they'd find was a whole lot of human. Dragon DNA burned in the ashing process, so the most the dummies would get were bits and pieces, a contaminated sample at best.

Ivar hummed. He couldn't wait until Bastian and his merry band of bastards clued in. The Nightfury's outrage—and the subsequent hunt for him—was going to be so much fun.

But there wouldn't be any fun tonight. No ashes, either. The humans were swarming like ants.

The best he could do was collect the scraps; little hits of information to use with Forge. Details. Ivar wanted them all, anything and everything he could turn into ammunition to stoke the lethal male's fire. He needed to direct all that rage. The death of Forge's female—Caroline what's-her-face—was the perfect foil.

As Ivar picked up the metal tinge of blood and acrid smell of death, he smiled. Forge would go mad with grief, murderous as he searched for his child.

And once he did, Bastian wouldn't stand a chance.

Leaving Ivar to do what he did best…continue his work in the lab, designing the perfect weapon to unleash on humankind.

———

Gravel crunched beneath the X-Trail's oversized tires as Angela turned into the Van Owens' driveway. Lights flashed farther up the lane, painting the trunks of tall pines in revolving yellow splashes.

Hmm. That was a pretty impressive light show...much bigger than she'd expected. Particularly since the sheriff had promised to keep the scene tight. Not more than fifteen minutes ago.

She sighed. Lovely. Just what she and Mac needed... another circus.

Double fisting the steering wheel, Angela tightened her grip to keep from swearing. Her partner was doing quite enough of that already, enough for both of them. And honestly? Two pissed off detectives at a crime scene was one too many.

With all the enthusiasm of a gutted fish, Angela slowed the SUV's roll and rounded the last bend. The high beams swung around, sideswiping a knot of police cruisers before ghosting over a hunk of burned-out metal. Still smoking, the wreckage threw black plumes skyward, washing out the details of the house behind it.

"Holy crap."

"Uh-huh." Mac scanned the mess through the windshield. "Welcome to Clusterfuck County, Ange."

No kidding. It looked like a bomb had gone off. The unfortunate victim? An ambulance with a twisted undercarriage and a scorched orange and white paint job. The house hadn't fared much better. From what Angela could see, the porch roof had collapsed inward to shake hands with the floor. And the windows? Gone. All of them shattered, leaving gaping wounds in the Cape Cod's face.

And yeah, wasn't that a lovely reminder of what lay inside the freaking place. On the drive out, Mac had filled her in: dead girl slit wide open, missing baby, AWOL nurse. Terrific. The combo was right out of a horror show. Now, all they needed was the guy from *American Psycho* to show up with his chainsaw to round out the picture.

First things first, though. The crime scene needed to be locked down.

There were too many cops standing around. Doing what? Nothing, but getting their yak on.

And wow...she'd laughed at Mac, calling him paranoid when he said he didn't trust the country yahoos. His words, not hers. But looking around now, she conceded the point. They *were* a bunch of yahoos.

Crap, she owed her partner an apology—the second one in the space of a week. And wasn't that going to suck?

Mac pointed to the right, toward a copse of redwood trees. Ah, a parking space. The perfect one, too...close enough for a bird's-eye view, far enough away to avoid contaminating the crime scene. But the real perk? No one hemming them in, which meant the possibility of a fast getaway if Sheriff Yahoo proved to be as stupid as his officers looked.

With an "atta-boy" for her partner, Angela turned the wheel, heading away from the congestion at the mouth of the lane. As the SUV bumped over uneven ground, she scanned the scene again. God, what a mess. Not the kind of case a cop wanted to catch this close to the weekend. And yo-ho-ho and a bottle of rum. All of a sudden, Sheriff Yahoo was looking a whole lot smarter than the two of them put together.

What in God's name had happened here?

Her brows drawn tight, Angela hit the brakes and threw the truck into park. Taking the keys out of the ignition, she tossed them to Mac. "Man, where are we? Kandahar?"

"Not enough dead bodies." Mac caught the airborne gift, cutting off the happy jingle of metal on metal mid-song. "We've got what—just the one, right?"

"Yeah, one dead girl, but..." Popping the latch, Mac pushed the door open and stepped out of the SUV. "Night's still young."

Angela snorted. Four a.m. was young? Her partner needed his internal clock reset. Then again, an insomniac no doubt dealt with a different set of criteria for determining what constituted early and late.

"So, what's your best guess here. Is it..." Angela trailed off, realizing her partner wasn't listening. Hopping out of the cab, she glanced over and got a load of Mac's expression. Oh, boy, she knew that look. He didn't wear it often, and seldom went that still, but when he did? Nothing good followed. "Hey...Mac."

Size twelves planted on the ground, he stood frozen in the V-shaped cove between the open door and truck frame. White-knuckling the roof edge, he stared at the sky above the Cape Cod, his gaze sweeping through the darkness, searching for something. A something Angela couldn't see, but experience told her not to discount. Mac's spidy senses were crazy accurate, much sharper than hers...when he wasn't having one of his episodes.

One eye on her partner, the other on the sky, Angela unVelcroed her Glock. Gripping the hilt, she kept it holstered and hustled around the front of the SUV.

"Talk to me...whatcha got?"

"Don't know...something's off."

Great. Here they went again. Trouble.

"What was your first clue?" she asked, keeping her voice light to bring Mac back onside. Every once in a while, he freaked her out like this. The last time, he'd seen some sort of shadow, felt breath on the back of his neck. Mac had hauled ass, moving with freakish speed after something Angela hadn't seen, much less felt. She'd chased him seven blocks that night. No way she wanted him to put in a repeat performance here...in the middle of nowhere with nothing but bush for miles. "A freaking bomb went off out here."

"Probably C-four," he murmured, his military mind coming back online. Thank God and all the angels, too. "And I'm not going anywhere."

"Good to know," she said and meant it. She'd had enough cardio lately, thank you very much. "Come on. Let's walk the scene. See what we got."

He studied the skyline for another heartbeat, then dragged his gaze away and tipped his chin in her direction. "Right behind ya."

With a nod, she folded the Velcro back in place and, securing her weapon, led the way up the lawn. After flashing her creds, she ducked beneath the yellow tape and peeled right to walk the perimeter. From the corner of her eye, she saw Mac go left, toward the sheriff and the tight knot of deputies surrounding him.

Thank God for small favors. Or rather, for Mac. He knew her strengths lay in the field—in picking up evidence at a glance, the small stuff that most detectives missed— not in interdepartmental schmoozing. Being a twenty- first century woman didn't mean automatic acceptance. Some of the old-timers still got their panties in a wad over a woman working homicide. And that just pissed her off...so, yeah. Her talking to Sheriff Yahoo wasn't a great idea.

With methodical precision, Angela let her eyes do the walking and worked her way down the side lawn, around the back corner of the house and what the—

It looked like a freaking tornado had blown through back here.

Snapped like toothpicks, a swath of trees lay flat, massive trunks torn in two. The track was at least fifteen feet wide and forty feet deep. Holy crap. Something huge had made that, a bulldozer maybe. Big problem with that theory, though. No tire treads or tracks, not a single one indicating any heavy-duty equipment had rolled through recently.

Angela kept going and found an ash pile. A massive one. Okay, so it was bigger than the ones they'd found in the city, but discovering it ticked the first box. Their guy had definitely been here.

She found a second pile as she walked the other side of the house, just to the right of a rundown garage. And then, something else.

An impression at the top of the driveway, beside the old tractor. Which, of course, the yahoo idiots were gum-flapping around. With a "do you mind, get the hell off my evidence," she examined the hole. About a foot deep, the long trench was U-shaped with a mucky bottom. Stranger still? The ice chips. The small fragments were all over the area: in the trench, around it, mixed in with the gravel.

Hitting her haunches, Angela picked up a chunk. The piece was smooth and even, perfectly formed, like something you took out of a freezer. Weirder still? The thing was thawing evenly, keeping its shape as it melted in the palm of her hand.

An eerie sensation ghosted up her spine. Something was really wrong here...in a crazy spooky kind of way.

And she hadn't even made it to the kitchen yet.

Angela blew out a rough exhale. Time to go. She'd avoided the body of her latest victim long enough.

Taking the steps two at the time, she avoided the rubble and stooped under the downed porch. A second later, she crossed over the threshold, boots crunching on broken glass, to head down the narrow corridor. She took a moment before moving into the kitchen, noting the red pool beside the island and the footprints drying in human blood on the ceramic tile. With a deep breath, she settled herself and took a wide path around the island, making sure to step carefully. The CSI unit would arrive soon. She didn't want any evidence compromised...needed every scrap to figure out what exactly had gone down here.

At least, she thought so until she got her first glimpse of Caroline Van Owen.

"Oh, my God," she whispered against the back of her hand. "The bastard."

Laid out on her back, the girl had been sliced wide open. Mac had warned her, but still...

Angela swallowed the awful taste in her mouth.

This wasn't their guy's usual MO. None of the other girls had been pregnant. But Caroline? Holy hell. Someone had...had...cut the baby right out of her womb.

Yeah, not at all like the first three victims.

So different, in fact, it made Angela sick. Stomach-turning, bile-tasting sick.

Crouched beside the island—mere feet from a black bag and strewn medical supplies—Angela forced herself into detective mode and reached into the back pocket of her chinos. As she snapped on her rubber gloves, her mind went critical, diving into the place that allowed her to do her job—the place that both her captain and her partner loved: the sinkhole of analytical thinking that once engaged, solved a crap load of cases.

Seconds passed into minutes. How many Angela couldn't say as she collected and analyzed...all without touching. Her brain was like a camera, snapping pictures that she would later recall with total clarity. Some labeled her skill a "photographic memory." Mac called it magic.

A soft scrape on the ceramic sounded behind her. Without looking away from the vic, she asked, "Any sign of the nurse?"

Mac cleared his throat. The rough sound echoed in the small space, telling Angela more clearly than words that her partner was on the same page. He hated what he saw as much as she did, the scene that had taken another girl's life.

Shifting a little behind her, Mac said, "Shoe impressions...size seven, maybe...behind the rusted-out Buick. Alongside more big boot prints."

"Military grade...like downtown?"

"Yeah."

"The smaller ones might be Caroline's."

"Could be, but my gut says no." Moving around to the other side of the kitchen, Mac hit his haunches at the opposite end of the island. A muscle jumped in his jaw as he met her gaze over the top of Caroline's body. "I think they belong to Myst Munroe, our missing nurse."

"Um-hmm." Picking up a discarded cell phone, she flipped it open. Yup, it belonged to the nurse. "Wrong place, wrong time?"

"Maybe." He tipped his chin toward their vic. "That's precision cutting...surgical, clean, no hesitation marks. Need a lot of training to do that."

"So, what are you thinking? Black-market baby?" Angela hoped not. The monster killing young women was enough for any duo to handle. That someone might have sliced up a woman to take her baby? Yeah, she wasn't going there until the evidence forced her to. Her eyes narrowed, she scrolled through the nurse's phone, looking at the history. "Got a nine-one-one call."

"A hang up?"

Angela shook her head. "Two minutes and twenty-seven seconds."

Mac's eyes narrowed as he stood to take the iPhone out of his front pocket. "I'll get the recording. And a BOLO out on Munroe's car."

"Get a warrant, too...for her place, financials. Everything." Angela snapped the cell phone closed and reached for the tag on the medical bag lying open beside the victim. With a flick, she flipped the name out and...what do you know? Myst Munroe was printed on the face in neat block letters, address included.

Yes, indeedie. Something smelled rotten in Bumpkinville.

And Angela's gut told her that Ms. Munroe was up to her eyeballs in it.

Chapter Fourteen

Myst woke up in a strange bed. Naked.

Alarm bells—the kind that killed brain cells—went off inside her head, shutting down her ability to breathe properly. As her choppy breaths grew louder, adrenaline joined the fun, ramping her heartbeat into catastrophic territory. She swallowed, forcing herself to focus. Yeah, a functioning brain would be good right about now. Maybe then she could figure out whose bed she'd face-planted in.

And where her clothes had gone.

Rubbing her eyes, she ransacked her memory, trying to remember the hows and whys. Nothing but fog came...and the shriek of panic.

Double-fisting the down duvet, she forced herself to breathe in and out—in then out—and turned her head on the pillow. Her vision stayed blurry a second then...

Thank God. She was alone.

Good news all the way around, but even better? The neighboring pillowcase was smooth, the pillow without a dent from oh, say, a head. Which meant, she'd crawled in by herself and stayed that way since landing, well, here. In the middle of a strange bed...that no doubt belonged to a strange guy.

She rubbed her forehead, struggling to remember. The missing piece was…right there. On the tip of her brain, but no matter how hard she stretched, she couldn't reach it.

"Okay…relax and think," she said to herself.

Which, in hindsight, was a bad idea, because upon that instruction an awful thought popped into her head. While it banged around in there, Myst swallowed hard. Had she been…been…God, she didn't want to say the r-word, but she couldn't shake the horrible suspicion. Her big mind blank could be drug induced. Rohypnol was a powerhouse narcotic, one that wiped memory clean with wide, ugly brush strokes.

Myst should know. She'd had a patient or two come into the ER looking lost and empty-eyed the morning after being slipped Roofies at a bar.

All right. *Breathe.*

That was an awfully big assumption. Huge, really, without proof. So, first things first…eliminate every other possibility.

Myst pushed up onto her elbows. A narrow wedge of light streamed across the carpet, coming from an open door to the left of the bed. A bathroom, maybe? Seemed like a good guess, particularly since a second door was closed tight on the other side of the room. As her eyes adjusted to the dimness, shadowed shapes formed: a dresser against the far wall, a bench at the end of the bed, a wide window behind tightly drawn shades.

But better than the semi-lit, somewhat sketchy decor? She really was alone…100 percent by herself. No one was sitting in the wide-backed armchairs in front of the window or lurking in dark corners or leaning against the wall across from the bed.

Relief hit her so hard she jackknifed into a sitting position. Blankets clutched to her chest, she took her investigation one step further. As she curled her legs underneath her she paid close attention. She and sex were nearly strangers. Had been for more than...what? Three years? Yeah, that sounded about right, so if she'd been...ah, sexually active last night, then certain muscles should be sore.

Right?

She nodded, liking the logic. "Yes, absolutely."

Myst came close to crying when she realized she wasn't hurting...at all. But the craziest thing? The one with sure wow factor? Other than the hole in her memory, she felt amazing: well rested, energetic, no headache. No headache? Man, that was a gift. She couldn't remember the last time she'd woken up without—

A knock sounded from across the room.

Her head whipped around. She stared at the door, traced its antique lines, not wanting to know who was bare-knuckling the thing from the other side. She'd just gotten used to the idea that she was okay, and now? Someone stood out there with every intention of proving her wrong.

A second knock echoed, stomping on the quiet like a herd of elephants.

Galvanized into motion, she scrambled over the side of the bed. As her feet hit the floor, she tripped over a throw pillow and, heading ass-over-tea-kettle, grabbed onto the top sheet. Still anchored to the mattress, the cotton did its job and kept her upright before she yanked the entire mess off the bed. The duvet and an assortment of other bedding went flying.

But, what did she care?

She wasn't going for homemaker of the year here. The goal was safety, and as she wrapped the bed sheet around her like a toga, she searched for a weapon. Whoever stood in the corridor wasn't necessarily her friend. She needed to be prepared to do...what exactly?

The heavy silver candlestick sitting on the bedside table caught her eye. One hand holding her makeshift dress, she snatched the thing off its perch. Curling her hand around its neck, Myst held it close, right up against her breastbone.

"My lady?" A crisp British accent came through the door, drifting on a polite wave of inquiry. "May I come in?"

Myst blinked. *My lady?*

The Brit waited half a heartbeat before the handle began to turn. Myst's pulse went ballistic, ratcheting up another notch when the polished pewter rotated and the space grew wider between the door and its wooden frame. She raised the candlestick, widened her stance, expecting an axe murderer to come through the door.

A cherub—compete with dark curls and innocent eyes—stuck his head into the room. "Oh, wonderful. I am so pleased you are awake. Good morrow, my lady." Completely ignoring the fact she was brandishing a candlestick like a battle axe, he pranced over the threshold. "Are you hungry, my lady? I have prepared waffles this eve and all have gathered in the kitchen."

Myst stared at him, mystified. Waffles? In the kitchen? Holy crap, who—

"Oh, my goodness me," he said as his flying fairy feet paused in the center of the room. He gave her an apologetic look, then smiled, flashing a gold front tooth. "Forgive me. Wherever are my manners? I am Daimler, and I am so very pleased to meet you, Ms. Munroe."

With a flourish, he bowed, twin tails on his tux flapping.

Okay, so Daimler—Mr. Starched-Pressed-and-Buttoned-Up—knew her name, but as far as monikers went, she didn't like that one. *Ms. Munroe* reminded her too much of her mother and, right this second, she didn't need to have an emotional breakdown as well as a mental one. "Ah, it's Myst."

The little guy stooped to pick up a small throw pillow. He came back up with a perplexed look on his angelic face.

She cleared her throat. "My name is Myst."

"Oh, my lady...thank you." His eyes went a little misty, like she'd given him a huge gift. "You honor me beyond measure..." Smoothing the pillow with his long-fingered hands, he gave her a wobbly smile. "Myst. Master Bastian said you were a female of great worth, but..."

As Daimler prattled on, he scurried around the bed, picking up the discarded duvet. Myst heard every word, but didn't care about any of them but one.

Bastian.

Bam.

Her memories poured back into her skull like water into a glass. Her eyes narrowed. The kidnapping jerk had kissed her. Last night. In the clinic. And...goddamn it. Why had she liked it so much? Exhaustion. Yes, that was a good excuse. She'd been so tired, and no wonder. After a night like that—after Caroline's horrifying death and her angel's near miss—she...

Holy crap. The baby.

Panic closed her throat for a second. Myst zapped herself with mental jumper cables.

"Daimler," she said, her tone sharp with worry. "Where's the baby?"

The butler hit the pause button on his mouth and the tidying routine. Standing with one hand poised in the air—in a gesture that reminded her of the guys from one of her favorite shows, *Queer Eye for the Straight Guy*. "Oh, no need to worry, my...Myst. The little one is with Master Bastian, of course."

"I need to see him...the baby," she clarified. Not Bastian. The rat-bastard. "Right now."

With a slight incline of his head, Daimler headed for the dresser and as he turned, Myst noticed something odd about him. The guy had pointy ears...like Legolas from *The Lord of the Rings*.

Holding tightly to her toga, Myst examined that bit of information. Although why it surprised her was anyone's guess. Bastian and his crew were at least half dragon. Why not have an elf for a butler?

"Here we are." Daimler turned and approached, clothes folded over his forearm. He laid black yoga pants along with a white tank top and purple hoodie on the bench at the foot of the bed. "It is my hope these will suffice, my...Myst."

"Thank you," she whispered in return, her terminal politeness coming to the fore. And why not? She wasn't angry with Daimler. It wasn't his fault that she found herself here, in a strange place with a half-dragon jerk.

"I will leave you to dress in privacy. When you are ready, the kitchen is just down the corridor...to the right."

When she nodded, Daimler did a quick one-eighty and headed for the door. As the latch closed with a soft click behind him, Myst reached for the clothes. She needed to get to the kitchen ASAP. Not that she wanted to see Bastian again. Not a chance. Her angel was there...and if the lair was anything like a human home? The kitchen would be at its heart. A prime place to engage in a little reconnaissance...and find an escape route.

Myst nodded. Good plan.

Time to take the bull by the horns and find a way out of the nightmare.

Chapter Fifteen

Rikar sat at the kitchen island, amazed he was still alive. He should be ashed out, nothing but a messy pile on the clinic floor. He deserved it a hundred times over for touching his friend's female. Okay, so he hadn't actually been the one doing the touching. Didn't matter. He'd crossed into uncharted territory, an abyss not many came back from.

The fact he'd woken up at all this evening was a testament to Bastian's control. Or love. Either way, he still couldn't believe...

Yeah, it was a mind fuck to the nth degree. Especially when he met B's gaze—across a stack of waffles and ocean of maple syrup—and got nailed with a don't-you-ever-do-that-again glare. If there'd been any doubt, that look sewed it up. Myst and her unbelievable energy were off limits. To him and every other male in the universe.

Bag it and tag it, CSI Willows. Case closed.

One with a slap-happy ending, too.

Or was it?

Try as he might, Rikar couldn't find any happiness in the situation. Sure, B had found a high-energy female that appealed to him: goal accomplished, a totally high-five worthy moment. But, palm slapping aside, the suck factor was there, too. His best friend was headed for a whole lot of hurt. Rikar knew it like he was sitting there, ass glued to

Fury of Fire

the stool, ignoring the others chowing down on Daimler's homemade waffles as he stared at Bastian, hoping for the best while fearing the worst.

Rikar guessed it was a question of degrees, of taking the good with the bad. God knew he wanted what Bastian wanted—a healthy race moving forward into the future. Warriors with strong backs and even greater determination, bringers of death to the Razorback rogues. But an equal part of him didn't want to hurt a female—or to see one hurt—to accomplish the goal.

The whole plan seemed back-assward to him.

After all, his kind needed females like Myst. Ones with high energy to keep them well fed and healthy. What would it serve to take one to mate, only to see her die in childbirth?

And the question was redundant. He already knew the answer, had gone round after round with Bastian so many times that he could hear the other male's voice inside his head. Females with strong energy produced more powerful offspring. Stronger sons guaranteed a lethal force, males like him and Bastian. Warriors who were gifted beyond the physical with genetically enhanced firepower.

The perfect examples? His ice. B's crazy-ass exhale.

Man, that lightning strike, psychochemical combo was some freaky shit. And that was before he got into the whole mind-meld thing his friend was packing. To have the ability to read and dissect the enemy's strengths and weaknesses from a distance was one hell of an advantage. Christ, that kind of up-front info came in handy in a firefight.

Playing with his fork, Rikar flicked a strawberry across his plate. He watched it somersault through the syrup with little enthusiasm. His hunger wasn't about food. He needed to log some personal time with a female, draw some energy to flush out the last of the poison.

Not that he was hurting anymore.

Nah, the anti-venom had done its job, and the gash on his arm? Nothing but a thin pink line on his skin, one that would disappear completely before the night ended. Still, a faint ache stayed with him, giving him a headache that jammed up his ability to concentrate. A little sip from the right female and he'd be good to go.

That was if B didn't ground him for the night.

Christ, he hoped not, even though protocol called for it. Warrior or not, an injury like he'd suffered wasn't taken lightly. Had it been any one of his comrades, Rikar would've been on board with a night off the fighting rotation. But no way he could stay home. Not tonight. He needed to stretch his wings or he'd go rat-shit crazy...especially with Myst in the lair. He needed to stay the hell away from her. There'd be no double jeopardy on that one. He went anywhere near her again and Bastian would kill him.

Rikar stabbed a piece of melon, wishing it was a Razorback's head. Wishing Bastian would start the freaking meeting already.

They were all here, in their usual spots around the kitchen island. Everyone except...

"Where the fuck is Sloan?" With a scowl, Rikar put his fork down before he did more than mangle a fruit wedge.

Sitting opposite him, forearms folded on the marble countertop, Venom raised a blond brow. "Temper, temper there, buddy."

"Sun's going down," he growled. Translation? Time to get out of Black Diamond and head downtown to hunt the enemy...and feed.

Wick murmured his agreement. Which amazed the hell out of everyone. The taciturn male never talked, rarely made any sound at all. He was more phantom than male, ghosting in and among the Nightfury warriors...with them, but not really. The only one who truly knew him was Venom, his bunkmate. Yeah, those males were tight—as close as he and Bastian were—but their history remained a mystery. Ven protected the male like a cub, refusing to share the hows and whys.

Fine by him. Rikar knew all he needed or wanted to know about Wick. The golden-eyed SOB was lethal, a sociopathic killer without conscience or reserve. The perfect male to have your back on a battlefield.

The newborn's cry started up like a siren on a fire engine. Soft at first, the unhappy sound gathered in strength until every male looked up from his carb overload to focus on the playpen on the other side of the kitchen. Looking like a blurry-eyed first-time father, Bastian pushed away from his stool and crossed to the floor-to-ceiling windows.

Tinted black, the glass panels were alive with movement and magic at the moment. Soon, they would lighten on their own, go from black to crystal clear, allowing moonlight to shine into the aboveground lair. The special feature protected them from the sun, allowing them to move freely during the daylight hours.

As he scooped up the infant and set him against his shoulder, Bastian strode back to his spot. Instead of sitting on his stool, though, he sat on the adjacent countertop, leaned back and tipped his chin in Rikar's direction. "Any word from the others?"

"Not yet." Rikar shoved his plate away. Fine china slid across marble on its way to meeting the butter dish. The pair kissed with a clink as he said, "They should arrive at The Gathering soon, though."

A furrow between his brows, Bastian rubbed the baby's back, his concern for the other members of the pack showing. As Nightfury commander, his friend carried a heavy burden...worried about them all. But what he hated most? Too much distance, and the fact that Haider and Gage were an entire continent away didn't sit well. With any of them.

"Fucking Archguard," he murmured, disgusted with the idiots responsible for the mess about to go down in Prague.

Venom snorted. "Arch-idiots, you mean."

Yeah, that sounded about right. The Archguard—the males who headed the five dynastic families and sat on the high counsel—*were* idiots. The good-for-nothing assholes sat on their aristocratic duffs, protecting their own interests while doing little to help the race. Christ, they had no clue what happened in the real world...the one outside the cushy, privileged society in which they existed.

Dealing with them was like talking to someone who lived in a bubble. Sound got through, sure. But it was just a whole lot of Charlie Brown...*wah-wah-wah—wah-wah.*

None of that mattered, though. Not in the long run, because however much Rikar wanted to kick the whole lot of them to the curb, The Gathering couldn't be ignored. All of Dragonkind revered the celebratory tradition. To not send a representative was akin to treason. So, Haider and Gage had made the trip. Now, all of them sat on pins and needles, praying the pair not only arrived safely, but made it back in one piece.

The heavy clip of footfalls sounded in the corridor.

Rikar shifted in his seat, releasing some of his tension. "About time."

Sloan jogged into the kitchen, red file folders tucked under his arm. The male threw him a dirty look. "Heard that, asshole."

"Can't take the heat? Be on time."

Sloan's dark gaze narrowed on him. "Get off my dick, Rikar."

Keeping his mouth closed, he bit down on a grin. Thank Christ for the dark-skinned SOB. Razzing Sloan always improved his mood. Though one look at B's expression told him to lay off.

"Sloan, whatcha got?" Bastian shifted the baby to his other shoulder.

Poor little guy squawked, the sound pissed off with a dash of I-Want-My-Mommy. Which had pretty much been his MO all day…fussy with a capital F. They'd each taken a turn feeding him, walking him with the bouncing rhythm he seemed to like. Well, almost everyone had taken the baby out for a spin. Wick didn't make the cut. No one trusted the male anywhere near an infant.

Their resident computer genius—hacker of impenetrable databases—tossed the file folders onto the center of the island. Red card stock slid across white marble, bumping into the maple syrup pitcher. "Trouble."

Venom reached for one of the files. "The normal amount or the oh-my-God-hide-the-kids kind?"

"The SPD kind."

"Fuck," he and Bastian said at the same time.

"Yeah, we got a pair of detectives up our ass." Flipping a chair backwards, Sloan slid onto the seat, forearms folded on the rounded chair back. "Three unsolved murders… all females, dark hair, early twenties. Cause of death…catastrophic organ failure."

Another round of "fucks" took a turn around the kitchen.

Sloan kept talking. "Oh and here's the best part. Ash piles laid out next to the victims. Wanna take a guess what that means?"

Bastian growled. The infant reacted with a startled cry. With a curse, B started pacing, up and back between the island and the bank of wall cabinets. As he patted the little guy's bottom to soothe him, B switched up his tone and murmured, "Ivar."

"Yeah, that's my guess, too," Sloan said. "I think it's a message."

"A big 'fuck you'?" The second folder in his hand, Rikar scanned the contents, picking up the detectives names: Ian MacCord and Angela Keen. He looked at their pics and bios. Huh, both homicide veterans. And hmm. The female was gorgeous, with dark red hair and intelligent hazel eyes. "You think he's that stupid? If he's leaving ash, he's taking one hell of a risk. If the humans get samples into the lab, they might find more than human DNA."

Venom sighed. "We're gonna need to clean this up."

"I'll do it," Rikar said, grabbing onto his escape hatch. No way was he staying home tonight.

"You sure?" Bastian's eyes narrowed, drilling him with a glare as he walked past with the kid.

Rikar nodded, smoothing his expression to hide his reaction. He hated when B gave him "the look." It was like getting nailed in the grill by a wrecking ball. "Hit the lab, scramble the results. Find the detectives and scrub 'em. No sweat."

His best friend eyeballed him for a second and then switched gears. "All right. Here's the plan. Wick, you're going out with me tonight. Venom and Sloan...pair up. And Rikar...do what you need to do, then get your ass back here. You took a hit last night. No fighting until you're one hundred percent."

Fucking hell. He'd just had his wings clipped.

Even so, Rikar kept his yap shut. If he argued, B would ground him for sure. And while the situation was less than optimal, at least he wouldn't be left behind. In the lair. With a female that belonged to his best friend.

"We clear?" Bastian gave him another warning glare.

"Got it," he said, not willing to push his luck. "And the baby?"

"Myst'll take him." With a quick inhale, Bastian glanced toward the corridor, then back to him. "You're gonna want to put on a shirt, man. Right now."

He scrubbed a hand over his bare chest. Shit, he hated clothing. It made him hot and itchy, something his frosty side didn't tolerate well. The only reason he wore shorts at all was so he didn't freak his friends out by walking around with his equipment dangling.

Then again, staying alive trumped being comfortable. And the status quo in the lair.

Yeah, he had a feeling a new "normal" was about to hit Black Diamond. But that tended to happen when a female dropped into the picture and fucked up the flow.

Chapter Sixteen

Fine art wasn't her forte. Myst always confused Monet with Manet, couldn't tell Degas from Renoir, but the one she'd just walked past was a van Gogh. She paused mid-step to study the painting more closely. Yeah, definitely á la Vincent...as in painted by the master, not lifted from the rack at the local frame shop.

God, the thing had to be worth a fortune.

Why that surprised her, Myst wasn't sure. She guessed she hadn't expected quite so much from Bastian and his cohorts. In hindsight, though, she should have.

Her bedroom alone spoke volumes. It was refinement and taste wrapped up in a beautiful package that boasted the best of everything, from the antique sled bed to the brass fittings holding the silk curtains away from the windows. The colors were spectacular, too, the palate of soft lavenders and darker grays wrapped in an envelope of creamy white.

A feminine oasis complete with walk-in closet and matching bathroom.

Standing in the middle of all that gorgeousness, temptation had rung her bell, urging Myst to hunker down and well...hide. The problem? She wasn't a chicken. Somewhere along the line, the *bok-bok* gene had skipped a few branches in her family tree, leaving her with the chromosome pairing of stare-'em-down and make-'em-pay.

"Fine time to find that out," she said to herself.

Flipping her hair over her shoulder, Myst got a whiff of ylang-ylang. She huffed. The scent was driving her crazy. Not that she didn't like to smell good, but the ylang-ylang came with an added bonus. Damp hair. As in...she'd taken a shower recently. One she couldn't remember.

And wasn't that a kicker?

Bastian had...God. Had he really bathed her?

An undeniable *yes* echoed inside her head, dragging her inch by uncomfortable inch toward humiliation. Myst dug her heels in, told herself to grow up, but embarrassment grabbed her anyway, then threw her over the edge. Feeling her cheeks heat, she hit herself with a whole lot of logic.

So what? He'd seen her naked. Big deal, right? She wasn't fifteen anymore and, reacting like a teenage girl when a man saw her N-A-K-E-D was just plain stupid. Not to mention unhelpful, especially since she'd decided not to hide...was, in fact, walking toward Bastian and not away.

But the thing was...stupid or not, she couldn't deny that it mattered to her. Bothered her on a purely feminine level. It made her feel vulnerable, at a distinct disadvantage in the silent war raging between them.

How was she supposed to look him in the eye and not wonder if he was picturing her without a stitch on? Which, in turn, would make her think of him that way and...

Well, it was bad all the way around.

Myst rubbed her temples. She needed a new game plan. One in which she stood firm and told him to take her home. One that included telling him what she thought of his my-enemies-are-after-you theory. She didn't need his protection. And honestly, the war between him and those other dragons didn't have anything to with her, so why would anyone be after her?

The easy answer? They wouldn't. Bastian was obviously overreacting, being overprotective after overblowing the situation.

And hallelujah. She was back on track, thinking about getting out, not being naked. With Bastian.

Still, the whole shower incident made her want to button up and armor down. Myst checked the zipper on her hoodie. Yup, the purple Lululemon was still zipped to her chin, covering everything vital. She took a second to smooth the front of her yoga pants, then frowned at the polish on her toenails.

Myst snorted. So much for looking tough. Yeah, because nothing said badass like bright pink nail polish and sequined flip-flops.

As she flip-flip-flopped her way along, Myst watched painting after painting roll by. The wash of color enlivened the white walls, sitting comfortably above the chunky chair rail and gleaming hardwood floors. Even out here—in a place that did nothing more than get a person from point A to point B—everything looked expensive. The mitered corners met with meticulous crispness. Each halogen lined up with its neighbor, blending into the all-white scheme, no scuff marks in sight.

The seamlessness made Myst uncomfortable. It was too perfect: no cracks or streaks of dust, no visible signs of weakness...anywhere.

Having grown up in a tiny, two-bedroom house—one that put the shabby in Shabby Chic design—Myst couldn't identify with that kind of wealth. It made her feel like a second-class citizen traveling in a foreign country without a passport. Still, she kept her feet moving, each flip-flop a steady echo against the beautiful backdrop.

The corridor wasn't the kind of place you sped through. It was too much like the The Met in New York City to gallop down like a runaway horse. She got the impression that if she sped up even a little, a guard—complete with museum uniform—would pop out of the woodwork and scold her.

Uh-huh, and there went her training again. All the politesse her mother had drilled into her on display for the gallery and…yeah, no one else to see.

Which was beyond unfair. Completely idiotic, really.

Her mother had died almost three years ago, yet Myst couldn't forget. All those manners clung like old perfume, refusing to fade, reminding her of that dark December day.

It was more than just the violence, though, that stayed with her. It was the little things—all the stepping stones of behavior that her mother had insisted upon brought her low, too. Not that they were bad things to live by, but…

She missed her mom.

Missed her laughter and generous ways. Missed her crazy bohemian ideas and the wisdom that always accompanied them. Missed the endless lectures too: about respect and honesty, about treating others the way you wished to be treated.

And wow. Bastian had obviously skipped that lesson.

Passing a huge painting of a battle scene—something Napoleonic, judging by all the rearing horses and red, brass-buttoned coats—Myst finally heard what she'd been listening for…

Her angel. And oh, boy, he didn't sound happy.

Neither did the male voices that came between the crying fits, all the stops and starts as the baby paused to take a breath.

Myst paused in the corridor. As much as she hated to hear him cry, she needed a second to compose herself. Walking in there unhinged wouldn't help her, wouldn't help him...wouldn't help anyone. If she showed any weakness at all, Bastian would eat her alive and she wouldn't get what she wanted.

Squaring her shoulders, Myst put on her best don't-mess-with-me face and, taking a deep breath, rounded the corner into—

She stopped short, flip-flops glued to the limestone floor, eyes riveted to...

The scary army in the kitchen.

Well, okay. Not an army, exactly, but...jeez. The four guys sitting around the kitchen island were huge: all mean looking and muscular, and now? Completely focused on her. As four sets of eyes narrowed, Myst felt hers go wide. Taking a step back, she crossed her arms, hugging herself in a protective gesture she knew looked weak. But she couldn't help it. The aggressive factor on these guys was off the charts.

Myst swallowed past her heart, now firmly lodged in her throat. "Ah, s-sorry, but I'm looking for—"

"*Bellmia.*" The deep timbre of Bastian's tone flowed like honey, surrounding her with warmth and sweet safety.

Myst rode the wave and, releasing a shaky breath, turned toward his voice, needing to see him. Seeing was believing, after all, and regardless of the rift between them, she trusted him to shield her from the biker gang making mincemeat of her with their eyes.

He smiled as he met her gaze, and all the embarrassment Myst thought she'd feel departed for places unknown. The whole shower thing was okay. He hadn't taken advantage of her. She knew it without asking. The need to take care of her was there for her to see—in his eyes, on his face—and for some reason, that made all the difference.

Leaning back against the countertop, Bastian stared at her a moment longer, then pushed away from his perch.

Without meaning to, she breathed, "Hey."

"Hey," he said, echoing her in word and meaning.

It was more than just a how-the-heck-are-ya kind of greeting. Somehow, the "hey" seemed profound, as if they were speaking a language no one else understood. Which scared Myst more than a squad of terrorists at close range... armed with rocket launchers.

Rubbing her upper arms, she watched Bastian cup the back of the baby's head, supporting his neck as he adjusted his hold. A blue blanket tucked around him, her angel let out an ear-piercing howl. The guys at the island cringed, rearing a little in their seats.

With a grimace of his own, Bastian patted the baby's bottom, no doubt hoping the movement would soothe the little guy. "Looking for him?"

"Yeah. And you, too. We need to talk about..." Pausing, Myst chanced a quick peek at their audience, who were now watching them with rapt attention. Like she and Bastian were the best show in town. "Umm—"

"Come and take him, okay?" Skirting the massive center island, Bastian crossed to her in a hurry. The newborn wailed, little fists pumping over the blanket edge as Bastian shifted him from his shoulder, preparing to hand him over. "He doesn't like me very much this evening."

"Or anyone else," one of the four muttered.

Myst smiled. She couldn't help it. The news that these big, tough guys were having trouble handling one little boy made them seem normal. Well, not quite, but still their grumbling was music to her ears. So were Bastian's blood-shot eyes as he got close enough for her to see them.

"Have you been up with him all day?"

"Pretty much," he said, sounding as tired as he looked.

Well, all right. Vindication. She might have had a shower without her consent, but he hadn't slept all day. Somehow, that seemed, well, if not quite a fair trade, it came really, really close. "Is he fed?"

Bastian nodded. "An hour ago."

Raising her arms, she accepted the newborn, feeling her heart lift as his slight weight settled warm against her. He stopped crying mid-wail, as though he knew who held him and was happy to see her. Myst cooed in greeting as she checked him out, making sure his vitals were good and his heartbeat strong. Red-faced from his temper tantrum, he grumbled at her baby-style and then blinked, looking up at her solemnly as if to say, "How could you leave me like that?"

A round of murmurs rolled through the kitchen.

"Wow," one guy said.

"How did she do that?"

"The hell if I know," a third voice answered, awe in each syllable. "Probably all that energy."

Myst ignored them and feathered her fingertip over the baby's check. With one last snuffle, he turned his face toward her and closed his eyes as she whispered, "That's a good boy. Go to sleep, angel. I'm right here."

With a sigh that sounded an awful lot like relief, Bastian peered over her shoulder. "You're good with babies."

"I love them."

"Good," he said, his tone so soft she barely heard him.

Someone cleared his throat, and Bastian stepped back, giving her room to breathe.

"Myst…you remember Rikar and Sloan?" With the slight head tilt toward his men, Bastian pivoted and, planting himself next to her, leaned back against the countertop. Huge black boots crossed at the ankles, he pointed to the biggest guy. "That's Venom. Wick's on the far end."

She nodded, because honestly, what else could she do? Rikar, with his pale eyes and dark blond hair, was unforgettable. The mocha-skinned Sloan was gorgeous with a capital G. Venom's laughing eyes and quick smile were no sloppy seconds either. Myst had seen all three in the clinic when she treated Rikar. But the fourth?

He scared the crap out of her.

It wasn't his appearance. Wick was as good looking as the other three, but…his eyes. Something about the golden hue set her get-out-of-town bell ringing. She'd always thought gold was a warm color. Wick proved her wrong. His gaze was raptor flat, his eyes lifeless pits that bordered on cruel. And his stillness—the absolute absence of movement—screamed predator.

Myst inched closer to Bastian, thinking they should have called the guy Fuse instead of Wick. Light him up and watched him detonate. Kaboom!

"Are you hungry? Want some waffles?" Bastian's shoulder bumped hers as he leaned around her to pick up a white plate. Nudging her with his hip, he urged her toward the kitchen island. "Sit down, *bellmia*."

Sit where? Across from crazy-eyed Wick? No freaking way. "Ah, I'm really not that hun—"

"Here." Venom slid out of his seat and patted the back of his chair. "You can have my spot, Myst. I'm done anyway."

Okay. What to do...what to do?

Running sounded good, but impolite, too. Besides, leaving now would only get her more of the same. A bird's eye view of the corridor when she needed the lay of the land... all the exits off the island. An X marks the spot sort of thing, and as she debated whether to be rude and walk away or play nice and take a seat, she scanned the wide archway on the other side of the kitchen. A dining room sat beyond and to the right of that? Double French doors.

Myst sat, murmuring her thanks to Venom.

"So...Myst." Planted in the archway, Venom propped his shoulder against one of the timber-beam posts. "You from Seattle?"

"Leave her alone, man," Sloan grumbled around a mouthful of waffle. He threw her an apologetic look. "Sorry. He's a total pain in the a—ah, butt."

Venom made a face. "What? Just curious. Nothing wrong with that."

Feeling as if she'd fallen into the *Twilight Zone*, her gaze bounced between the two men. "I was born in LA. My mom moved us up here when I was four."

"Ooh, a Cali-girl." Without warning, Venom started singing his version of "California Gurls" by Katy Perry, fingers snapping to the beat.

"Christ," Rikar said, sounding disgusted even though a smile threatened.

Sloan groaned, both hands over his ears. "Please, God. Make it stop."

The comment pushed Myst over the edge and, unable to hold it back, she huffed. As soon as she laughed, Venom stopped serenading them to grin at her. God, they were almost charming. Except for Wick, who just stared like he was busy taking her measurements for a roasting pan.

"Here."

Warm with a hint of maple syrup, Bastian's breath curled against the side of her neck. His heat came next, gloving her shoulders as his arms came around her from behind. Surrounded by his scent, Myst breathed him, staring at the plate loaded with waffles and fruit slices that he set in front of her.

Utensils made an appearance next, clinking against marble. With slow precision, he straightened the silverware next to her plate, prolonging contact with her. Myst wanted to argue, to push him away, but...wow. The guy was delicious, all hard muscle and glorious heat.

He hummed next to her ear, like he knew what kind of effect he had on her. The rat. "Eat your breakfast, baby."

Her mouth went dry. Myst swallowed, working moisture back, and stifled a shiver. God, he was dangerous. And she was playing with fire. No matter how attractive she found him, she couldn't allow herself to go down that road. It was full of potholes, ones deep enough to lose herself in if she let him charm her.

Rotating her shoulder, she bumped his chest. The silent message was simple...back off. No slouch in the brains department, Bastian stepped away, giving her the room she needed to adjust her hold on the baby. After she settled him, she picked up her fork and realized...

Bastian had cut her waffle into neat, bite-sized squares. As he drizzled syrup over her breakfast, Myst bit her tongue, resisting the urge to thank him. But she wanted to so badly that her teeth ached. Under normal circumstances, she wouldn't have hesitated. After all, he was feeding her, caring for her in a way that felt too good for words. All that Dr. Feel-good, though, was a problem. A potential pothole in the making.

The little things mattered, and something small like, oh, say gratitude (pothole number one) would turn into trust (pothole number two). Trust would inevitably circle into closeness, then take a nosedive into curiosity (potholes number three and four). And curious was not where Myst wanted to be with Bastian. All that would lead to was more nakedness. Which would...

Yeah, no use going there. Hot, wild sex needed to stay off her radar.

A knowing light in his eyes, Bastian nudged her plate. "Eat, *bellmia*."

With a nod, Myst speared a bit-sized square. The outside crunched before her forked pushed through to the fluffy center. As she brought it to her mouth, she almost moaned. Yum. It was pure heaven, melt-in-your-mouth delicious. The second bit of sugary perfection made her close her eyes. Man, oh, man, who knew a waffle could taste so good? Daimler was a wizard...the god of culinary delight.

"So B..." Shifting in his seat, Rikar looked away from her as she took another bite. "Time to vote?"

"Sounds good," Bastian said, his voice deepening as he watched her eat. "You're up, Rikar."

"Hang on a minute." Chasing a drop of maple syrup, Myst licked it off her bottom lip. As Bastian drew a long breath, she asked, "What are you voting on?"

"The infant needs a name." His focus trained on her mouth, he watched her chew for a second before dragging his gaze back to hers. "I thought you might like to help us find the right one for him."

"For real?"

Bastian nodded.

A half-eaten piece of waffle in her mouth, overwhelmed by Bastian's generosity, Myst got a little misty-eyed. The giving of a name was serious business, the first in a long line of important decisions that would ensure her angel's welfare. A name meant love, signaled caring and longtime commitment.

And wow. How much of a sap was she?

Still, as she glanced down at the sleeping infant, she couldn't deny the sentiment...or how much she appreciated the gesture. By including her in the process, Bastian was giving her a gift. One she didn't know how to repay except by...

Oh, great. A little thing...the first pothole in what she suspected would be a long line of them. "Thank you."

His mouth curved. "My pleasure."

"Hmm...all right." Pale eyes narrowed, Rikar rubbed his hands together. "Attila."

With a gasp, Myst threw him a look of outrage.

Rikar glanced at her, all doe-eyed innocence. "What? It's a great name."

"If you're a mass murderer, maybe," she countered, unable to believe he would suggest such a thing. Attila the Hun? Forget it. No way she would allow them to name her angel *that*.

"She's gotta point, buddy." When Myst thanked him, Venom grinned at her, then threw his preference into the ring. "I vote for Torture...then we can call him Torch for short."

Myst stared at him, open-mouthed. He couldn't be serious. What kind of name was Torch? A bad one, that's what.

"Nah, too obvious. What about Ironhide?"

Rikar snorted. "You can't name him after an Autobot, Sloan."

"Why not?" Sloan frowned at his friend. "*The Transformers* is an awesome movie."

Myst bristled. "No way I'm voting for—"

"Viper," Wick said with a barely audible growl that made her skin crawl.

"I like it," Rikar said. "Good one, man. It's a definite contender."

Over her dead body. Which pretty much summed up how she felt about every suggestion they made, as names like Blitz and Hemlock made the rounds. Dear God, had they lost their flipping minds? Imagine naming a precious baby Grim. *Grim,* for pity's sake!

"Mayhem," Bastian said, finally tossing his choice in the ring.

Myst stared at him. "You can't be serious."

"Man, that's a good one, too." Venom scratched the top of this head. "I can't decide...Viper or Mayhem. So, which one?"

"None. Neither!" She glared at the lot of them.

"Well, if you're going to KO all our ideas, female," Sloan said, looking affronted, "make a suggestion."

Chewing on the inside of her bottom lip, Myst thought fast. She needed to come up with something...right now. If she didn't, the great barbarian horde would choose one of those awful names and—

She had it. The perfect one. "Gregor."

Five pairs of eyes narrowed as they mulled over her choice.

"It's Scottish...a strong name," she said, talking fast to convince them. "It was my grandfather's." Her voice went soft as she remembered the gentle man who'd helped raise her. Never having known her father, Grandpa G had been her lifeline, a solid role model in her unconventional upbringing. "He fought in the war. I had all his medals framed. They're hanging on the wall in my apartment."

Okay, so that was a little more personal than she intended, but...really. Her angel deserved a better name than *Viper*. And if telling them a bit about Grandpa G—the war hero—helped sway them? Well, she wasn't too proud to fight dirty.

But, as the silence stretched and Bastian's friends continued to stare, Myst wondered if she'd made a mistake. She didn't know these guys or what they were capable of... although, the word "ruthless" came to mind. Maybe sharing family history or anything else was a bad idea. Maybe she should listen to her early warning system—the one ring-a-ling-linging inside her head—and run for the nearest exit. Because sure as she was sitting there, they didn't look happy with her suggestion.

Chapter Seventeen

As far as strategies went, Myst's was ingenuity in action. Beautiful, yet oh, so simple it sounded something like... *if at first you don't succeed, guilt your opponent into caving.* Add a dash of feminine hope. Sprinkle in some bone-crushing dismay. Toss the whole dish with pleading violet eyes and...voilá, Bastian and his warriors had a recipe for disaster.

A cocktail called *pretty please* with a cherry on top.

"So..." Bastian glanced around the island and clamped down on the urge to laugh. For the first time ever, his warriors were speechless, unable to say no to the female who sat staring back at them. It was karma...payback with a knuckle-grinding punch. "Gregor, huh?"

"It's a great name..." she paused to fuss with the baby blanket, then looked right at him. And wham, he got the full effect of those baby blues. The second part of Myst's plan had just been deployed. Clever, clever female. Bastian's lips twitched even as he resisted the urge to adjust what was happening behind his fly. "It suits him, don't you think?"

"It's a human name," he said as she tilted her head, continuing to give him strong eye contact. Bastian shifted in his seat, becoming more uncomfortable by the second. God, what a female. She knew exactly how to play him. Still, he refused to give in without a fight. Okay, so he would give her what she wanted in the end—guaranteed—but that didn't mean he had to be a pansy about it. "And he's not—"

"Caroline was human and so is he. At least half, right? I know he's fathered by..." She worried her bottom lip with her straight, white teeth, nearly sending him into orbit. Man, he loved her mouth. "I mean, that's why he's here... because he's one of you? But, he's human, too, and I know my *friend* would like my choice."

Well, all right then. Sucker punch time. She was fighting dirty, slamming her trump card down on the table, the one labeled "mother and friend." Which meant, they were off and running. Cuz, honestly, two could play that game.

Although, he would have to wing it and hope for the best. His brain wasn't working right. The reason? Most of the blood was no longer in his head. Hell, more than half of it had headed south on the desire train about five minutes ago.

Folding his arms on the countertop, Bastian took a deep breath, needing his calm-cool-and-collected back. Yeah, that and a tub of cold water. He glanced at Rikar. Right. No help there. His best friend was trying to keep from cracking up. The warped SOB had one stupid sense of humor.

Bastian glanced at the steel-framed wall clock across the kitchen. A little over thirty-six hours to go. So little time to make her want him...to make her accept him.

Sloan cleared his throat, no doubt wanting him to get a move on.

Still holding up the archway, Venom shifted behind him, the scrape of his boots against stone sounding loud in the silence. "B, maybe we could—"

"I'll make you a deal, Myst," he said, cutting off his warrior's capitulation. He didn't care that Venom had problems denying a female anything. The big male would have to hang on...and bite holes in his tongue while he was at it. Bastian refused to give up his advantage. "I'll give you the name Gregor if you give me something in return."

Suspicion glinted in her eyes. "What?"

"His full name...the one recorded in the annals...will be Gregor Mayhem and—"

A round of appreciative—and relieved—murmurs rose in the kitchen.

"And?"

"Your word that you'll stay here and spend every waking hour of the next three days..." He paused for effect, wanting her to feel the weight of his resolve. "...with me. No escape attempts."

Her mouth fell open. After a second, she snapped it shut. "That's not fair. I saved his life. I should get to—"

"You want the name? That's the deal, but be careful, *bellmia*. Think hard. Once you give your word..." He stared at her from beneath his brows, warning her by deed and word. "I'll hold you to it."

Stuck between what she wanted and his conditions, Myst broke eye contact to glance down at the infant. Pretending to fuss, buying more time, she adjusted the blanket and then, as though unable to help herself, she stroked the Mohawk running down the center of the baby's head.

A second passed into more while Bastian held his breath. Forcing her ran contrary to everything he believed, but he needed her close without having to fight to get her there. It was imperative...vital to him like food and water was to continued good health. He yearned for her in a way that crossed all the self-imposed limits he lived by. He couldn't leave her anymore than he could stop breathing.

The deal closer, though…the absolute best? Bastian knew that if she gave her word, Myst would keep it. Even if she didn't want to.

After a minute of chewing on her bottom lip, she met his gaze. A moment in time turned into infinity as he looked at her…as she looked back at him.

"Three days." Her voice was whisper soft, all the considerable brainpower behind her eyes assessing, unearthing layer after layer as she searched for the catch. The trap in which he wanted to ensnare her. Bastian almost felt badly that she would never figure it out. Not until it was too late. "After that, all bets are off?"

Bastian nodded, watched her think, all but tasting victory.

"Fine, but…" Sounding unhappy but resigned, she tossed out a challenge of her own, "*Be careful* what you wish for, Bastian. You might not like what you get."

"Impossible," he murmured, allowing everything he felt for her to show in his eyes: all the heat and longing and neediness he always kept hidden from view.

As color stole into her cheeks and she broke eye contact, Bastian killed the urge to roar in satisfaction. He'd won. The next three days belonged to him. And whether she knew it or not, Myst was now his forevermore.

With careful, precise movements, Ivar grabbed one in a long line of stainless steel handles and pulled on the refrigerator door. The thing resisted for a second, clinging to the metal frame before it opened with a suctioning slurp. His hands steady, his heart racing, he slid the test tube holder onto the top shelf. Seven vials wobbled, clinking together as lip met glass lip. Still white-knuckling the handle, he held his breath, waiting for the volatile contents to settle.

Which was beyond ridiculous.

The biohazard suit he wore was airtight. An impenetrable beast with layer upon layer of protection. Why he even bothered to suit up was a mystery he'd yet to solve. Dragonkind didn't react like humans did to contaminants. Or viruses.

Better to be safe than sorry, though. He couldn't afford to become infected—for more than just the obvious reasons—and those bugs were serious monsters. Ones he wasn't 100 percent sure he could control.

Ivar smiled behind his mask as he let the fridge door swing closed. Forget necessity. Experimentation. Innovation. Yeah, those two were the real mothers of invention.

Soon, though, his science project would need to be tested, and the outcomes analyzed. Seal a few of his worker bees in the vault—a secure, airtight chamber connected to his lab—and take one or two of the monsters out for a spin.

Humming "Born to Be Bad," Ivar crossed his all white workspace. Seamless and pristine, the room pleased him more than the entire Razorback lair put together. It was his sanctuary, his place of solitude. A place no one else dared enter.

And yeah...the fear factor really got him off. His warriors didn't understand his science, which was the best part of the whole operation. He could do whatever he wanted to down here: no holds barred, no questions asked.

The airlock hissed, the double-wide glass panel sliding open as Ivar approached. Pride hit him chest level as he stepped into the decontamination chamber. His little worker bees had done a stellar job. His laboratory was perfection, from the high-tech toys and stainless steel countertops to the smooth, shiny walls. One thing, however, irked him.

The chamber.

Sure, it came signed, sealed, and delivered...but only in size small.

Four by four feet square, the Decon chamber barely contained him. Was too tight a squeeze for even his considerable comfort level. Jesus, the thing felt more like a box than what it was...a necessary step en route from the lab to the lair. Thank God he didn't suffer from claustrophobia. Otherwise, getting in and out of his sanctuary would be H-E-L-L. And he had enough on his plate without adding that to the mix.

Leaving the soothing quiet behind, he stood in the center of the Decon. As the door closed and locked behind him, the blowers got busy. The violent rush of air tugged at his suit as he waited for the sophisticated system to give him a thumbs-up and let him go. The light went from red to green above the second door. A second later, the lock released with a click and the glass panel facing him slid open.

Fresh air rushed in. Halle-fucking-lujah. The stagnant air inside the chamber always bothered him. It smelled too much like death. Or rather, the absence of life.

Taking a deep breath, Ivar willed the bio-suit off his body. Standing naked in a center foyer that looked a lot like his lab—without all of the long worktables—he rolled his shoulders, then got busy stretching out his muscles, one long limb at a time.

The knots bracketing his spine uncurled as he conjured his clothes. Ivar sighed. The wide-legged sweats and loose-fitting tee-shirt felt like heaven, the cotton equivalent of paradise after an afternoon spent in the confining heat of the bio-suit.

As the Nikes settled on his feet, Ivar put the sneakers to good use and crossed the vestibule. Without slowing, he punched through the double doors. The suckers swung with a soft squeak, dumping him into the half-finished corridor.

Ivar paused to examine the hinges. His eyes narrowed. The brackets weren't installed properly, and now the metal pins were bent. Who the hell had—

A tingle rushed the length of his spine. Ah, good. The ruined hinges would have to wait. His XO had news for him.

Turning right, Ivar headed for the unfinished end of his home. As he walked, the hum of machinery and the clank of metal echoed in the deep. Male voices rounded out the symphony, telling him the humans were hard at work digging the last section of the lair.

Desperation hung in the air around them. Ivar smelled the stench of it through the concrete walls. Could feel the humans' heartache, the awful homesickness that drove them. All were united under one goal—building his lair as fast as possible and going home to their families. Each wanted to restart his life and feel the sun on his face. It was sad, really. The pitiful creatures really believed the lies he told them. His busy bees didn't have a clue they would never again see the light of day.

He almost felt bad about it. Almost, but not quite.

Stepping out of the corridor and into his office, Ivar got a load of his XO. Up against the far wall, Lothair was lit up like a Christmas tree, his gaze glowing from a good feed.

Lucky bastard.

Ivar rolled his bad shoulder, working out a cramp as he crossed his office. Still in the drywall stage, the room looked like death, the unfinished walls and concrete floor giving everything a gray tinge. Well, everything except his desk. The antique walnut piece was an absolute stunner with thick, hand-carved legs and intricate curlicues on the front panel. The matching chair wasn't bad, either.

Skirting the corner of the monstrosity, Ivar raised a brow. "Good hunting last night?"

"A coed." Lothair pushed away from the wall with a hum, like he was remembering the female and loving the picture. "Unbelievable mouth. Even better ride."

"Gonna give me her address?"

"No."

Ivar laughed. Shit, he couldn't blame Lothair. He didn't like to share, either. Then again, the females from whom he fed usually ended up dead. Like that brunette last night. What a waste. She hadn't been worth the effort. He was already hungry...less than twelve hours after he'd taken her.

With a frown, he nudged his chair out and sat down. As he settled into the cushions, he tipped his chin in Lothair's direction. "What's up?"

"Forge is on his way down."

"You blindfolded him?"

"Yeah. Drove him in circles for an hour, too. No way he can track us here."

"Good." And it was. He didn't want anyone to know where to find their lair unless fully committed to the cause. Forge, included. Eyeing his XO, Ivar picked up a letter opener. Made of polished ivory, the smooth surface slid against his palm before he tossed it above his head. He watched it rotate end over end, then reached out and grabbed the hilt mid-spin. "So…you sticking around to see the explosion?"

A smile ghosted across Lothair's face. "Thought I might enjoy the show."

"It'll be a good one," he said, not bothering to hide his anticipation. Or the fact he liked Lothair's desire to participate. The younger male made him proud. He really did.

An echo sounded in the corridor, the heavy footfalls coming closer by the second.

Ivar grinned at his XO, then wiped his expression clean. Forge didn't need to see that he was jazzed; that he loved the fact that a freak turn of events had provided the very thing he needed to get the powerful male on his side.

"Ivar?" The deep bass came from the other side of the door.

"In here."

With a forceful shove, the door rocketed inward, banged against the wall and…stayed there, door handle buried in the Sheetrock. Ivar didn't care about the damage to his wall. He was more interested in the male coming over the threshold. Amethyst eyes aglow, Forge dipped his head beneath the doorframe, then stopped short, standing just inside the room. The male always did that…came in, but never committed to sharing space with him.

The indecisiveness annoyed the hell out of Ivar. The distance was like a physical manifestation of Forge's mental state—of his inability to commit to the Razorback cause.

Always direct and to the point, the male said, "What the fuck?"

"Got some news." Holding the warrior's gaze, he stood and moved around to the front of his desk. Expression appropriately grave, he sat on the edge and crossed his arms over his chest. "I wanted to tell you myself."

Forge tipped his chin, telling him without words to let it fly.

So, Ivar did. Got down to the nitty-gritty and explained exactly what had gone down with his female. He left nothing out, neither scent nor sound; retelling the female's brutal death with perfect recall. But more important than the how was the why. And as Ivar talked, he laid the blame on thick, putting Bastian in the hot seat.

"No." Forge shook his head. Unsteady on his feet, he backpedaled and, as his shoulders hit the wall, fumbled for his cell phone. The one he'd bought to keep in touch with the female. "I just saw her...shared a meal with—"

"I am sorry," he said, surprised that he meant it. The pain in Forge's eyes was too real too deny. Jesus, the male had actually loved Caroline what's-her-name. "But we'll get your son back. Lothair and I have already started searching...we'll hunt the Nightfuries down and find—"

Forge went off like a bomb, the agonizing roar unlike anything Ivar had ever heard. As the male went ballistic, magic surged and furniture flew, spinning around the office like a tornado had just touched down.

So much for Ivar's matched-set office furniture. His desk was already in two pieces, and the chair? Nothing but kindling. Not that it mattered. Forge could tear the place apart for all he cared, because after months of work, Ivar had the male exactly where he wanted him.

Mad with grief, burning for revenge, Forge would do what he'd never been able to...track Bastian and make him suffer before he died.

Ivar smiled as he and Lothair took cover in the hallway.

Yippee-ki-yay. Let the games begin.

Chapter Eighteen

His radar up and running, Bastian walked into the Gridiron with Wick on his heels. Music thumped, the heavy metal vibe rolling up hard as he paused on the edge of the crowd and scanned the interior of the nightclub. Kitted out Goth style, everything was black and mirrored with stainless steel accents. Not that he cared. He hadn't flown all the way downtown for a lesson in interior design.

The enemy was here. Or had been. He could smell them. Trace amounts of brimstone cut through the sharp scent of alcohol and...huh. Bastian took another whiff. The scent was upscale, posh with a capital P—a fancy oil some dragons liked to rub on their scales.

Bastian stifled a snort. Freaking pansies and their nasty spa treatments. Wicked vain, all of them.

Not that he was complaining. The scent trail made his job easier. Made tracking them a softball pitch in a hardball game. Every once in a while, though, Bastian wished the idiots would grow an imagination and try something new. The club scene was getting old. But predictable was just that... *predictable*. The Seattle strip was prime hunting ground. An environment fit for blending, for finding females with the best energy.

Which got his crank on.

He hated the downtown core and the cloying sweetness of the clubs. All the female perfume sloshing around in a vat of human sweat and stale alcohol. Not to mention the overcrowding. Man, that was the worst, even though no one ever came near him. People always tripped over themselves to get out of his way.

Tonight was no different.

After getting a load of him, the humans scattered left and right, opening a path wide enough to drive a Humvee though. Fine by him. Anyone touched him tonight and he'd go off like a fricking bomb.

He didn't want to be here in the filth and squalor. In the bump and grind. See all the sex happening in dark corners. Or watch the humans pour poison down their throats and shoot toxic waste into their veins.

He wanted to be home. With his female.

Bastian growled, disgusted with himself. Myst's pull on him was insanity squared. But the tug—the alluring need—made him imagine her beneath him. She'd be unbelievable, magic with all that soft skin sliding against his and... shit. He kept picturing them together: entwined, tangled up in silk sheets, her head on his shoulder while they loved and talked and—

He needed to get a grip. A big one before he completely lost control of the situation. And his fantasy.

Yeah, on paper that argument worked great. In the real world? Not so much. The power of his attraction to Myst was impossible to ignore. Its grip was too strong. So he was stuck...jammed between what was right and what he wanted.

Wasn't that fun? Uh-huh, a whole barrel full of laughs.

And the entire reason he wasn't at Black Diamond tonight.

He needed some space. She did, too. Rushing her wouldn't do either of them any favors. Especially since he refused to let her go.

Not for the reasons he'd given her—although those were pretty compelling. No, it was much worse than Ivar and the Razorbacks' threat. Bastian couldn't return her to the human world because he literally *couldn't*…like he had a physical impediment or something. A stop button that got smacked every time he thought about taking the easy way out.

Which meant one thing. He'd bonded with her. Taken to her so fiercely that his dragon side was digging in, building trenches to defend his territory.

Man. Was that even normal?

He didn't know. The bonding had happened so fast. He'd met Myst what…a day ago? Yet he recognized that she belonged to him and, as much as he hated to admit it, Bastian knew he was hers, too.

And didn't that suck.

What he had with Myst was destined to be short-term. He knew it. Biology confirmed it. She would never survive birthing his son. And getting her pregnant was inevitable. Even if he sent her home—hell, to the other side of the planet—he wouldn't be able to stay away when the Meridian realigned. Not now that he'd tasted her. His biological imperative would drive him to find and claim her.

All Dragonkind males went a bit nuts when the energy field shifted and the Meridian surged. Bastian and his warriors were no different. Twice a year, at the fall and spring realignments, Daimler locked them in the vault one level below the lair's underground facilities. It was twenty-four hours of ball-breaking, teeth-grinding hell. Not that any of them ever complained. It was better than the alternative—or had been until he'd made his decision to find a female and be the first to sire a child.

A great plan. Until he met Myst.

Now he was upside down and backwards...totally turned around about his decision and what it meant for his female.

His fist cranked in tight, Bastian rolled his shoulders as he made his way through the club, trying not to think about what the next three days would bring. But it was hard. The ache wouldn't go away. As heaviness settled like a dump truck on his chest, Bastian forced himself to keep moving as he scanned the crowd, looking for Razorbacks. And a fight. He needed a muscle-stretching, claw-grinding, bloody brawl.

Bastian snarled, low and soft. Where were they? Hiding in dark corners? He sensed at least two, but couldn't see them. Couldn't pinpoint them within the thick heat and stench of the Gridiron. Hell, he hoped there were more than just two. A full squadron of enemy warriors was just what the doctor ordered tonight.

Climbing the stairs to the VIP section, he focused on the back hallway. Long and narrow, the corridor streamed past the bathrooms on its way to the emergency exit and the alley beyond.

Shitkickers rooted to the floor, Bastian stared at the reinforced steel door and sent out feelers in a surge of energy. Letting his magic roll served two purposes. One, it broadcasted his location, a kind of come-and-get-me beacon the enemy would hear and follow. And two? The magical ping would bounce off any Razorbacks in the area and send that information back to him. Within seconds, he would know their strengths and weaknesses. Probably their shoe sizes, too.

Ousting an entwined couple from a booth with a mental zap, Bastian slid into the seat. Rocking a fierce expression, Wick grabbed a chair and, flipping it backward, straddled the thing. Golden eyes roaming the dance floor, the male folded his arms on the chair back and settled in.

"They're here," Wick said through mind-speak.

"I know." The ping came back, giving Bastian an impression. Two males. One young, the other much older. Good. Two inexperienced idiots wouldn't be much of a challenge. *"Got two closing in fast."*

"What's the word?"

"Watch the bigger one. He's rocking Scald." Bastian's lips curved up at the corners. Not bad. Scald was an interesting weapon. Natural napalm mixed with venom, the toxin slid underneath scales. The highly flammable stuff was deadly when mixed with fire. And what do you know? *"The second breathes fire."*

A hard gleam in his eyes, Wick nodded.

A waitress stopped in front of their table, wearing a tray and not much else. One hip cocked, she ran her gaze over Bastian. He endured her inspection, thinking she wasn't nearly as pretty as Myst was.

Jesus. What was wrong with him?

No way should he be thinking of his female now. That kind of mental side trip screwed with a male's focus and got him killed.

Registering his non-interest, the waitress glanced at Wick. She flinched and shuffled sideways, fear surging in her scent as her gaze ping-ponged back to Bastian. No surprise there. Wick might be a handsome male, but unless he applied himself, the females ran scared.

Holding her tray in front of her like a shield, she asked, "What can I get you?"

"Johnnie Walker, Blue. Neat." He hitched his thumb in Wick's direction. "A lager for my friend."

Wick raised a brow, no doubt wondering what he was doing. Bastian ignored him. The enemy males were a few minutes off yet. He wanted to blend in, and two guys dressed in black leather sitting in the VIP section without a drink didn't qualify as camouflage.

Reaching into this pocket, Bastian took out a wad of cash. He peeled off three Benjamins and set the bills on the tabletop. "Keep us good and poured. Got it?"

"I'm yours all night."

Uh-huh. Bastian knew that before she said it. If he wanted to he could raise her skirt right here and do her on the tabletop. Funny, a day ago that might have amused him...interested him, even. Not now, though. There was only one female he wanted, and she was at home. Sitting in his kitchen eating waffles.

God, he was so screwed.

Hips swaying in her barely there skirt, the waitress returned from the bar and set their drinks down, Bastian's in front of him, Wick's on the edge of the table. Close enough for the male to reach, far enough away so the female stayed out of range. Not that Wick cared. The warrior never touched alcohol. It was against his principles or something.

A tingle swept the back of Bastian's neck. *"Show time."*

Wick growled and, eyes on the swarm of human bodies, shifted in his seat for an easy exit.

The dancing throng parted like the Red Sea, opening a wide swath. Strobe lights flashed. Head and shoulders above the rest, the male came through the crowd. Locating them at the back of the club, the Razorback's mouth curved. He stood unmoving for a moment, boots planted in the middle of the dance floor, a challenge shimmering in his gaze.

Bastian didn't take the bait. He couldn't start a fight inside the club. Sure, memories could be wiped, but humans were slippery creatures. One might escape his net...with a cell phone picture or two. Not something any of his kind wanted to see on CNN. Dragonkind needed to stay hidden, an unknown in the human world. Otherwise, the inferior race would weapon up, like it had in past centuries. And honestly? Government-sanctioned dragon slayers were just plain annoying.

When neither he nor Wick moved, the Razorback reached out and snagged a female. Using the blonde as a shield, the rogue pulled her in tight and, cupping the nape of her neck, touched his mouth to the side of her throat. Wick tensed, ready to let fly as the female buried her hands in the enemy's hair, tipped her head back and gave up her energy.

Bastian grabbed Wick's forearm to keep him seated. So the Razorback was feeding. Big deal. He wouldn't drain the female...not here. The most he would get was a sip. One that wouldn't help him in the end.

Downing the JW in one swallow, Bastian relished the burn and got to his feet. Only one male had entered the club. The other was still outside...waiting.

Which was excellent news. He hadn't gone up against a male rocking Scald in a while. Oh, yeah. This was going to be all kinds of fun.

Chapter Nineteen

The Razorback backed away from the female as Bastian crossed the VIP section. His gaze riveted on the male, he kept his pace smooth and unhurried. No sense startling the jack-off. He didn't want him to bolt.

Running and hiding was not on the menu. Not tonight. Screaming and begging, however? Yeah, that would do. At least, for starters. The dying would come later, but right now, he needed the pair to sing like a couple of songbirds.

With Ivar on a killing spree and the cops involved, he was after information. A whole lot of it. The kind only a Razorback could provide...like: where to find the sadistic SOB responsible for stirring Dragonkind's pot with a shit stick. The result of all that churning? Over a century of war and a fractured community, one in which males picked sides and committed their sons to the cause...rogue or Nightfury.

The Archguard sat on the fence, not knowing which way to jump. The council's lack of leadership put it on the brink of sanctioning the worst genocide the planet had ever known.

Forget the Holocaust. Forget the Congo and Darfur. Ivar's agenda would wipe out all things human.

At least, that's what Bastian suspected.

Was he 100 percent certain? No. All he had right now was a whole lot of nothing. A handful of suppositions coupled with a gut feeling that pointed to the undeniable possibility.

What he needed now was to prove it. A tall order? Maybe. But he knew Ivar. Had trained alongside him in the Transylvanian pack before the male had gone rogue. Ivar's obsession with science made a crack addict's habit look like a trip to Disneyland. And like a druggie, the twisted SOB got a contact high from the destructive forces science could wield.

Humankind was an incredibly frail species. Case in point? Cancer and HIV. Both diseases ravaged their race while nothing touched Dragonkind.

But no matter how many times he warned the Archguard, the lofty males sat on their duffs and did nothing. It was a wait-and-see strategy that would get them all killed. Dragonkind needed human females to survive. Without them, they would all die...in an agonizing manner that made the bubonic plague look merciful.

Ignorant fools, every one of them.

Reaching the stairs to the VIP lounge, Bastian slowed his roll. The closer he got, the more skittish the Razorback became, like he regretted signing up as the bait-and-switch guy. Well, too bad. The pinhead had started the game and Bastian wanted to play.

"I'm going out back." Wick veered left behind him, heading for the narrow hallway and the emergency exit beyond. *"Gonna take a look-see."*

"Keep me posted."

Bastian watched the Razorback fade in behind the bar. Well, at least the little bugger was making it interesting.

Putting the bar between them was an obvious strategy. The freaking thing was huge...and annoying as hell. The biggest nightmare in a place that specialized in them, the structure formed a perfect circle beside the dance floor. Three deep, humans thronged the countertop on all sides. Clad in thin, transparent stone, the marble bar face was backlit...a glowing 360-degree free-for-all of bumping bodies wrapped in the thump-thump-thump of heavy-duty bass. And that wasn't the only problem. High stools sat around its periphery, elevating those seated into visual interference.

The scene provided the perfect cover. If he didn't move fast, the Razorback would be out the other emergency door before—

Too late. Pinhead was already running.

Unleashing his speed, Bastian gunned it for the front door. *"Watch out. The little shit bolted."*

"Your ETA?"

Bastian jumped over the black cord stretched across the club entrance. The bouncers cursed and females waiting in line shrieked as his feet connected with the sidewalk at the bottom of the stairs. *"Airborne in thirty seconds."*

"Perfect," Wick said and meant it, too.

Great. Just what he needed. Wick on the warpath, playing it solo.

Then again, he couldn't blame him. He and Wick suffered from the same affliction: outnumbered-itis. The lethal male loved it when the odds leaned heavily in the Razorbacks' favor. Or at least, he enjoyed the perception... and the enemy's surprise when he upended their sorry asses.

The idiots. There was something wrong with their math. When would they learn that more bodies never equaled certain victory?

Pausing on the street corner, Bastian scanned Yesler Way, looking for some privacy and space. He needed to get airborne and being smack-dab in the middle of the Seattle club district was too public. Sure, he could go invisible, cloak himself to get the job done. But disappearing into thin air in front of a crowd wasn't the best idea. All those humans owned handhelds: iPhones and Blackberries with video capabilities.

Not exactly the kind of impression he wanted to leave.

Taking a sharp left, he turned into the parking lot. Perfect. Privacy, space, and leverage all wrapped up in one.

Without slowing, Bastian hurdled a concrete barrier. Two strides later, he leapt onto the roof of a tricked-out SUV. Metal groaned, dimpling beneath his boots as he launched himself skyward. Shifting to dragon form at the top of his jump, his wings caught air and he climbed, surging above buildings and rooftops.

"Wick...on my way."

"No hurry."

Bastian snorted. Even out of breath, the male never said quit. At least now, though, Wick talked to him. The first couple of times out together, the warrior hadn't said boo. Not even when he'd been in trouble, outnumbered four to one in a firefight.

Cloaked by magic, Bastian buzzed the Space Needle, flying fast toward the waterfront. The warehouse district and train yards were a favorite of Wick's. Crazy as it seemed, the male loved to fight near heavy machinery. Hurling locomotives and front-end loaders at the enemy was fast becoming a hobby for him.

True to form, he found his warrior in aerial claw-to-claw combat over the PRS rail yard. And right below him? A dump truck. Shit, it was only a matter of time before the thing went flying.

The pair of Razorbacks attacked in tandem, keeping Wick's hands full. Thank God. Dodging enemy claws was hard enough without getting nailed in the grill by a Freightliner.

Casting his invisibility cloak wide, he added his magic to Wick's, ensuring they stayed hidden from view, and banked right. He needed an opening, a small window of opportunity to join the fight. If he engaged too soon, he'd hit Wick. If he went in too late? His warrior would end up injured. So he flew around the periphery and waited…and waited. And waited for Wick to let him in.

With a spectacular flip, Wick dodged claws and spiked tails. Avoiding the smaller dragon's fangs, Wicks' gold and black scales flashed as he delivered a bone-crunching uppercut. The bigger dragon reeled, head snapping to the side.

Finally. He had his window.

Engaging fast, Bastian sideswiped the bigger male. The razor-sharp blade of his tail bit deep, slicing through green scales. As blood welled on the enemy's side, Pinhead bared his fangs. Fantastic. The Razorback was about to treat him to a bit of—

Pinhead exhaled on a hiss.

Scald shot between the fucker's fangs. Bastian banked hard. A second before the napalm hit, he tucked his wings and rotated, spiraling into a supersonic spin. As the venomous stream rocketed beneath him, he got a whiff of it. Wicked cool. The stuff smelled nasty: like gasoline and dirty socks mixed with something sweet. Kind of like Buckley's cough syrup. Which made sense: Scald could steal the company's slogan, "It tastes awful. And it works."

The dump truck went flying, giant tires spinning as it hurtled through the air. With a twist, Bastian took cover, diving toward the railway tracks. The red Razorback wasn't as quick and—

Crunch! Metal met scales, snapping bone with a sickening crack.

Jesus. The takedown was a thing of beauty. Wick's aim was bang on, as usual. Though how he managed to get a hold of the Mack in the first place was a total mystery. One Bastian wanted to solve, but...

Now was not the time.

Wings extended, using a crane's boom as cover, Bastian flipped, resetting his strike angle. He needed to take the green dragon alive. Answers...he wanted some before he killed the Razorback. And what do you know? Pinhead was on board with the plan. Struck stupid, he watched his comrade fall from the sky. As the red dragon hit the ground—a truck in place of his head—and ashed out, the remaining rogue roared.

More Scald hit the airwaves.

Bastian rocketed into a side flip. Pinhead had just made a dumb-ass mistake. Speed and agility equaled maneuverability...all huge advantages in an aerial dogfight. The Razorback had obviously missed the memo. Relying on Scald, the male hung in midair, a stationary target with a huge bull's-eye on his chest.

Napalm streamed by, a mere inch from his wing tip. With an abrupt shift, Bastian cut his flight short and...

One potato. Two potato. Three potato, four...

He broadsided the rogue, hitting him like the freight train he knew Wick wanted to throw. The strike drove the male backward. As the Razorback's head whiplashed, Bastian grabbed his wings just above the elbow joint. His talons sank deep, digging past scales to find flesh as he applied pressure. Pinhead squawked and twisted, flailing to break Bastian's hold.

Too little, too late.

He bent the Razorback's wings back. Bone snapped and the sound ricocheted, echoing off steel-clad warehouses, joining the male's scream of agony. Enemy claws raked him, tearing at his shoulder and chest. Bastian tightened his grip and, without mercy, flew toward the ground. Pinhead's spine collided with concrete with a gruesome crack. Jarred by the impact, a rusty pile of railway ties rattled and the Razorback gasped, blood bubbling up his throat to seep from the side of his mouth.

Applying pressure, he pushed the Razorback's pain threshold. "Where is he?"

Wick touched down beside him. Golden eyes narrowed, the dump truck-wielding male sat like a cat, tail wrapped around his front paws, the tip twitching as he watched and listened.

Broken and bloodied, the green dragon wheezed, "L-lab. Always...the l-lab."

"Doing what?"

"Don't..." The Razorback coughed, fighting for each breath. "K-now. Don't...go... in there. Bad s-shit."

Wick bared his fangs. *"Proof positive."*

"Not enough for the Archguard," Bastian said in mind-speak, frustration seeping into his tone. *"They won't take my word for it."*

"Imbeciles."

B snarled in agreement. The Razorback moaned, the sound so awful Bastian took pity. Grabbing his horned head, he twisted, breaking his enemy's neck in one clean snap. Limp in death, the rogue's green scales ashed as he stepped off and...

Bastian's eyes narrowed as a prickling rush rattled over his scales.

Wick's head snapped toward a break between two warehouses. The alleyway between the two buildings was narrow, but wide enough to see the ocean beyond. "B..."

"I feel it."

Sidestepping, he got low and, using the railway ties as cover, he let his magic roll. Something was out there. Something big. Something he couldn't identify, but...

Fog rose off the surface of the water. Wisping out, the thick brume frothed, creeping over the breakwater along the shoreline. Ethereally beautiful, power hidden in its depths...magic as lethal as Rikar's ice mist. The spikes running down the center of Bastian's spine vibrated, rattling, warning him.

"Get airborne," Bastian said, a second before a fireball lit up the night sky.

Like a long-tailed comet, it streaked over the top of a warehouse and...Jesus. Fire-acid. The deadly combo ate through scales, burning dragons from the inside out.

"Go. Go. Go."

Unfurling his wings, Wick leapt skyward.

The fireball rocketed into a pair of giant fuel tanks behind them. Diesel geysered sky-high, then ignited, the orange fireball mushrooming with the force of a nuclear bomb. The shock wave blew Wick sideways. A horrific clang echoed as his skull met the side of a building.

Bastian saw him crumple a second before the explosion threw him backward, introducing his ribcage to a healthy dose of steel. Bones cracked, giving way as he was body slammed by a front-end loader. Pain spiraled, biting into his torso. Sucking wind, starved for oxygen, Bastian rolled.

Air or no air, he needed to move and stay clear of the fire-acid. The poisonous gel was everywhere, mixing with diesel, throwing off black smoke and toxic fumes. Fingers of flame rose like mini-tornados, racing across fuel soaked dirt and...

Agony licked over his hip.

God, he was on fire. But worse than that? He was coated in acid from knee to shoulder along his left side. Forget the pain, he had bigger problems here. The acid worked fast, would take him apart scale by scale to reach the vulnerable muscle beneath. Once that happened, he'd lose his ability to move, becoming a sitting duck for the enemy to pick apart from the sky.

And he'd lost his wing mate.

In a heap on the ground, Wick still hadn't moved.

Molding his wing to his side, Bastian smothered the last of the flames. The gruesome smell of burnt skin rolled with the smoke, making bile rise in his throat. He swallowed it, ignoring the pain as he scanned the terrain. He couldn't stay here. Wick needed time to shake off the strike, which meant he must get to higher ground. Find a defensive position and hammer the enemy when they flew in low.

The fuckers wouldn't know what hit them. But first? He needed to get his ass in gear.

Unfolding his wings, Bastian leapt skyward. His left wing didn't catch air, sending him sideways, flapping like an injured eagle. Jesus. He couldn't lift off. One of his wings was fried, acid eating holes in the webbing.

Smoke swirled as the ambushing SOB swept in from the ocean like the grim reaper. Deep purple with a blue underbelly, the dragon bared his fangs. Bastian snarled back and, crouching low, tucked his injured wing in tight. Yeah, he might be down, but that didn't mean he wasn't deadly.

The Razorback circled the rail yard: one, twice, a third time. Bastian waited, conserving his energy. He would only get one shot at the big male...a single exhale of his poisonous electro-pulse. But one was all he needed. If he hit Deep Purple in the face...game over.

"Tell me where he is and I'll be merciful." Carried on smoke, Deep Purple's voice rolled on an accent. The thick brogue could only mean one thing. The male came from the other side of the pond...from the Scottish pack. What the hell was he doing in Seattle? "I'll kill you quickly. Return your ashes to your kin."

"Sporting of you." Pivoting on his hind legs, Bastian kept pace with the male circling above him.

"Where is he?"

"Who?"

"The infant."

Bastian stifled a growl. The rogue wanted the baby... just another male to turn into a mindless Razorback solider. Deep Purple landed on the steel edge of the warehouse opposite him. Less than fifty feet away, he perched and waited, stalling for time. With a weapon like fire-acid, the male knew exactly what was happening beneath Bastian's scales.

Smart. Deadly. Deep Purple was a lethal opponent with the patience to match. As a warrior, Bastian admired him for it. As a Nightfury? He wanted to rip the rogue apart. Gregor Mayhem belonged to his pack now. Nothing would change that.

"You can't have him."

Deep Purple didn't like the news flash. "Tell me or—"

"Or what? You'll kill me?" The spikes along Bastian's spine rattled, chiming against one another as he prepared for imminent attack. "Not a very effective way to locate the infant."

Razor-sharp talons scraping steel, the male moved forward. "I'll rip you to shreds...like you did my..." Moisture glinted in the male's eyes as his chest heaved. Bastian's eyes narrowed. Interesting. Deep Purple was in serious pain, the emotional kind. He recognized the devastation, the total mental breakdown, before the male hid it behind aggression. This wasn't about Razorback business. Deep Purple was here for himself. "You murdered her...my Caroline. You—"

"Is that what Ivar told you?"

Wings flared outward, the Razorback snarled at him.

"Nightfuries don't hurt females, warrior," Bastian said. "We tracked a nine-one-one call. She bled out before we could reach her."

"You lie!" With a pain-filled roar, the male breathed in, telegraphing his intention.

Bastian inhaled, filling his lungs with smoky air. The electro-pulse rocketed from his throat, hammering the Razorback's fireball midstream. Fire-acid sprayed backward in a blinding arc of blue-white flame. The psychochemical, lightning combo of Bastian's strike slammed into the enemy dragon's face. As Deep Purple roared, the poisonous gas in the air ignited.

Heat and sound went supersonic.

The explosion flashed bright white as it blew the Razorback off the roof. Hurled backward, Bastian slammed into parked railcars, scattering them like dominos from a box. Underneath the heap of twisted metal, shards of shrapnel cut deep into his damaged scales. Hot and wet, blood welled, running down his side and...

God. That hurt.

"Get up," he growled at himself. Shit, even his voice was shot, nothing more than a rasp on thin air. Then again, that made perfect sense. He couldn't breathe around the pain expanding inside his chest. "Get...up."

Flailing, he used his tail to toss railcars left and right. If he didn't get on his feet, he was dead. Wick, too. The fire was burning out of control, consuming everything in its path. He needed to reach his warrior before the flames did. But...the smoke. He couldn't see a fucking thing.

Sirens sounded in the distance.

Humans. The cavalry was coming.

Using his talons, he dug deep, dragging himself out from beneath the train pile. As he rolled to his paws, his left leg buckled. Fantastic. Just what he needed. A broken bone. With a hop, Bastian sucked wind and stumbled sideways. His body wasn't working right. His vision was tunneling, the pressure behind his eyes becoming worse by the second. It clawed at him, dragging him down until his head felt sloppy and loose on his shoulders.

No. Hell, no. He refused to pass out. His invisibility cloak was down. The fire department and police were coming. If they found him here...

Jesus. He needed to stay with it.

But as he fought, clawing his way toward his fallen comrade, Bastian couldn't stop the inevitable. His injuries pulled at him, sapping his strength. He was out of time and energy.

His luck had just run out.

Chapter Twenty

The Crime Scene Investigation facility was a fascinating place. Lots of people. Lots of activity. Kind of like a human beehive full of lab rats.

If that made any sense. Which it didn't but, what the hell? The analogy worked for him, so Rikar went with it.

With his arms crossed, one leg bent, his boot planted against the wall, he leaned back to watch all the buzzing. He shouldn't be here. It was an "authorized access only" area. At least, that's what the sign said before he walked past the front desk. The humans would've freaked out if they'd seen him, but with his magic up and running, they hadn't. So here he stood—invisible—in the wide, central corridor, getting the lay of the land.

What he needed was a map. With titles of the labs and descriptions of the tests performed in each. But with Sloan in a snort over his performance in the kitchen earlier—sensitive bugger—Rikar wouldn't be getting any directions through mind-speak from his buddy. Ah, well. Teasing their resident computer genius was worth the trouble. Maybe in the future, though, he'd plan it a little better. Like for a time when he didn't need his friend's help on a mission.

His eye on a pretty lab technician, Rikar uncrossed his arms and pushed away from the wall. Time to take a stroll. Maybe introduce himself to an evidence bag or two labeled "ashes." And the female was his first stop. With her above-average energy, she'd take the edge off his headache; heal him up nice and quick.

The added bonus? Information. She'd tell him exactly where to go to find what he wanted.

With a thought, Rikar ditched his leathers, conjuring a pair of Dockers and a blue button-down to take their place. A holstered Glock on his hip, he clipped an authentic looking SPD badge to his belt front. And booyah, he was ready for his meet and greet with the pretty lab rat.

And yeah, he was a big, fat liar.

Females hated that. He knew it, and had she meant something to him, Rikar might have felt badly for what he was about to do. But such was Dragonkind's MO: hit and run, love 'em and leave 'em…fast. Preferably with no memory of the loving.

He'd remember, though. Which was more than enough for both of them.

Rikar slid in behind a group of males as they walked past him. With a mental flick, he lifted his invisibility cloak and blended in, using them for cover. No one noticed his sudden appearance. Then again, humans never did. They were too busy rushing from place to place, heads down, yapping on cell phones that would eventually give them brain tumors.

Christ, it was a helluva way to live.

But that wasn't any of his business, was it? The female technician, however? Hmm, yeah. In about thirty seconds she'd be all business, closing up shop to take a meeting with him.

He got a birds-eye view of her through the glass and… thank God for floor-to-ceiling glass walls. She looked even better up close.

With a quick glance, Rikar surveyed the CSI offices again, looking for a private space to take her. Laid out with precision, all of the labs lining the corridor looked the same: sliding glass doors, stainless steel countertops, high-tech equipment, and low-backed swivel chairs. Man, Sloan would love this place...which was another difference between him and his buddy. The male would've spent hours snooping around. But no way, not him. Rikar couldn't wait to get out. The lab was suffocating, confining...like being in a freaking fishbowl. All the little fishes on display for the world to see.

Rikar breathed in through his nose and out his mouth. He should've expected his reaction to the squat human building. Small spaces gave him the creeps. But the female? She would make him forget for a while.

Dark hair pulled away from her face, she was bent over her worktable, looking good enough to eat. And as she filled small vials with clear liquid, Rikar imagined filling her from behind. He'd tip her hips up and...oh, yeah. That was exactly how it was going to happen.

Reaching her lab door, Rikar peeled away from the group and turned into her fishbowl.

Without looking up, she said, "Whatcha got?"

Hmm, nice voice...husky but all business, with a hint of the South. Louisiana, maybe. Realizing he was empty-handed, Rikar conjured an evidence bag just like the ones he saw open on her table. He rustled the plastic. "Something looking for a home."

That got her attention. Turning her focus away from her science experiment, she gave him what he wanted...eye contact. And bingo. Instant attraction: pupil-dilating, mouth-parting, female hormone-surging chemistry. She was totally into him…or rather what he looked like. Fucking A. He was so totally on board with that.

"Hey." Rikar smiled, sending a whole lot of I-want-you-too her way. He pointed to his chest with one hand, lifted the plastic baggie with the other. "New guy. Not sure where I'm going…or who to give this to."

"That happens." She smiled back and racked a test tube. Stripping off her rubber gloves, she came around the corner of the countertop toward him. "The lab's like a big maze… confusing the first visit or two." Less than three feet away now, she held out her hand, and Rikar got his first taste. She smelled good, so fresh and new. "Let me see what you've got, and I'll point you in the right direction."

"Why don't you take a break instead?" Reaching out, he cupped her outstretched hand in his, putting them palm to palm. "Get to know me a little better."

"Umm…" She blinked, her soft gasp music to his ears. He laced their fingers together. "I'm not supposed to—"

"No one will ever know," he murmured, laying it on thick. With a gentle tug, he walked backward, pulling her toward the door. "Time for a break…don't you think?"

And just like that, he was in…leading her by the hand down the corridor.

Cloaking them both, Rikar hid them from the eye in the sky—all the cameras that humans liked to install everywhere. He didn't want anyone to see where they were headed. He wanted to lay the female out, sure—take the edge off by feeding—not get her fired.

Yeah, and wasn't he a peach? A lying paragon about to bang a female blind and leave her just as fast.

Rikar pushed the thought aside. It was what it was...he would get her off, take what information he needed, and get gone.

Finding an empty office, he tugged her inside, locked the door and, when she offered her mouth, he went to work blissing her out. He didn't ask her name. She didn't ask his. Thank Christ. He wasn't in the mood for pleasantries. Not that he ever was, but as he took her good and hard—made her beg before letting her come—he wondered what it would be like to have a female of his own. To have someone waiting for him at the end of each night. To hold her close after he loved her each day...to not have to hunt anymore.

Wishful thinking.

He would never be like Bastian. That male was strong—above board—ready to sacrifice his own happiness for the good of the race. Rikar was too selfish for that. Too aware that losing his heart to a female would end more than just badly.

So this was it. A fast fuck with a beautiful stranger in too public a place was as good as it would ever get for him.

Half an hour later—well fed and orgasmed out—he left the pretty lab tech in a blissed-out heap and headed down the corridor. He was looking for Chuck, the skinny, wild-haired geek who occupied the last lab on the left. And, thank you God, no long search and retrieve necessary. The kid was in his lab, the purple streaks in his acid-blond hair a dead giveaway.

Stepping over the threshold, Rikar slid the glass door closed behind him.

"Hey, bro," Chuck said, all surfer-dude, glancing up from his microscope. "What up, man?"

Rikar tipped his chin at the evidence bags cued up on the techie's workstation. "Looking for the results on the ash samples."

"Sorry, dude. Haven't got to 'em yet. Everything's cued up, but big-time backlogged. Brian's out sick tonight."

"S'all right." Rikar came in close, getting into the lab rat's personal space. The male squawked, protesting when he grabbed him by the scruff of the neck. Chest to chest now, he took control of the human's mind, calming the male. "Look at me, Chuck."

Vacant-eyed, the human complied.

"Are all the samples in the box? No stragglers?"

Almost boneless in his arms, Chuck relaxed on a sigh. "Nah...that's all of 'em."

"Good," Rikar murmured as he got busy rooting around inside the human's head. With a gentle wash, he scrubbed the male's mind clean: taking his memory of the ash samples, telling him that he'd never seen or heard of them. If the two cops showed up before Rikar got a chance to scrub them, there'd be a whole lot of what-the-hell-do-you-mean-you-lost-our-evidence? But, hey, that wasn't his problem, was it?

After sitting numbed-out Chuck in a chair, Rikar crossed the lab. Peering inside the box, he studied the samples for a moment, noting times and dates. He raised a brow. Ivar had been busy. There were at least six samples sitting there, giving him the Ivar salute. Rikar grabbed the entire load. Sloan would want to test them. Though, Gage—the Nightfury's biochemical expert—would've been the better choice. But that wasn't going to happen...not with Gage off protecting Haider's back at the Archguard's fucking festival.

Whipping up a backpack, Rikar stuffed the samples inside and headed for the door. Time to get the hell out of

Dodge. Chuck would come to in a couple of minutes, along with the female he'd pleased. Besides, the fishbowl effect was starting to get to him. Nothing was big enough in the human world. Everything they built seemed compact, substandard in size and—

"Rikar."

Bastian's voice came through mind-speak loud and clear. But shit. Something was wrong. His best friend didn't sound right. *"Here."*

"Need you." Bastian coughed, the harsh rasp sounding wet, like the male was choking on something. *"Wick's down. I'm...in...deep shit."*

"Where are you?"

"Rail yards. Humans...coming."

"Hold tight."

"Hurry," Bastian said through the static.

The connection between them snapped, cracking like brittle wood. Fuck. His best friend *was* in deep trouble if he couldn't hold the link to mind-speak.

Moving like an F-18, Rikar rocketed past the front desk and out CSI's front door. As he shifted and took to the sky, his wings blew a huge gust of wind. Air hit the parking lot with the force of a hurricane. Alarms shrieked and humans came running, weapons drawn, as cars went flying, flipping end over end.

Metal crunched against metal, and electricity arced, sparking as an SUV took out a telephone pole.

Rikar ignored the auditory soundtrack and climbed, uncaring of the damage he left behind. Normally, he avoided the hurricane routine. Tonight, though, he would've leveled the building if necessary. His best friend needed him. The humans could go to hell.

The wailing sirens were getting closer. In another two minutes the humans would be on top of him. The nightmare scenario hammered Bastian, prodding his get-up-and-go. Too bad his adrenaline was pretty much tapped out. He could've used a shot of it right now.

Reaching deep, he dredged the last of his reserves, forced himself to keep moving. Pain tightened its grip, tearing at him like barbed wire. His vision wavered. Bastian blinked as his mind followed suit and shorted out, flickering like an overloaded electrical circuit. It was like getting the plug pulled on his cerebral cortex. And as mental acuity went down the drain, he landed in Blanksville. What did he need again? Something important. Or maybe it was *someone*.

That thought sparked another.

Yeah, definitely *someone*.

He groaned. That was it. He needed to go home...to her.

Digging his claws in, Bastian dragged himself another few feet. Wet earth pushed between his talons, mounding over his knuckles. The fuel-soaked ground burned the raw patches of flesh exposed by his shot-to-shit scales. He didn't care. He had to find Wick and get them both back to the lair.

The harbor beyond the bank of warehouses was the only option. And yeah, that was going to be a bitch. Especially the saltwater part.

Bastian cringed. He hated the swimming almost as much as he hated elevators. But with his energy stores gone, he couldn't cloak himself, never mind Wick. The dark inky water would do what he couldn't: provide enough cover until Rikar performed his knight-in-shining-armor routine.

Dragging his broken leg, Bastian crawled over a burning pile of timber. His eyes stung from the smoke as he squinted to get a line on Wick. The male had to be close. The building he'd been introduced to skull first was just ahead and—

Something shifted behind him.

Bastian spun, his bladed tail arching wide. The dark shadow ducked and lunged, coming straight at him. He caught the load in the chest. Anguish rippled through him as he lost his footing and...fuck. He was going down. Would die for making a rookie mistake.

Goddamn it. He knew better than to assume anything in a firefight. The Razorback wasn't dead. Or retreating from the truckload of humans less than a mile away. The rogue had played it perfectly. Was practically on top of him, coming in for the kill.

With an agonizing twist, he followed the SOB's movement. The second before he moved in, Bastian filled his lungs, set to hammer the enemy with another electro-pulse. A huge talon struck. Flipping him up and over, the male grabbed him by the scruff of the neck.

Bastian snarled and reared, striking with his claws.

"Shit!"

Jesus Christ. Bastian's knees went weak as he switched to mind-speak, *"What the fuck, Wick?"*

"Sorry." The warrior swayed above him, stumbling sideways. *"I'm not...shit. Can't see. My eyes are fucked up."*

Headlights flashed, the fire truck behind the halogens roaring into the rail yard.

"Shift." With a groan, he moved from dragon to human form. His muscles screamed, but he hung on. He couldn't pass out. Wick needed him. *"We gotta move. I can't fly, but my vision's good."*

As Wick shifted to human form, he slung Bastian's arm around his shoulders. *"Which way?"*

"Right…twenty feet to the warehouse. Head for the water."

Aligned from shoulder to hip, naked as a pair of fifty-dollar whores, his warrior dragged him toward the corner of the building. His burnt skin slid against Wick's and Bastian gagged, nearly passing out as agony yanked his chain.

Stay awake. Don't black out.

He was dangerously weak, so far gone he couldn't get his legs to work, never mind manage a pair of leathers. Not that Wick minded. The male had problems of his own, and being naked was the least of them. The head injury coupled with the blindness was screwing with his speed, making him stumble under Bastian's weight.

Rounding the corner of the warehouse, Wick lost his footing. They went down, face-planting into the steel barrels stacked against the wall.

"Fuck me," the male groaned.

Shouts sounded, the rise of male voices joining the roar of the fire. God, they were close, barely one hundred feet away. Bastian heard the zing of fire hoses and the clank of steel as humans got busy fighting the blaze.

"Go. Leave me and…" Black spots in his vision, Bastian rolled onto his back. Rough asphalt pressed into his side, grinding small stones into his burns. *"Go."*

"And fuck you, too." Pupils contracted to pinpoints, golden eyes glowing like headlights, Wick hauled him to his feet.

Bile hit the back of Bastian's throat, but he got with the program. As he made his broken leg work, he cursed himself. He was an idiot. Not only had he screwed up the fight, now he'd insulted Wick. No Nightfury got left behind…ever.

Blind, deaf, or dumb, it didn't matter. His warrior would sooner cut off his own arm than abandon him.

Carried by Wick, they stumbled forward under Bastian's direction. There was a ton of debris lying around: rotting square timbers, steel rods, and broken pieces of concrete slabs. Maneuvering around an old boat carcass, they reached the pier. Rough wood scraped the soles of his bare feet. Thank God. They'd made it...were almost out of sight.

Crooked and bent from years of neglect, the end of the dock twisted up to one side. Wick stumbled as he hit the incline, but he kept going, the smell of ocean salt galvanizing them both. And oh, shit. This was going to hurt.

"Hang on to me," Wick said, wisps of fog curled around their feet. *"Don't let go."*

Bastian tightened his grip on his warrior. Muscles flexed around him as Wick lunged, pulling him headlong off the end of the pier. Splashdown hit Bastian like a sledgehammer, dragging him under. And as the ocean closed in, filling his mouth and nose, salt water attacked, invading his wounds. Pain went from debilitating to apocalyptic. In full body spasm, he twisted, screaming in silence as darkness swallowed him whole.

Chapter Twenty-one

Sirens wailing, emergency vehicles raced down Alaskan Way, the street running parallel to the waterfront. Rikar watched the bumper-to-bumper light show from a mile up, flying fast as he scanned for his brothers. Cold Seattle air rushed against his scales. Thank God. The CSI offices had been hot as hell.

Why did they do that? Crank the heat up when a two-degree downshift on the thermostat would save a boatload of energy and cost them less, too. It was annoying, not to mention senseless. Wasn't that why they invented sweaters? To take the chill off?

Rikar shook his head. There he went again, letting his mind wander to keep the fear at bay. Bastian wasn't answering. He'd sent out a dozen pings, trying to connect and...

Nothing. A big fucking doughnut hole. Not even static in the mind-speak arena.

Which meant one of two things. His best friend was either unconscious or...dead.

A chill skated beneath Rikar's scales. He couldn't lose him. Not Bastian. Anyone else and he'd cope, deal with the loss and grieve. But not his best friend.

Still cloaked, Rikar broke cover. Slicing through storm clouds, he dropped fast and came in low, approaching the rail yard from the water. Whipped by the wind, the harbor threw up ocean spray, reducing visibility. Terrific. Great night for a fricking storm. His friends were out there—needing him—and Mother Nature was in her usual West Coast snit, getting in his way, pissing him off.

Breathing deep, Rikar caught the smell of chemical smoke. A second later, he saw it through the mist, black plumes billowing across the roof of the nearest warehouse. He circled right—ignoring the human circus of wailing sirens and squealing tires as they roared over the bridge and onto the scene—to take a closer look.

Holy shit.

Lit up like a war zone, the entire rail yard was on fire. Melting steel and burning timber littered the debris field, surrounding a massive crater. The whole area had gone nuclear, a dragon-style face-lift of shredded fuel tanks, rail-cars and...

A totaled dump truck. Yup, Wick had definitely been here.

Reconning the area, Rikar sent his magic rolling in search for his friends. The ping spread like an invisible net, molding over land and sea, steel and concrete like living radar. From his bird's-eye view, he watched firefighters work and circled a second time, hoping for a signal.

Again...nothing.

He had to get down there. His brother might be trapped under the rubble. And the humans working fire hoses? Totally FUBARed. He didn't have time to scrub memories, and that left one option...death.

Which sucked on so many levels.

Not that he minded killing humans. Even though he avoided humankind whenever possible, criminals weren't off-limits. For a very good reason. Serial killers and rapists hurt females, something a Nightfury never condoned. So yeah, capping one of those idiots turned murder into justifiable homicide. But icing a bunch of cops and firefighters? Man, that was just plain wrong.

Invisible to human eyes, Rikar drew up short. He hovered for a moment, wings spread wide above the males below. Heavy dread settled in his chest as he took a deep breath. Ice crystals formed in his mouth as he bared his fangs and—

A faint ping slid over his scales, circling the horns on his head.

Rikar's focus snapped toward the harbor. He closed his mouth, swallowing ice. The sound came again. The static was soft, fading in and out, barely a signal at all, but...it was definitely there.

Christ, they were in the water, the last place a dragon wanted to be. None of Dragonkind were strong swimmers. Well, except for water dragons, but Rikar discounted that myth. He'd never seen one, never mind talked to one.

Reversing direction, Rikar flew toward the center of the bay. Waves bashed the breakwater, spraying thirty feet in the air. The mist coated his underbelly, then wicked away, falling like raindrops from his scales.

"Bastian!"

"Down."

Wick? Holy Christ. *"Where are you?"*

"Can't hold him...much longer. Current's...too strong," Wick rasped, the weakness in his voice nothing like the usual harsh tone.

"Hold tight, buddy." His head on a swivel, Rikar scanned the inky waves. Seconds ticked into more, triggering his internal alarm. The water was too black, hiding his

comrades beneath choppy spray and rolling whitecaps. Jesus, he couldn't find them, not in the dark like this. He needed more...a tracking device to lock onto and hold. *"Wick, man. Talk to me."*

Silence came back, revving Rikar into panic mode. *"Wick?"*

Nothing. No heavy breathing, rasps of pain or—

A yellow flash of light whipped Rikar's head to the left. Like Morse code, the blinking light found a rhythm and...

Had Rikar been the weeping kind, he would've cried. Thank God for Wick, the tough, wicked-smart SOB. The male was blinking, using his golden gaze as a beacon in the dark.

Shifting mid-flight, Rikar rocketed toward them. Coming in low, mere feet above the white caps, he spotted them. Holding B around the chest, Wick bobbed in the waves, fighting to stay afloat. Without slowing, Rikar arced his wings and drew his front talons back. He wouldn't get another chance. Wick might go under and not resurface if he missed.

As the next wave crested, he struck. His talons plunged and caught. With a snarl, he climbed, pulling them free of the icy chop.

He heard Wick's gasp of pain, but didn't slow as he hauled ass for the lair. Both males needed care, but Bastian? His best friend's life force was dangerously low. He needed a serious energy infusion. If he didn't get it soon, he wouldn't survive.

Flying fast and hard, Rikar reached altitude. With the city below and storm clouds gathering above, he felt the first raindrops and started to pray. For the wind to push him east toward Black Diamond. For the lightning to hold off.

And for Myst to survive Bastian's energy-greed when Rikar placed his best friend in her arms.

Christ, his wish list was way too long. And when a male got greedy, something always went wrong.

———

Three days. A whole seventy-two hours of Bastian and nothing but Bastian, so help her God. Had she really agreed to that?

Yes.

The word slithered through her mind, the "S" turning into a long-tailed hiss. As the special brand of poison sank deep, Myst rubbed a slow circle on her temple. She deserved the Idiot of the Year award...and a plaque. One that said, For Going Above and Beyond the Call of Stupidity.

Okay, maybe that was a bit harsh. She'd been pinned, after all, pushed to the wall by Bastian and his crew, but still...

Baby name or no baby name, she should have stuck to her guns and demanded that he take her home. But oh, no...what had she done instead? Promised not to escape. Made a pact with the guy who'd not only kidnapped her but had flown her to the secret lair of a dragon-slash-human military unit.

Or whatever they called themselves. Nightfuries. Or something.

But that was only half the problem.

The real crinkle—the one that had her tied in knots— was tantamount to self treason. A betrayal on all fronts: moral, intellectual, and emotional. And even though she wanted to deny it, Myst wasn't into lying, especially to herself.

Which left her with one doozy of an admission.

She only half regretted being taken by Bastian.

Myst let the cupboard door close with a bang. Yeah, she really, *really* deserved that stupidity award.

But Bastian. He was just so…so…intriguing and smart, gentle in ways that drew her. And let's not forget gorgeous. Throw in his scent and…wow. She was in real trouble, and that was before she remembered how he looked at her. The amped-up intensity in his eyes coupled with affection made her feel important and precious, maybe even a little loved.

She'd lost her flipping mind.

No way should she be romanticizing Bastian. What did she really know about him, anyway? Not much beyond what she'd seen, and most of that landed in the just-plain-crazy column of her running tally.

God, she needed a drink.

And not one of those fruity concoctions, either. She wanted a strong one, something vicious tasting with lethal alcohol content. The problem? She wasn't much of a drinker. When stressed, she went straight for the hard stuff…70 percent chocolate.

Oh, baby. What she wouldn't give for some Lindt right now. Or some M&Ms. Plain or peanut, she didn't care. Either one would do.

Standing on her tiptoes, Myst peered into a top cupboard. She pushed a package of raw almonds to the side so she could see to the back. Nothing. Nada. And that was the last in a long line of ultramodern cabinetry to check. The entire kitchen was full of organic, whole food that no one in her right mind would want to eat. And she was a nurse, for pity's sake…totally game for the health food scene.

What was wrong with these guys? Did they have something against junk food? Obviously, no one in the house ever suffered from PMS.

And wasn't that a shame.

She needed someone to talk to...someone with enough estrogen to counteract the heavy dose of testosterone that lived in the house. But Daimler had put the kibosh on that idea fifteen minutes ago, informing her she was the only female for miles. For miles! God, that sounded ominous. Though, come to think of it, she should probably be happy about the intel. After all, if she was the lone kidnappee, the Nightfury gang couldn't have any other victims chained up in their dungeon.

Or somewhere equally scary.

But then, scary was a matter of opinion, wasn't it? A question of degrees, and her compass had been spun in the wrong direction. True North? Yeah, right. Try upside down and backwards. That's what Bastian did to her. Now she couldn't tell which way was up, how to get out, or whether she wanted to.

Three days.

Of Bastian.

God help her.

With a frown, Myst abandoned her quest for chocolate and turned toward the floor-to-ceiling windows. Framed by huge timber beams, the glass panes had lost their opaque sheen, allowing her to see through to the garden beyond. Fall flowers bloomed along flagstones paths. Huge trees and well-groomed shrubs swayed in the night breeze, moonlight painting their leaves with a silver brush.

A lovely prison. Yeah, Black Diamond was absolutely that: modern, beautiful, well designed, but a prison all the same.

Pausing beside the kitchen island, Myst glanced at the baby sleeping in the crook of her arm. Was Gregor worth all this? Worth the kidnapping, all the fear, and now, her promise to stay in a place she knew was dangerous?

Disgusted with herself, she shook her head.

Of course, Gregor was worth it.

He was life affirming, an innocent caught in a horrible net. Which begged the question…how could she possibly leave him?

The answer was obvious. Everything inside her said no. She didn't want to leave Black Diamond without him. Yet she couldn't take him with her, either. Bastian had made that clear. Gregor was only half human; the other half was pure dragon.

So…

She couldn't raise him on her own. He needed to be with people who understood him, knew his history, and were able to teach him about the challenges of his nature.

With a sigh, Myst brushed his cheek with her fingertip. How unfair. Holding him was heaven, but in three days, she'd be forced to give him up. Never see him again. The thought left her stuck in the middle…jammed between her world and his. And in that small space, there was no compromise or easy way out. It came down to one thing…a choice.

Stay or Go. Her life for his.

Her throat went tight and, skirting the island, Myst walked toward the playpen. She needed to put him down… just for a while. Cuddling him wasn't helping her. It made the ache worse. Made the thought of leaving him harder to bear and the idea of keeping him seem less like a sacrifice. But he wasn't a puppy. Adoption was serious business, and she had a decision to make.

Releasing her hold, she forced herself to lay him down. As she adjusted the blanket and tucked him in, she traced the whorl of his tiny ear, listening to him breathe. Limited time. They were destined to have limited time together, and she wanted to remember everything. From his beautiful baby smell and the softness of his skin to the way he looked bundled up, so small and perfect, in his playpen.

A knot the size of Seattle settled on her chest and pressed down. Myst breathed through it and withdrew, putting the distance she needed between them.

Time for some fresh air.

She could what-if herself to death later. Right now, the garden looked like the perfect escape. She could lose herself among the tall trees and flowering shrubs for a while to think and plan...and snoop.

Bastian's home was enormous. A timber-framed monster with more square footage, locked doors, and coded entries than she could cover in one evening. But memorizing the layout was less important than finding transportation. She needed a car to get the heck out of Dodge.

And where did most people keep their vehicles?

In a garage.

Daimler—bless him—had already let drop that the garage wasn't attached to the house. So plan A included getting outside. The garden was the perfect cover for some covert snooping. Too bad she didn't have any training in that department. A little Navy SEAL would go a long way right now.

But much as she liked to call him one, Bastian wasn't an idiot. She'd seen him speak to Daimler when he left the kitchen. Ever since then, the little elf had gone household commando on her. Out of sight, he dogged her every move, watching like a hawk and—

Surprise, surprise. She wasn't alone.

Myst pivoted toward the butler's pantry. The scraping, almost imperceptible sound came again. Jeez. Daimler wasn't any better at the covert thing than she was. Bless his heart, though, for trying.

"Daimler?"

With a joyful hop, the butler burst through the swinging door, leaping into the kitchen. An icing-covered spatula in his hand, he waved it above his head, circling the thing with flourish. "Yes, my...Myst? How may I be of assistance?"

Fighting a smile, Myst stared at him. Good God. The guy was agile...and funnier than any episode of *Queer Eye for the Straight Guy*. Thank goodness for Daimler. He was better than a hit of Prozac for the doom and gloom department.

"You can stop following me around, you know. I'm not going anywhere." At least, not tonight. In three days, however? Watch out. By then, her plan would be rock solid, and she'd have the keys to the fastest vehicle in Bastian's garage.

"Oh, I'm not—"

"Save it, Daimler."

The spatula drooping, he went from joyful to crestfallen. "It was not my intention to invade your privacy, my lady."

"I know."

"Master Bastian is concerned...this being your first night at Black Diamond. He wanted to stay, but duty called him away from you."

He wanted to stay...with her.

Six words. Alone, they were nothing special. Together? They almost sent her over the edge. As it was, she was barely hanging on to her don't-fall-for-him rule. But every time she turned around, Bastian was doing something she liked. Something thoughtful and nice. Which just burned her butt. Why couldn't he get with the program and act like an axe murderer or something? It would've made her life a whole lot easier if she actually *wanted* to get away from him.

Right. Escape. That's what she should be thinking about.

Taking a moment, Myst reshuffled her deck—the one labeled priorities—and got back in the game. Time to sit down at the table and play a round of What's Bastian Up To? with the hand he'd dealt her.

And Daimler was the perfect foil. Too honest for his own good, the elf would tell her what she needed to know with a few well-placed, seemingly innocent questions.

"The house is beautiful," she said, tone casual with just the right amount of curiosity thrown in for good measure. "And huge. How many square feet?"

"Oh, goodness me." With a twirl, Daimler retreated toward the pantry.

Myst blinked as he spun like a top and, bumping the door with his butt, disappeared into the room beyond. As the door closed with a swoosh behind him, she sighed. Great. She was worse at the covert thing than she thought. Somehow, she'd tipped him off. Now, she wouldn't get her questions answered and—

The elf barreled back into the kitchen, a cake stand complete with cake in one hand, a glass bowl filled with white icing in the other. "Including the underground lair?"

She nodded and, stepping up to the island, slid onto the high-back chair closest to where Daimler was setting up shop.

"Hmm…" Armed with the spatula, he iced the sides of the cake. Myst's mouth started to water. Man, that smelled good…carrot cake and sugary icing. The junk food of champions. "Twenty-three thousand square feet…give or take."

Holy crap. The place was much bigger than she thought and…

God, that cake was driving her crazy. Reaching out, Myst rescued a drop of icing about to fall from the edge of the bowl. As she brought it to her mouth and sucked the sugar from her fingertip, she hummed. Daimler was awesome…one of the finer rarities on Earth. "Not including the garage?"

Daimler's gold tooth flashed as he chuckled. "Would you like a piece?"

Uh-huh. The guy was in full deflection mode, turning the conversation around on her. Myst wasn't daunted. Two could play that game. "God, yes. I'm dying for something sweet."

"I knew you had a sweet tooth," he murmured, looking pleased.

Turning toward the bank of cupboards, he flipped one open. A white plate made an appearance as he drew a drawer open. Utensils and plate in hand, he returned to the kitchen island. He cut a generous slice, slathered it with more icing than was legal before setting the entire sugar-high down in front of her.

She took her first bite and moaned around the mouthful. "You are a culinary wizard."

He smiled. "And you are a very curious female."

Busted.

Swallowing her second bite, Myst covered her tracks. "Don't you think I should be? I have a life outside of all this,

Daimler. One Bastian took from me. How will I learn about you...about *them*...if I don't ask questions? If I'm going to live here—be happy here—I need to understand certain things...like how they operate, what's off-limits, what's not...don't you think?"

"Master Bastian warned me you are very clever."

"Oh, come on. Tell me a little bit about the house... about them. What can it hurt?"

"Not a thing." Spatula working double time, Daimler kept his focus on his work, making pretty swirls on the cake-top. "As long as you ask the male who is now responsible for you, my lady."

"Excuse me?" She stilled, a bite of carrot cake halfway to her mouth. The male responsible for her. That didn't sound good. In fact, it sounded a lot like a master-slave mockup. One practiced in, oh, say...the flipping twelfth century. Well, fat chance. No way she would allow that. If Bastian went medieval and treated her like a second-class citizen, scales or no scales, she would skin him alive. "You mind explaining that?"

Smart guy that he was, Daimler backpedaled, dropping the blame in his boss's lap like a hot potato. "Master Bastian's orders. If you wish to know something, you are to ask him."

Uh-huh, and *Master* Bastian could go to hell. "Well, he's not here to answer any of my questions now, is he?"

"I am sorry." His gaze on the cake, the tips of Daimler's pointy ears turned bright red. "I know the hours he is away from you will be taxing, but there are many activities to occupy your time. The game room holds many things of interest, and as our guest you may—"

"Guest, my foot."

"But, my lady, if only—"

"Forget it. You aren't going to convince me, Daimler." White-knuckling her fork, Myst locked eyes with the elf. Daimler was her best chance of uncovering Bastian's plans. God knew Bastian would never tell her. He was too quick... too smart to show his hand before he played it. "What is he up to? Why am I really here?"

"I do not know what you mean, my lady."

"Yes, you do." Silver clinking against expensive china, her fork collided with the edge of her plate. "Don't you think I have a right to know...to decide for myself?"

"You must ask Master Bastian these questions, Myst," he said, his tone so quiet she barely heard him. With a sigh, his gaze returned to hers. Myst shivered, seeing the terrible sorrow in his eyes. "Please, my lady. It is not my place to tell you."

His sadness spooked her. Warned her. Made her want to run.

Dear God, what did Bastian intend to do to her? Panic closed her throat as an awful thought crossed her mind. She wasn't getting out of Black Diamond...ever. Not unless she made it happen. And promise or no promise, she needed to do it now...before Bastian got his gorgeous self back home. Before his charming, fast-talking ways made her agree to some other stupidity.

He could do it, too...make her want to stay with him. Convince her to give up everything she'd worked so hard to accomplish. And she knew exactly how he'd do it.

Gregor.

He'd use the baby to manipulate her into agreeing to more time...just enough to snare her, making it impossible for her to get away.

Myst shook her head. She couldn't let that happen. Couldn't give Bastian the chance to sucker her in. Once he got hold of her, she knew he'd chew her up and spit her out.

Guaranteed.

Regardless of his seeming concern and affection, she wasn't one of his kind. That had come across loud and clear while she argued with him about Gregor's name. Which made her disposable, didn't it? A plaything with the added bonus of an expiration date when he got tired of having her around.

Holy crap. She needed to leave. Right now.

Feigning a calmness she didn't feel, Myst pushed her plate away. The French doors stood on the other side of the archway, less than thirty feet away. Once she crossed into the garden's narrow footpaths, the thick foliage would provide all the camouflage she needed to double back along the side of the house. The garage had to be out front, close to the driveway.

The second she found it—and a car—she'd head for the city. Seattle would hide her. At least, for a little while. Long enough to figure out what to do, where to go…how to live so Bastian would never find her.

She glanced at Daimler. "Thank you for the cake."

"Of course."

Her footwear clipped her heels, the flip-flop sounding loud in the silence as Myst slipped off her chair. Stepping away from the island, she gestured to the playpen, vise-like pressure squeezing around her heart. "Would you mind watching him for a while? I need some fresh air."

"Are you all right, my lady?" Daimler leaned toward her, concern on the planes of his elfish face. "I didn't mean to—"

"Myst!" The deep voice boomed, echoing like canon fire up the corridor.

The thunderous crack made her jump. Her kneecap collided with the corner of the steel chair leg. With a curse, Myst rubbed her knee, but she was already moving. She knew that tone. Had worked too many shifts in the ER to not recognize the urgency...the frantic desperation of whoever was shouting.

Something had gone wrong.

Just as she rounded the counter, Venom sprinted into the kitchen. Putting the brakes on, he slid to a stop in front of her. "He needs you."

"Who?"

"Bastian." Breathing hard, he stared at her, the irises of his ruby-red eyes growing smoky and intense. "He's injured. It's bad. Will you come and—"

"Where is he?"

"Rikar's bringing him."

"To the clinic?"

"Yeah. They're almost here, but you should know—"

"Later." Adrenaline hit Myst like jet fuel. Kicking off her flip-flips, she rocketed past Venom, entering the corridor at a dead run, her mind working in one direction. Bastian was hurt. He needed her. "Venom...move it! I need to set up triage. Show me how to get down there."

She heard the huge guy shift a second before she saw him. Moving like an organized hurricane, Venom hit his stride, long legs working overtime as he passed her in the double-wide hallway. Myst upped her pace, pumping her arms, bare feet keeping time with the thundering echoes of his footfalls.

Rounding a corner, she skidded to a halt behind him. This couldn't be right. There was nothing but wall-to-wall paneling, a dead end that—

Fancy wainscoting retreated into the sidewall, revealing a set of shiny elevator doors. The stainless steel sliders opened. Venom stepped inside the steel box. Right behind him, Myst watched as he hit the down button with the side of his fist. Smooth and silent, the elevator descended, giving her a moment to breathe...and think.

God, what had Daimler baked into that carrot cake? Drugs?

Yeah, that would explain her dramatic about-face.

Two minutes ago, she'd been scared senseless, ready to run, to leave Bastian behind forever. And now? She wished the elevator would hurry the hell up. She needed to get her hands on him and make sure he was all right.

No doubt about it. She was officially AWOL, her priorities on the wrong side of the proverbial fence.

Chapter Twenty-two

Standing behind the one-way glass, Angela watched Jennifer Lopez's look-alike pace on the other side. Interrogation Room One could do that to a person. Cramped and stuffy, the dingy space felt more like a coffin than a room, but...

That was the point.

Interrogation 101...drive suspects crazy. Make them want to spill their guts before a single question got asked.

So far, the tried and true seemed to be working. Her suspect was antsy. The problem? Angela didn't know if Tania Solares deserved her stay in Homicide's little patch of heaven. She should probably feel guilty about that...about putting the brunette in the hot seat and leaving her there to stew. And she would. Later. And only if she cleared Ms. Solares of any wrongdoing.

But right now? She was a person of interest in a homicide investigation. One who'd called in sick, ignored the messages on her cell phone, and been in the wind all day.

The behavior upped the voltage on Angela's suspicion meter. What had Myst Munroe's BFF been doing? Helping her friend get out of town?

The kicker, though? The thing that absolutely floored her? After combing the city for Solares and coming up empty, their quarry had walked into the SPD precinct about—Angela checked her watch—oh, about half an hour ago.

"Are they out of their flipping minds?" Solares muttered.

Probably, Angela thought as she glanced at her notes on Solares. The stats read like a rap sheet without the criminal element: twenty-eight years old, lived alone, a landscape architect with a shoe fetish.

Okay, so she'd made up the shoe thing, but…really. It didn't take a brainiac to figure it out. Solares was more than just fashion forward. The brunette was a force of nature. A one-woman wrecking crew in her pinstriped pencil skirt, button-down top, and black stiletto boots.

Gucci, most likely.

Angela stole another look at the gorgeous footwear. Yeah, definitely. That leather looked butter soft.

So did Mac. At least, in the head.

She caught a glimpse of her partner's expression from the corner of her eye. No doubt about it. His killer instinct was nowhere near *killer* at the moment.

Angela stifled a snort. The guy was practically drooling. Had been since the gorgeous Ms. Solares walked her curvaceous body into their less-than-elegant office. Under normal circumstances, Angela would've found his reaction to the brunette funny.

Not today.

Right now, she wanted answers, not a testosterone-induced stupor. She didn't have time to screw around. Four women were dead. A baby was missing. And with their prime suspect still at large? Yeah, Mac needed to get with the program. Because, like it or not, the BFF would be talking to them. Dishing all she knew on the mysterious Myst Munroe.

Snapping the leather-bound notepad closed, Angela headed for the door. She bumped Mac on the way out, brushing his shoulder with hers. "You gonna keep it together in there, Irish? Or am I doing this alone?"

"I'm good." A sheepish look on his face, he followed her out the door. "You're leading, though."

Her mouth tipped up at the corners. Yeah, like there'd been any doubt of that. With his trademark cool-guy demeanor out of commission, Mac was more liability than asset in the interview process. Still, she wanted him with her. Mac's skill at picking up cues—interpreting subtle shifts in body language—made psychic ability look like child's play.

Cranking the knob, Angela pushed the door wide and stepped into IR one. Stale air peppered with the smell of spearmint greeted her as Solares spun on three-inch heels. A grim look on her face, the brunette plopped her Versace handbag on the scarred tabletop. Snapping her gum, she drilled Angela with her dark brown eyes.

"What's going on?"

"You're a hard woman to find, Ms. Solares." Angela met the brunette's gaze head-on, giving as good as she got. "Where've you been all day?"

"Around." Solares crossed her arms over her chest.

Hmm...and wasn't her body language interesting? Defensive and nervous. Maybe even a little guilt-laden.

Good.

Uncomfortable was exactly how Angela wanted her.

Hard-ass wasn't really her style. Mac always handled the rough-edged interviews, but that didn't mean Angela wasn't good at it. Putting the thumb screws to a suspect was part of the job. As necessary a weapon as the Glock holstered at the small of her back.

"Detective Keen, Homicide." Brushing the bottom edge of her leather coat aside, she flashed the badge clipped to her belt before tipping her chin in Mac's direction. "My partner, Detective MacCord."

Solares frowned. "Homicide?"

Walking toward the table set in the center of the room, Angela paused beside a plastic chair. She glanced at the monstrous handbag now crowding her interview real estate. The big-ticket item suited the woman. Solares was high profile and higher maintenance. Normally, not a problem for Angela. This one, though, was whipcord smart. Intelligent in the way a knife was sharp. And as Solares's eyes cut to where she stood, Angela felt the sting.

Which pissed her off enough to pull her bad cop routine.

"Have a seat, Ms. Solares," she said, her voice a lethal combination of I'm-not-playing and don't-mess-with-me as she pulled out a chair.

Boots rooted to the pitted floor, Solares' eyes narrowed. "Why don't you tell what this is about first?"

With the one-way mirror behind her, Angela set her notebook down beside the Versace and pointed to the chair opposite her. "Sit."

"Holy cr—do you know how long I've been here, waiting?" Solares paused, no doubt to unclench her teeth. "Of course, you do. You're the one who put me here."

Angela raised a brow, but stayed silent. If she opened her mouth right now, an apology for the tough-guy routine might fly out. Then where would they be? Eyeballs deep in No-Answersville with a potential suspect riding shotgun, that's where.

Mac shifted behind her, the scrape of his boots loud in the quiet, as he used his size to back her up.

A good thirty seconds ticked past before Solares backed down. "Oh, for God's sake."

Taking two steps, she grabbed the chair back and yanked. Metal screeched across wood before being slammed down a few feet from the edge of the table. With a grace that belied her attitude, the woman sank into the plastic seat. Crossing her arms over her chest, she settled in, her chin set at an obstinate angle.

With a murmured "thank you," Angela slid into the chair across the table and opened her notebook. She started with the usual questions. Had Ms. Solares seen her friend? Talked to her? Did she know where she might be? When the answers came back no, no, and no, Angela moved on. "Tell me about Myst...habits, history. How long have you known her?"

"Look, I came down here to file a missing person report." A crease between her brows, Solares crossed her legs, foot bobbing in the breeze. "I was telling the other officer everything when I got hauled over here. What's going on?"

"Just answer the quest—"

"Please," she said. "Just...tell me. Myst's in trouble, isn't she?"

"What makes you think so?"

"Well, I'm here...*here!*...in an interrogation room with *you*." Worry in her dark eyes, she raised her hands, palms up, the gesture one of helplessness. "I don't know what happened, but...I spent all day looking for her. I've checked her apartment, called her boss, talked to the nurses at the hospital. No one's seen or heard from her since...oh, God. I knew something would go wrong. Had a feeling, you know? I tried to talk her out of it but..."

Mac moved into her line of sight as Solares's voice trailed off. Propping his shoulder against the wall, her partner tipped his chin, telling her he was back online. Thank God. She didn't like flying solo.

Angela raised a brow. "But?"

"She promised to check in...after, you know? Myst never breaks a promise and she always...*always*...checks in. I waited up. I've called and called...but everything goes to voice mail." Brushing her hair behind her ears, Solares shook her head. "It doesn't make sense. If she could reach me, she would. Something is really wrong. She would never let me worry if she could..."

The woman's voice broke, and Angela took pity. "Listen, Tania, we're—"

"You don't have a clue, do you?" Her dark brown eyes filled with tears.

Angela tightened the grip on her pen to keep from reaching across the table to take the woman's hand. It was hard. She understood that kind of panic...was too well acquainted with death not to recognize the upheaval of a missing loved one. And as Solares glanced away—crossed her arms, uncrossed her legs, fidgeted, and then recrossed everything to keep the pain at bay—Angela felt herself crack. The woman in front of her wasn't guilty of anything other than caring about her friend.

"God," Solares whispered, wiping beneath her eyes. "I told her not to go out there...to just leave well enough alone."

"To the Van Owen house?"

"Yeah. But Myst wouldn't listen. She was so worried about Caroline."

"Why?"

"Something about test results and missed appointments." Glancing up, her gaze sharpened as she met Angela's. "And that jerk of a boyfriend."

"Caroline's?"

"He was awful to Caroline, you know? Abusive. Myst didn't go into detail, but it didn't sound good and now..."

"What?"

"Myst's dead, isn't she? That asshole killed her."

"There's no proof of that, Ms. Solares," Mac said, entering the conversation. "Do you know the boyfriend's name?"

"Umm...Ryan something." Frowning, she chewed on her bottom lip. "Brady, maybe?"

Angela scribbled down the name, hope blooming hard. An abusive boyfriend equaled a solid lead. The guy had a history of violence and a motive—the baby. So, where did the missing nurse fit in? Was it a wrong time, wrong place scenario? Was she a hostage or the next victim? Maybe. Maybe not. But one thing for sure? Myst Munroe needed finding.

"This is such a nightmare." Solares rubbed her upper arms. "Just like before."

Before? Angela tossed a loaded look at her partner. "Come again?"

The J.Lo look-alike blew out a shaky breath. "It's like what happened to her mom...except, well, Myst isn't dead in her kitchen."

"What?" both she and Mac said, echoing each other.

"Yeah." Her gaze bounced from Angela to Mac then back again. "You didn't know?"

Mac shifted. Pushing away from the wall, he crossed the room, pulled out a chair, and joined them at the table. His gaze riveted on Solares, he murmured, "Fill us in."

"Her mom was murdered three years ago," she said. "The cops said it was a robbery. A bunch of Dana's important papers, her computer, and backup files were stolen. Research. From her work at the biotech."

A scientist. Wow. Another piece to fit into the Myst Munroe puzzle. "What was her mother researching?"

"Genetics, I think. Something to do with DNA splicing and gender. I didn't understand any of it. I'm a landscape designer...my world revolves around plants, not science." Playing with her ring, Solares spun it around her middle finger. "Myst came home from work and found her. Dana had been...sliced up...tortured, the detective said."

Angela sat back in her chair, analyzing the new information. Was it important to their case? God only knew, but honestly? Every little bit counted. Sooner or later, all the pieces would come together to give her what she needed, a trail of facts that led to a murderer. "Was the killer ever caught?"

She shook her head. "I think that's been the hardest part for Myst...the not knowing. No closure. The constant wondering. Do you think her mom's murder has anything to do with her...being missing?"

"We're running down every lead." Pushing his chair back, Mac stood, a clear indication the interview was over. "Thank you for coming in, Tania."

Solares snorted and got to her feet. "Like I had choice?"

Angela's lips twitched as she joined the pair. Whatever the brunette's shortcomings, courage wasn't among them. Taking a card from her notebook, she handed it to her. "If you think of anything else, call me."

With a nod, Solares accepted her offering. "Will you let me know if anyth—"

"Don't leave town." Mac gestured toward the door. "We'll be in touch."

Sticking the card in the top of her bag, Solares grabbed the straps and, high heels clicking, skirted the table on her way to the exit. As she opened the door, she glanced over her shoulder. "Whatever you think she's done, detectives, you're wrong. Myst would never hurt anyone. She doesn't have it in her. She still has nightmares about her mom's death."

Uh-huh. Well, that remained to be seen, but at least talking to Solares hadn't wasted their time. As the brunette disappeared from view, Angela let her killer instincts out of the box. She had new leads...two good ones to chase down.

The boyfriend was priority one, but checking him out wouldn't take long. And then? The biotech thing. Genetic research, DNA splicing coupled with a missing baby. Coincidence? Angela's gut told her no. So many things about the case didn't add up: not the murders or the ashes. Throw in the science angle and...yeah. Those pieces were related. All she needed to do now was find the link, the string that connected the whole.

She glanced at Mac. "Feel like a trip down to Archives after we check out Ryan Brady?"

"You know me...cold cases turn me on."

"Not curvy brunettes?"

"Them, too," he said, grinning.

Angela rolled her eyes and, snatching her notebook off the table, whacked him in the arm. As he recoiled and went "Ow" with feigned injury, she headed for the door. The big goof had no shame. Then again, most men didn't—

The screech of guitars erupted, blaring from Mac's back pocket. Digging out his iPhone, he brought it to his ear. "MacCord."

She stepped over the threshold. Mac growled, "What the hell do you mean *lost?*"

Uh-oh. That didn't sound good.

Putting on the brakes, Angela swung back into the room.

"Well, find it. Or I'm coming down there." Mac disconnected and shoved the phone into his pocket.

Yikes. Now, there was a threat and a half. No one wanted Mac coming to see him, especially unhappy. "What's up?"

"I put a call in to the lab…wanted the results on the ash evidence." Blue eyes full of pissed off, Mac ran a hand through his hair. A bad feeling hit her gut level. She nodded anyway, needing to hear his news. "It's gone. The fuckheads down at the lab can't find it."

"Goddamn it." Every time they caught a break, the case whiplashed, throwing them from bad to worse.

Angela pinched the bridge of her nose. She felt a headache coming on.

Chapter Twenty-three

The frosty air hit Bastian like whiplash. His head jerked, throwing his body into cramping lockdown. The spasm rippled, screaming down his spine as consciousness flickered. Fuck him. He was on sensory overload, a jagged piece of real estate no dragon wanted to occupy.

An abrupt shift yanked his chain. Agony spun him around, stretched him thin, shackling him to the whipping post in his mind. The lashing pain came fast and furious, and, with a groan, he reached for something solid. His hands found warm scales. Bastian tightened his grip on the claw wrapped around his ribcage. It wasn't his own. At least, he knew that much, but...

God. He couldn't breathe.

Clawing through the haze fracturing his thoughts, Bastian forced his chest to expand. Oxygen. He needed some. Right now.

Sucking wind, he fought for purchase, shifted in the talon and tried to open his eyes. Jesus. What the hell was wrong with his eyes? The fuckers wouldn't open.

He tried again. His eyelids lifted, giving him a nothing but blur. "Fuck."

"Almost there, B," the familiar voice came through mind-speak.

"Rikar?"

"I gotcha."

His best friend's voice steadied him. Memory rushed in, surfing on a wave of information. The rail yard, the explosion...and that purple SOB. Bastian growled. The bastard had gotten the drop on them. The thought pushed another forward. They'd made a run for it. He and—

"Wick?"

"Here." The deep growl came from his right.

Fighting the need to vomit, Bastian forced his eyes open again. He was flying. Correction...Rikar was flying. He and Wick were dangling, passengers in a one-dragon parade.

Bastian's vision flickered, black spots playing connect the dots. *"You...all right?"*

"Fuck, no. And you're a fricking train wreck."

Stood to reason. He'd been ass-planted by a fleet of railcars.

And a truckload of fire-acid.

White wings stretched wide above them, Rikar changed course, coming down through thick clouds. The dip jarred Bastian, firing up his pain receptors. He bit down on a groan. His broken leg really hadn't liked that, but... God. The burns were worse. With each flight shift, his side screamed, drawing more energy from his center.

Not that he had much left.

He was dangerously weak, so close to going under it scared him. Not something he wanted to acknowledge, but he'd never been here before: injured and reliant on another. Didn't matter that it was Rikar. Best friend or not, Bastian always looked after himself.

The weakness took him out and weighed him down. Without assistance, he'd never make it back to the lair... where another problem existed.

Myst.

He craved her. Needed to touch her. Wanted her hands on him and the soothing comfort of her voice in his ear. Hmm, he could already taste her. Bastian swallowed, the movement compulsive, like an addict imagining his next fix. And he was addicted. In need of his female's energy to the point of gluttony.

Shit. He was way too hungry. Had fallen off the edge into energy-greed.

The state was beyond dangerous. One all his kind feared. And no female wanted to encounter. Not if she wished to keep breathing.

"Rikar."

"Hang tough, B. Waterfall in thirty seconds."

"No...not..." Bastian shuddered, desperate to make his friend understand. He didn't want to hurt Myst, but if he touched her...Jesus. He'd drain her dry, take her life force to preserve his own. It was simple biology, survival of the fittest bred into all Dragonkind males. *"Don't let me...don't let—"*

His best friend banked right. The motion swung Bastian around and anguish bit deep, sucking the air from his lungs. He gagged, fighting his stomach's one-way tide to refocus. But the rough flight wasn't making it easy and, as treetops gave way to the river and Rikar turned north toward the waterfall and Black Diamond, Bastian knew he was in trouble.

He could feel her now. Sensed her essence as strongly as he did his own. Ravenous with thirst, his dragon rose deep inside him and zeroed in, marking its prey. Bastian fought the instinctive response, tried to shackle the need. The beast overrode reason—rearing, snarling, declaring its intent.

Bastian closed his eyes and, for the first time in his life, started to pray. He asked for strength and, cursing his nature, dug deep to find his humanity. Myst needed his protection. Deserved lightness and good, not the shadows he'd given her.

Or the pain he was about to inflict.

———

Bastian could go to hell if he thought Rikar would choose a female over him. No way would he let his best friend die. It didn't matter that neither of them liked the game plan. Or that he felt badly for Myst. Reality was a ball-breaker with a big attitude.

Bastian needed her. So, yeah. Myst was on the hook.

Banking like an F-18, Rikar came around the last bend in the river. The tumbling roar of the waterfall met him, spraying a cloud of mist into the night air. Without slowing, he sliced through the cascade into the tunnel beyond. Water wicking from his wing tips, his sonar lit up like the Fourth of July, pinging off the rock face as he navigated the narrow passageway. The LZ lay just ahead. Beyond that? The underground lair...and his friend's salvation.

Coming in fast, he drew up short, floated above the landing zone for a second, then touched down softly. His back claws scraped granite, throwing up stone dust. Wick cursed as his bare feet met stone. The male stumbled sideways into the hatchback. Bastian's legs buckled, sending him to the cavern floor.

Rikar shifted, moving from dragon to human form. Concern riding him hard, he crouched, coming down beside Bastian. The male groaned and, planting his palms, pushed away from the ground. Careful of his injuries, Rikar slid to his friend's good side and helped him up.

Electricity sparked as Venom came through the cavern wall. Ruby eyes aglow, the male swept the scene and, giving the f-bomb a workout, ran toward Wick.

Rikar slung Bastian's arm around his shoulders and turned them toward the lair's entrance. "Where is she?"

"The clinic." Wick in his arms, Venom met his gaze over-top of his buddy's head. "I didn't warn her."

"Don't..." In obvious pain, Bastian groaned. "Rikar... don't..."

"You need her."

"I'm too...hungry." He recoiled, struggling as Rikar half-carried, half-dragged him across the LZ. "Don't... please. I'll...kill her...can't..."

"I'll stay with you. If shit gets critical, I'll pull her free."

"Bull...shit. You won't be able—"

"Fuck off." With a snarl, Rikar muscled his best friend through the invisible barrier. Static electricity surged, raising the fine hairs on the back of his neck. Another step and he was through, boots planted on the polished concrete of the interior corridor. Thank God. He was seconds away from getting Bastian what he needed. The clinic was up the hall. Myst was in there, waiting for her male. "I'm not letting you die."

Chin to his chest, Bastian shook his head. "Rikar, please. Please."

Rikar ignored the begging. In that moment, he didn't care. He would give his best friend what he needed...risk of a dead female or not.

The double-wide glass doors to the clinic slid open, and—

"Oh, my God!" Wide-eyed, Myst sucked in a quick breath seconds before her bare feet took flight. "Rikar, we need to get him into the clinic. I've got—"

"No! Stay away!"

The desperate denial echoed against concrete, but Myst didn't slow. Like a female hurricane, she raced down the hallway, her eyes riveted on Bastian. Thank Christ. The faster she got to him, the faster he'd lose the battle and stop fighting. Still, as she came within range, Bastian reared, trying to retreat. Rikar held firm, strong-arming his best friend into the female's path.

Her proximity wrecked Bastian.

Deep-seated instinct surged, shoving B toward his female. With a snarl, he lunged at her. Rikar let him go, watched his friend wrap her up hard. As his broken leg gave out and sent them sideways, Myst gasped. The shocked sound lasted less than a second before Bastian caged her: pressed her back against the wall, put his mouth to her throat, his hands searching beneath her tank top. As skin met skin, she arched and energy surged. Wild heat exploded, knocking Rikar back a step and...

Jesus Christ. The female, she...she...

Was bleeding white-hot energy.

Twisting, she tugged at Bastian, pressed herself closer, welcoming the male who held her.

"*Bellmia...*"

"Here." Small hands in his dark hair, her mouth parted as B thrust his thigh between her own. With a hum, she made room for him, wrapping her legs around his hips.

Ignoring his injuries, Bastian groaned against her throat, drawing hard on her energy. "*Bellmia*...mine."

The pair were extraordinary. Beautiful. Like nothing Rikar had ever seen. And Christ. He was just standing here, watching them…like some kind of perverted voyeur. But, he couldn't leave. Still had to get them into the clinic.

God knew Bastian wouldn't make it on his own. And Myst? Man, she was already out of it: energy-overloaded and pleasure-bound gone.

But as he steadied Bastian—careful not to touch his wounds or Myst—and moved the pair along the corridor, the center of Rikar's chest grew tight. He'd lied to his best friend. Looked him in the eye and…

Bastian would never forgive him.

And Rikar wouldn't blame him. He didn't deserve a free pass on this one…was in the wrong on so many levels: for ignoring B's wishes and forcing him toward Myst, for lying, for not pulling the female to safety before Bastian took too much.

———

She should be doing something. Shouldn't she? Myst frowned as the mental merry-go-round went round and round, spinning her from one thought to the next. She could've sworn there was *something*. A list she wanted to check. A task she'd started and needed to finish, but…

Her brain was gone. A blank slate that turned inward, chasing its tail inside her head. The endless loop lured, left her foggy, making her give in to the warm, heady rush. As the siphoning current gathered her up, she rode the wave, gasping as another round of pleasure rolled through her.

God, it was so good: the floating, the burn, the blur of oblivion.

She wanted more of the pleasure-bound sensation. And then more after that, but she couldn't indulge. Not now. Not without solving the problem first. It was mission one, critical to, well...something. Or someone.

Yeah, that was it.

A person needed her. Someone really important.

She shifted, locking down on the internal flow. The streaming rush narrowed, shutting out sensation until nothing but a trickle remained.

"*Bellmia*...no. Open. I need..."

As the rough voice rose on dark pleasure, the pressure at her throat increased. Gasping, she fell into the sucking rhythm and the hardness between her thighs. God, *that* was unbelievable: delicious, undeniable, beautifully intense. So good she struggled to catch her thoughts—and keep them straight. Delight closed the gap, drawing her back into mindless pleasure. With a sigh, she gave up and settled in, moving closer to the hard heat surrounding her.

"Yes, baby...yes."

Hmm...what a voice: deep, wicked, full of promised ecstasy that guaranteed a wild ride. And God, she wanted to take that trip, but...with whom?

The question was probably important. One she should, no doubt, find the answer to, but...hell. The pitch and swell was just too good. And so was that groan. Delicious and desperate, the sound was deeply male and, oh...wow.

Bastian.

Oh, yeah. She was with him. He was with her. She could feel him now: his hands against her bare back, his mouth on her skin, his body strong against hers and—

Myst frowned. Wasn't he...she seemed to remember...

He needed help, and she was set up, trauma kit ready to go in the clinic. Her hands tightened in his hair. "Bastian..."

"Easy," a guy said as the world went topsy-turvy.

As her head spun, Myst touched down, her spine connecting with something soft. A bed? A gurney? She didn't know...didn't care. All she knew was that Bastian needed help...the kind a trauma hospital specialized in giving.

"Help...hurt...need doctor."

"Shh...it's all right."

Oh, God, the stranger didn't understand. Myst shook her head, desperation taking root inside her. He needed to go for help. She didn't have the strength to let Bastian go... to call his friends. Something was wrong with her. She was tapped out, muscles and mind so unresponsive she struggled to put two thoughts together.

She struggled to open her eyes. "No...help him. He's hurt...burned."

"Relax, female. You're helping him," the guy said, all soothing tones and easy rhythm. Cracking her lids, Myst got a blurry impression of a face. Pale eyes glowed from the masculine planes and angles, shimmering like blue stars. "He needs you. Hold onto him."

Her eyes drifted closed. All right, she could do that... fat lot of good it would do in the end. She'd seen Bastian's injuries. He needed medical attention, not her. But as he settled heavily against her, sucking hard at her throat, her mind floated up, winged out, leaving her with one thought. The stranger was right. She must hold on...keep Bastian close.

She could save him if she held on tight enough.

Chapter Twenty-four

Consciousness hovered inches away. Or was it miles? Bastian couldn't tell. Didn't know much beyond the fact he was down. Flat on his back in a cold, dark place that he couldn't remember landing in.

Not good on any level. A downed dragon was a dead one.

Shifting position, he tested his surroundings, struggling to put the puzzle together. One plus one didn't equal two. Everything felt wrong, thick with haze. His built-in sonar was bent, receiving more static than viable information. Shit. He needed to move, knew it with an urgency that shoved through the fog, galvanizing him.

He dug deeper, searching his senses for information. His muscles twitched, racking him with sharp spasms. Cutting off a groan, Bastian sucked in some air and, reassured by the movement, drew another lungful. The in-out routine sidetracked the pain, shifting it from scream-worthy to teeth-grindingly brutal.

Thank God.

He didn't have time to screw around. He needed to get mobile and out of wherever he'd landed—or face-planted, which was a safe bet, considering how much his head hurt—and reach...

What...the lair?

His brows collided. No. Not home. He must help *someone*.

Ignoring the lethal ache between his temples, Bastian gathered his magic. Heat crackled like electricity, racing through his veins until his fingertips tingled. He held the wild surge tightly for a moment, letting the power buffet his internal control, before he let it go. Like a powerful riptide, the magical stream blanketed his surroundings, bouncing off obstacles, bringing information back with each ping of sound.

A room. A bed. The soft beep of machinery from somewhere nearby.

Bastian uncurled his fists. Moving with slow precision, he pressed his hands into the mattress. Pain flickered at the movement, but the cotton gave, brushing against his palms. He curled his fingers, grabbing handfuls to ground himself.

Safe. Jesus Christ. He was safe and—

A scraping sound came from his left.

Fighting dry-mouth, Bastian croaked, "Rikar?"

"Hey."

"Where..." He cracked his eyelids.

"Recovery room in the clinic." An indistinct blur, his best friend adjusted the blankets, covering Bastian's bare chest.

Finished with the fuss routine, Rikar moved away from his bedside, footfalls loud in the quiet. The sound of rushing water filled the space. Bastian swallowed. He could almost taste it, feel the cool, wet slide down the back of his throat. The desperate quality of his need reminded him of another time and place. One he'd never revisited and didn't want to now.

But as the faucet continued to flow, the sound triggered visceral memory. Jesus. He couldn't stand it going back there. To the time after his father's death and before his transition. He'd been so vulnerable, at the mercy of other males and the new pack leader's cruelty, always hungry, thirsty, and caught between powerful males who didn't give a damn about him.

Needing to forget, Bastian shifted on the mattress, welcoming the pain. As the burn moved through him, the sheets rustled and memory faded, turning his attention away from his past and into his injuries. The weight of his limbs reassured him. He was all there, nothing vital missing. Thank God. The tightness along his left side and the faint ache below his knee he could accept. But a missing limb?

Yeah, not so much.

Now, all he needed was his brain back. He felt like a lobotomy patient, complete with blank memory. Nothing jived. His head was fuzzy, a messy jumble of fragmented thoughts that didn't fit together.

Hoping movement would help slide the pieces into place, Bastian pushed up onto one elbow. The sheet slid, pooling at his hips as he drew a deep breath and opened his eyes. Fluorescents nailed him, bright lights shooting straight to the back of his brain.

"Shit."

With a snick, the lights went out. Good old Rikar. The male had always been quick to understand and even faster on the trigger.

Rubbing his brows, Bastian tried again. The second he opened his eyes, his focus went pinpoint sharp, his night vision kicking in to help him. Across the room, Rikar pivoted, pushing away from the bank of stainless steel cabinets. A furrow between his brows, his friend met his gaze. Bastian went on high alert. Something was wrong, more than just the normal, everyday stuff.

Cup in hand, pale eyes intense, his friend returned to his bedside. "Thirsty?"

The polite inquiry cranked Bastian one notch higher. Rikar was never polite. Direct as a sledgehammer to the forehead? Yeah, okay, but he never danced around a problem. Right now, though? His best friend was chewing on one and, by the looks of him, it didn't taste good.

Attention trained on his friend's face, Bastian reached for the glass. What the hell? His hand shook. And his arm felt like a lead pipe, heavy and uncooperative. Ignoring the rattle and shake, he drank deeply, draining the cup dry before handing it back to Rikar. As his first in command grabbed hold, Bastian tightened his grip, connecting them as he drilled his friend with a look.

"Spit it out."

"I'm sorry…" His brows drawn tight, remorse flickered across Rikar's face. "I'm sorry. She's…she's—"

"Holy fuck." His mind snapped back online, clicking the puzzle pieces together. Adrenaline hit him like a freight train. He jackknifed, coming off the bed in a single surge of movement. "Myst!"

As his bare feet hit the floor, his left leg buckled. Bastian barely noticed, catching the edge of the bed, scanning the room. Empty, but for him, Rikar, and the king-size bed. Where the hell was Myst? She should be with him, not alone in the lair.

Bastian lurched forward, ignoring the pain. He needed to find her. What if…oh God. If he'd taken too much of her energy she would be in pain. Was that what Rikar didn't want to tell him? Was she hurting and—

"Oh, Jesus," he whispered, his throat so tight he could hardly breathe. And as fear picked up his heart and slammed it against his breastbone, he hated himself for what he was... for what he needed from the female he wanted so badly to protect. "Where is she?"

Reaching out, Rikar steadied him when he rounded the end of the bed. "B...listen to me. Just—"

"Tell me." Bastian turned on his friend and grabbed him by the throat. With a vicious shove, he pushed Rikar backward until his shoulders hit the wall behind them. Pinning him, Bastian got right in the male's grill. "Tell me where or I'll fucking end you. I'll fucking—"

"She's in the next room, but B...you need to be prepared." Rikar glanced away. "She's not doing well...her vitals are meandering downward. All her major organs are slowly shutting down."

"God damn son of a bitch...you promised to pull her free." Bastian's voice broke, grief and self-hatred overwhelming him. "You promised!"

"Jesus Christ!" Pale eyes alive with pain and fury, Rikar grabbed Bastian's wrist, lessening the pressure on his windpipe. "Yeah, I made the call and saved your life. And you know what? If I had to do it over? I'd fucking do it again."

Bastian's fingers flexed around Rikar's throat. In that moment, he didn't care that he loved the male like a brother. The pain of losing Myst was too much. He was fractured, split wide open, less of a male for what he'd done to her and...he wanted someone to pay. To hurt as badly as he did.

"Yeah...go ahead," Rikar said, reading his intention. "Take your best shot. I won't fight back...but it won't change a fucking thing."

Nose to nose with his best friend, Bastian snarled.

Tears in his eyes, Rikar raised his hands, palms up, body unresisting...a sacrificial lamb to Bastian's rage. "You're more important than her, B. Without you, Dragonkind—the whole race—is fucked. Do you think the fucking Archguard will keep it together when you're gone? Jesus! The European packs follow your lead. Is one female worth your warriors' lives...all of Dragonkind's future?"

The dutiful answer? No. No one was worth the destruction of his kind. But his heart said something different. Myst was more important than anyone or anything. He needed her like he needed air, and now, he couldn't breathe. And it was his fault...all of it. Had he done what she asked, Myst would be safe in her own world. But he'd been selfish—believing he could take without giving in return—and for his sins, she would lose her life.

With a hoarse sound, he pushed his best friend away. Rikar murmured, the sound full of anguish and, scrubbing a hand over his eyes, let him go. Without a backward glance, Bastian limped across the room, heading for the recovery suite next door. He could hear the bells now, the beep-beep-beep of the heart rate monitor that had pulled him from his dream.

Myst was in there, plugged into that machine. No way would he let her die alone.

"Bastian. For what it's worth, I'm sorry."

Bastian ignored the choked apology. He couldn't forgive his best friend. Not now. Maybe not ever.

———

Smooth wood slid between his fingertips as Rikar drew the pool stick back and let the thing fly. Cue ball cracked against cue ball, the sound rising above the Def Leopard tune playing in the background. The number five ball rocketed across green felt and sank into the corner pocket. He straightened away from the table and glanced toward the U-shaped bar.

Yup, the redhead was still there, perched on a stool, sipping her drink. Straight up cranberry juice without the kick of vodka. The virgin cocktail told Rikar a lot about the female. One? She was a health freak, looking after her kidneys with a tumbler full of red, tart, and juicy. And two? She valued control too much to pour alcohol down her throat.

Too bad. A drunk female would be easier to handle.

Especially this one.

Angela Keen, of the gorgeous hazel eyes, was no dummy. Whipcord smart, she was hardcore, a homicide cop with suspicion in spades. As he walked around the pool table, Rikar saw it in the line of her shoulders, in the way she scanned the bar. Watching, waiting, searching the shadows for trouble. Even her seat choice was telling: back to the wall, face to the door, body poised on the edge of the stool. Relaxed, but ready. A she-warrior with the physical and intellectual chops to make a male pay.

And hell, that just turned him on.

Grabbing the microbrew from the edge of the table, Rikar took a long pull. When that didn't help, he adjusted his baseball cap and pulled at his pant leg, making more room behind his button fly. The Sevens were his favorite non-fighting gear. Dark denim worn in to perfection, the jeans fit like a dream, style and comfort wrapped into one. Tonight, though, they felt too tight in all the wrong places.

Man, he was so cooked. He'd known she was pretty from the picture in Sloan's file, but...

He hadn't expected to be attracted to her. Not like this. Christ. She hit every marker on his considerable list. The one entitled, "Fuckable." He'd never experienced anything like it. The need to possess and control—to dominate—had him by the throat. And all he'd done so far was look at her.

Look at her and covet.

She was power personified. Plugged in to the Meridian like Myst was, but in a different way. The redhead's energy was jewel-like. Hard and gleaming, the current flowed through chilly intelligence and icy resolve. The combo wound Rikar tight. He wanted a taste. Wanted to feed his frosty side with the raw burn of all that arctic energy.

Which was just freaking perfect.

The last thing he needed was another complication. And Angela Keen was trouble under athletic curves.

Rikar flexed his hands around the pool cue and lined up another shot. As ball met pocket, he sighed. Other than his aim, nothing about tonight was hitting the mark. Not hunting the female cop. Not finding her. Certainty not the mind-scrub. He wasn't even halfway there. Christ, he was all the way across the bar, using the pool table as cover, trying to decide how to approach her. Without losing his cool.

Shaking his head, Rikar grabbed the microbrew by the neck. Fuck it. No time like the present. She was almost finished with her drink. If he waited any longer, she would slip away, hop off that barstool and head for the door. Rikar needed to intercept her before that happened. Following her home wasn't a good idea.

Not unless he wanted to end up like Bastian. Tied to a female he couldn't resist.

The thought made him flinch. Allowed the pain he'd stuffed deep down earlier in the evening to rocket to the surface. God, it hurt. The whole situation was a mind fuck, but Bastian's hatred was the worst.

His chest went tight as he replayed Bastian's reaction. Dropping the f-bomb, Rikar cursed himself and the awful choice he'd been forced to make. His best friend's life for the female's.

Christ. He wished there'd been another way. Wanted to undo it, but...

Second-guessing himself wouldn't change anything. He'd made a choice. Had hurt a female to save his best friend and...fuck. He hated himself for it. Could hardly stand to be inside his own skin. But consequence was a bitch. So he would stand firm at the whipping post and take every last lash. He deserved it...all the blood and pain. Bastian's fury was justified. He only hoped his best friend found mercy enough to forgive him someday.

Rikar snorted and took another swig of his beer. Yeah, right. Like that would ever happen. He'd seen the devastation. The awful emptiness in Bastian's eyes as he'd turned toward the door, toward the female lying in the hospital bed on the other side.

Bastian loved her. There wouldn't be any easy up and over for his best friend when it came to Myst.

His focus on the pretty cop, Rikar shook his head as he slid his cue stick into the slotted wall rack. How the hell had his friend fallen into that trap? And so fast. Bastian was the strongest male he knew. Tight in the head, solid in the heart, his friend never allowed the emotional side of his nature—aka the human side—to rule him. Okay, so they shared certain DNA markers with humankind—and, God knew, the humans went wild for the lovey-dovey BS—but that didn't explain his friend's reaction. Something far bigger than chromosome pairing was at work here.

And Rikar itched to know the what, how, and why. Maybe if he could answer those questions he'd be able to free Bastian. Maybe then he'd get his best friend back. But answers weren't coming tonight. A trip to the Archives to study the texts would have to wait. Right now, he had another female to deal with. Rikar sighed, wanting to hang his head.

Deal with. Right. Traumatize was a better word. It seemed more in keeping with his MO lately.

Yeah, he was a fucking peach. Pillar among males.

Chapter Twenty-five

Swirling ice in her almost empty glass, Angela watched the big guy approach from the corner of her eye. She'd wondered when he would make his move. He'd been staring, checking her out from across the bar for at least fifteen minutes.

She would've been flattered. Really. Had she been an airhead without the sense God gave her.

Something about the guy was, well...off. Not wrong, exactly, just different in a way that raised her radar, got it blipping like a warning shot across a warship's bow. Or maybe it was more meteorological. Like an oncoming storm, Mr. Rough-and-Tumble rolled toward her, his "hot" factor whipping her hormones into a frenzy.

God, was that what she was feeling? Molten attraction? The urge to unlock her long neglected libido's cage and let it out to play? Sure seemed like it.

Angela took a sip of her Cran-Raz. Mixed with ice, the cold slide felt good going down. Keeping an ice chip, she cracked it with her teeth. The sharp sound chilled her out, helped her take a breath and control her heart. The steady thump-thump-thump was ridiculous. Especially considering she didn't know the guy.

But, man, he was something. Male beauty and strength wrapped up in one crazy-hot package.

Skirting a couple of chairs, he walked between tables on a direct collision course with her position at the bar. The closer he got, the more intrigued she became. Mr. Rough-and-Tumble was a walking contradiction. Big, yet graceful. Handsome without being pretty. Casual body language covering lethal ability and iron will. How did she know? She saw it in the way he moved. Recognized the aggression—and potential brutality—in the coiled strength of his body. In the swing of his arms, the angle of his shoulders, and in each controlled stride. An enforcer, maybe. Or military.

Yeah, definitely. The SEALS or Delta force. Maybe even the Green Berets. The guy had seen action...and plenty of it.

Didn't explain why he was here, though. In McGovern's, a cop bar on the outskirts of town.

He slid in next to her, taking the elbow room to her right. And...thank you, God, he smelled fantastic, like spicy cologne and hardcore male. One whiff of him and her libido went first-grader on her: hand raised, butt dancing in the chair as her hormones screamed, "Pick me! Pick me!" Which was just plain crazy. No way should she be reacting to him like that. Her brain had obviously been short circuited by one too many handfuls of salted peanuts.

Angela pushed the bowl of Planters' finest away and, glancing at Mr. Rough-and-Tumble, raised a brow. "Looking for trouble?"

His mouth curved up at the corners; he took a handful of nuts. "Nah, just a pool game. You play?"

"Depends."

"On what?"

"Whether or not you like to lose."

He laughed, flashing straight, white teeth. "You're that good?"

"You wanna find out?"

"Yeah," he said, eyes intense as he popped the peanuts into his mouth. Angela swallowed as he chewed, reining in errant urges—ones that included full body contact as she licked the salt from his bottom lip. "I really do."

His voice came out low, almost purr-like, and Angela shivered as the vibration slid up her spine. Wow, he was a wet dream with the body to back it up. It didn't take a rocket scientist to figure out that he'd be good in bed...so unbelievably hot and—

Holy hell, what was she doing?

Cozying up to this guy was a big mistake...one she shouldn't make. Mac would kick her butt if he found out. Which was almost guaranteed. Yeah, McGovern's might not be busy tonight, but the bar held court for its regulars. She recognized the cops in the corner booth. And just her luck, they were old school, throwbacks from the glory days when women were receptionists instead of detectives.

For some crazy reason, she didn't care. Not tonight. Right this minute, she wanted to ride the edge—let go and live dangerously for a change. The blond sitting beside her would give her that. She knew it like the chill in her glass. He was a flesh-and-blood opportunity. One she couldn't pass up without at least exploring...if only for an hour or two.

Setting her glass down on the damp napkin, Angela pivoted on the stool seat. Knee to knee with him now, she studied him, absorbed the chiseled planes of his face and the pale blue of his gaze. Hmm, his eyes were incredible, the color of ice...of the unspoiled glaciers she saw on the

National Geographic channel. Icy, yet warm. Another paradox. One that upped her interest in him.

She held out her hand. "Angela."

"Rikar." He stared at her hand.

A heartbeat passed before he raised his own. As his palm met hers, a prickling rush slid through her, ramping up sexual attraction, shoving sanity aside. He sucked in a quick breath and pulled back, letting her go. The second his skin left hers, she wanted the feeling back.

A little breathless from his touch, she asked, "No last name?"

"Not tonight." He slid off his stool and tipped his chin toward the pool tables. "Maybe tomorrow, though."

Angela clamped down on a smile. He was a tease. Using a string-along strategy designed to not only heighten her curiosity, but keep it in orbit. Somehow, she wasn't surprised. Rikar was a player, a guy who understood the finer points of the game. Fine by her. She held the ball and controlled the field. No was no, after all, and instinct told her Rikar would respect her decision...either way.

Sliding off the stool, she followed him, enjoying the view from behind. Man, he moved well, male power coiling, releasing with each step, making her imagine what he'd feel like mouth to mouth and skin to skin.

And, oh, boy. Was she actually thinking about this? Considering taking Rikar home? After a measly fifteen minutes of watching and thirty seconds of talking? Jeez. She needed her head examined. But even as she told herself that, temptation called, urging her to answer. She hadn't been with a guy in...what? Close to two years. Not from lack of wanting, but from lack of time...and trust. Other than Mac, trust and men didn't coexist well for her. And, well, no way she would sleep with her partner. She didn't want Mac that way.

But Rikar?

Angela blew out a long breath. Yeah, he was perfect. With his pale eyes, skull-trimmed blond hair, and ripped body, he was number one on her list of stupid things to do on a Friday night.

Wiping damp palms on her dark jeans, Angela studied the cues hanging in the wall rack. She made a show of it, buying time to collect herself. The guy standing quietly in her shadow rattled her more than she wanted to admit, and honestly? Acting like an idiot came in at minus two thousand on her personal Richter scale.

Cue balls clinked together, rolling on the table as she picked her weapon, a beautiful dark piece with light wooden inlays. As she turned, Rikar positioned the balls on the white dot and lifted the rack, leaving a perfect triangle behind.

He tipped his chin in her direction. "Your break."

"Magnanimous of you." Chalking the end of her cue, she moved to the end of the table.

"Maybe I just wanna see you bend over. You've got a very pretty ass."

"Nice try, hot shot, but I'm not that easily distracted." At least, under normal circumstances. Rikar's compliment, though, cracked her wide open. She liked the fact he saw her as a woman, complete with curves and white-hot need. After years on the force, the cops she worked with considered her one of the boys and treated her like one. Thank God...on so many levels. Her job was hard enough without adding a sexual angle.

Grinning like the devil she suspected he was, Rikar walked toward her end of the table.

"Stay where you are." She pointed the end of her stick at him. Yeah, he might like the way she looked in her jeans, but that didn't mean she'd give him a free show.

Eyes intense in the low light, his chest expanded then released as he breathed out. Just loud enough for her to hear over the retro '70s music, he said, "You gonna make me earn it?"

"You have no idea."

With her hand braced on the table, Angela pulled the stick back and let it fly. As the chalked end struck, the white ball shot down the table, cracking the colorful triangle wide open. Stripes and solids ricocheted, bouncing off felt bumpers, heading toward pockets and…

The blue ball rolled into the middle pocket.

Solids it was.

As she worked her way around the table, sinking shots like a pro, Rikar stood by, the butt of his pool cue planted on the wooden floor, watching, waiting for her to make a mistake. But she hadn't lied. Pool was her game. A family tradition learned at her father's knee.

Minutes ticked into an hour and, as she beat Rikar time and again, he teased her, made her laugh, kept her guessing. And God, she enjoyed every second of it. Soaked up the attention. Loved that he wanted her and wasn't afraid to show it. Even when it meant losing one game after another.

Yeah, he was a good sport: charming, clever, and… watchful.

Something about *that* made the cop in her wake up. The way he watched her was on par with how she studied suspects. In a word?...probing. Okay, so the examination was mixed with desire, but...

Just like him, it was a little off. Wasn't right, somehow.

Why? She didn't know, but her observation changed the game plan. No matter how much he interested her, she couldn't abandon caution so completely. Other women would've done it, but she'd seen too much—been to too many bloody crime scenes—to trust without knowing. So, no. Taking Rikar home wasn't an option for her. Not tonight. Not until she got to know him better.

He racked another round.

Angela leaned her pool cue against the side of the table. "Look, I've got to get going. Wanna save round two for another night?"

"I don't have another night, angel."

Brows drawn tight, she stared at him. "What do you—"

He struck so fast Angela didn't see him move. One second he stood at the end of the table. And the next? His hands were on her, one wrapped around her wrist, the other against the nape of her neck. Her training kicked in, shoving her into defense mode. But it was too late.

Out-muscling her, Rikar picked her up, moving them back into shadows. She bucked, brought her knee up, aiming for his groin. He shifted, using his legs to trap hers. She screamed for the cops across the bar. They would hear her. Old school or not, they would come and—

"They can't hear you, angel." Rikar brushed his mouth against her ear and, tone full of regret, whispered, "Can't see you either. We're alone here."

"D-don't..." Helplessness rose, choking her with fear as she fought to break his hold. Rikar held firm, pinning her arms and legs, pressing her shoulder blades into the wall at her back. Oh, God. He was too strong. She couldn't escape and...

He'd rape her, here in the shadows, in plain view of a bar full of cops. Why couldn't they see her? Why weren't they rushing to help her?

Tears blurred her vision. She screamed again. "Get off me...get off—"

"Easy. I want you, yes...but this isn't about sex. I won't touch you that way. I'm not going to hurt you."

"Go to hell," she said, knowing he lied. A guy didn't pin a woman down to have a friendly conversation. "Get your hands off me."

"I'm sorry," he said, looking like he actually meant it.

Angela didn't believe the lame apology for a second. She knew better. The sick SOB was a predator. The kind of scum she hunted and put away every day. She should have listened to her instincts. Something about Rikar hadn't added up from the start. If only she'd paid better attention.

His eyes started to shimmer.

Angela's breath caught as the silvery light expanded until his entire iris glowed. The blue wave lit up the darkness and...oh, God. Rikar was more than a criminal. He wasn't normal. He was...something else.

A chill slid along her spine. "What are you?"

"Relax, angel. Let me in and I'll take it away...make you forget." Transferring both of her wrists into one of his large hands, he cupped her jaw and raised her chin. Angela tensed, twisting against him. He dipped his head. His mouth brushed her pulse point. She shook her head, denial locked in her throat as something unlocked deep inside her. A gate opened, flooding her with sensation. The heated curl settled belly low as pleasure surged, spreading through her limbs. "That's it, love...help me make you forget."

She wanted to tell him to go to hell, but couldn't find the words. They were gone, taken by bliss on a warm wave. As she went weightless in mental fog, Angela floated, listened to Rikar groan. Felt him settle snug against her as he nestled into the curve of her throat.

The super-charged current intensified until her fingertips tingled. Angela didn't care. He felt so good and...

That was wrong, wasn't it?

Shouldn't she push him away?

She frowned, trying to catch hold of the thought. Yeah, definitely. She never let a guy get this close. But she couldn't make herself move. Couldn't remember a thing as she closed her eyes, tipped her head back and let Rikar have his way.

Chapter Twenty-six

Bastian couldn't feel a thing as he pushed the door open. Not the hard edge of the knob in his hand. Nor the cold floor beneath his bare feet. He was numb, frozen from the inside out, unable to feel anything but anguish.

The turbulence kicked up all kinds of garbage, stirring the debris in his mental junk drawer. Unpleasant things surfaced, the longing for Myst among them. He hadn't thought himself capable of needing a female to the exclusion of all else. But the thought of losing her...

The pain of it knocked against his ribcage. Pushed inward until he couldn't breathe. Reminded him of what he'd done. Damning him with the truth.

Forget the Razorbacks. He was his own worst enemy.

The proof of it lay unconscious across the room.

Afraid to look at her, Bastian stood on the threshold, head bowed, a death grip on the doorjamb as he transferred his weight to his uninjured leg. The one broken in the fight hurt like bitch, but the bone was already knitting. He'd be as good as new in less than twenty-four hours. His heart, on the other hand? Jesus, that wasn't so simple. No amount of dragon DNA would heal the gaping wound torn in his soul.

A beep broke through the silence. The soft, repetitive sound drifted, carrying the scent of clean sheets and...lavender. The room smelled like Myst: the sweetness of her skin and fragrant shampoo. The one he'd used while in the shower with her.

The memory made him lift his head. She needed him now as she had then. He couldn't abandon her. Yeah, it would be easier to leave...to protect himself and avoid the pain. Part of him wanted to, but he wasn't a coward. She needed him, so he would stay until she didn't need him anymore.

Taking a deep breath, Bastian opened his eyes. Even in the dim light, his eyesight was perfect, providing details, quick snapshots he wished he couldn't see. Freaking night vision. He could do without the perfection today, because... God forgive him. She was so pale. So small and still in the center of the big bed.

Covered by the sheet, she lay on her side, arms curled against her chest, blonde lashes like crescent moons on chalk-white cheeks. Bastian's throat went tight. She shouldn't be like this: drained of life, waiting to die.

He wanted to go back. Reverse the clock and change the last twelve hours. The Razorback would've killed him quickly, left him ashed in the rail yard, just one more messy pile for the human police to clean up. Given a second chance, he would've taken that route and protected Myst. But it was too late now, and no amount of wishing could alter the facts.

His female was dying.

The need to blame Rikar lit him up from the inside out. Made him want to nail the selfish SOB. But taking his loss out on his best friend's hide wouldn't change a thing. Myst would still be here, unconscious and looking too small in the center of the big bed.

His eyes stung as he half-limped, half-hopped across the room. Bastian wiped the moisture away with the back of his hand. He never cried, but now, in the awful wash of dimmed halogens, black despair grabbed hold. He had done this... killed her as surely as if he'd buried a knife hilt-deep in her heart.

Bastian swiped at his eyes again and, taking a ragged breath, stopped at her bedside. He watched her chest rise and fall, thankful for each breath she took. Each one gave him more time with her. Not enough to say good-bye— there would never be enough hours in the day for that—but maybe he could soothe her. Bring her some small measure of peace at the end.

The bump and scrape of chair legs skittered through the quiet. Raising his fists, Bastian pivoted, bracing for the threat.

"Sorry." Sloan pushed to his feet, hands raised to the side. "I didn't mean to..."

As the male paused, Bastian dropped his fighting stance and tipped his chin. "You've been sitting with her?"

Sloan glanced away, color tingeing his cheeks. "I didn't want her to be alone."

At the end.

He didn't need to hear the words to know Sloan thought them. The dark-skinned male knew better than most about loss...about pain. Eleven years, and still he mourned his female and son. And now? Bastian finally understood. Was already living that hell, and Myst wasn't even gone yet.

"Thank you," he said, his voice rough with gratitude. "For staying."

A frown furrowing his brow, his warrior nodded. Planted on the opposite side of the bed, he rubbed the back of his neck. "I know you're pissed, B, but...don't be angry with Rikar."

Fantastic. Just what he needed: a peacemaker. Shit. Now all he wanted to do was hit something. Rikar was his first choice, but the male standing across from him would do in a pinch.

"We need you. I would have done the same in his place." Dark eyes full of regret, he met Bastian's gaze head on. "I would've hated it. But, like Rikar, I would've done it anyway."

Bastian shook his head. He couldn't do this. Not now.

When he didn't answer, Sloan headed for the door. As he came even with the end of the bed, he hesitated, boots squeaking on linoleum, and changed course. Bastian tensed as his warrior came alongside him. He didn't want to be touched. Didn't deserve the comfort, but as Sloan's shoulder bumped his in a show of support, he broke, inhaling a shaky breath as tears blurred his vision.

Raising one massive hand, Sloan cupped the nape of Bastian's neck. Taking strength from his warrior's touch, Bastian reached for Myst. His fingertips brushed her jaw, slid against her skin, traced the sprinkle of freckles on the bridge of her nose. So beautiful. His female was hands-down the most beautiful thing he'd ever seen or had the privilege to touch.

He stroked her cheek, brushing the damp strands of hair away from her temple. "I'm sorry. I didn't mean to hurt you."

"Ah...Bastian?" Sloan retreated a step, his hand dropping from his shoulder.

Focused on his female, Bastian didn't acknowledge the interruption. He was too busy memorizing her face: the curve of her cheek, the softness of her skin, the shape of her mouth. All the small details that would sustain him... that needed to last a lifetime.

His friend knocked the side of his arm. "B."

With a growl, he glanced over his shoulder, hammering the male with a load of leave-me-the-fuck-alone. "What?"

"Jesus, man. Look at her."

Still cupping her cheek, Bastian drew a gentle circle on her temple. He stared at Sloan. The male pointed at Myst. Frowning, he switched focus, scanned her face and...his heart paused mid-beat. What the hell? Was she—

"Oh, my...holy shit, B. Get in. Get into bed with her."

He froze as Myst took a deep breath and turned her face into his hand. "*Bellmia*? My baby...can you hear me?"

"Screw that...move your ass!" With a quick arm thrust, Sloan shoved him.

Bastian's injured leg buckled, pitching him forward. With a quick twist, he tunneled his arm beneath Myst, wrapped her close and rolled, protecting her from the brunt of his weight. The wires connecting her to the machine tangled, wrenching her shoulder into an unnatural position.

Giving the f-bomb a workout, he unwound the mess and, seeing the marks on her skin, snarled, "What the fuck, man?"

His attention on the monitor, Sloan ignored him.

Myst whimpered, scissoring her legs against his, tucking her head beneath his chin. Bastian murmured, used his voice to soothe her, and slipped his hands beneath her tank top. As his palms connected with bare skin, she hummed, turning her face into the base of his throat. He drew her closer, touching his mouth to the curve of her shoulder as he whispered her name.

"Sloan...what's happening?"

"I don't know, but...she's reacting to you. Her color is better and...get her out of those clothes. I think you need to be skin to skin with her." Dark eyes narrowed, Sloan studied Myst for a moment before switching his attention back to the monitor beside the bed. He tapped the glass, following the green blip across the small screen. "Her heart rate is evening out, too. What are you doing...feeding her?"

Bastian didn't have a clue. He didn't much care either, but—

An electroshock blindsided him, hitting him chest level. Bastian twitched and tightened his grip on Myst as the current spread, corkscrewing in a heated twist around his torso.

Jesus. The Meridian.

Like a switch being flipped, the energy went live, roaring through him without prompting. Okay. That was different. Usually he controlled the energy surge, opened the connection from Meridian to female, and drew what he needed. Right now, though, his well was capped. He wasn't feeding. Myst was the one linked in, creating the bond between them.

Shifting a little, he relaxed into the sensation. The current settled deep, gentling as his dragon responded and rose, channeling the energy flow from him to Myst.

One hand flat against her bare back, Bastian pushed the sheet out from between them. He cursed as he got tangled up in the wires again. "Sloan...get this shit off her. I can't strip her if—"

"On it." With quick hands, Sloan peeled the electrodes from Myst's skin. "Good to go. Do you need—"

"Turn around."

The second the command left his mouth, Bastian knew it was stupid. And possessive as hell. He shouldn't care if anyone saw her naked. Not when her life hung by a thread. But he couldn't control the need to keep her for himself.

He didn't want another male near her, never mind looking at her.

As Sloan spun to face the wall, Bastian got busy stripping her down. The white tank top went first. As it cleared the top of her head, he tossed it aside. Trying not to look at her bare breasts, he slid his hands beneath her waistband. Soft skin met his palms. God, she was naked beneath here, too. No panties, no barriers between them as he rolled the black pants down her thighs, off her feet, and kicked them to the end of the bed.

With a flip, he covered them with the sheet and wrapped his arms around her. Drawing her in, he put them chest to breast, tangling his legs with hers. She moaned, and Bastian hugged her closer, turning his face into her hair. As he kissed the soft waves, the current between them increased, tugging at his energy center. He gave it up, letting her take from him.

God, it was extraordinary. And a little strange.

He was feeding her, providing what he normally took. Though it was different, somehow. A gentler kind of nourishment, male to female instead of the other way around. He'd never heard of such a thing...hadn't known his kind was capable of feeding another.

Was this some kind of ancient rite, one Dragonkind had forgotten?

He didn't know, but as his hands traveled, stoking along Myst's spine, he vowed to find out. He needed to visit the Archives and read what his ancestors had written. And he would. As soon as he got his female back on her feet.

———

Mont Blanc in hand, red leather-bound notebook in his lap, Ivar leaned back in his new chair and propped his feet on his makeshift desk. The folding table wobbled, threatening to collapse beneath the weight of his boots. He ignored the sway, too busy scribbling in the margins, adding detailed notes to the complicated formula.

He needed to get it right this time.

Ivar snorted, wishing solutions were like dogs. Those four-legged fuckers always came when called. Science? Not so much.

Each experiment followed its own protocol, precise steps that took time to develop and implement. Success came after measured results and evaluation, not the other way around. Soon, though, he'd solve the mystery. Crack the code and unravel the genetic mapping of Dragonkind's fertility cycles. Once he did that? He'd be golden...have what he needed to start phase two of his project.

Phase one was already underway.

"Christ...underway. Barely," Ivar muttered, retracing the genetic codes, frustration getting the better of him.

Patience wasn't one of his virtues. He liked tangible results: the faster, the better. But even with the deck stacked, speed wasn't in the cards. Which was problem number...oh, he didn't know. Maybe 207? Number one on the list involved Bastian. The Nightfuries were a pain in the ass. That crew was hunting Razorbacks hard: killing his warriors, searching for him. Meanwhile, what was he doing? Sitting on his duff, waiting for clinical trials to begin, for his warriors to find the right residents for cellblock A.

All right. So the lack of progress wasn't exactly their fault. High-energy females were a rare breed, harder to find than four-leaf clovers.

Doodling in the side margins, Ivar sighed. He needed six—just six, although, he'd settle for five in a pinch—to get his breeding program off the ground. After that? He'd find more to add to the pot, but until then...

He refused to rush things or get ahead of the data. Mistakes happened that way. And right now? He couldn't afford to make any.

Ivar tossed his Mont Blanc onto the notebook in his lap. As the pen settled in the vee, he reached out and grabbed the journal sitting open on his desk. The leather-bound book was his bible; 179 pages of formulae and scribbled notes containing secrets he'd yet to unlock. His mouth curved, he smoothed the dog-eared pages, loving the textured paper and...the blood spatter.

Hmm, yes. The three-year-old blood blissed him out every time he touched it. Each droplet reminded him of the battle. He'd fought dirty that night—done the unspeakable in Dragonkind circles—to possess the journal. The one he held along with the six others locked in his safe.

Although, if given a do-over, he would've taken the scientist instead of gutting the female in her kitchen. Had he known how difficult genome typing would be...the sheer effort it would take to decipher her notes and create the serum? Hell. He would've locked her up and thrown away the key. Forced her to work in his lab until she found a way for Dragonkind to produce female offspring.

With her expertise, she might've done it. But she was long gone, leaving him to discover the answers on his own. He must find a way to unlock and alter dragon DNA. The problem? Magic was a bitch to break through, and with the tendrils roped around the quadruple helix of chromosomes? He was fighting an uphill battle.

But not for long. His latest formula looked promising; possessed the potential to break through the genetic markers and allow males of his kind to sire daughters. Dragonkind needed females of their own. Without them, his race would remain dependent on humans. Which meant he couldn't kill all of them. At least, not without starving his kind to death.

So, here he was...back at the beginning. Starting over.

It all came down to patience. Yeah, that and a kick-ass game plan.

Step one? Develop the breeding centers, both in his lair and in Europe. If he couldn't annihilate the humans all at once, he'd use them...breed them to feed his kind while he mapped the genomes and found answers. Only the strongest humans would be imprisoned in the centers, ensuring pure bloodlines and that each female born possessed the best energy. Once the centers were full and producing, he'd release his super bug, wiping the weakest of humankind from the face of the earth.

Hmm. He loved a good plan, and speaking of which, his lab awaited. Time to put phase one to work.

Setting the pen aside, Ivar flipped both notebooks closed. Journals in hand, he leaned forward and opened the wooden box sitting in the center of his desktop. A small, stainless steel tube glinted under the overhead lights. Ivar hummed as he picked it up. Seesawing the thing between his thumb and forefinger, he studied the curvy container. It was so ordinary. Unremarkable, but for the deadly nature of its contents.

With a smile, he fisted the tube. Man, he could hardly wait to see what his little monster could do.

He lifted his boots from his desk and, ignoring the squeak of his new armchair, pushed to his feet. His footfalls echoed on the concrete floor, shattering the quiet as he rounded the edge of the table and headed for the door.

Turning into the corridor, he mind-spoke to his XO. *"Lothair…status?"*

"Five in the chamber. We're good to go," he said, the soft beep of computers in the background. *"ETA?"*

"Five minutes. Lock it down."

Anticipation carrying him forward, Ivar strode toward the airtight vault. Apartment, though, was probably a better description for the chamber. With enough space for nine, the place was decked out with the best of everything: soft beds, three roomy bathrooms, and a fully stocked gourmet kitchen connected to a plush living area. Yup, only the best for his lab rats. He figured it was only fair. No sense making them suffer the indignity of squalor along with the agony of a slow death.

Or not.

Who knew? It might take his worker bees just minutes—not the hypothesized days—to die.

The smell of fresh paint in the air, Ivar rounded the last corner. Seven strides later, he hung a right, rolling into the vault's control room. One shoulder propped against the far wall, Lothair stood next to the observation window, his gaze trained on the humans locked on the other side.

Without glancing away from the test subjects, he shook his head. "They think they're going home. A decontamination area, I said…before we take them to the surface."

"You're a good liar." Throwing his XO an amused look, he headed toward the high-tech computer system.

"Better than you."

No shit. Lothair could charm the hooves off a goat if he wanted to. Ivar grinned, setting his journals on the granite countertop surrounding the touch-screen control panel. As he scanned the screen, he went to work, running the usual tests.

All of the levels in the vault read as normal. Airlock sealed tight...check. Temperature a balmy seventy-five degrees and closed-circuit ventilation system operational...double check. Cameras on and microphones rolling...triple check.

All right. Take one of "Experiment Super Virus" was good to go.

With quick fingers, Ivar punched his personal security code into the digital keypad. The rotation of robotics hissed and a glossy black panel slid open in the wall to his left. Opening his hand, he stared at the tube resting in his palm. He breathed deeply, savoring the moment before relinquishing his baby. With a whispered "God speed," he set the viral beast inside the robotic hand and watched it retreat into the wall.

The control panel lit up, waiting for his final thumbs-up.

Pushing away from his perch, Lothair moved to stand shoulder to shoulder with him. Ivar met his XO's gaze and tipped his chin. His friend nodded, reached out, and tapped the green button, setting the process in motion.

Computers geared up, the whirl of mechanics soft accompaniment as the plunger depressed, releasing the virus into the apartment.

Nothing to do now but wait.

"Got a gift for you." Digging into his leathers, Lothair pulled a piece of paper from his back pocket and handed it over.

"Christmas comes early?"

"Today's a big day. Figured I'd check item number two off your wish list."

Clean edges and crispy paper crinkled as he unfolded his gift. He saw the female's picture first and...hell. Wasn't she pretty? Myst Munroe, female of the kick-ass energy. A beautiful little blonde with violet eyes and a mouth meant for sucking. Yum. He loved the fair-haired ones. Especially if all that fairness extended south, to the neat triangle between their thighs.

He read the list below her DMV address. A nurse practitioner. Huh. Figured. Bastian always went for the clean, preppy ones. No Gothed-out females with spike collars and fishnets for that male.

"Where is she?" Ivar shifted his hold on the paper and traced the female's face with his fingertip.

"Denzeil's running down all the angles. So far, there's no trace of her."

"Bastian's keeping a tight leash on her."

"Looks like it. But from all accounts, she's strong-willed. He won't be able to contain her forever." A gleam in his dark eyes, Lothair smiled, and not in a pleasant way. Ivar almost felt sorry for the female. His XO relished a challenge and, when the male went after something, he did so with single-minded focus. It wouldn't be long before Bastian's high-powered female was exactly where Ivar wanted her... behind bars in cellblock A. "We've got cameras in her apartment now. Denzeil's monitoring the human authorities and their databases. The minute she sticks her head out, we'll get her."

Ivar refolded the paper and tucked it away. He'd look at her pretty picture later. Right now, he needed to plan. Map out every detail, imagine all the things he'd do when he finally got his hands on Myst Munroe.

Jesus, he couldn't wait to taste her.

Chapter Twenty-seven

Myst surfaced from sleep like a submarine, smooth and easy, but with a rushing awareness that startled her. Her limbs twitched, coming online as her brain rocketed into the ON position. As her eyes flipped open, she frowned.

Wow. This was weird. Completely upside down and backward.

Usually, she woke up blurry-eyed. In an incoherent scramble that left her stumbling around while her brain fired on all the wrong synapses. The result was less than fun. Her fail-safe solution? Coffee. And loads of it.

But this morning? Or evening. Man, she didn't know what time it was, but...

Wide awake didn't begin to describe her. She was on uppers without downing the drugs. Jazzed for no apparent reason. It was a little scary, actually. So strange alarm bells went off inside her head.

She rubbed her eyes and shifted, registering the softness beneath her and that she lay curled on her side. On board with the super perky rise-and-shine routine, her vision sharpened. Glossy white cabinets and a stainless steel countertop glinted in the low light. A round table broke up the space, sitting between the bank of cupboards and the bed. Two metal chairs sat at odd angles alongside, like they'd been pushed out of the way in a hurry.

She noticed the equipment next.

Lined up like soldiers, a collection of machines stood shoulder to shoulder against the wall and...wow. Nothing but the best for this unit. The medical equipment was state of the art, the most expensive models on the market. Not that the person using them cared. The heart-rate monitor was a complete travesty. Wires and electrodes hung to the floor in a messy tangle that just made her mad. Someone needed to kick that nurse's—or intern's—butt. That machine helped save people's lives and—

Wait a second.

What was she doing in a hospital? Okay. Stupid question. Part of her job involved spending time in hospitals, but she'd never been a patient. Until now.

Myst squinted at the pale walls, looking for a clue: a picture, a diploma, signs of any kind. Nada. A big, fat blank. Just like her memory.

Man, this was getting old. She could do without the whole "can't remember the next morning" routine. Especially when every time it happened, she ended up eyeballing someone else's sheets. With a sigh, Myst stretched, arching her back to work the kinks out and...

She was naked. No hospital johnny. Just skin on cotton. Again.

Her mind came back online in a hurry. Holy crap. Bastian. It had to be. Every time she closed her eyes around the guy, she woke up without a stitch on. Which wouldn't have been all that bad if he stuck around after he'd gotten her that way.

Whoa. Wrong thought. Ah...wasn't it?

Chewing on her bottom lip, Myst tried to decide. She wanted him—no denying it—but was sleeping with him the smart thing to do? She knew herself well, could feel the fall coming. She didn't do casual sex. At least, not well. The one time she'd tried, she'd ended up getting hurt, wanting something the guy wasn't prepared to give.

She sighed, admitting she was in too deep.

But the worst was knowing Bastian wanted her, too. She could see it every time he looked at her. And when he looked at her, she forgot where she was, what she was supposed to be doing...namely saying *no*.

With a groan, Myst flipped the sheet back. Time to get up.

"Bellmia?"

The sleepy murmur drifted over her shoulder. A strong arm followed, snaking around her body from behind. She twitched in surprise, gasping when he pulled her in tight. His chest touched her first, pressing against her back a second before the rest of him followed. Oh, God. She had him, full-on contact; his breath warming the side of her neck, his strong body up against hers.

Her eyes drifted closed, and she leaned back, relaxing into his embrace. Wrong thing to do, she knew. She should be shrugging out of his hold, telling him off...giving him the heave-ho. He was, after all, taking a truckload for granted. But as he fit her to the curve of his body, she lost the will to resist along with her voice. He felt too good, not even the threat of future pain overrode her desire for closeness.

He needed her. And she wanted to be needed.

Shifting into a shoulder roll, Myst glanced over her shoulder. Sleepy green eyes met hers and...oh, man. Sexy, naked, sleep-rumpled man alert.

"Hi." Her voice came out on a husky whisper.

"Hi back." Bastian's mouth curved up at the corners. God help her. The guy was dangerous when he smiled. "How do you feel?"

"Umm...good. I'm good." She dragged her focus from his lips and met his gaze. Hmm. His irises were the most incredible color: bright green, blue, and hazel flecks in a unique blend that was all Bastian.

Releasing a long breath, his eyes drifted closed. He murmured low, speaking a language she'd never heard before. One that was beautifully rhythmic, and as the rolling R's and long-drawn S's filled the quiet, she realized he was praying. Or thanking someone.

She shuffled sideways, turning in his arms until she faced him. Bad idea if she planned to escape, but her heart wasn't much into getting free at the moment. And as she cupped his cheek, she didn't care if she got burned in the end. Here and now? Yeah, that's what mattered, and being with him like this felt too right to avoid.

She traced the ridge of his cheekbone with her fingertips. "Hey...are you okay?"

"Perfect." His deep voice rumbled, and she shivered as he opened his eyes. His gaze shimmered in the low light, heating her up, making her want. With a soft growl, he kissed the center of her palm.

Steady girl. Take it slow...breathe.

She took the advice, breathed in then out. But her gaze drifted, wanting a sneak peek. And with the sheet down around his hips? Oh, boy, he was beautiful: smooth skin poured over ripped muscle and solid bone. Stroking her free hand over his shoulder, she leaned away just a little. She needed more, a better view of his chest and the taut six-pack below.

Myst froze mid-look. She frowned. The skin around his ribcage was pink. Not raw exactly. More like scalded, as though someone had poured hot water on him and—

"Oh. My. God." Planting her hand on his shoulder, she pushed, applying pressure. He rolled onto his back. She came up onto her knees, eyes searching his chest and belly. God, there was a strip of pink skin running from his ribcage to the top of his thigh. He'd been burned. She remembered now, and the memory made her frantic as her gaze ran over him. "You were hurt. I came out of the clinic and…God… Rikar brought you in and—"

"I'm all right, Myst."

She shook her head, stripping the sheet all the way off him. Bastian grabbed for her hands. She avoided his grasp, checking his thigh and knee. He winced, muscles flexing up hard when she touched his shin. "Your leg. It's broken and…" On her knees, she forgot about being naked and straddled his uninjured thigh. Looking around, she scanned the recovery room. "Where's my bag? I need to—"

"Baby, look at me." Propping himself on one elbow, he cupped her face with his free hand. His touch stopped her in mid-flight, keeping her planted in the middle of the bed. As he met her gaze, he stroked her cheek, soothing her. "The bone is knitting. The burns are almost gone. By tonight, I'll be good as new."

"But…how?" Her brows drawn tight, she stared at him. "How is that possible? I saw you. Your injuries…oh, my God, Bastian. They were terrible."

"I'm half dragon, love. My kind heals fast."

The reminder of what he was should've sent her running. Or at the very least, backed her up a step. Crazy that it didn't. But all she saw was the man and the way he treated her. With respect, affection, and passion. The fact he wasn't entirely human was less important...a bit of an afterthought. Hardly worth her attention at all.

And wow. Go team Myst. Way to think outside the box.

"Are you sure?" Still worried, she examined his side again. "I think I should check you anyway. Just to make sure and—"

"How about I make you come instead?"

Myst blinked. Well, okay. That effectively shut her up. And got her thinking, because...holy crap. That was the best offer she'd had in years. She bit her bottom lip, a little unsure, but mostly? Loving the idea of making love to him.

It had been so long. Eons since she'd allowed anyone to touch her. And here she was, naked in bed with Bastian wanting her. She was so tempted, and he was...a freaking sex god or something. No way he could look and smell like he did if he didn't have some powerful mojo working for him.

Myst swallowed when his gaze dropped to her lips. He paused, his own mouth parting, his breath coming faster, his eyes drifting lower. He skimmed over her: first her breasts, then her belly, and finally, the curls between her thighs. Heat bloomed, pooling at her core as he licked his bottom lip as though he was imagining what she tasted like there.

Desire sent her sideways into the path of anticipation as his gaze returned to hers. She shivered, seeing the wildness in him—all the pleasure he promised without words. And as he reached out and curled his hand around her wrist, she leaned toward him instead of away. Allowed him to tug her off balance, onto her hands and knees above him.

Still propped on one elbow, his mouth a hair's breadth from hers, he taunted without touching. "Say yes."

Need made her lose her mind. It was the only explanation. The only reason she closed the distance between them. There were so many questions left unanswered. So many things she needed to know about him. About Dragonkind. But common sense had flown, and as her lips brushed his, Myst whispered the one word she never should have, "Yes."

———

As Myst leaned in, Bastian's heart went jackrabbit, pounding the inside of his chest. Her trust floored him. The gentle brush of her mouth ruined him. And lust? Hell, that bastard lit his fire then poured gasoline on the flames.

The result? Passion's equivalent of a Molotov cocktail.

Boom. Lights out. Good-fucking-night.

Which wasn't his MO at all. He was always in control with every female he spread beneath him. But not with Myst. She was different. Special in a way he found hard to describe, but felt just the same.

Her hands on his skin. Her soft mouth against his. Her scent in every breath he took. Jesus. He couldn't get enough.

Inhaling hard, he dragged her into his lungs, struggling to keep it together. To let her touch him. To give her all the time she wanted to explore.

But...oh, man.

Each caress cranked him higher until nothing existed but him, her, and the wicked pleasure she gave him. Which was backward on every level that counted. He should be the one touching her, taking the lead—blowing her mind, making her beg—not the other way around.

Except, he shouldn't be making love to her at all.

Not without telling her the truth of his kind. But he couldn't stop kissing her. Couldn't slow down long enough to tell her he had something important to say. His drive to please her had taken over, pushing him past the point of no return. Which was so unfair—to her, not him. She deserved the truth before he laid her down and loved her hard. Should know how much she meant to him.

There were so many things he'd left unsaid. She had a right to know about the energy exchange. About how Dragonkind males sustained themselves. About what he took each time he touched her, but…

Goddamn it. She tasted too good. Felt too right poised above him. And the current of energy flowing between them? The Meridian turned incendiary, burning a trail through his veins. And as Myst lit him up she linked in, completing the connection until energy flowed in a continuous loop, from her to him then back.

Addicted to the power she wielded, Bastian moaned and, elbows planted on the bed, tipped his face up, seeking more of her. With a hum, she kissed him softly and, in that moment, he copped out. Knew he wasn't going to tell her the truth about himself. Not now, when he had her naked in his arms.

Fuck. Could he be any more of an asshole?

Probably. But the fear of losing her made him that way. Rejection was a high-flying bitch without brakes. Once it was airborne, pain followed closely behind. No way would he risk it without making love to her first. Later. They would talk later…after he had the taste of her on his tongue and her scent on his skin.

One afternoon with her would never be enough. He knew it, but didn't care. A few hours were better than none at all. So, selfish or not, he would take her. Store the memories away to reach for another time just in case she never let him touch her again.

Shifting his weight onto one elbow, he snaked his other arm around her. He drew her closer, smoothed his hand down her spine, then moved up again, exploring from hip to shoulder. God, she was exquisite. So beautiful with her lithe curves and pale skin. Brains and beauty. Softness and strength. Sheer perfection wrapped up in one female.

His. Every magnificent inch of her.

Bastian groaned as she tilted her head and deepened the kiss. The caress was slow, thorough, more exploratory than true conquest. So far. But it was only a matter of time. She would own him body and soul after this. Maybe she already did. He'd lost the battle the first time he'd laid eyes on her. In that crappy little house in the middle of nowhere.

Ironic, wasn't it?

For all his physical strength, he was the weakest of their pairing. The most needy, the one begging without words to be taken...used hard and loved long. He wanted to be mastered—at the mercy of his female while she demanded everything from him. Hmm, he already craved the chains. Had opened his mouth wider, becoming slave to her conqueror when she flicked her tongue over his bottom lip, gifting him with a little taste and truckload of tease.

"You like that?" She nipped him with the sharp edge of her teeth.

Bastian's muscles fisted up hard, curling his hips off the mattress. "More."

"How much more?"

"Anything...all you want."

"Just the answer I was looking for." Smiling against his mouth, she cupped the back of his arm. With a gentle tug, she slid his elbow from beneath him. "Lie back for me."

The instant his shoulder blades touched down, rustling on cotton, she delved deep, invading his mouth, rewarding him with her sweetness and...oh, man. She tasted decadent—like a summer storm, clean, driving rain and heat lightning—but it wasn't enough. He needed her scent all over him, and his on her. Possession wasn't good enough. Only domination would do...hers over him, his over her. He didn't care as long as he ended up buried to the hilt inside her.

In the next thirty seconds.

With a groan, he tunneled his hands through her hair. Cupping the back of her head, he drank deep, eating at her mouth. Small hands pressed to his shoulders, she shifted, throwing one leg over to straddle him. His shaft kicked as she settled: knees on either side of his hips, the tips of her high, tight breasts brushing his chest, her tongue deep in his mouth.

Spreading her thighs wider, she rocked against him. Her slick heat bathed his skin, arched his spine, pushed his hips up. Bliss bit deep then whiplashed, nailing him like a body shot to the chest. Fighting for control, his hands flexed in her hair. She rolled her hips again.

Jesus. He wasn't going to make it. Was losing control. She was too hot. So ready he felt her slide, wet and creamy, against his abdomen.

"Myst...baby." His erection pulsed. He arched, an instant away from orgasm. "I'm going to come. I can't...Jesus...I'm going to...oh, fuck."

"Shh...settle down."

He drew a desperate breath, throbbing hard, on the verge and then—

A miracle happened.

His body calmed, obeying his female without question.

Bastian shuddered. Holy shit. How had she done that...with nothing more than a whispered command? A moment ago, he'd been a nanosecond from losing it. Now? The urgency no longer ruled him. His fire was banked but burning...leaving him hard and ready, but in control again.

Awed by her, Bastian whispered her name.

She murmured back, praising him, and drew his hands out of her hair. His fingers twitched, and he growled as he lost contact with the silken waves. Using the pads of her thumbs, she stroked the insides of his wrists and pressed his arms above his head. "Keep them there. You don't touch me until I tell you to...got it?"

No way. Unfair. He shook his head. "I need—"

"Got it?" She laced their fingers together. Brushing a kiss to the corner of his mouth, she pressed the backs of his hands into the mattress.

"You're killing me."

She smiled. "Give a little to get a lot. My way first...yours second."

Second? Forget that. Try third...maybe even fourth. Making love to her twice would never be enough. He nipped her bottom lip, protesting the conditions. But...if she wanted her way first, so be it. He'd get what he needed before he let her go.

"Deal?"

"Devil's bargain." He rolled his hips against her bottom. She gasped and tipped her head back, riding the undulation. "I'll make you pay for it later, *bellmia*."

"Promises, promises."

With a satisfied hum, she released her hold on him and retreated, taking her mouth from his. Which drove him crazy. In that moment, all he wanted was another taste of her, to tangle his tongue with hers and slide between her thighs.

Oh, yeah. That's exactly what he needed. Her beneath him. Him deep inside her.

Forgetting his promise, Bastian followed her retreat.

She pushed him back down. "A deal's a deal, Bastian."

"Fuck."

"Um-hmm." Her eyes full of mischief, she rocked her exquisite ass against his abdomen, giving him a magnificent view of her pink-tipped breasts as she shifted astride him. "We'll get to that."

Please, God. He wouldn't last much longer. Not if she kept—

His muscles flexed as she trailed her fingers down the underside of his arms. Fingers spread wide, she continued down, caressing his chest, circling the hard points of his nipples. Bastian fisted his hand in the sheets. The little vixen. She was teasing, testing his resolve...pushing him past his limits into uncharted territory.

He never submitted. Ever. But with Myst, he allowed the domination. Forced himself to endure her exploration while she discovered where he was most sensitive, made him arch and groan...and curse. But when she shifted down his body, inner thighs brushing the outside of his, leaned in and—

Oh...Jesus.

Her mouth touched down on his chest, right over his heart. He undulated beneath her, egging her on, enjoying the heat of her mouth on his skin. Delight followed each caress, shoving him into pleasure so intense that he could hardly breathe. It was torture, and he loved every second. She was a female worth worshiping, and as she bathed him in heat, he spoke to her in Dragonese, praising her in the language of his kind.

"You're so beautiful, Bastian."

He whispered her name like a benediction.

She answered with heat and, flicking him with her tongue, reached between his thighs. She found him on the first try, wrapping her hand around his erection. With a groan, he gave the f-bomb a work out and surged beneath her.

Showing no mercy, she stroked him, each pull a rhythmic, soul-stealing draw. She paused to pay special attention to the tip of his shaft, drawing out the pleasure. His balls fisted up tight, and he growled, long and low, throbbing in her hand, fighting to hang on and...wait for her.

But...fuuuuck. He was so close.

Twisting beneath her, he rasped, *"Bellmia,* please...let me touch you."

Stroking him one last time, she lifted her head. As her gaze met his, she set her mouth to his and whispered, "Green light."

On a snarl, he released his death grip on the sheets. His arms came around her so fast she gasped as he reversed their positions. Mid-flip, he latched onto her breast and, suckling the beaded tip, spread her beneath him. Securing her hands in one of his, he drew her arms above her head and held her prisoner.

"Payback's a bitch, *bellmia*."

"Bastian..."

Her husky murmur nourished him, and not wasting a second, he settled deep, hips between her thighs, erection against her heat. Still at her breast, he nipped her gently. With a moan, she arched, asking for more. He gave it to her, laving the sensitive peak before lifting his head to pay equal attention to its mate.

Soft skin slid against his and need spiked, spiraling into explosive sensation. As it raged, Bastian burned for her, listened to the sexy sounds she made, reveled in the way she clung to him, loved the way she begged for his kiss. Unable to deny her, he returned to her lips, tangled their tongues, tasting her deep.

Hmm...beautiful female. So welcoming and hot...so incredibly demanding.

Wrapping her calf over his hip, she undulated, opened her mouth wide, giving as good as he gave her. The roll and release pushed her hips up, and...oh, yeah. He got bathed in slick and creamy heat.

Temptation called. Bastian shifted, releasing her wrists to slide down her body.

"Oh, yes...please," she murmured as he pressed his mouth to the soft swell of her belly. "Bastian...yes."

"Where do you want me, baby?" Licking over her hipbone, he headed south and, grasping her knee, pushed her thighs wide. And...oh, God. She was beautiful here, too. So pink and slick.

He brushed her damp curls with his fingertip. "Here?"

"Please."

"Mouth or fingers?" He kissed the inside of her thigh, giving her time to decide—because...shit. No way around it. He would have both before he finished: her taste on his tongue and his fingers deep inside her. Questions was... which did she want first?

He flicked her with his tongue, working his way closer to her core with each stroke. "Tell me, love."

"God..." She panted, tight nipples rising and falling on frantic breaths. "Anything...please, just—"

He dipped his head, spread her slick folds, and licked deep. He groaned as he got his first taste. Hmm...yeah. A feast for a starving male.

Pressing in, he worked his tongue deeper: exploring her softness, coating the back of his throat with her cream. With a wild cry, she jerked beneath him, hands flexing in his hair, begging him for the pleasure. He flicked the little bud at the top of her sex. Playing, cranking her high, he did it again and again, circling with the tip of his tongue.

"Bastian!"

He tongued her again then settled in—holding her down while he stoked, drawing on her sensitive flesh. With a whimper, she caught his rhythm, rocked against him, asking for more. Lured by her scent, undone by her taste, he upped the stakes and slid one finger deep. She pulsed inside, fisting up tight, moaning when he set a pace designed to drive her wild. He stretched her gently, slipping a second finger into her heat, and sucked harder with his mouth.

Spread wide, deep in the pleasure, she threw her head back. Hips churning, back bowed off the bed, she came in a screaming wave of energy. As she throbbed around his fingers, the blast hit Bastian dead center, splitting him wide open. Ferocious need stepped through the fissure, killing gentleness in one broad stroke.

Bastian tried to hold on, to cage the undeniable urge to take her hard and fast...without mercy or feeling. He wanted inside her so bad that...Jesus. He didn't trust himself not to hurt her. Couldn't control the animalistic need and—

She came again, clinging to him, sobbing his name. Her need pulverized restraint, sending him over the edge with a snarl. Spreading her beneath him, he rose above her. As she panted, riding another wave of delight, she wrapped her legs around him, inviting him home. He thrust deep, buried himself to the hilt inside her with one powerful stroke, then roared in ecstasy when she clenched hard and held him tight.

Home.

Fuck, yeah. He'd finally come home.

Chapter Twenty-eight

Shifting the precious bundle in his arms, Rikar willed the door locks open with a thought. The deadbolts double clicked, and he shook his head. He'd lost his frickin' mind. Bringing Angela home was a bad, bad, *bad* idea. But leaving her at the bar—surrounded by males sucking back Budweiser—hadn't been an option.

Not with her like this. Sleeping hard after the mind scrub...and his feeding.

Shit, he hadn't meant to do that. Taking her energy hadn't been part of the plan. As far as he knew, his agenda had read: Angela Keen, quick mind scrub; Ian MacCord, wash, rinse, repeat if necessary. Not stay out all night getting your ass kicked by a gorgeous redhead with serious pool skills.

Rikar snorted. Trust a female to screw up a perfectly good plan.

He glanced down at her, trying not to brush the top of her head with his mouth. But, man...it was hard. Her hair was so soft. He knew it firsthand from when he'd buried his fingers in the fiery strands, pressed his thigh between her legs and her back to the wall, and drank deep, taking his fill.

Now, she lay content in his arms, curled like a kitten, head on his chest, hands tucked inside his leather jacket, her scent all over him.

Fuck, she was pretty.

He sighed, flipped the handle, and shoved the door open. The security system fired up, beep-beep-beeping a warning. He deactivated it with his mind, but his boots stayed planted on the paisley carpet in the corridor. He stared into the dark hole of her condo, unable to turn away, but not wanting to go in. There was no doubt a bed in there. And he'd have to get close to it to lay Angela down. Dangerous territory for him right now.

He blew out a long breath. Maybe he could leave her sitting in a chair or propped up on the couch and avoid the bedroom all together?

Now who was a jerk?

Him, that's who.

Christ, leave her sitting upright, getting a kink in her neck? What the hell was wrong with him?

Unlocking the clamp down on his legs, Rikar crossed the threshold. He kicked the door closed behind him, shutting out the light from the corridor. His night vision fired up as the condo plunged into darkness around him. Huh. Pretty sparse…not much to look at in the small, upscale apartment.

He walked past a galley kitchen on his left and into the small living room. Long couch, two rattan chairs, a flat-screen TV mounted on the wall. No area rug, no pictures hanging on the washed-out walls, nothing but hard surfaces and floor-to-ceiling, steel-framed windows with industrial blinds on them. Nothing that would tell him who she was or what she liked to do in her off-hours. Then again, maybe she didn't have any. Cops were notorious workaholics, spending more time on the job than in their real lives.

The place was blissfully cool, though, like she'd cranked the heat way down. Score another point for Angela Keen. Her tally was now somewhere in the range of plus bazillion on his sliding frosty scale.

Glancing right, he found a narrow hallway. The bedroom was somewhere down there. He glanced at the couch. No way he'd leave her there. She'd wake up with a chill and...

Yeah. He soooo needed to get the hell out of here.

A death grip on his urges, he hit the hallway, turning sideways so her feet didn't bump the wall. Two doors faced each other across the corridor. A quick check through doorway number one and he located the bathroom. He went right, shouldering the door open, heart picking up pace, pissing him off as he crossed into her personal domain.

Her scent was stronger here, as though she spent all of her time in the small twelve-by-twelve-foot box. Rikar swallowed, breathed in through his nose, out his mouth, and rounded the foot of her bed. The thing was compact, just like her. A steel-frame double with silky-looking sheets and no other embellishments. No throw pillows. No fancy quilts or embroidered anything. No nonsense...just like her.

Man, he liked that about her. Clean, simple, straightforward on the outside, beautifully complex on the inside.

Okay. Enough of that bullshit.

This was an in-and-out mission. And not the sexual kind.

She sighed as he set her down. He watched her snuggle in, the muscles across his abdomen pulling at his hipbones, fisting his balls up tight. Yup. No doubt about it. Time to get the hell out of Dodge, but...

With a curse, he grabbed the heel of her boot and pulled it off her small foot. He attacked the second, dropping it beside its mate on the floor, and went to work on the duvet. Drawing the covers down, he tugged them from beneath her and then brought it up, wrapping her in the warmth of silk and feather down.

Her eyes drifted open.

Rikar froze, his hands in the covers beneath her chin as he got nailed by her hazel gaze. The impact almost floored him.

"Hey," she said, the greeting slurred by sleep and the aftereffects of the feeding. She blinked once, a slow up and down. "You staying?"

"No." But man, he wanted to. He brushed the hair away from her temple instead, fingertips lingering on her soft skin. "Go back to sleep, angel."

Her eyes drifted closed, dark lashes on pale cheeks. "Tomorrow?"

"Yeah, tomorrow," he said, lying through his teeth, trying not to feel good that she wanted to see him again.

As sleep pulled her under, Rikar straightened and spun toward the bedroom door. Escape was priority one. Nothing else he could do. No sense making another mistake. He'd made enough tonight to last a lifetime. Now he needed to get back to the lair. Back to reality before daylight hit and he got fried by the sun.

Thirty seconds later, he was out of her apartment and in the corridor, door double-bolted behind him, security panel beep-beep-beeping as ADT reengaged the system. He breathed a little easier. His she-cop was safe, locked up tight behind the steel doors and concrete walls.

His. Right. He needed his head examined. A total frickin' reboot. One he was likely to get when he got home and had his hardware rewired by Bastian and his nasty grief-vengeance combo.

Man, payback was a bitch.

"Don't think about it," he growled at himself, cranking the door to the stairwell open.

He went up instead of down, taking the stairs three at a time. The underground garage where he'd parked Angela's Jeep wouldn't get him anywhere but...well, underground. Not exactly where he wanted to be right now. He needed air and plenty of height to unleash his inner dragon.

The beast was jonesing to get out. Wanting to stretch his wings, work out the frustration, and forget about the female. About how good she tasted. And where he'd left her.

Moving as though he had rockets strapped to the bottoms of his shitkickers, he came out onto the rooftop. Arms and legs pumping, he sprinted across the blacktop and, planting his foot on the raised roof edge, swan dived his way to freedom. He let himself fall, cold air blasting his face and neck. Halfway down, he shifted. White scales flashing in the moonlight, muscles stretched to the maximum, asphalt rising fast. Fifty feet from the ground, the wind caught, lifting his bulk as he banked hard, missing the corner of a skyscraper by inches.

Some fast flying and twenty minutes later, he sliced his way through Black Diamond's underground tunnel. Water wicking from his wing tips, he pulled up short and landed on the LZ. As his talons scraped stone, he glanced at Myst's car.

Fuck him, but he'd have to do something about the Honda. Namely, get rid of the thing. He didn't want to see it every time he came home. The reminder of her stay in the lair—of his best friend's love affair with the female and the fact that it was his fault Bastian had lost her—was too much to bear.

With a growl, Rikar flipped his wings. The spikes running down his spine rattled and water droplets flew, reflecting like diamonds in the light of the floating globes. Or like tears. Rikar shook his head, telling himself to get back in the game...that turning his ass around and flying away wasn't the answer.

No way would he pull a disappearing act. He owed Bastian better.

Shifting into human form, Rikar strode toward the lair's magical entrance, wrapping his leathers around his body. The fighting clothes suited his mood, and if he was going to get his ass kicked, he might as well do it right.

Sensation washed over him, pricking his skin as he walked through the solid stone wall and stepped into the corridor beyond. He stood there a moment, a whole lot of nothing ringing in his ears. Which was freaking eerie.

Normally, Sloan cranked up the volume, thumping out tunes in the pre-dawn hours. A little Jay-Z or Tupac. Sometimes Nine Inch Nails or, if he felt like old school, Led Zeppelin. Anything—even pansy-ass Neil Young—would've been better than the ball-busting silence. But no luck there. The lair was quiet as a tomb...or a funeral home.

Too. Perfect.

His hands fisted, Rikar bowed his head and forced his feet toward the clinic door. In contrast to the howling inside his head, the glass sliders opened without a sound, closing the same way behind him. Moving with purpose now, he swept past the examination table and pushed through the double doors at the back of the triage room.

A long hallway lay beyond, stretching out for what seemed like miles. Doors, planted like blank faces in the wall, marched along the corridor's right side. Bastian was laid up behind the first, flat on his back in the big bed, recovering from brutal injury. Man, he'd never seen the male like that, and it scared him.

Which cranked his screw the wrong way.

He couldn't imagine the lair without the big male. Didn't want to, either. But losing his best friend hadn't happened. He'd made sure of it. Hadn't he?

His throat went tight, guilt and loss biting deep.

God, he hadn't wanted to hurt her. Given a choice, he would've saved his friend another way. But wishing and wanting wouldn't change a thing. It was what it was. End of story.

Steeling himself for Bastian's reaction, Rikar pushed the recovery room door open and...

Got a whole lot of nothing except mangled sheets in the center of an empty bed.

What the hell? Yeah, Bastian was a fast healer. They all were, but he shouldn't be on his feet yet. Should still be sleeping, recovering...healing. Then again, Myst's energy was unbelievably powerful. As potent as the she-cop's and...

Whoa. Not going there. Not now. Not ever. He'd done right by Angela and put her to bed. Alone. No way would he allow her to linger in his mind.

A soft sound in the next room brought his head around. Without thinking, he strode toward the connecting door and cracked it open.

Rikar's jaw dropped as he saw the couple on the bed. His mind took a quick snapshot: naked, mouths fused, Myst's hands in Bastian's hair, him between her thighs, her legs wrapped around his hips. Her moans of pleasure. The flex and release of his best friend's spine as he rode his female good and hard.

Holy shit. Holy shit. Holy, holy shit.

Yanking the door closed, Rikar wrenched his hand from the knob as though the thing was on fire and stumbled backward. He took another step. And then another. Feeling like his brain had just exploded inside his skull. When his legs collided with the side of the bed, he sat down, breathing hard, the image of the pair burning a hole in his cerebral cortex.

He scrubbed his hand over the top of his skull trim. "Jesus Christ."

"What's your problem?"

With a full body flinch, Rikar's head snapped to the left.

Sloan stood on the threshold, filling the door to the corridor with his bulk, a tray loaded with food in his hands. "You look like you've been poleaxed."

He felt like it, too. A pickax to the head wouldn't have stunned him more. "Don't go in there."

"They awake?"

"Yeah...and busy."

His buddy's mouth curved up at the corners. "Get an eyeful?"

"Shit," he muttered, trying to exorcise the image of Bastian and...Christ. Like that was going to happen anytime soon. "What the fuck is going on?"

"I don't know, but..." Shaking his head, Sloan rolled into the room, footfalls silent on the linoleum floor. The smell of homemade bread and the sweet tang of Daimler's raspberry jam drifting, he slid the tray onto the table, then turned, linked his arms over his chest, and planted his ass against the stainless steel countertop. "He fed her, Rikar. The second he touched her…man, I've never seen anything like it."

Rikar's brows collided. B had done *what?* Head still ringing from the earlier sneak-and-peek, he threw a load of WTF in Sloan's direction.

"Yeah, I know. It was freaky…the energy going from B to her," Sloan said, the confusion in his tone mixing with awe. "She's totally fine now. I checked them an hour ago. Both were sleeping hard."

"Not anymore." Rikar rubbed the back of his neck. Jesus, B had fed her. *Fed a female.* Totally unheard of, never mind, well…crazy. He didn't know how else to categorize it. It was off the charts…way out in who-the-hell-knew territory.

His brows cranked down hard, Rikar pushed to his feet and headed for the door.

"Good." Shoving away from the table, Sloan followed. Was right on his heels, a large, looming male, as they entered the corridor. "B deserves a little R & R."

Rikar snorted. *R & R?* Not exactly what he would've called it.

"Daimler's rockin' roast beef for the morning meal." Still shadowing him, his buddy punched past the double doors to the clinic a second after Rikar crossed the threshold. "You game?"

He shook his head. "Later."

"Where are you headed?"

"The Archives."

Time for some research. He needed to know what was going on with Bastian and his female. The crazy feeding stuff? Yeah, he so wanted answers, and the tomes—written by Dragonkind's forefathers—were his best bet. Who knew? Maybe he'd get lucky, find the key, and unlock the mystery.

———

With one last body shiver, Myst collapsed on Bastian's chest. Her ear pressed to his heart, she listened to the thump-thump-thump. Her mouth curved as she snuggled in, contentment that had nothing to do with physical pleasure and everything to do with emotional satisfaction stealing through her. She'd ridden him good and hard, had made him beg this time instead of the other way around.

Hmm…what did they say about payback?

Satisfaction widened to a full-on grin.

Bastian's arms came around her, and with a sigh, Myst relaxed into his embrace, wondering at the tally. Was it four or five now? She'd lost count sometime after the second round of lovemaking. She had a good excuse, though. He distracted her completely. Yeah, with loads of mind-numbing sex, but the time spent talking in between, too.

The man liked to ask questions. He wanted to know all about her: her likes and dislikes, interests, fears, about her job, where she lived…absolutely *everything*. Right down to what kind of ice cream she went for at the local parlor. Myst snuggled a bit closer, giving him an affectionate squeeze. The guy was incurably curious. But then, she wasn't much better, asking him all kinds of questions in return.

And he hadn't disappointed.

She now knew his favorite color was purple, he loved spicy food, Rugby was his game, and gangster movies were his favorites. Among other things. And the more she found out about him, the farther she tumbled down the I'm-falling-for-you slope.

Which meant? Grass stains and a whole lot of messy emotional grime.

But, God, he was hot. Macked out, so fierce in bed he made her beg. And she wanted more. Lots more. But... maybe not right now. She was suffering from serious body drain that only a full load of carbohydrates would cure. Yeah, that and a nap.

Myst yawned as Bastian drew lazy circles down her spine. Smoothing his hands over her hips, he cupped her bottom and, with a hum, she arched. Umm, she was sensitive. Her skin on fire from the time spent under and above him, from the exquisite pressure of having him deep inside her.

"God..." She squirmed, nestling her head beneath his chin when he palmed the back of her thighs. His fingers pressed inward and she gasped, muscles quivering as he caressed her with light, teasing strokes. "Are you always like this?"

"Like what?"

"Insatiable."

Laughter rumbled up from his chest, making her smile. "With you? Par for the course, love."

And there it was...the compliment she craved. Stupid. Brainless. Way too needy. But she couldn't help it. She needed to know that she pleased him. That he wanted her even now...with the wild passion fading and the quiet setting in.

Dangerous. Moments like these were dangerous. The in-between time when everything could—and usually did—go wrong.

Slipping sideways, Myst dismounted, pulling free of his body to settle at his side. Her head on his shoulder, arm slung across his chest, leg curled over his thigh, she tried to switch tracks. She didn't want to doubt him or attach any expectations to the last few hours. Disaster lay in that direction, one full of excuses and empty promises. The inevitable "I'll call you tomorrow, baby. We'll do dinner."

She didn't need that crap—or the lies—and Bastian's intensions in the aftermath shouldn't matter. He'd been generous to a fault. Had made her come so many times his skill blew her away. But even as she told her herself that physical pleasure was enough, she didn't believe it. She wanted more. Casual sex wasn't her thing, and would never satisfy her.

Not when it came to Bastian.

Self-preservation urged her to deny it, but what good would that do? Something powerful was going on between them. On her end, at least. Myst felt the connection, the all-encompassing draw as it pulled her into his orbit. Tethered there, she revolved around him, yearning for commitment while simultaneously fearing it.

It was craziness squared. Emotional Russian roulette with all the chambers loaded. No way around it. She was going to take a bullet on this one.

"*Bellmia?*"

Myst swallowed past the lump in her throat. "Yeah?"

"Brace yourself."

"What for?"

She yelped as Bastian flipped and the room pinwheeled. One up and over. A second time with the speed roll. The flash of ceiling-mattress, ceiling-mattress was all she saw over his shoulder. Like a circus performer, he dismounted, feet landing on the floor, arms locked around her.

She sucked in a quick breath. "Holy crap, you—"

He cut her off with a quick bend and toss. She gasped as her abdomen connected with his shoulder. Hanging upside down, butt in the air, and hair a tangled mess in her face, she growled at him.

"Shower time, love." His arm curled around the backs of her thighs, he caressed her bottom with his free hand, then gave her a gentle slap.

"Hey!" She twisted to get a feel for his trajectory. She spotted the closed door across the room. "And what? You couldn't just ask me?"

"More fun this way."

"Caveman."

"Baby, you have no idea." Turning his head, he nipped her hip.

And oh, boy. Long live the Neanderthal.

She caught a glimpse of white tile as the bathroom door swung open. Without slowing, he crossed the threshold. The water came on without him touching it, but she didn't care. Magic. No magic. What did it matter? All she wanted was for him to unleash his inner caveman and...

Oh, God, that was good.

She parted her thighs a little more, moaning as he stroked her with his fingers. He went deep, touching just... the right...spot...and stepped into the shower enclosure. Warm spray rushing over her spine, he withdrew from her core and swung her off his shoulder. Her feet didn't hit the floor, though. Between one breath and the next, he wrapped her legs around his hips, pressed her back against the tile wall and—

"Oh, yes...pleeease," she whispered, tilting her hips into his, welcoming his possession.

Thrusting deep, he took her mouth, flicking her with his tongue, setting a pace that drove her wild. But despite her impatience, he kept it slow, circled deep, heightening her pleasure with each stroke, delivering his taste, making her gasp. Her hands clenched in his hair, a second away from begging, she sucked on his tongue. Yum. He tasted like a man should: dark spice, erotic heat, hardcore domination in each stroke and release. And as his skin slid against hers, Myst yearned for more than just the physical. She wanted everything, the best kind of forever with the man in her arms.

Orgasm came fast, rushing her into ecstasy. She sobbed his name, shuddered around him, reveling in the ache deep inside her. He upped the pace, hips rolling into hers. She held on tight, rode the wave, and whispered to him, telling him he was beautiful, that she couldn't get enough, how much she needed him. His breath hitched and, muscles flexing beneath her hands, he dropped his head to her shoulder and throbbed deep inside her.

A while later, he raised his head. His green eyes shimmering, he kissed her gently and pulled free, setting her feet on the tiled floor. She swayed. He smiled, snaked an arm around her to hold her steady, and reached for the soap. One last kiss, and he started to wash her. With a satisfied sigh, she let him, enjoying the soapy glide of his hands and the fresh scent of Dove in the air. Thorough as always, he didn't miss a spot, massaging her sore muscles, working closer to her center until he touched the sensitive flesh between her thighs.

When she flinched, Bastian frowned. "You're sore."

"Only a little." Running her hands down his back, she licked a water droplet from his skin.

He nipped her earlobe. "Forgive me. I was too rough with you."

"No...you were perfect."

He grinned. "And you...exquisite. But no more today. You need time to recover."

Circling with gentle fingers, he rinsed her clean then stepped back to turn the soap on himself. Unable to help herself, she watched him, tracking the southbound suds across his chest and six-pack to...oh, man. He was beautifully made, so strong in all the right places.

"No fair, *bellmia*. You keep looking at me like that and..." His gaze glowed as he watched her admire him. The connection between them sparked, raising awareness until she could hardly breathe. Crazy. Totally nuts, but tender or not, she wanted him again. Reading her right, he shook his head, leaning around her to turn off the water. "Now, who's the insatiable one?"

"Can't help it," she said, wanting to chase the droplets across his chest with her tongue. "You're so fricking hot."

He laughed. "Later. Rest and recover, *bellmia*. You'll need all your strength for tonight."

Picking her up, he opened the glass door and stepped onto a bath mat. Chilly air raised goose bumps on her wet skin and, with a shiver—and absolutely no shame—she snuggled into Bastian's chest. He snagged a towel from the metal wall rack, wrapping her up before he grabbed another and went to work on her hair. And like a four-year-old, she let him. It felt so good to be taken care of...to be the recipient instead of the giver for a change.

"Bastian?" Fighting the hypnotic pull of his fingers in her hair, she stifled a yawn. "What's tonight?"

He gave her a sharp look of surprise. "Nothing."

Myst stilled, his quick denial raising her radar. A guy's "nothing" was the equivalent of a woman's "fine." Not good on so many levels, and as she stared up into his face, the link she felt between them flared, gifting her with insight, telling her he wasn't being honest, that he wanted her question buried six feet under. The rushing sensation intensified into a warning. She tugged at the towel, wrapping the fluffy terry cloth under her arms and over her breasts like armor.

What to do? Let it go or confront him?

She didn't want to push, but it wasn't in her nature to ignore important issues. She was a take-the-bull-by-the-horns kind of girl, and if she wanted something permanent with Bastian, she needed to stay true to herself. No hiding—not for her, not for him.

Reaching out, she spread her fingers on the damp skin over his heart. "Bastian...please, just tell me."

He shifted his weight from one foot to the other, like he was suddenly uncomfortable in his own skin. A muscle twitched in his jaw, and he said, "The Meridian realigns."

"What's that?"

"A biannual occurrence. It's an...important event for my kind." His fingers flexed in her hair a second before he let her go and stepped back to snag another towel.

She studied him, trying to get a bead on his mood. "Like a celebration?"

"I'll explain everything later." Wrapping the towel around his waist, he turned toward the door. "I called Daimler. He's coming with clean clothes for you."

Uh-huh. There it was...the deflection. The 180-degree turn in the distraction department. But man, it was effective. The topic switch up worked, rocketing her into how-did-he-do-that territory.

How had he called Daimler? There were no telephones anywhere she could see, and she'd been with Bastian the whole time. Okay...admittedly, she'd been in a pleasure coma most of the afternoon, but still, she would've noticed something as significant as a cell phone.

"We don't use phones, Myst," he said over his shoulder. "You won't find any in the lair."

No phones? Crap. There went plan B. She wouldn't be calling Tania anytime soon.

Padding on bare feet, she adjusted her towel and followed his retreat into the bedroom. "Okay. Then how did you—"

"We call it mind-speak." He dropped the towel, and she got a terrific shot of his ass before...

Her mouth dropped open. Between one breath and the next, he was dressed: leather pants, black muscle shirt, big boots on his feet.

He rolled his shoulders, his expression so serious she got the impression he was worried about her reaction. "We have a few tricks like that, *bellmia*."

No kidding. The ability to get dressed with a thought was, well...cool. And weird. But she must be getting used to all the weirdness. His ability didn't bother her all that much. She knew he was different, had accepted the magic as part of the man. "Can you do that for me? Save Daimler the trip?"

His mouth curved as the tension left his shoulders. Crossing to where she stood, he pulled her in his arms. Giving her a gentle squeeze, he murmured, "You are an outstanding female."

Her heart flip-flopped, somersaulting inside her chest. Myst slapped it into submission. She was already in enough trouble here. No sense upping the stakes into idiot territory and translating his praise into "I love you."

"I have to go." Dipping his chin, he kissed the top of her head. "Wait here for Daimler. Eat something. You need your strength. I'll see you at the evening meal. All right?"

No. Not all right.

She wanted him to stay with her. Which made her let him go. Clinging to him wasn't a good idea. Not even close to practical. He couldn't spend all his time with her, but as he headed for the door, her heart didn't listen to reason and hung onto him. Myst let it go, knowing she would never get it back.

An awful hollowness expanded inside her chest. This wasn't like her. The fall-in-love, needy, clingy crap was someone else's MO. She was the smart, practical one: strong, independent, tough. Raking her wet hair away from her face, Myst felt the pressure build inside her. It pushed at her boundaries, threatening to geyser into an emotional explosion.

She needed space. And clarity. A little fresh air—some time outside in the garden—was a definite must. Otherwise, she'd lose her mind like she'd already lost her heart to a man who didn't love her in return.

Chapter Twenty-nine

With a growl, Bastian slammed the thick volume closed, resisting the urge to hurl the fucker across the library. He punched the tabletop instead, leaving a dent the size of his fist in the steel top. As metal clanged, reverberating off floor-to-ceiling bookcases and polished concrete floors, he shoved his chair back and stood.

Legs spread and feet planted, he snarled at the stacks of leather-bound tomes. Useless. All of them.

None held the answer he sought. Jesus. He'd left Myst—in nothing but a towel—for this? Abandoned his mate to spend a day alone in the lair while he'd come to the Archives on a Hail Mary mission to find answers that would never be his.

He'd had such high hopes, but found nothing but dead ends. And time was running out.

Hanging his head, he ran his hands through his hair. He laced his fingers and pressed down on the back of his head, trying to keep it together. His neck muscles stretched, screaming as the knots bracketing his spine got yanked. Bastian welcomed the discomfort. It distracted him, stalled the pressure that was turning his skull into a pressure cooker.

Imminent explosion. He was a nanosecond away from total meltdown.

He couldn't forestall the inevitable. A future in which he didn't hurt Myst. The answers he needed to keep her safe didn't exist, and the Meridian would realign in...

Releasing the hold on his neck, he glanced at the clock across the room. In less than six hours.

"Christ." His voice bounced against concrete and steel, playing ping-pong in the silence.

He already felt twitchy, the need for his female like poison in his veins: pervasive. Incurable. Catastrophic. He was staring down the barrel of a loaded gun with no way of avoiding the bullet. But worse? He was the one with his finger on the trigger.

Resentment boiled up until Bastian tasted it on the back of his tongue. There was no way to negotiate it. The Meridian was a force of nature, a phenomenon his magic couldn't touch, and like all of Dragonkind, his mating instinct would kick in the moment the energy bands merged. The biannual occurrence created a twelve-hour window, one in which his body shifted into high gear with singular purpose.

To spawn the next generation of strong sons.

Necessary to carry their race into the future. Hell to a bonded male in love with his female.

Bastian curled his hands into fists. "Jesus fucking Christ."

Wasn't life grand?

The hungering was the reason he and his warriors had Daimler lock them in the vault twice a year—at the spring and fall realignments. Seven hundred feet below the surface, the crypt was a work of art. A steel cage with electronic locks surrounded by miles of hardcore granite. And inside? Full living quarters kitted out with the best of everything.

Usually, the vault worked like a charm. Kept the Nightfuries contained, giving them the space they needed to control the hunger as the energy surge flipped the fertility switch and the meter started running.

Not this realignment, though.

Masterpiece though it was, Bastian wasn't sure the vault would hold him. He wanted Myst too much and would tear the reinforced steel apart to reach her.

So, where did that leave him?

Could he fight the pull—his very DNA? Find a way to dampen the hungering and his need, make it somehow manageable?

As restlessness fired up his neuro pathways, Bastian paced. His boots thudded against the floor, echoing in the quiet, bringing small comfort, but no relief. Round and round he went, circling the table in the center of the room, looking for a solution.

Maybe if he locked himself down. Got Daimler to tranquilize his ass and turn him into a zoo exhibit...

Yeah, that might work. No guarantees, though. He was a strong male—his magic potent both in and out of dragon form—but a terrible plan was better than nothing. It was worth a shot to keep Myst safe and—

"Knock-knock."

Without slowing his roll, Bastian glanced toward the door.

Rikar stood on the threshold, shoulders filling the space between the jambs, a slim leather-bound book in his hands. "What...don't feel like playing?"

Bastian's eyes narrowed. "Who the fuck's there?"

"Your sorry-as-shit best friend." Pale eyes locked on Bastian's face, Rikar stood tall—boots planted, spine straight, shoulders back—like he was preparing for something unpleasant. Probably a good bet, given Bastian's level of pissed off.

Swinging left, Bastian strode past tall bookcases jammed with thick volumes, moving away from Rikar. Pacing toward his friend wasn't a good idea. He wanted to hit the male so badly his knuckles ached.

"Look, B. All I ask is that you hear me out." His expression grave, Rikar strode into the library. As he slid the journal onto the table, he said, "I offer you *grevaiz*, Commander."

"In here?"

"We can go to the LZ if you want. More room out there."

Bastian clenched his hands. Great. Just what he needed. A *grevaiz*.

The ritual was time honored, a warriors' tradition. An offering of first strike when one male had wronged another. A way for the offended to be appeased, and the offender, forgiven. The rite supposedly allowed healing, but as he stared at Rikar, his anger faded. He didn't want to hurt his best friend. Yeah, yesterday he would've taken the shot and skinned the male alive. Right now? He needed his buddy like a lifeline.

"She's all right, Rikar," he said, flexing his fists to release the tension. It didn't work. He still ached, inside and out. "Fully recovered."

"I heard and…I'm glad. But…" A furrow between his brows, Rikar stared at the floor, offering what he believed he owed. "I still offer first strike."

"I don't want it." Much as it killed him to admit it, Bastian said, "I would've done the same to save you. Now, enough with the bullshit. I need your help."

Rikar tipped his chin. "Shoot."

"Tonight...when the Meridian realigns, I want you to tranq me. Daimler's getting a truck load of the drug and—"

"No fucking way."

Bastian glared at his friend. "You *owe* me this. I don't want to hurt her, but I won't be able to stay away."

"And what? You think the vault's going to hold you?"

"It'll work. All I need—"

"Even pumped full of drugs, B, you'll get out." Rikar crossed his arms over his chest and shook his head. "And fuck up the rest of us."

Hell. He hadn't thought of that. If he hammered a hole in the vault, he would provide his warriors an escape hatch. And where would they go? Into the city—juiced with need and hungry as hell—to find the nearest female. With a curse, Bastian kicked a chair out of his path and completed another circuit around the room.

"You can't avoid it, Bastian. She's here. You've bonded with her. There's no escape for you." he said, honest as always.

Stopping in front of a bookcase, Bastian grabbed the shelf at eye level and leaned in, the pain of circumstance tearing him apart. "What am I going to do? How can I keep her safe?"

A chair scraped along the floor behind him. "Come and sit down, B. I think I found something that will help."

Taking a shaky breath, he pushed away from the bookcase and approached his best friend. "What did you find?"

Rikar pointed at the journal he'd set on the table. "Found it in the vault...mixed in with frickin' Charles Dickens. Interesting story in there about a Dragon Queen."

"A what?"

"Yeah, pretty cool stuff." Knocking on the red cover with his knuckles, Rikar parked his ass in the chair opposite him. "Don't know who wrote it…don't know if it's true, but it might explain the connection you share with Myst. Why you were able to feed her."

"Sloan," Bastian murmured.

His best friend nodded. "He filled me in. Now, he's looking through the computerized annals, searching for more info. Maybe he'll get lucky and find something, but the journal? Christ, I'm gonna kick the Scottish pack's ass for keeping *this* from us."

The Scottish pack? Those bastards were a tight unit. Closed to the outside world, they didn't like outsiders—dragon or humankind—and sure as shit didn't share information.

Bastian grabbed the chair he'd booted out of his way and sat. He tipped his chin in his buddy's direction. "Hit me."

"One of their females gave birth to three sons. All sired by the same male…the pack's commander."

Three. Twins were rare, but…

"Triplets?"

Rikar shook his head. "The first two were born seven years apart. The middle and youngest son…ten years between them."

His brow drawn tight, Bastian stared at his friend, not understanding. He heard the words, but their meaning couldn't be. Females died on the birthing bed without exception. Myst's patient—and the bloody mess she'd walked into—was proof positive of that. "It can't…how… Jesus, the female survived?"

"Yeah. And according to this? She lived nearly three hundred years, dying when her mate did...an instant kind of thing. He was killed in battle. She died within minutes of him. In their lair fifty miles away." His friend leaned forward, bringing their heads closer together. "Christ, Bastian. I think the two were energy-fused...like you and Myst."

He shook his head. "It's a myth."

"Is it?" His eyes like blue flames, Rikar leveled him with his gaze. "Myths are formed around kernels of truth. You're connected to her...have been from the moment you saw her in that kitchen." He tapped the book again and continued, "How would we know whether it's true or not? Our kind are notorious for the hit and run...love 'em and leave 'em fast. We never stay long enough to create a lasting bond. I think what you've found with Myst is so rare that the knowledge of it has been lost over time. The few who knew failed to pass it on."

"Fucking Scots," he growled, feeling like he'd collided with a concrete wall, skull first. Shoving a stack of tomes aside, Bastian planted his elbows on the tabletop and fisted his hands in his hair. He pulled at the strands, battling the ache and the unknown. If what his friend said was true...if the theory held? God. It opened up a whole new world—the possibility of keeping Myst in his life. "Are you sure about this? You've got to be—"

"Shit, B." Reaching out, Rikar wrapped his hand around Bastian's wrist and squeezed until Bastian raised his head and met his gaze. "You can feed her energy...healing energy. Do you know what that means? With you present, there's a good chance she'll survive birthing your son."

A *good* chance. Not a 100 percent one. "When did this happen? How long ago did the Dragon Queen die?"

"The journal dates from over a hundred years ago."

"Are her sons still alive?"

"The two eldest died in battle with their sire, but the third might still be alive."

"Name?"

Releasing his wrist, Rikar grabbed the book off the table edge. Leather creaked as he cracked the spine and flipped through the pages. Near the back, he pulled out a long piece of paper folded into four equal parts. He unfolded it like an accordion, and Bastian caught a glimpse of black ink sprawled into the branches of a family tree.

Rikar traced his finger over the bottom half. He stopped on a name. "Forge."

Bastian sat back in his chair, his mind churning over a plan.

"What are you thinking?" Rikar asked. "The Scottish pack won't answer a summons. And no way we can get to Scotland without some serious—"

"We don't need to jump the pond." The thick burl of the Highlands ringing inside his head, he replayed a recent conversation. "You know the fucker in the rail yard...the Razorback rocking fire-acid?"

"Yeah."

"From the Scottish pack."

The corners of Rikar's mouth curved. "We need to cage him. Find out what he knows."

"Um-hmm." Bastian stared at the rows of books over his friend's shoulder, seeing them, but not really. His mind was fully engaged, turning over the plan, looking at it from all angles. He needed to clip Deep Purple's wings. The only way to do that? Reel him into the kill box...close enough to zap him with some serious voltage and lock him down.

No easy feat. The enemy male was smart. Caging him would take real effort and tons of planning. Yeah, that and time. Something he didn't have. At least, not until tomorrow night when the realignment was over.

"So, we bait him." Slouching in his chair, Rikar crossed his ankle over his knee and turned the journal over in his hands. "Can you get him in the pipe? Will he even come?"

"He'll come." Chasing an itch, Bastian rubbed his shoulder blades against the backrest, his strategy crystallizing. "He won't be able to resist. We've got something he wants."

"What?"

"His son."

Not that he would give Gregor Mayhem to the male—to a freaking Razorback. No way. Never mind that the Nightfury code of honor forbade it. He was more concerned with his mate. Myst would skin him alive, and…well, well, well, look at him go. He was suddenly into pleasing a female. Especially given the chance he might get to keep her for a lifetime.

Yeah. Hope sprang eternal and all that jazz.

But even as Bastian made light of it—was afraid to believe she would survive birthing his son—he prayed it was true. *Please, God, be merciful.* He wasn't asking for much. One simple thing. That's all he wanted. A family: a mate for him, a mother for his son.

Clinging to the hope, Bastian pushed to his feet. He needed to see Myst. He didn't have much time, and she deserved every bit of his before the realignment. A real date. A shared meal…or something. Anything to make her feel special.

As he rounded the end of the table, Rikar handed him the journal. Smooth, red leather slid across his palm. He

stared at it a moment, knowing he'd read it front to back—
in search of more hope—before he laid Myst down tonight.
Gripping the slim volume, he glanced sideways at his best
friend, a brow raised in question.

Keeping pace, Rikar strode with him toward the door.
"The rest of us will be locked down in an hour. You'll have
the lair to yourself. Have fun tonight."

"Asshole."

"You know it." Slapping him on the shoulder, Rikar followed him into the hallway. "Relax, B. Even out of control in
the hungering, you won't hurt her."

Bastian nodded, praying his friend was right, but not
really believing it. He had control issues around Myst. And
that was before the hungering got ahold of him. He'd never
been with a female when the Meridian surged. Had no idea
what he'd do...or how rough he'd get when need grabbed
him by the balls.

Chapter Thirty

Her plan got shot to hell right out of the gate. Myst shook her head, marveling at Daimler's cleverness. The elf was magic in the distraction department...a lifelong member of "Oh, I need your help with just one more thing." And she'd fallen for it. Had spent hours searching Web sites, scouring the Internet for baby stuff.

Now, Gregor had more paraphernalia than was strictly legal.

Well, all right. Setting her angel up with the best had been fun, but the unfortunate causality in the whole mess? Her alone time. She hadn't gotten any yet, but things were looking up. Daimler had left five minutes ago.

Hallelujah.

Time to snoop.

Careful to keep her movements steady, she shifted Gregor in her arms. Fast asleep after his bottle, he snuffled then settled, his cheek against her shoulder as she crossed the nursery. With gentle hands, she laid him in his crib and adjusted his blanket beneath his chin.

"Sleep well, angel," she murmured before snagging the baby monitor off the nightstand.

Tiptoeing across the room, she entered the corridor on the fly. She didn't have much time. Daylight was fading, and the Nightfuries would roll out of bed soon, beating feet toward the kitchen and Daimler's rack of lamb. The elf had hemmed and hawed for the better part of the morning, trying to decide what spices to put on the damn thing. Now she could smell them, the delicious mix of flavors making her mouth water.

Not wanting to bump into the chef extraordinaire, she headed in the opposite direction. No way did she want to be anywhere near the kitchen. Bastian would no doubt show up there along with his crew, and right now? She didn't want to see him.

He'd lied to her.

All right. Maybe calling him a liar was a stretch. But crap, not much of one. She kept replaying the time they'd spent together—avoiding the sex, because…God…remembering the way he touched her sent her into fricking orbit—and she realized that he'd left a lot out. Case in point? The Meridian. What was it exactly? What did it do, how did it operate, why did Dragonkind need it? But the big one, the question to end all questions? How did the Meridian involve her?

Deep down, she knew she was mixed up in the middle of it.

Her first clue had been Bastian's reaction. He'd avoided the issue, giving her token answers. And as he skirted the subject like a pro, her BS meter had thrown all kinds of red flags. Now her conspiracy theorist was neck deep in what-if land, kicking out theories that made her doubt everything.

Strange, but when she was with Bastian the voice in the back of her head went silent. The second he left her alone? *Wham.* Uncertainty came rushing back.

Raking her hand through her hair, Myst jogged up a set of shallow stairs. Her flip-flops clacked on the marble treads, echoing in the quiet as she paused under a huge archway. Her breath caught, the magnificence of the space taking her by surprise. Perfectly round; the room boasted a domed ceiling painted with a fresco. Dragon warriors took flight from its center, the colorful array of strength and power flashing above the bright light of the rotunda. The curved walls were similarly adorned, each panel between the marble half columns showcasing a single dragon. She recognized Bastian right off, the midnight blue scales and green eyes a dead giveaway. A white dragon with gold flecks occupied the spot beside him, the pale blue eyes telling her it was Rikar.

Remarkable.

Awe made her shiver and, as the fine hairs on her nape rose, she crossed the space, examining the mosaic-tiled floor. The intricate pattern swirled, forming a crest of some kind. A foreign language surrounded it, curling around the emblem's outer edge. Myst crouched to stroke one of the letters with her fingertip. After tracing the loop, she stared at the fresco depicting Bastian.

God, he was beautiful—in and out of dragon form—and no matter how hard she tried to deny it, she yearned for him. Totally crazy. Completely stupid. But true in every way that mattered.

With a sigh, Myst pushed to her feet and got herself moving. Three archways—identical to the one she'd just passed through—stood ready to take her deeper into Black Diamond. She chose the one across from her and, after trotting down another set of stairs, entered a large living room.

The ceiling soared twenty feet above the space, looming over furniture groupings. One entire wall contained windows, the brilliance of the setting sun muted by heavily tinted glass. Myst skirted the end of the pool table, walking past the cue racks to run her hand along the back of the couch. Butter-soft leather sliding against her palm, she approached the fireplace. Double-sided, the hearthstone rose in a sweep toward the ceiling. Space flowed on either side of its massive foundation, creating two equal passageways into the dining room beyond.

Jackpot. The French doors leading out to the garden. She'd come full circle, slipping beneath Daimler's radar.

Tiptoeing past the fireplace, she hid behind its stone facade, using it for cover as she peeked into the dining room. From her vantage point, she had a clear view of the archway leading into the kitchen. No elf in sight. Thank God. So far so good.

The smell of roasting lamb in the air, Myst prayed for quiet floorboards and, skirting the enormous table, made a beeline for the double glass doors. Outside, the trees swayed, waving her along, making Myst imagine the colorful leaves acting as lookouts in her personal getaway movie.

Except, she wasn't trying to get away.

She'd given Bastian her word. Three days. He'd asked for three days, and foolish or not, she intended to give them to him. But as she opened the door and stepped out onto the patio, a pang of anxiety unfurled in her belly. This wasn't betrayal. She wasn't being unfaithful to Bastian—or her promise—by being outside the lair.

Myst frowned. Right?

Her feet rooted to the flagstone, Myst rubbed her upper arms, fighting the urge to go back inside and confess her sins. Which was just plain crazy. All she wanted was some fresh air, a little time alone to think and...to locate the garage.

And there it was, an honest thought at last.

Yeah, and she'd accused Bastian of lying. Her conscience told her she wasn't any better. Despite her promise, she'd explored the house, searching for the best way out. Her actions spoke more of preparation than curiosity and, standing in the shadow of Black Diamond, she faced an inescapable truth.

She had one foot in and the other out.

Half of her wanted to commit and stay with Bastian while the other half itched to run. Hiding would be easier but more painful. No matter how she sliced it, Myst knew she would miss Bastian—her craving for him was too hard to ignore. Somehow, she'd fallen hard, gotten in too deep to ever get out unscathed.

A gust of wind tugged at her, playing with her hair as she looked to the sky. A storm was coming. The fury of it didn't surprise her. About the same time each year, Seattle suffered through a doozy and the cleanup afterward. Downed trees and severed electrical lines were par for the course, and the least of the problem. She always felt supercharged during Mother Nature's fantastic crash-bang show: unable to stay still, like she had an overabundance of energy and no viable outlet.

Usually, she did something stupid.

Last year, she and Tania had gone running, a full-on sprint fest through rain-soaked streets. Trotting down the patio's steps, she walked into the garden, taking the pathway to her right, wondering what Tania would do without her this year. Her best friend was high-strung, a little neurotic at the best of times. But during what they'd come to call the Fall Storm, Tania got so edgy she was prone to idiocy.

She needed to call her friend, if only to hear her voice and make sure she was all right. But Bastian had told her the truth about the phones. In the hour that she'd searched, she hadn't found a single one.

Following the dirt path, she brushed her hands over some leafy ferns and walked parallel to the house. Black Diamond was a monster, a timber-framed structure that went on and on. The wing she could see sprawled out, taking up ground space with rustic majesty. She kept an eye on it, looking for a way to skirt its perimeter and find the front of the house. She'd already tried the front door. Talk about Fort Knox...the thing had more deadbolts than a maximum security prison. Ones that didn't budge, no matter how much muscle she put into it.

A few minutes later, she found what she sought: a break in the shrubbery and a narrow trail along the side of the lair. She studied the thorny ground cover and then glanced at the flip-flops on her feet. Work boots would've been better, but beggars couldn't be choosers. Barefoot, it would have to be.

Holding her footwear in one hand, she stepped carefully, tiptoeing through the bramble, ignoring the small scrapes against her skin. With one last hop, she landed on the trail and peeked around the side of the house.

Bingo. An outbuilding dead ahead.

The smell of rain blew in as thunder rumbled and the wind picked up, tugging at her clothes. Myst ignored the warning and, slipping her footwear back on, trotted down the path toward the building. *Please, let it be the garage.* She needed to know where it was...and the kind of vehicles housed inside.

As she came even with the front, lightning forked overhead. The hair on her nape lifted, sensation tingling down her spine, gravel crunching beneath her feet. She moved right, running across the driveway and...

Thank God. Big, industrial-sized doors.

Set in a row, seven garage doors stood shoulder to shoulder, waiting patiently to be opened and, as one second ticked into the next, Myst tasted freedom. It was a moment away: the simple press of a button, a quick search for the keys. And standing in the growing darkness, she imagined the steering wheel in her hands and the roar of the engine as she drove away from Bastian's home. A heavy weight settled on her chest, the pressure vise-like and painful.

Moisture pricked the corners of her eyes. How could this have happened? She'd finally found the right man, the perfect one for her and...Goddamn it. Fate left her with a terrible choice. Give him up and reclaim her life. Or stay and lose everything.

Myst hung her head. *Guess he wasn't so perfect, after all.*

The soft scrape of footfalls sounded behind her.

With a sigh, Myst raised her head to stare up at the storm-swept sky and watched the angry clouds tumble. She should've paid better attention. The tingle she'd felt earlier wasn't storm-driven. It was about Bastian, and the fact she could track him when he was near.

She glanced over her shoulder. Serious green eyes met hers, unraveling her one thread at a time.

"What are you doing out here, Myst?" His tone was soft, barely rising above the wind.

"Exploring."

"Are you done?"

When she nodded, he held out his hand, palm up, inviting her to come to him. She stayed still a moment, holding his gaze—hesitating—then gave in. She wanted him too much. But as she slid her hand into his much larger one, she called herself a fool. Her love affair with Bastian wouldn't end well and still, like a lamb to the slaughter, she went to him without a fight.

———

Standing on the threshold between the French doors, Bastian scanned the dining room. The thing was lit up, candlelight bouncing off polished silver and hand-cut crystal. A stark contrast from the beer-drinking, trash-talking poker game the table saw every Saturday afternoon. Usually, the place smelled like a locker room and the cheezies Wick liked to munch on while he kicked their asses at five-card stud.

Daimler had outdone himself. Yet again. But then, the *Numbai* was all about pleasing those he served. Well that, and food.

The male never missed a beat in the kitchen. Was always experimenting, serving new dishes, everything gourmet-style. Which was a good thing. Daimler kept the males of the lair satisfied in the eats department while making sure each got the nutrition he needed to stay in prime fighting shape. Although, Bastian could do without the curlicue garnishes. A steak was a steak. All that other crap was just window dressing.

Tonight, though, Bastian appreciated Daimler's flare for high drama. The male might drive him crazy with marzipan flowers on cupcakes, but he knew how to throw together an intimate evening for two.

His fingers still laced with Myst's, he gave her a gentle squeeze. "Hungry?"

"I could eat." Her breath caught as she got a load of the table. "Wow."

Untangling her hand from his, she stepped around him. While he mourned the loss of her heat, her gaze skimmed over the candelabras, pale linens, and the two place settings arranged at one end of the long table. Drifting to a stop, she cupped the back of an upholstered chair. Silence stretched, drawing him tight before she turned to look at him.

Wariness in her gaze, she asked, "Wine me, dine me?"

"I thought we could share a meal."

"You want a news flash?"

"Sure," he murmured, watching her closely, trying to gauge her mood. Pensive. Too quiet. On edge. Not exactly the reaction he imagined when he asked Daimler to set up the romantic evening.

"All this?" One hand picking at the piping on top of the chair, she gestured toward the table with the other. "You don't need any of it, Bastian. I'm a sure thing."

Her admission should've pleased him. Bastian found himself worried instead. Her confusion clouded the air around her, warning him better than words. She was thinking about running. He didn't blame her. The world he lived in would never be easy for her. It was isolating for a female, a strange place with different rules—and Myst was essentially alone in it. No other females to talk to or spend time with... no one to help guide her from old life to new.

A pang hit him chest level. "And that scares you... belonging to me?"

"Yes...no...I don't know," she said in a small voice, sounding lost.

"It's all right to be unsure, Myst," he said, needing to reassure her. What they shared *was* strange, and as he moved away from the door toward her, Bastian struggled to find the right words to tell her that he understood. "The feeling between us is unexpected. A little overwhelming. For me, too."

Her grip on the chair tightened as he stopped behind her, close but not touching. When she shivered, he lost the battle. His urge to comfort her was too strong. He needed her in his arms. Murmuring to her in Dragonese, he used his voice to soothe and drew her in, wrapped his arms around her, fitting her back to his front.

A shudder rolled through her into him. "You've never..."

"No." Dipping his head, he burrowed into her hair, filling his lungs with her scent. "There has never been another for me. Only you."

"Okay. That's good. Really good, but...what now? I mean...God." The words came out on a quiver, giving voice to her panic. Like a living thing, she vibrated, on the verge of bolting. "It's only been four days. *Four days!*"

"I know."

"I mean...jeez. So little time and I'm..." With an abrupt shift, she turned in his arms. She shook her head, unease in her eyes as she searched his. "Half nuts. A giant mess over you. Totally wrecked. It can't be—"

"Normal? No, love, it isn't."

Thank God. He loved the way he affected her, and what he felt for her in return. The sheer strength of their bond empowered him, gave hope where none existed before. And as he held her close, he wanted to sink deep and wallow in it. He needed to show her that what they shared was right and true...meant to be on a cosmic level that crossed borders and trumped species.

"What we share...the connection we have?" Keeping one arm around her, he cupped her face, brushing her skin with featherlight strokes. "It's powerful and very rare."

A furrow between her fine brows, she stared up at him. In her gaze he saw everything he'd felt over the past day: confusion, curiosity, fear of the unknown. And yet, even though she was afraid, she accepted his touch, waiting for him to continue. She wanted the truth. He needed to tell her, but...

Where should he start?

At the beginning? Near the end?

Emotion wasn't his strength. Yeah, he felt it, but he'd always kept it caged, avoiding vulnerability like an axe to the head. But with her in his arms and a pleading light in her eyes, he couldn't deny her. She deserved the best of him.

Taking a deep breath, Bastian reached for his magic. It came when called, flaring along his spine and in his fingertips. Holding her gaze, he tapped into her energy, connecting them on the emotional plane. There, he laid himself bare, allowing her to see everything: his love and respect for her, all the need, want, and hope for their future.

Her breath caught and tears filled her eyes. "I see you."

Bastian's heart stopped mid-beat, just hung inside his chest. *I see you.* English words with Dragonkind meaning. In the tradition of his kind, the words carried ancient weight: It was an acknowledgement of worth, respect, and undying devotion.

I see you.

The truest compliment one could give to another.

The question was...how had she known? Connecting them emotionally was one thing, her ability to read his mind quite another. But her acknowledgement wasn't random. He saw the understanding in her eyes and...Jesus. Was the energy-fuse that strong?

The possibility blew his mind, sent him reeling in directions he hadn't considered.

"*Kalim, bellmia,*" he said, speaking to her in his own language, returning the sentiment without hesitation. "I see you, too."

She nodded, the tension leaving her on a long exhale. "Bastian, will you do something for me?"

"What?"

"Be honest with me. Tell me everything I need to know to understand you. Your kind. The world you live in." A worried look on her face, she chewed on her bottom lip. His gaze dropped to her mouth, and...oh, baby. What a distraction. It sent him on a mental side trip, making him remember how good she tasted. How badly he wanted inside her again as she said, "I can't stay here without understanding what it will mean for me. There can't be any secrets between us."

Bastian frowned. No secrets? Talk about a foreign concept. Dragonkind was secretive by nature...needed to be to survive in a world where humans outnumbered dragons by thousands to one. But Myst was his mate. He wanted to trust her. To share his life. To open his heart without fear or reservation.

Question was...would she want him after he told her about the hungering? About his fertility cycle, the uncontrollable need, and the risk to her?

Fuck Rikar and this theory.

Nothing was certain. Except one thing. Myst would run from him if she knew the entire truth.

So where did that leave him? Cooked. Yeah, that about summed it up.

"Bastian?"

"Share a meal with me, *bellmia*," he said, stalling for time. "Let me feed you as a male should and...I'll explain."

At least, a little. Mostly all, but...some truth was better than none. Right?

Closing his eyes, Bastian buried his face in her hair and, breathing her in, hugged her tight. God forgive him. He was selfish. The lowest of the low to take what should be hers by right to give.

But complete honesty was a commodity he couldn't afford. Not tonight.

Not until the hungering passed and he settled onto an even keel again.

———

The chocolate soufflé looked delicious. Too bad Myst couldn't taste a thing.

Despite Daimler's talent and the gourmet meal, everything tasted like sawdust. Her taste buds had gone on strike, picketing the entrance to her mouth: little signs raised, jostling for airtime, lobbying for another dish altogether. One that started with a B. And ended with an N.

Myst swore she could hear the little buggers chanting... give us a B. A. S. T. I. A and N!

Shifting in her seat, she searched for relief from the physical discomfort and blocked out the mental noise. For the fifth freaking time. The insistent voice occupying the back half of her brain yelled louder. Her heart revved up another beat, thump-thump-thumping against the wall of her ribcage. She fidgeted some more and twirled her fork in her fingers, watching the silver sparkle in the candlelight.

God, what was wrong with her? Feeling supercharged by the Fall Storm was one thing. The restlessness she understood. But the crazy sexual need?

She'd never felt anything like it. And it was getting worse.

Each moment walked her closer to meltdown. The urgent rush buzzed in her veins, making her hypersensitive, imprisoning her on lust's razor-sharp edge. She tried to shut it out and be sensible. But fantasy wouldn't leave her alone. Was it normal to envision leaping over fine china to wrap herself around Bastian?

Her eyes half closed, Myst nearly moaned as the image flooded her mind. Hmm, that would feel so good: sitting in his lap, him deep inside her while she stroked his tongue with her own.

Heat bloomed between her legs. She squirmed again, accusing herself of nymphomania. But, man, there was just something about Bastian. She was hyperacute, aware of him on a level she'd never experienced before and…

Yeah, so much for restraint. She was officially pathetic. Had ticked all the boxes on her love-struck stupid list. Now, she was falling down the rabbit hole with no way of ever climbing back out.

Terrific. Just…peachy.

Camouflaging another squirm, she stabbed her soufflé. She imagined it was her libido. The thing needed deflating before she embarrassed herself. Attacking Bastian wouldn't go over well. Mr. Starched-and-Pressed would keel over in a dead faint if she ruined his culinary masterpiece. Yeah.

That would be good for a lecture...or five. Daimler would have a cow and then send of her off to etiquette school to learn some manners.

Still, she considered it. Getting dressed down by the elf might be worth it. Whip cream had arrived with their dessert and...

She bit her bottom lip. God, he would taste good slathered in heavy cream. Swallowing past her sudden case of dry mouth, she glanced at Bastian from the corner of her eye. Staring at his plate, he cleared his throat and shifted in his chair.

His chest muscles rolled, drawing all kinds of attention from the peanut gallery inside her head. They urged her on. She stalled, drawing circles in icing sugar with the tines of her fork. When that didn't work her, she took another tack.

"So, energy-fused, huh?" she asked, desperate for a distraction.

White-knuckling his fork, Bastian stared at his soufflé and nodded. "The bonding is rare for my kind. I thought it was a myth. Until I met you."

The compliment relaxed her a little, and she smiled. He was being honest with her, even though he found it hard. She understood, knew talking about his race, revealing secrets long kept, trusting her with the truth was difficult for him. He'd hesitated at first, the truth coming in stilted stretches of conversation. But true to his word, he explained as they ate, pausing only to allow Daimler to set course after course in front of them.

She had so many questions.

He answered them all, telling her about the Meridian, how its energy bands ringed the planet and held everything in place. It was fascinating, really. The vertical ribbons ran north to south, joining at the poles. Thin threads spread over the globe with magical netting, connecting all living things in a continuous loop. And surprise, surprise…she understood the interconnected landscape. Had felt it all her life, sensing more than believing that every organism—big or small—affected the next. The circle of life approach—the idea that all things turned inward, renewing themselves with the seasons—appealed to her.

And Dragonkind? Their history and origins captivated her.

Born of the goddess Mother Earth and the Dragon God, the race's beginnings were right out of an A&E movie. Bastian told it perfectly: like a bedtime story, full of twists and turns, deceit and betrayal. He cranked up the tension in all the right places, telling of the Dragon God's affair with a wood nymph…and the goddess's reaction. Her weapon of choice? A curse that tied Dragonkind to her world—the earthly plane and the energy in it. But worse—at least in Dragon God's mind—was the way she'd done it. She'd taken the ability to produce female offspring from Dragonkind, forcing the males to submit to human women not only to survive, but to procreate.

Brilliant. Revenge with flare. An ancient goddess with a modern woman's attitude and the guts to get even. And really, what woman couldn't get behind that brand of kick-butt justice?

Gathering all the factoids up, Myst categorized the information, filing everything away in the correct mental file folders. "And I'm high-energy?"

"Very. The most powerful I've ever seen." Bastian chased a blueberry around the edge of his plate. "I hadn't known what being full felt like until I touched you."

Okay. She had to admit the whole feeding thing threw her. Unsure how she felt about it, she chewed on the inside of her lip and sorted through the mental minefield. When nothing exploded in the psychological sphere, she frowned. Maybe she could accept his hunger and the way he satisfied it with a little more information.

Digging into her dessert, Myst carved a hole in its center, making a mess of the pastry with no intention of eating it. "You could hurt me while feeding, couldn't you?"

"I don't want to hurt you," he said, squishing the poor berry with his fork.

"I know." And she did...deep down where instinct ruled and common sense took a back seat. Regardless of the risk, she trusted him: to keep her safe, to take only what he needed and...

What do you know? Her uncertainty shifted, and all of a sudden, the energy feeding seemed okay. Erotic in a way that made her shift in her seat again. Bastian needed her, and she responded to that truth of discovery. A humming started deep inside her, the desire to provide all he required becoming clawing desperation. She wanted to be the *one*... the only woman to love him, feed him, hold him in her arms.

"Bastian," she whispered, her need for him tossing her into a void of uncertainty. "Please, look at me."

A muscle twitched along his jaw. He shook his head. "Not a good idea."

"Why?"

"I'm wound too tight," he said, his voice so deep she barely heard him. "I look at you...I'm coming across the table at you."

The news flash stopped her cold. Then heated her up.

As the inferno got cooking, she stared at him in open-mouthed astonishment. What was wrong with her? She'd been so busy hiding her own reaction she hadn't noticed his. But she was noticing now and...holy crap. He was one big ball of sexual energy. Throwing off so much heat, she could smell his arousal.

And suddenly, his physical distance—the strict no touch, no eye contact policy—during dinner made sense. Myst swallowed as her gaze drifted over him, picking up small details and body cues. Color burnishing his cheek-bones, tension vibrated through him. One hand curled around the arm of the chair, he had the thing in a death grip, threatening to rip it right off the upholstered side. And as Myst watched, his chest rose and fell, the rhythm so fast she couldn't stand it.

Screw etiquette. She needed him. Right. Fricking. Now.

With a soft growl, she shoved her dessert aside. He glanced up, heat making his eyes shimmer in the low light. Thunder boomed, rattling the windowpanes, and she leapt from her seat. She went up and over, sending plates and utensils flying. Fine china collided with cut crystal, skidding across the tabletop.

Bastian groaned and drove his chair back. The thing hit the wall with a thud, and he stood, catching her mid-flight. Relief came in a blinding wave as she made contact. She slid her hands into his hair. The soft strands pushed between her fingers, driving her headlong into desire. With a desperate moan, she took his mouth, slipped her tongue deep inside to devour him.

He didn't deny her, gave her all she demanded, satisfying her one wet stroke at a time. He murmured in between kisses, praising her as his hands tunneled beneath her waistband. As his palms met her skin, she surged, begging him without words to strip her bare. Nipping her bottom lip, he answered the call, pushing the pants off her hips.

The black fabric slid down her legs and hit the floor. A second later, his thigh pressed between hers and...

Oh, yeah. Naked, beautiful man.

He'd pulled the disappearing clothes trick. Now, they were skin to skin, nothing between them but heat and desperate need.

"Bastian, now! I can't wait...now, please."

"*Bellmia*...my beauty." His eyes glowing like twin emeralds, he swept the plates off the table. They crash landed on the floor, splintering into shards as he sat her down on the table edge. "Spread your legs...wider, baby. Let me in."

Lying back, she arched her spine, twisting against the tabletop, and let her knees fall open. He growled, moved in and, hooking her legs over his forearms, grabbed her hips. She sobbed his name as he thrust deep, burying himself to the hilt inside her. Delight echoed on her wild cry, rippling out in a spastic wave that went on and on and on. She moaned when he retreated and came back.

Again and again: giving, taking, possessing her so completely she didn't know where he ended and she began.

He set a fast pace, and she begged for more. Unzipping her hoodie, he pushed her tank top up, baring her breasts. Arching her spine, she presented herself like a gift. The heat of his mouth closed around her nipple, and she burned for him: urging him on as he suckled, rolling his hips, working himself deep inside her. Bliss came and Myst took it all— loving Bastian's fierceness, craving every part of him, knowing she would never get enough.

Chapter Thirty-one

The storm blew itself out as the Meridian normalized just before dawn. Bastian's greediness settled along with it, shifting him from single-minded need into caring mode. Myst was exhausted, on the verge of sleep in his arms, needing a bed and about twelve hours of REM to recover from their night together. But he couldn't make himself move. He wanted to stay camped out in front of the fireplace in the nest of blankets he'd made for them on the living room floor.

He should feel bad about that. About the hours spent on hardwood and the Oriental rug: loving her, pleasing her, being pleased in return. And he might have if Myst hadn't been as needy as he—so demanding he hadn't had time to move them to the couch, never mind his bedroom.

"Too far away," she'd said. "I need you. Please, don't stop."

And God. There'd been no resisting her. Or denying himself.

He'd taken full advantage, lost all control, drowning in his desire for her. With the morning sun, though, came the reckoning. And as the windows shifted, moving from clear glass to dark tint, protecting him from the ultraviolet rays, regret taunted him in the reality of a new day.

He would have to tell her. Everything.

The thought scared him. He hadn't told her the whole truth, and her reaction to his omission wouldn't be fun. But he wasn't a coward. He'd created the mess. Time to man up and take the poison pill.

"Myst?" Not wanting to startle her, he skimmed his hand over her shoulder, down her arm, enjoying her soft skin way too much. *"Bellmia?"*

She hummed, rousing with an enticing stretch. He swallowed, watching her breasts rise and fall, nipples tight as she turned onto her back. Coming up onto his side, he cupped her cheek, ran the pad of his thumb over lips swollen from his passion. Hmm...he'd kissed her so much last night. Deep and hard. None of the kisses soft or gentle like she deserved. Dipping his head, he brushed his mouth against hers.

Her lips parted to accommodate him. "Again?"

"No. You need to sleep and...we need to move."

"Uh-uh. Let's stay here. Play a little more."

"Insatiable." Hiding a smile, he shook his head and kissed her again. "And no can do. We gotta go."

With another stretch, she half-groaned, half-growled, and opened her eyes. Bastian sucked in a breath as he got nailed with her sleepy violet gaze. Unable to help himself, he kissed her again, slipping into her, tasting her with his tongue. Her hands slid into his hair, cupping the back of his head, holding him close, accepting him as she had all night.

In-fucking-credible.

Unbelievably beautiful.

Myst was more than he deserved.

He flicked the corner of her mouth as he pulled away. He should tell her right now. Rip the lid off his sin like a

Band-Aid. Let her get angry. Explain everything to her...
Rikar's theory about the energy-fusion and that Bastian
might be able to protect her throughout the pregnancy—
and when she went into labor with his son.

Bastian closed his eyes. *Might.* It was one helluva word,
wasn't it?

"Bastian?" Myst stroked her fingers through his hair.
"What's wrong?"

Unable to force the confession past his throat, he shook
his head.

"Don't lie to me," she said. "I can feel your sadness.
You're in pain. Tell me why."

"I...last night..." he trailed off as his throat went tight.
"It's nothing."

She went still beside him, her gaze sharpening on his
face.

Shit. She was reading him, using their connection to fer-
ret out the truth. He slammed his mental doors, trying to
shut her out, protect her and himself until he found the
best way to tell her. But that was a load of BS. There was no
best way.

He cleared his throat and shifted to get up. She tightened her grip, keeping him in place. In full panic mode, he
reached for an excuse. "Daimler will be here soon...to start
breakfast. My warriors will be coming in, too. We should
move."

She didn't budge, holding firm. "No secrets, remember?
Tell me."

"Fuck," he said. "I'm sorry. I don't want to hurt you."

"You've never hurt me."

"I did last night. I did—"

"No, you didn't."

He took a breath, feeling like he was suffocating. "I don't want you to hate me. But, it's done and I can't undo it. I can't—"

"Bastian." Concern in her eyes, she stroked his cheek, trying to calm him. "Just tell me."

"I didn't tell you the whole truth about the realignment. God forgive me, baby...you're pregnant," he rasped. His hand fisted in the blanket beside her, his chest heaved. But the physical meltdown was nothing compared to the emotional trauma and, as Myst's eyes went wide, he knew he would never forgive himself. "I got you pregnant. I'm sorry...Jesus...I'm sorry."

"Love, listen to me," she said, her voice soft. "I'm on birth control. My periods have always been screwed up. I get a shot every few months to help regulate it. So I can't be—"

"You are." He spread his hand over her belly, filling the space between her hipbones. "I can feel him already... quickening inside your womb."

She shook her head. "That's not possible. I'm..." she trailed off and sat up. Planting her palms on the floor, she scooted backwards, away from him. "No. I can't be."

He reached for her.

She retreated faster. Grabbing a blanket, she held it in front of her like a shield, warning him away.

Desperate to make her stay, he tried to explain. "I can help you, Myst. Because of our bond...the energy-fuse... there's a good chance you'll survive the—"

"Survive?" Shock flared in her eyes.

"*Bellmia*, please. Listen to me. I think—"

"You think? You *think*?" She shot to her feet. Tripping over the rug edge, she stumbled, then caught her balance. "You did this without asking me? Knowing I could *die*?"

Jesus, he was botching it...making her panic, pushing her away with every word. His heart a tangled mess, Bastian stood and faced her. "I know, and I'm sor—"

"You say sorry one more time and I'll..." the words trailed off, drifting into nothing as she wrapped the blanket around her torso.

Helplessness swamped him. He was losing her. "I didn't know what else to do. With the Meridian and...Jesus. Had I told you that I'm only fertile during the realignment and that you would conceive, you would have run. And...fuck, but I couldn't let you go and...I didn't want to force you. But that's what would've happened."

She retreated another step.

"Myst, you saw me last night. How out of control I was... how many times you had to slow me down, take control so I didn't get too rough. If I had chased you down, I would've hurt you. I wouldn't have meant to, but I would have and—"

"You don't know that, Bastian," she whispered, her face ashen, her eyes hollow as she stared at him. "I might've stayed, but you chose to keep secrets from me. After I asked you not to, and you swore that...oh, my God. You promised me. You *promised*."

"I know." He held his hands out to the side, begging in word and deed. "Let me make it up to you."

"You can't."

"Please. I'll do anything...give you—"

"I can't do this." Tears in her eyes, the smell of despair and betrayal spiked in her scent. "I can't...stay here."

With a sob, she broke eye contact and spun. Skirting the hearthstone, she fled into the dining room, the blanket flowing like a cape in her wake. She was in full panic mode: the chest-heaving, feet-flying, intellect-consuming kind that would send her into danger. And it was his fault. He should've found a better way to tell her, given her time to rest and recover from the night.

Choking on self-hatred, Bastian sprinted after her. He needed to catch her before...

"Myst...don't!"

"Stay away from me," she yelled, already on the other side of the table.

He leapt the antique, desperate to reach the door before she did. But she was faster. Grabbing the handle, she yanked the door open. Sunlight flooded the room, hammering him with UV rays. Pain blinded him, burning the backs of his retinas. Shielding his eyes, he threw himself sideways, into the darkest corner, out of the sun's deadly path.

Seeing nothing but spots, feeling nothing but agony, Bastian roared her name. But even as he begged her to come back, he knew she wouldn't. He'd hurt her more than she could bear. She was already gone. He could feel the distance widening between them.

———

Gravel bit into the bottom of her bare feet as Myst raced across the driveway. Pain lanced her, shooting up the backs of her calves. She didn't slow. Freedom lay less than ten feet away...a beacon of hope with industrial-size garage doors and cedar siding.

God, it all looked so normal. So safe. Nothing unusual about the structure except the circumstances that sent her speeding toward it.

Pregnant.

Her head pounded as words echoed inside her, making panic the only thing she knew. *Run faster.* She needed to run faster. Maybe then reality would fade and leave her with nothing but a healthy dose of denial. She wanted it layered on thick, like smudge on a windowpane, so she couldn't see beyond into the light. Clarity and acceptance wouldn't give her anything but more tears.

Each breath rasping in her throat, she glanced over her shoulder. Bastian wasn't there. Thank God. If he got ahold of her, she was cooked. He'd drag her back and imprison her. She checked behind herself again, afraid he was on her heels. The rational side of her knew he couldn't be. Daylight prevented him from following her. She'd learned that last night while they talked…when she thought he was being so honest with her.

She was a fool. He'd lied to her…again. This time with catastrophic consequences.

A sob caught in the back of her throat. She couldn't be pregnant. It wasn't true. She used the best birth control money could buy. But with the magic and Bastian and…

Oh, God. Anything was possible.

How…okay, not how. She knew the *how.* The next question was why. But she knew the answer to that one, too. He hadn't wanted to force her, and as crazy as it sounded, she understood his logic. The Meridian had driven them both over the edge, but Bastian had been out of control. So wild in the height of the storm she'd used quiet words and gentle touches to bring him back from the brink. He'd always listened, dialing down his desire before he'd gotten too rough with her.

But it had been close a number of times. So, yeah, on some level she accepted the reason behind his lie. Could even find honor in his actions.

God, what did that say about her...that she was deranged? Suffering from some form of delusion? Or was it love? Love, after all, made people do stupid things. Like forgive a man when he deliberately withheld crucial—and life-threatening!—information.

Yeah, no doubt about it. Stupiditis was a definite part of her mental package. But at least she was clearheaded enough to diagnose the problem and administer the psychological antidote: a healthy dose of self-preservation by way of escape. Which meant she needed to keep moving. Time wasn't on her side.

The layout of Black Diamond, either.

The lair was a labyrinth, a system of interconnected tunnels spreading like a spiderweb beneath the house. She'd bet her eyeteeth that one lead to the garage. And that Bastian was racing down it right now.

The thought made her run faster. She zeroed in on the door set beside the larger ones, slowing her pace. She reached for the knob.

Please, God, let it be...

The door opened on the first crank, swinging on well-oiled hinges. She plunged over the threshold, her bare feet slapping on smooth concrete, her eyes adjusting to the darkness. She stood shivering for a moment, the afghan doing little to protect her from the cold, and scanned the interior. A key box. She needed to find where they kept all the keys, but...

Talk about *Mission Impossible*. She couldn't see a thing, and the place was huge, much bigger than the garage doors implied.

Spinning around, she looked for a light switch. Bingo. A set of five. She flipped them all, the buzz of electricity crackling in the silence. As industrial-grade fluorescents flickered to life, she spotted the garage door openers mounted further down the wall. She hammered them with the side of her fist. Gears ground in motion, rattling chains, lifting the huge metal doors off the concrete floor. Sunlight flooded into the room.

"Fuck."

Well, that answered that question, didn't it? Secret tunnel into the garage? Check.

Bastian cursed again as the doors continued to rise. Scanning the back of the structure, she stepped into a bright patch of sunshine. As it warmed her shoulder blades, her eyes adjusted to the light, and she watched Bastian dive behind a tall tool cabinet, his arm shielding his eyes. She covered her mouth with her hand, her heart so heavy it sank inside her chest.

God, she was hurting him, wielding his weakness like a weapon, pushing him away one UV ray at a time. Still, she stayed in the sun, refusing to give up her defensive position. She needed out. His lies hurt too much for her to forgive so easily. And as the emotional ache expanded to encompass the physical, she didn't know if she'd ever be able to accept his apology.

So, where did that leave them?

She couldn't stay, and he refused to let her go. The standoff left them on opposite sides of the fence, her need for space warring with his desire for closeness. Her right to freedom, though, wasn't one she would debate. The decision was hers to make, not his.

"Bastian, I'm sorry." Man, the irony. He was the one who'd hurt her, and she ended up apologizing. "Please... just stay there."

"Don't go. *Bellmia,* don't." His voice drifted from the darkness, the ache in his tone undeniable. "We'll work it out."

"I need space." Her throat closed, tightening around each word until she could barely push them out of her mouth. "I'm going home."

"You are home."

"For how long?" Her breath hitched as she lost the battle and tears escaped, rolling down her cheeks. "Until I go into labor and die?"

"You're not going to die!" His shout echoed, bouncing off the steel structure as she wiped her cheeks. The mop-up helped clear her vision. She scanned the walls and...found the keys.

Thank God.

She eyed the metal hooks. There were eleven of them, an equal number of keys hanging on the wooden board. She did a quick count, skimming over vintage cars until her gaze landed on an SUV. The Denali sat in the third spot, so logic—and Daimler's tendency for extreme organization—told her the truck's keys were on the hook number three.

Careful to stay in the sun, she kept her eyes on the back of the garage and hotfooted it toward the keys. Bastian was quick. He could pull a fast grab-and-go—haul her into the tunnel and the lair before she knew what hit her. With slow deliberation, she reached out and grabbed the set she needed. Metal rattled then settled in the palm of her hand.

"I won't let you die," he repeated, his tone as desperate as she felt.

"That's crap and you know it. You can't protect me...not from this."

"Rikar thinks I can, because of our bond, and—"

"How many women survive?" Moving fast, she headed for the SUV's driver-side door. "Tell me! How many?"

As her shout echoed, Bastian stood up. Protecting his eyes with his hand, he stayed deep in the shadows, following her movements, walking with her, marking her progress as she stepped up to the Denali. Her hand curled around the handle.

"Myst..."

"They all die, don't they?" Her grip tightened on the door pull. God, she wanted to hit him so badly. Maybe then he'd hurt as much as she was right now. "Just like..."

Caroline.

Her mouth parted, and Myst went completely still.

"Oh, my God." The test results. The ones with all the anomalies. Caroline's blood work had been bang-on until the twenty-eighth week of her pregnancy. After that, something strange started to happen...a surge in dragon DNA maybe? A hormonal shift of some kind—maybe even a magical one—that protected the baby, but hurt the mother?

Her mind whirled as she stared at Bastian. Purpose grabbed hold, infusing her with hope. Okay, so it was a Hail Mary pass, but...

She needed to get to the hospital and access Caroline's medical file. Instinct told her the clues lay in the blood work. Maybe the techies had isolated the platelet problem. Maybe the ME had noted something odd in the autopsy report. A small detail. A tiny clue. That's all she needed to set her on the right path. The one that would help her find the answer that might save her life.

Myst cranked the SUV's door open. "I have to go."

"Stay...give me another chance."

"No," she whispered, fighting the compulsion to let him persuade her. Even now—pissed off and hurting—she wanted to touch him...to hold him close and be held in return. "Bastian, please. You need to let me go."

"I can't," he said, eyes shimmering in the gloom. "I love you, Myst. I can't let you leave knowing you won't be safe out there."

More tears fell. He loved her. No fair. It was all she ever wanted and, yet she couldn't stay. Finding the truth—discovering what killed Caroline—was more important than pleasing him right now.

"You don't have a choice," she said, her voice raw with regret. "And neither do I."

With a pitiful hiccup, she slid into the seat and slammed the door behind her. Jamming the key into the ignition, she cranked the engine. She heard Bastian roar, saw him lunge toward her in the side-view mirror and, with more desperation than will, threw the SUV into gear. Before he stopped her, she put her foot down, peeling out of the garage on squealing tires and a truckload of hurt.

As she shot into the sunshine where he would never be able to reach her, she whispered, "I love you, too."

But she knew with certainty that it was too little, too late.

———

Plastic crinkled as Ivar stuck his hand into the bag and pulled out two pieces of bread. His stomach rumbled, running on empty after the realignment and a long night filled with pleasure. Well, at least, his own. The female hadn't been so lucky.

He'd dumped her an hour before dawn. In an alley across town. Another dead body for the cops to find. Oh, goody.

With quick hands, he slapped together his sandwich. Mustard got slathered on first. The thinly sliced meat and cheddar went on next, then lettuce and tomato. He liked a little crunch with his ham and cheese. Pressing down on the protein-feast, he grabbed a knife and sliced the whole mess in half.

The first bite made him groan, the kaleidoscope of flavor hitting his tongue just right. Turning away from the kitchen island, he held the half sandwich in one hand and opened the fridge with the other. He went for the 3 percent and, cracking the top, drank right from the milk carton. As he chug-a-lugged, Lothair jogged into the room with a laptop under his arm.

Interesting.

His XO was usually on a slow roll: his pace always even, a never-in-a-hurry kind of male. Ivar took another bite. Lettuce crunched between his back molars, sounding loud in his ears. His mouth half full, he said, "What's up?"

Lothair's black eyes flashed. "Got something you should see."

"Oh, yeah?"

He tipped his chin as Lothair set the Mac down on the granite countertop. With a flip, his XO opened the computer, waited a second for the thing to fire up, then tapped in a password. The inside of an apartment took shape on the screen. Loft-like, the space was open plan: kitchen, living, dining, and bedroom all in one. Three windows with arched tops set in a brick wall marched down the far side of the room. An old warehouse, probably. One with good bones and enough luck to be converted into condos instead of becoming landfill.

Ivar liked the idea. Recycle. Reuse. Refurbish instead of tearing down. Good move on the developer's part. Way better than the ugly condo towers with which the humans ruined the skyline.

"So," Lothair said, fingers moving rapid-fire on the keyboard, "the cameras I planted fired up a minute ago. Thought you should see—"

"Bastian's female." His hand tightened around his snack, squishing the guts out of the thing. Tomato juice dripped onto his palm, and Ivar dragged in a breath, eyes riveted to the blonde female as she came into view. She said something to someone in the corridor then turned and closed the door. The lock snicked, and she leaned back against the wood panel, both hands covering her face. "She's crying."

"Trouble in paradise?"

No doubt. His best guess? Bastian had taken her when the Meridian realigned. Rough play always upset females of worth. Well, most of the time. Some of them were into BDSM. Which was okay for other males, but not him. Yeah, he enjoyed killing, but taking a female's energy didn't mean smacking her around. When he drained them, they always died peacefully...with pleasure, even.

Leaning closer to the screen, he watched her wipe her eyes and adjust the... "What's she wearing? A blanket?"

"Looks like it." Lothair leaned in, and together they watched Myst Munroe make a beeline for the bedroom. As she disappeared through the only interior door, his XO murmured, "Bastian had some fun last night."

"Shit." So much for plan A. Planting his own child deep in her womb wouldn't work now. Not if she already carried Bastian's son. But Ivar was nothing if not adaptive. A pregnant female was useful...especially as bait.

Ten minutes later, Myst came out of the bathroom, towel wrapped around her body, damp hair pulled away from her pretty face. She headed for a chest of drawers and...

"What is she—"

"Scrubs," Ivar said as she dropped the towel. The terry cloth crumpled around her feet, and his breath hitched. Hmm...she was a beauty: all pale skin, slight curves, and high, tight breasts. He set his sandwich down on the plate, growing thick behind his fly. "Where does she work again?"

"Swedish Medical."

Ivar glanced at the clock across the kitchen. Seven hours until darkness. Until he got his hands on Myst Munroe. "Brief everyone. I want them all up to speed and ready to go as soon as the sun sets."

"Forge is still MIA."

"I'll keep trying him." Not that the big male would answer. Forge had gone postal, completely off the grid.

"You think he'll come around?" Lothair asked, eyeing his ham and cheese.

"No clue."

Picking up the mangled half of his sandwich, he shoved the other half toward his XO. As they shared his snack, his mind turned inward, toward his plan and away from Forge. No sense crying over spilled milk. The warrior was of no use to Ivar in his present state of mind. Tonight's plan required precision and control, not a male with suicidal tendencies on a paternal mission.

And if push came to shove? He'd take the warrior out along with Bastian. At least then he'd have a matching set of urns for his mantelpiece.

Ivar smiled. He loved it when a plan came together.

Chapter Thirty-two

The medical center smelled as it always did...like chemical soup and bad aftershave. The obnoxious mix clung, coating the back of Myst's throat. She swallowed the toxic taste, wishing she was anywhere but here—back in a place where everything looked normal, but nothing was the same.

Bruised on the inside, she wanted to curl up for a while. Find a quiet place and, well...cry some more. But pride wouldn't let her, refusing to allow her out of the pity park. A shame, really. She could've used a break from the I'm-pissed-at-Bastian merry-go-round she was riding.

God, she was sick of it. Tired of herself and him...of everything and everyone.

Even the potted palms in the lobby annoyed her. She glared at the collection as she passed. And if looks could kill? The stupid trees would be dead as doornails...horticultural examiner's inquest pending.

Throwing the palms one last scowl, she skirted the backlit direction sign and crossed the lobby. Her nursing shoes squeaked on the polished floors, sounding louder than usual, raising her pulse, making her sweat.

"Relax." Wiping her damp palms on her scrubs, she glanced around, trying to look calm. "Act normal. Just another day at the office."

Uh-huh. Right. Like every day started with a surprise pregnancy and a quest to steal medical records. The entire thing was Bastian's fault. "The big jerk."

I love you, Myst.

His words floated through her mind and, against her will, she recalled the timbre of his voice, the look on his face...the pain in his eyes. Goddamn it.

"Focus," she hissed at herself, getting rough with her bag as she adjusted the strap on her shoulder. "Stop thinking about him."

The woman sitting at the U-shaped information desk threw her a strange look.

Skirting the receptionist's command post, Myst shrugged by way of explanation and said, "Man trouble."

Snapping her gum, the woman nodded. "I hear ya, honey. No good sons of guns most of the time."

The Texas drawl made Myst smile and, strangely enough, settled her down. No sense being nervous. She'd made up her mind. Blatant law-breaking aside, she needed Caroline's medical file, and the best place to get it was the fourth floor...where the doctors held court in corner offices.

Her plan? Find an empty one with a computer.

Fifteen minutes tops—a let-your-fingers-do-the-walking kind of deal, followed by a quick print job and...voilá. Instant information.

Mangling the fringe on her bag, she wound the small strip of leather around her finger and scanned the main corridor. She didn't want to run into anyone she knew. Considering the mobile nature of her job, the chances were slim, but nurses worked shifts, rotating around the clock. A change in schedule might put her face-to-face with one of her colleagues.

And wouldn't that be fun?

At best, those she worked with on a regular basis would know she was MIA. At worst? The police were looking for her, asking other nurses about her habits, digging into her life to solve the mystery of Caroline's death and Gregor's disappearance.

Either way, she was screwed.

The sound of laughter came from behind her, echoing off the foyer's high ceiling. She glanced over her shoulder and—

Perfect.

A gaggle of nurses, lunch bags in hand, walked out of the sunshine and into the building. As they passed, Myst slid in behind them unnoticed, an individual among a group. The best kind of camouflage.

Listening to them chatter, she soaked in the normal rhythm of their day. Less than a week ago, *this* had been her life. Now, it felt empty, rounded out by a hollowness she couldn't define. Strange how a person could change so much in such a short amount of time, but reality didn't pull any punches. Which left one option, didn't it? Move forward. Put one foot in front of the other and get on with her life. The question now? Did she walk toward Bastian or away from him?

Shaking her head, Myst pushed the decision away. Baby...no baby...she couldn't deal with the mess right now. Not when she felt so raw inside that it hurt to breathe.

The group stopped in front of a bank of elevators. Myst broke away from the group, headed around the corner, and found the stairwell. As she climbed the steps she forced herself to focus: picturing the fourth floor, imagining the offices, which ones had receptionists she'd worked with, which ones didn't.

The fourth-floor wall sign came before she was ready. Standing on the landing, Myst rolled her shoulders to loosen up tense muscles. She could do this. A quick in. A faster out, and she'd have the information she needed.

Grabbing the metal knob, she pulled the door open and stepped into the corridor. The lock clicked behind her, sounding loud in the silence. She turned right, registering the pale yellow walls and the blue doors. Like books on shelves, they lined up in perfect symmetry, bracketing the hallway on both sides. The drone of voices came from behind some of the doors: patients waiting to be seen by doctors, nurses asking questions, the ringing of telephones mixing with the buzz of fluorescent lights.

The further she walked, the quieter it became. The OBGYNs were housed on the far end. And they were the best targets. Hospital calls came in frequently, pulling them out of the office and into the birthing center. Add that to the fact it was lunchtime and...

Bingo.

Just what she needed: a suction cup stuck to a door with a plastic sign hanging from its hook. Complete with black numbers and red hands, the clock read 12:30 p.m., and the notation beneath it? *Be back soon.*

Myst checked her watch. She had twenty minutes before the receptionist came back.

Looking both ways, she made sure the corridor was empty, then reached for the knob, praying—

The door opened on the first try. Thank God. She'd hoped like hell, but receptionists were tricky creatures. Some locked up the office like they had a pot full of gold beneath their desks. Others were more laid-back, assuming patients would take one look at the sign and head to the coffee shop to wait out the allotted time.

With one last look to make sure she was alone, Myst slipped inside. All the lights were on, the cloth-covered chairs with their worn wooden arms on display as much as the magazines on the side tables. Behind a half wall across from the waiting area sat the receptionist's desk. White file folders with colorful tabs lay in the out-box. A bigger pile leaned in a lopsided tower in the in-box, a testament to the overworked, underpaid medical secretary.

Some things never changed.

Shouldering her bag, she jogged into the doctor's private office. An old computer occupied one corner of the cluttered desk surface. As Myst swung to face the monitor, she grabbed the mouse without sitting down. The screen saver's starbursts faded, giving her a plain black background with the prompt for a username and password.

The moment of truth. Had the hospital shut down her access? Did the administration even know she was gone?

Chewing on her bottom lip, she sat down in the swivel chair. Her hands shook as she typed, half afraid the computer would sound the alarm and screech *thief, thief, thief!* She tried twice, fumbling her way over the keyboard, deleting her password and retyping it, visions of the inside of a jail cell in her mind's eye.

Finally getting it right, she paused, her finger poised above the enter button. With a "please, God," she hit the last stroke. The computer thought for a moment, then...wham. She was in.

Perched on the edge of the chair, Myst typed her patient's first and last name. Caroline's file popped onto the screen.

She double clicked it, hope racing fear to the finish line as she hit the print button, then scrolled through the notes.

"Please, let it be here. All I need is...holy crap."

Her mouth parted as the lab results came up. She leaned closer to the screen and read the report again. When the sight didn't convince her, she shook her head and whispered, "Hemophilia."

Was that even possible?

The blood disease was considered a male one, a genetic disorder passed from mother to son. It wasn't developmental. A patient was born with it, something to do with the X chromosome and—

"Oh, my God." She cupped her hand over her mouth to stifle a moan. Oh, no...no, no, no. Hemophilia was treatable. With the right medication...had the test results come through...if she'd only known, she could've saved Caroline's life.

Setting her elbows on the desk edge, she palmed her head and stared at the screen, running through the chart one more time. Goddamn lab technicians. They should have been faster with the results. If only they'd...

But that wasn't fair.

She knew it even as she cursed them. Like everyone in the medical system, the people who ran the samples were inundated with requests...too many to test and not enough time. The reasons why, though, didn't make her feel any better. No amount of understanding in the world could erase the awful facts.

Her patient had died of a *treatable* illness, leaving a little boy without his mother.

Feeling hollow inside, she sat in the empty office, listening to the thunk-thunk of the old printer as it spit out page after page. When the screen saver came on, she swiped her cheeks and pushed up the sleeve of her Patagonia to check her watch. Ten minutes and counting. She needed to move, couldn't sit on her duff waiting for shock to fade and her brain to reboot. The receptionist would be back soon. Better to take the printouts and—

Laughter sounded in the hallway.

Myst froze, hearing the metallic snick of the knob and the hiss of hinges as the door opened and the voices grew louder. She caught a glimpse of a white doctor's coat. Jumping to her feet, she grabbed Caroline's file from the printer tray. As she stuffed the pages in her bag, she made a beeline around the desk edge.

God help her. They were back early, and she was in a whole mess of trouble.

———

The precinct smelled like burnt coffee and bad attitudes. The first made Angela's stomach churn. The second, she understood, because...hey. She was the biggest source of stay-the-hell-away in the open space she shared with the other SPD detectives.

Reading the signs, no one spoke to her. Although, a couple of the braver ones arched eyebrows, throwing speculative looks her way. Yeah, inquiring minds wanted to know. Hers included. She couldn't remember a flipping thing from last night.

Okay. Not quite true. Her memory was tossing out a couple of tidbits: pale blue eyes and the letter R.

R. Angela frowned. Was it the beginning of a name? An address?

Slumped in her chair, she rubbed her forehead and watched the flurry of activity through her lashes. Per usual, the bullpen was hopping: guys talking on the phone, shuffling paperwork or typing more up, drinking the sludge they called coffee. She'd wait, thank you very much. No way that stuff was hitting the bottom of her stomach. Not if she wanted to keep it down.

She felt Mac's presence before she saw him. Like always, he blew in like a hurricane, scaring the residents, making them pack up their stuff and hit the road. With a smile, she watched the mass exodus, appreciating the noise reduction as the other detectives suddenly found something more important to do.

Her partner set a Starbucks down on her desk blotter.

"Bless you," she murmured, reaching for the cup of joe.

"Long night?" Perched on the corner of her desk, he took a sip of his coffee.

A creature of habit, he ordered the same thing every time: extra large black, no cream, no sugar. Angela liked the predictability. Night or day. It didn't matter. Comfort existed in their caffeine ritual, and she never deviated either, always went for a latté, heavy on the steamed milk.

Taking a sip, she sighed and settled back in her chair. "Yeah."

He grinned. "About time you had some fun. Anybody I know?"

Good question. One she couldn't answer and since admitting that wasn't an option, she lied, "No guy involved."

"Uh-huh."

She glared at him. "You think I'd be this pissy if I'd gotten laid?"

"Depends on the guy." Enjoying the tease, Mac's blue eyes twinkled as he shrugged. "If he wasn't any good—"

"Oh, shut up." Plunking her coffee down on her desk, she reached for a manila file folder. "Tell me what we've got today."

Mac's expression got serious in a hurry. "Just came from the lab."

"Body count?"

"I didn't kill any of the idiots," he said, enough growl in his voice to register on the animal kingdom's sliding scale.

"Bravo, Mac." When he snorted, she smiled. Score one for team Angela in the payback department. Freaking guy... asking her whether she'd gotten some action last night. "Welcome to the civilized world."

"They lost the ash samples, Ange."

She blinked. What ash samples? They had...holy hell. Her brain was in serious misfire mode if she couldn't remember a running tally of the evidence. What had happened last night? Something strange. Something...

God. Why couldn't she remember?

Combing a hand through his dark hair, Mac pushed away from her desk edge and headed for his own. Jammed up against hers, their work spaces faced off, and as he sat down, she met his gaze. "The stuff's not there. It's like—"

"Someone took them?"

"Exactly, but there's no evidence of it." He shook his head, frustration making him restless. "I went over the camera's digital files frame by frame. Nothing out of the ordinary."

Angela frowned. "An inside job."

"Yeah...maybe. IA's all over it, talking to the techies, but that doesn't help us."

No, it didn't, and neither did the holes in her memory. Flipping the case file open, she said, "All right. Let's go over everything again. Maybe—"

Mac's cell phone screeched, and she winced. Man, she really wished he'd change that ringtone. It was hell when she had a headache.

"MacCord." As chatter came through the earpiece, Mac went still in his seat. The hair on the back of Angela's neck rose as her partner's eyes narrowed. "Yeah...good job. Sit on her until we get there."

Mac closed his phone with a snap. She tipped her chin, a *tell me, tell me, tell me* written all over her face.

"Guess who just showed up at the medical center?"

It didn't take a brainiac to guess the answer. Their prime suspect. Ms. Munroe was back on the grid.

"Security got her locked down?" When Mac nodded, she grabbed her leather jacket off the back of the chair and headed for the door. "Let's go. I'm driving."

Chapter Thirty-three

The LZ's floating globes flickered, swaying into each other, threatening to short out as Bastian paced beneath them. Magic crackled in his fingertips, along his spine, lighting him up from the inside out. He was losing his mind. Needed to get out of the lair like a guy buried alive needed to get out of a coffin.

The suffocating smell of cave pressed in, the must, dirt, and stone dust closing his lungs. He breathed deep, forced air in, and then breathed it out. Uncurling his fists, he flexed his fingers. His knuckles cracked, snapping under the pressure as he strode across the cave: crisscrossing the open space, coming inches from the granite edge, footfalls echoing in the vastness.

Four sets of eyes ping-ponged, following his progress. Bastian ignored them all. He didn't give a shit what his warriors thought. All he wanted was out.

"How much longer?" he snarled, coming an inch from Sloan's boot tip.

Propped against the Honda's back tire, plugged into an earbud, laptop across his thighs, Sloan's fingers flew over the MacBook's keyboard. "Fifty-three minutes and change."

"Fuck." Screw the sun. He needed to find his female now before—

"Forget about it, B." Planted on the hood of Myst's car, legs dangling over the front wheel well, Rikar nailed him with his sit-your-ass-down glare. Bastian hated that look. It was like getting plugged in the chest with a forty-four magnum. "You get fried by the sun, and she's on her own out there. Is that what you want?"

Double fuck. "The Razorbacks—"

"Can't go out in the sun, either," Rikar said. "There's no play here but to wait."

"Sit your ass down, Commander." Venom's ruby eyes flashed in the dim light. Backing Rikar up with muscle, the big male pushed away from his lean against the cave wall. "We wait."

Wick, per usual, didn't say a thing. Just watched, golden eyes fixed on him, prepared to move if Bastian shifted form and dove for the LZ's ledge.

Jesus Christ. He was surrounded by a bunch of jack-offs. Serious ones, preparing to back up their threat and tie him down for another fifty-three fucking minutes. And honestly? He appreciated the loyalty, but...

His female was out there, alone and vulnerable. So pissed off at him she was likely to do something stupid.

Rikar sighed and, swinging his legs up, dismounted, landing beside the car. As his feet touched down, Bastian got tense. He and Rikar were tight, but right now? He didn't want his friend anywhere near him.

Widening his stance, Bastian cranked his fists and rolled his shoulders, screaming *stay away* the only way he could... with a shitload of body language.

"Ease up, my man." Rikar's boots brushed over the uneven granite floor, pace steady, approach slow. Bastian watched him from the corner of his eye, killing the urge to turn away. Yeah, he was wound too tight and didn't want to be touched, but he wasn't a coward, either. And as Rikar came alongside, he allowed it, accepting his friend's comfort as he cupped the back of his neck. "Look, I know you're afraid for her. I totally get that. But she's safe right now... among her own kind in the daylight. The Razorbacks can't touch her."

Bastian shuddered, imagining the worst. "If they get to her first...if they touch her...Rikar, I don't think I can—"

"You can handle it. By morning, she'll be back in your arms." Rikar squeezed the nape of his neck. "You can track her energy, and we're smarter than those fuckers. We'll get her back, B."

His chin against his chest, Bastian closed his eyes and pictured Myst. Saw her violet eyes and beautiful face. Felt her warmth. Heard her laughter. Rikar was right. If he got himself fried—like he almost had in the garage this morning—Myst would be a sitting duck. Vulnerable in a world she didn't understand.

"We good?"

Bastian nodded and, raising his head, looked his best friend in the eye. Their gazes clung a moment, silent understanding passing between, like it always did.

Rikar slapped him on the shoulder. "Now...strategy. We've got two targets tonight: Myst and the Scot."

"I'll look after my female," Bastian said, starting up with the pacing again. "I'll make sure she's safe, then we go after Deep Purple."

His arms crossed over his chest, Venom snorted. "Pansy-ass name, but it suits him. I like it."

Rikar huffed and glanced at Wick. "You ready?"

Nodding, Wick patted the military-grade case sitting on the ground beside him.

Black with big, steel latches, the thing housed Gage's latest invention—Dragonkind's equivalent of a Taser. The weapon packed a one-two punch—a combo of high-voltage electricity and neuro-inhibitors that put a dragon out for the count. Once they zapped Deep Purple, they'd have an hour to get him in a cage.

"Oh, shit," Sloan said.

"What?" he and Rikar said, their voices echoing together across the cavern.

"We've got a bit of a snag." Pressing on the earbud with his finger, a frown on his brow, their computer tech listened hard. "I've been monitoring the police chatter, scanning for any more murders, listening in on the detectives."

Rikar perked up. "The she-cop?"

"Yeah," Sloan said, looking up from the MacBook. His dark eyes meet Bastian's. "The male just got a call. They have an APB out on Myst, and they just found her."

Bastian eyes narrowed. "Where are they taking her?"

"King County precinct."

His hands curled into fists. As his knuckles went white, a picture formed, and Bastian imagined beating the hell out of the male detective. Taking comfort from the image, he slowed his rolling, forcing himself to think instead of react. The cops wouldn't hurt her. Yeah, they might scare her a little, but the police followed certain rules: human rights, equal treatment, no corporal punishment allowed. Still, the idea they'd lock her in a room and threaten her...

Just thinking about it made him want to rip their heads off.

"Time?"

"Forty-three minutes."

Jesus. Was the clock screwing with him, moving slower than usual? It felt like it, but as Bastian stalked to the other side of the cave, giving his shitkickers a workout, he kept it together, visualizing the fastest route to the police station. Sloan wasn't the only one scanning human databases for intel. And he'd bet his fangs that Myst was now on the Razorbacks' radar, and Ivar knew exactly where to find her.

———

Steel closed with a snick behind her, shutting Myst on the wrong side of locked door. The chill in the air nipped, raising goose bumps on her bare arms. She rubbed her biceps, wondering if the cold was some sort of interrogation technique: take her Patagonia, toss her into fridge-like conditions, and wait for her to crack.

Detective MacCord seemed like the type. The guy was hardcore, a lethal combination of skill and intensity with added value...violent tendencies. Kind of like Bastian and the crew at Black Diamond, only different—a toned-down version of kick-ass with his dark hair and stormy blue eyes. The only consolation? Detective Keen read as genuine; concerned, even. Then again, maybe it was all an act—a good cop, bad cop routine designed to pull her off balance.

Myst huffed. As if the room wasn't doing that already.

Man, the place was right out of *Law & Order.*

Standing just inside the door, she hugged herself a little tighter, fighting shivers and the urge to cry. God, how had it come to this? With her imprisoned in a twelve-by-twelve-foot box with beige walls and a one-way mirror? Although, it could've been worse. At least, the interrogation room had a window. Okay, so there were bars crisscrossing in front of the glass, giving off a criminal vibe, but light came through, making her feel less claustrophobic.

Skirting the table and chairs in the center of the room, Myst walked toward the window. The view sucked, but she wasn't interested in the asphalt lot with the police cruisers parked between yellow lines or the building beyond the chain-link fence across the street. Daylight was fading, the sun hanging low on the horizon.

The orange glow warmed her, and as she stared at it, she saw the hard angles of Bastian's handsome face and his shimmering green eyes. Despite all the seesawing confusion, she wanted to go back to that place, when he'd held her and she'd felt safe. Right now, he was trapped inside Black Diamond—probably out of his mind with fear for her—but not for much longer.

Propping her shoulder against the cinder block wall, Myst watched the sun sink lower and whispered, "Bastian, I'm right here. Please find me. Please...*find me.*"

She repeated the SOS, feeling selfish, knowing she had no right to expect a rescue, much less ask for one. Not after the way she'd treated him in the garage. God, the look on his face as she put the Denali in gear and...

Myst closed her eyes.

Yeah, he didn't owe her a thing, but she asked anyway. Sent the distress signal over and over—hoping the connection they shared would bring him. Sent it until her temples throbbed and it became a running chant of desperate *pleases* inside her head.

Which just pissed her off.

She should be able to save herself, goddamn it. Relying on someone else to ride—or rather, fly—to her rescue seemed, well...old school. Totally medieval or something. The problem? She couldn't see a way out of the mess. Out of the police station. Out from under the law's thumb and away from two very determined detectives.

The door clicked behind her.

She drew a deep breath, preparing for confrontation as a spicy scent drifted into the small room. Men's cologne. Detective MacCord was back.

———

Compassion wasn't high on the list of priorities for a suspect. At least, it shouldn't be, but today? Angela found it hard not to wince as she stepped into IR two behind her partner. Myst Munroe looked ragged, and not just around the edges. Her exhaustion went deeper than that, beyond the physical to a place dominated by soul-deep weariness.

Angela could relate.

She felt a lot like that herself right now, her mind playing tricks, showing her pieces of the puzzle while hiding others behind a wall of impenetrable mental haze. The other cops thought she was hungover, a little off her game, fighting a post-binge headache. She wished it were true, then she wouldn't have to face the real problem. Something had gone terribly wrong last night.

The tip-off? She could see the holes in her memory. Actually, *see* them…pinpoint and isolate the lapses; was able to surround, but not touch them. Her brain had put the information inside a box and sealed it tight. And that *R*. It kept at her, sending her round and round on the mystery merry-go-round.

God, she had a headache.

Rubbing the bridge of her nose, she bypassed Mac and set her legal pad on the table. As intended, the paper made a slapping sound, echoing a little in the small room.

Usually, that was enough to get a suspect's attention. Myst didn't even flinch. She was fixated, staring out the window, looking like she'd just gone ten rounds with a pair of mental boxing gloves.

Compassion grabbed hold again. Angela slapped it back down. She didn't have time to play nice. Not with a baby MIA.

Her eyes narrowed, she studied the woman she suspected of cutting a baby from his mother's womb for profit. Angela frowned. Myst didn't fit the profile. From all accounts, she was kind, caring, willing to go the extra mile for her patients. The late-night phones calls, the home visits, and the conversations over coffee all supported those facts. So, what the hell happened out there? How had Caroline Van Owen ended up dead on her kitchen floor?

Grabbing the back of a chair, Angela pulled it away from the edge of the table. The metal legs squawked against the tile floor. Mac made a face, but she got nothing from Myst. No reaction at all. Just quiet stillness, firm focus…like she was watching for something.

"Ms. Munroe," she said, raising her voice.

"I'm sorry," she said, her gaze fixed on the setting sun.

Interesting. If this kept up, she and Mac would have a confession sewn up in five minutes flat. "For what?"

Her brows drawn, Myst stepped away from the window. She rubbed her upper arms, and Angela clenched her teeth. Yeah, it was cold in the room. The interrogation tactic was one they used often: better to keep a suspect uncomfortable and on edge than comfortable and well fed. Still, she hated turning the screws on this girl, and as Myst turned to face them, she almost apologized for the cops' asshole-ish policy.

"For any trouble I'm about to cause you." Lifting her chin, Myst met her gaze, then bounced over to Mac's, only to come right back. "Just thought I'd get the apology out of the way beforehand, you know?"

About to cause you. Not had already caused. Her cop radar flipped on, completing a revolution on her suspicion grid. Studying their suspect, Angela patted the back of the chair. "Take a seat, Ms. Munroe."

With a nod, she stepped toward the table. Three strides later, wearing wariness like a flak jacket, Myst sank into the seat. "What time is it?"

Still standing just inside the door, Mac's brows collided. He threw her a silent what-the-hell. When she shrugged, he glanced at his MTM watch. "Seven thirty-one."

"You should probably clear out." Twisting her blonde hair into a makeshift knot at her nape, Myst glanced at the window. "He'll be here soon."

"Who?" Weird. The conversation was right out of a mental patient's playbook. The problem? Angela didn't think Myst fell into the nuts category. The woman was tired, sure, but not crazy.

"Doesn't matter. You won't remember anyway." Planting her elbows on the table, Myst leaned forward and dropped her head into her hands.

"No harm in telling us who he is, then," Mac said, his voice coaxing as he approached the table.

Angela threw her partner a WTF look. She'd never heard that tone from him before. At least, not in an interrogation room. Usually, he hammered suspects with the cold, hard facts; striking fast and with brutal intent. But as he pulled out another chair, she got the feeling his playbook had just expanded to accommodate damsels in distress.

With a flip, he turned the chair backward, straddled it, then reached out and wrapped his hand around Myst's wrist. Which freaking floored Angela, and as her brows got busy shooting skyward, she watched her partner pry their prime suspect's hands away from her face. Okay, he was officially off the grid, four-wheeling it into dangerous territory. But Mac's instincts were always bang-on, so she backed off and stayed out of it, waiting to see if Myst would respond to the "nice guy" routine.

Leaning in, he cupped both of his big hands around Myst's. "Where's the baby?"

"I'm so sorry," she whispered, holding onto Mac like a lifeline. "I tried so hard to save her, but...I couldn't and..."

As Myst trailed off, Angela's throat went tight. Haunted. The woman was haunted by the memory, reliving it frame by frame. She could see it on her face—in her gaze—the force of it so powerful Angela ached for her.

As the swell rose inside her, she slid into the last chair. "What happened that night, Myst?"

Squeezing her eyes closed, Myst clung to Mac's hand, then took a breath and raised her chin to look right at Angela. "Caroline was already on the floor...in a pool of blood...when I got there. God, there was so much and I called for help, but..." Myst shook her head and took a shaky breath. Angela breathed with her, empathy rearing its ugly head again. "She flatlined and I...didn't have a choice. The ambulance was too far away. He would've died if I hadn't..."

"He?" Mac murmured.

Their suspect nodded.

"Listen to me, Myst." Folding her forearm on the table-top, Angela leaned in. God, they were close...so damned close to getting the answers they needed. To getting the baby back safely. "You need to tell us where he is."

"He's safe."

She shook her head. "You're going to have to do better than that."

"I wish I could tell you more, Detective Keen, but I can't. He's with people who care about him...who will raise him right. That's all you need to—" She flinched, cutting the words off midstream as she rocked backward. Flinging off Mac's hand, her head snapped toward the window. "Oh, my God."

Mac stood, reacting to the terror in Myst's voice. His eyes narrowed on the window. "What is it?"

"We need to get out of here." Shooting to her feet, Myst skirted the edge of the table.

Angela leapt after her. No way would she let the woman pull a fast and fly. Not with a baby in the wind and more questions than answers. Reaching out, she grabbed the back of her prime suspect's shirt and yanked, pulling her off balance.

As she stumbled backward, Myst yelled, "You don't understand! I can feel them out there. It's not Bastian, and I can *feel*...oh, God...no."

The building rocked on its foundation.

Angela lost her footing, stumbled back a step and...holy hell. A dark shadow settled over the window, blocking out the night sky. Something hissed and glass shattered, blowing into the room like shrapnel, ripping into her upper arm. The pain barely registered before the blast picked her up and threw her. She went down hard, taking out Myst, hitting the floor butt first. They landed in a heap, her teeth slashing against the inside of her mouth. She ignored the taste of her blood, shouted for Mac.

"Ange, incoming," he roared as flames licked through the shattered window. "Get her out!"

Choking on toxic fumes, Angela ripped the Velcro away from her Glock. Screw his instructions. No way would she leave her partner. Not while they were under attack.

Screaming at Mac to stay clear of the window, she dragged Myst toward the door. She would shove the nurse into the bullpen with the other detectives then—

Huge black talons curled around the steel-framed window.

Time faltered, tripping into slow motion. Frame by frame, Angela watched the impossible unfold. Felt her heartbeat and the adrenaline rush. Smelled the smoke. Heard Myst scream and the animalistic growl as cinder block gave way, crumbling like dry earth beneath scaled talons and sharp claws. The thing snarled, fangs bared, black eyes flashing as it exhaled. Like pressurized gas, acrid air streamed through the hole in the wall. The blast picked Mac up and threw him through the one-way mirror.

As glass shattered and her partner disappeared, Angela palmed her Glock. With a battle cry, she pulled the trigger, emptied the entire clip into the monster clawing its way through the precinct wall.

Chapter Thirty-four

Heavy footfalls bounced off metal, echoing down endless corridors created by Port of Seattle authorities. Stacked like Legos beneath the open sky, shipping containers read like a maze, the twists and turns hemming her in until Myst didn't know which way was forward or back. The nasty trifecta herding her between the boxes' high walls added to the effect: suffocating her, closing the cage, marching both her and Angela toward a man-dragon neither of them wanted to meet.

Ivar.

The leader of the Razorbacks was in the shipping yard somewhere. Waiting.

Suppressing a shiver, Myst twisted her hands, fighting to loosen the zip-tie cuffs around her wrists. Made of thick plastic, the edges dug in, rubbing raw patches on her skin. She didn't care. Time was running out. The dark-eyed SOB leading them into the heart of the shipping yard wasn't slowing down, and with a pace that quick? It wouldn't be long before she came to face-to-face with the head psycho.

Angela bumped her from behind. Losing her balance, she stumbled forward and tossed the cop her best what-the-hell glare. The detective kept coming, nudging her with her shoulder, pretending to lose her footing, and understanding struck. An act. Angela was acting her ass off, trying to stay close. With her arms crossed in front of her chest, she went along and tripped again, praying Angela had a plan.

The cop was smart…had lots of training. Maybe she'd figure out how to get them both the heck away from the bastards holding them prisoner.

The detective listed sideways and, bumping her again, whispered, "Get ready to run."

Crap. That was her *plan*?

Under normal circumstances, it would've been a good one. Excellent, even. The only problem? Myst didn't know which way to go. They'd taken so many turns she was hopelessly lost. The next kink in the plan didn't make her feel any better, either. The guys surrounding them were fast, able to shift into dragon form in a heartbeat. No way they'd be able to outrun them.

But, God…what other choice did they have? Meeting Ivar wasn't an option she wanted to entertain. Not after all Bastian had told her about the bastard.

Swallowing, Myst forced moisture into her mouth, trying to forget what her captors were capable of, but the last half hour played like a bad movie in her head. The interrogation room, the explosion, and smoke. The screaming and gunfire. Sharp claws ripping through the police station wall. The tug and pull of being dragged backward through the hole by her legs. Angela being hauled out on her belly, too. The terrifying flight over the city and…the rough treatment when they landed.

Angela stumbled into her again.

"Which way?" she asked, glancing at the lead asshole to make sure he wasn't listening.

"Next alleyway between containers…you go left." Her eyes sharp, Angela scanned the narrow corridor. Stacked three high, the containers blocked any chance of escape. And with the Razorbacks in front and behind them? Yeah, the whole situation looked like a Hail Mary pass on an impossible playing field. "I'll go right."

She shook her head. "We stick together."

"We'll have a better chance if we split up. One of us might get out."

"But—"

"Find Mac." Angela whispered, glancing at the pair of Razorbacks trailing them. "Get to my partner, he'll—"

A growl sounded behind them. "Making plans, females?"

"Myst's feeling sick." Quick on her feet, Angela shrugged, playing the lie like a pro. "Just trying to calm her down."

Asshole number one snorted. "Weak female. Don't know why Ivar wants her."

"She's high-energy, Denzeil," the lead asshole said, glancing over his shoulder. The chill in his gaze touched her, freezing her with fear before it slid over Angela. "They both are...good breeders."

"So what, Lothair..." The third Razorback paused, a thoughtful look on his face. "They're lab rats?"

"With fringe benefits."

Denzeil's nostrils flared. "Who gets the redhead?"

"Me." The corners of Lothair's lips lifted as he stared at Angela. "Can't wait, either. Maybe I'll fuck you before Bastian and his band of bastards show up. Got time before he tracks the signal and comes for his female."

Bait. Myst's stomach rolled. She was bait, and like chum thrown into shark-infested waters, Ivar would use her to lure Bastian into a trap. And regardless of the danger, he would come. Try to pull her out instead of letting her go...like he should, like she deserved. She'd abandoned him and yet...

God forgive her.

He would come, tear the shipping yard apart to reach her. She knew it like her own heartbeat and, as each thump slammed into her chest, two thoughts tore her apart, shredding her down the middle.

The first sounded like hope, a plea and prayer for rescue. The second hit with a one-two punch, equal parts guilt and dread. Her decision to run instead of talk to Bastian about a reality she didn't understand might get the man she loved killed. And for a split second, she wanted to wish the love away, because without it Bastian wouldn't feel compelled to come after her...would've remained safe, far away from Razorback claws.

The consequences of her action sliced deep. Pain spilled out, filling her so full she snarled at Lothair, a "Screw you" poised on the tip of her tongue. Angela kicked the side of Myst's foot and shook her head, the message clear. *Don't react. The more you do, the more ammunition you give them to hurt you.*

With a small nod, Myst acknowledged the wisdom, but it almost killed her. She wanted to launch herself at Lothair's back and snap his neck. Yeah, it went against everything she knew about herself and her nature but...she could do it. Her knowledge of the human body gave her an edge. All those nice, neat vertebrae were easy to crack if you knew what to do.

The alleyway between containers came into view.

She heard Angela draw in a deep breath and then blow it out, preparing for escape. Myst did the same, filled her lungs and let it go, enriching her muscles with oxygen. The second she started to run, she couldn't stop. Couldn't look behind her. Or slow down.

His footfalls echoing, Lothair continued straight down the corridor.

And Myst got ready.

The instant they reached the gap between containers, they bolted in opposite directions: Angela right, Myst left. The Razorbacks behind them shouted, raising the alarm. Adrenaline screaming through her veins, Myst's feet flew. The thud of heavy boots sounded behind her. Hot breath washed over the back of her neck, and she dodged, zigzagging to avoid capture. A huge hand flashed in her peripheral vision. She changed direction, skidding around a corner into a narrow alleyway.

"Shit," a voice said, full of pissed off behind her.

The skitter of sliding feet sounded as he put on the brakes. Myst huffed in triumph as the Razorback collided with the container. Another curse joined a clang, banging around between the steel boxes, echoing into the night.

Without looking back, she sprinted toward the end of the ally and freedom: each footfall hammering against asphalt, her chest heaving so hard she couldn't hear anything but her own ragged breath. She chanced a look over her shoulder. Rubbing the curve of his shoulder, Denzeil stood between the steel walls—thighs spread, boots planted—blocking the end of the alleyway, but...

He wasn't moving. Was just standing there, eyes shimmering in the gloom, an awful smile on his face.

Terror flooded her, washing through her veins. Oh, God...no. Mind-speak. The psycho was communicating with someone. She could see the spike in energy. As his red aura flared, she came even with the end of the container and—

A huge hand shot from around the corner.

Sucking in a sharp breath, Myst skittered sideways and ducked low. She heard a growl. Felt the grab and pull as he fisted his hand in the back of her shirt. With a flick of his wrist, he tossed her into a dead-end alleyway. She twisted as she stumbled, trying to get her feet beneath her. She must find a way around him, but as he approached, a massive shadow against the rising moon, Myst knew she didn't stand much of a chance.

Making twin fists, she brought her bound hands up. "Stay away!"

"No chance of that, female." Dark red hair pulled away from his face, black wraparounds concealing his eyes, his mouth curved at the corners. "But I like your style."

"You won't like it when I snap your neck."

"A fighter." He grinned, flashing his straight white teeth. Flexing his fists, he came within striking distance, daring her to hit him. "I like that, too. It'll make taming you far more interesting, don't you think?"

As far as taunts went, that was a good one. Especially since the bastard accompanied the words with movement. Step by step, he moved in for the kill, crowding her, pushing her back into a corner she held no hope of fighting her way out of. "It won't happen. I am Bastian's."

"I know," he said, an undercurrent of excitement in his tone. His nostril flared, and Myst realized she had said *exactly* the wrong thing. "But possession is nine-tenths of the law, and I have you now. Do you think he will want you back when I am through with you? After I have ridden you hard…taken everything a female can give a male?"

Balanced on the balls of her feet, Myst kept pace with him, pivoting, keeping him in sight as he circled her, looking for an opening. The soft tissue of the nose. Raking his eyes with her fingernails. Booting him in the balls. All viable options. The last one, though, was her favorite. "I'll never give you the satisfaction...Ivar."

"You already have." He walked around her again, staying just outside her strike zone. "Owning you, fucking you, feeding from you...seeing you locked in cellblock A with my daughter growing in your womb? That's all the satisfaction I need."

Daughter? Myst frowned. What the hell was he talking about?

Keeping her guard high, she stared at him from between her fists, mind working overtime. Dragonkind didn't produce girls so...

The answer hit her like a sledgehammer.

Ivar was a scientist and, like her mother had always done, dealt more in results than reality. *All things are achievable through scientific experimentation.* How many times had she heard that growing up? She'd lived the obsession—knew exactly what had driven her mom—and saw the same commitment in the man backing her into a corner.

She met his gaze through the dark lenses hiding his eyes. "You're manipulating chromosomal DNA."

"Smart female," he murmured, a sick sort of approval in his expression.

"It won't work. You're chasing—"

He struck so fast she didn't see him move. Grabbing her by the nape, he buried his fingers in her hair. Fear lit her up, making her vicious. With a twist, she slammed her bound fists into him. She connected: once, twice. The third time he cursed as his sunglasses went flying. The Oakleys clanged against the shipping container. Myst screamed and struck again. His eyes flared, shimmering with violence, illuminating the darkness with a pink glow.

"You son of a bitch."

Lashing out again, she thrust her knee up, aiming for his groin. He shifted and, without mercy, cranked her head back, raising her onto her toes. With a curse, she held the tears back, refusing to show weakness or acknowledge the pain, and kicked him again. He took the hit on the thigh and shoved her against the container wall.

Cold steel bit into her spine and reality hit hard. She couldn't win. He was too strong. "Get off me...get off me!"

"Lesson one...don't tell me what to do," he said, aligning their bodies, pressing in until he pinned her. Unable to move, she turned her head away, gagging as he dipped his head. The warm rush of his breath touched a second before his mouth brushed her cheekbone. "Lesson two? Give me what I want, and you'll live."

"I'm not giving you a thing."

His lips curved against her skin. "Hmm...female. You smell so good. Bet you taste even better. Give me a sip, sweetheart...a little taste of all that energy."

Her stomach rolled. She swallowed, fighting to keep the bile down. "Go to hell."

Ivar snarled, the sound hissing next to her ear. Fear ripped through her, gathered speed, twisting her energy into the force of a hurricane. For once, she let it go, embraced the wildness she'd always felt, rode the whipping wind inside her, settling into the eye of the storm. From its center, she controlled the tempest, defining the boundaries as Ivar cranked her head back and dipped his head.

Feeding Bastian had taught her well. She knew what the connection felt like, and how he opened it. Now, all she wanted was to shut it down. Her energy belonged to the man she loved and no other. No way would she allow Ivar to take what didn't belong to him.

Ivar pressed his open mouth to her throat. He sucked hard, drawing on her skin, searching for the conduit to reach what he wanted. Myst tightened her grip on the energy stream as it surged behind her mental barricade. A pause. A momentary shift inside her, and the Meridian retreated, respecting her right to rule it.

"What the fuck?" Ivar jerked then retreated, shock in his pink eyes.

"The energy is mine." Meeting his gaze head-on, she watched surprise turn to fury as she threw his words back at him. "And possession is nine-tenths of the law, asshole."

Baring his teeth, he shifted his grip. His hand tightened around her throat, cutting off her air supply. As she wheezed, struggling against the choke hold, he growled, "You'll give me what I want, female. I'll beat you to fucking death to get it."

The threat should've scared her, but it didn't. No matter how rough he got, she wouldn't give in. Bastian was coming. She could feel him now. The vague impression of him was hazy—faraway, but closing fast. It gave her strength. Enough to fight as Ivar dragged her toward an open shipping container at the end of the aisle. And as the metal doors clanged behind her, she opened her senses and sent out a call meant solely for Bastian, praying he reached her in time.

———

Leading the Nightfury warriors, Bastian came through the clouds. Condensation wicking from his wing tips, he leveled out over southern Seattle, city lights nothing but pinpricks below him. Flying fast, he sent his signal out in a wide sweep. Each ping looped back, directing him as scent, sound, and sonar fed him information.

The police station had been a bust. Thirty seconds circling the scene told him everything he needed to know. The precinct wall had a hole blown in the side of it, and the cops didn't have a clue.

But he did.

Ivar. The rogue prick.

Bastian growled, baring his fangs in the cold night air. The male had taken Myst. Now she was in the hands of a psychopath without an off switch.

Inhaling deep, Bastian exhaled long and slow. He needed to keep it together. Losing his mind wouldn't help his female, but if Ivar touched one hair on her precious head...if that asshole...

Fuck no. He couldn't go there. Fear was useful only when turned to a purpose, and so he shaped it, honing it into a lethal weapon to use against the enemy.

No mercy. There would be no mercy tonight.

Dropping down low, he skimmed skyscrapers, mining the electrostatic bands to find Myst. Her energy was like a radio wave, a magical bandwidth with a unique signature that he could lock onto and—

His head snapped to the right. South. He needed to fly further south. She was down near the waterfront, among ocean freighters and concrete piers. Bastian banked hard and snarled in triumph. He could smell her now. Feel Myst as she sent out her energy to link with his own. He murmured in his mind, praising her through their connection, hoping she could hear him. Feel him. And know he was coming for her.

"Got her," he said, mind-speaking to the five flying behind him in V formation.

Rikar answered, *"You locked on?"*

"Port of Seattle...the shipping containers."

"Interesting place for an ambush." Rolling through the cloud cover, Venom's green scales flashed as he took up the wingman spot on Bastian's right.

Wick came up on his left. *"How many?"*

"A fuck load." Bastian's eyes narrowed. *"I sense seventeen."*

"The Scot?" Per usual, Rikar took the shadow position, moving up and over to fly above Bastian's spine.

"I don't feel him among them," he said as Sloan completed the fighting pyramid and flew in beneath him. Surrounded on all sides by his warriors, Bastian dipped low, increasing his speed as the shipyard came into view. Spread out over a square mile, the Port of Seattle was a huge enterprise: a tangled web of shipping containers, cranes, concrete docks, and cargo ships. He zeroed in on the most remote section. *"Wick...you ready?"*

Gold and black scales glinting in the moonlight, his warrior patted the electro-magnetic gun strapped to his forepaw. *"If the fucker sticks his head out, I'll nail him."*

"Christ...a full sentence, Wick. What the fuck?" Rikar grinned, showing fang as the others laughed.

"Fuck off," Wick said, getting back on his usual roll...two syllables.

Bastian ignored the byplay, too focused on Myst to join in their pre-fight ritual. Shooting the shit before battle settled his warriors, moving them into battle-zone mentality. But with his female in the mix, he didn't want calm. He wanted rage, and as she reached out for him, he locked on, following the road map she drew him. His chest went tight. X marks the spot. Yeah...right there. He could practically see her. Less than a mile away, she was hidden in a shipping container at the back of the lot.

"Show time, boys." Dialed in, he fixated on his female, reading her energy. It was still strong, her life force undiminished by the fear he sensed in her. As relief rushed through him, the lethal side of him took hold, pushing him into brutality. *"Go in hot. Take all the motherfuckers out. Understood?"*

"Fucking A," his warriors growled as a unit.

Following Bastian's lead, they came in over the water, flying over a freighter and in between industrial cranes. A rumble sounded as Razorbacks—hidden behind steel and concrete—took flight, launching into a blitz attack, filling the moonlight sky with flashes of colorful scales.

Flipping up and over, Venom broke ranks and rotated into a spiral. He inhaled deep and exhaled smooth. With a hiss, poisonous gas rolled out in front of him, a combo of neuro-toxins and vaporized fuel. Bastian rolled hard, getting the hell out of the way. As he changed course, the toxic cloud blanketed the sky, stalling Razorbacks in mid-flight, stealing the air from their lungs an instant before Wick breathed out. Blue-white flame streamed from his throat as Wick lit the fuse on Venom's special brand of poison and...

Kaboom!

Steel groaned as the blast went nuclear, rolling out in a toxic wave. Shipping containers flew like cardboard boxes, flipping end over end. Blown out of the sky, three Razorbacks fell, ashing out as the others scattered. Bastian jacked up the invisibility cloak, wrapping the shipyard up tight. The only human he wanted to see tonight was Myst and, well... now, that she carried his child she wasn't 100 percent human anymore. And as he engaged a Razorback, slicing through scale and bone to snap the rogue's neck, he couldn't help thinking, "Fantastic, just one more thing to fuck me up."

Myst wasn't going to like it when he told her that.

———

Trapped inside the shipping container, Myst scrambled as Ivar came at her like a heavyweight boxing champion. She veered right. He countered and, swinging his arm, backhanded her. The strike sent her sideways, snapping her head back, and as her cheek throbbed, her blood flowed, filling her mouth before sliding down her throat. She gagged, but didn't buckle. No way would she bend. The bastard could hammer her into unconsciousness, but she wouldn't give him a single drop...not one ounce of the energy surging inside her.

Ivar raised his hand again. This time she saw the whites of his knuckles and a closed fist, not an open palm. He was running out of patience, and she, out of time.

Stay strong. Stay strong.

The blow hammered her in the ribcage. She listed sideways and fell, hitting the steel floor with a thud. Pink eyes glowing with a fierceness that terrified her, Ivar reached down, fisted his hand in her hair and hauled her to her feet.

"Give me what I want."

Even knowing she fought a losing battle, she struggled anyway, refusing to let him win; to be a victim and go down without a fight. "No."

"Fucking female," he said, breathing hard, ripping at her hair with his grip.

"Asshole male," she rasped as he pushed her face-first into the wall. "You like hurting those weaker than you, don't you? You get off on it. What happens, Ivar, when someone is as strong as you...do you run and hide? Yeah, that's your style, isn't it? It's why you won't take on Bastian. He'd kick your ass...and you know it."

With a growl, he shook her. Her head snapped back, and Myst reevaluated her strategy. Taunting him wasn't the best plan. But, God. What else could she do? She needed to buy time...enough for Bastian to reach her. Keeping Ivar pissed off and engaged with her meant that he wasn't out organizing his warriors. From what she knew, the Razorbacks required leadership in a fight. Without a strong leader pulling the strings, Ivar's warriors would fold, allowing the Nightfuries to breach their defenses. Once behind enemy lines, Bastian and the others would take the enemy out one by one.

At least, she hoped so. She didn't know how much more of Ivar she could take.

"No answer, Ivar? Are you so afraid of my mate that—"

"Shut the fuck up." Shoving her against the wall, he pressed his chest to her back, crushing her between himself and the steel wall. As she struggled, he kicked at her feet, spreading her legs to thrust his thigh between her own. The invasion pressed hard muscle against her core. Pressure banded around her ribcage, stealing her air as he growled, "Maybe I've been going at you the wrong way. Maybe I should just fuck you instead."

Oh, God...no. A beating she could endure, but rape? Would she be able to hold onto the energy...to hold it back and deny him as he assaulted her? Myst squeezed her eyes shut. *Stay strong. Stay strong.* She repeated the mantra over and over, biting down on a whimper as Ivar slid his hand beneath her shirt.

His palm settled flat on her bare belly. "Now, who's the one with no answer?"

Fighting his hold, she screamed, rage driving her. The battle cry echoed, and she pushed against the wall with her bound hands. "Screw you!"

"Absolutely...let's get to it."

Hot breath in her ear, he tugged at the string holding her scrub bottoms in place. She bucked, flailing against his immobilizing hold, rebelling against his touch. The knot slipped. The cotton covering her hips slid an inch. Unable to hold them back, tears flooded her eyes. But Myst refused to let a single one fall. She wouldn't give Ivar the satisfaction. He could go to hell. Bastian would send him there then—

Boom!

The explosion sounded a second before the blast wave hit. Metal groaned as the shipping container rocked, sending Ivar back a step. Thrown with him, Myst stumbled and then crumpled when Ivar dropped her. Hinges whined, the shriek of rusty steel reverberating in the enclosed space a moment before the door opened.

Lothair stuck his head inside. His dark eyes found Ivar. "Nightfuries...coming in fast."

"Good." His mouth curved up at the corners, he glanced at Myst. "He's taken the bait. Is the C-four set?"

"Yeah."

"Get that bastard in the pipe. Let's blow the horns off his fucking head." Ivar's pink irises flashed, and Myst went tense with dread. Without taking his gaze from her, he pulled another flex cuff from his back pocket. As he approached, she rolled in the other direction, trying to get up. Not that she had anywhere to run. Not with Lothair blocking the exit, and Ivar bearing down on her like a freight train.

Just as she made it to her feet, he grabbed her ankle and yanked. She cried out, hitting the floor hard. Kicking out with her free foot, she aimed for his head. He dodged, slipped the plastic cuff around her ankle, and then went after the other one. Within seconds, he caught her, immobilizing her feet like her hands.

"Be a good female and stay put." Patting the top of her head like a dog, he smiled, pushed to his feet, and headed for the door. As he joined Lothair, he glanced over his shoulder. "I'll be back to finish what I started later, sweetheart."

The double doors banged behind him. She heard a series of clicks and...

Oh, no. He'd locked her in, securing the door from the outside.

Curled on her side, a terrible chill sank deep, seeping into the place where hope lived, obliterating it with one sure stroke. Myst closed her eyes. Without that lock, she might've had a chance. Even with her hands and feet bound, she could've inchwormed her way to freedom. Gotten out the door and into the alley between containers. Now? She was screwed...stuck waiting for a rescue that might never come.

"Bastian," she whispered, finding solace in the sound of his name. "I'm here. Right here. Find me."

Before Ivar comes back.

She didn't voice the words. Couldn't bring herself to say Ivar's name. Not out loud. It seemed a kind of sacrilege, a way to give power to the enemy, and crazy or not, she refused to perpetrate the betrayal. From now on, he would be known as "the asshole" in her heart and mind.

Fighting to stay calm, Myst rocked against the steel floor. The back and forth motion helped clear the fear-induced fog. Little by little, her mind sharpened, allowing her to play out different scenarios. The game of "what if" made her feel more prepared, gave her answers to implausible questions. "If he does that, I'll do this."

Another explosion, closer this time, made the container sway. As it shifted and groaned, vibration rumbled beneath her, rattling her bones. Pain followed, reminding her of the beating. The bruises, she could handle. The fear of Ivar coming back? Not so much.

Against her will, her teeth started to chatter. Sensation flickered, ghosting down her spine. Bastian. God, he was close. So very close.

Rolling onto her back, she stared at the corrugated roof and screamed his name over and over, choking on the tears she couldn't hold back any longer. Each shout came out on a sob and, twisting her wrists, she struggled to break the plastic cuffs. All she needed was a little leeway. If she could get one hand out. If she could just…

"Come on. Come on." Stupid flex cuffs. The things worked better than ropes and chains. The plastic didn't give at all. "Goddamn it."

She tried her legs, flexing her feet to get her shoes off. Maybe without the Reeboks she could—

An unearthly shriek sounded overhead. Myst froze and looked up at the ceiling, afraid the asshole was coming back for her. She flinched as a clang rippled through the air. A low growl came next, then the sound of claws raking steel. Myst worked faster, rocking like a mental patient as she fought imprisonment and her terror.

Something sprayed the back wall of the container. Breathing hard, she pushed onto her knees, praying that whoever had set up camp on the other side of the wall was on her side. She heard the sizzle first...then saw the fire. A thin line flared, cutting through the steel like a welding torch, drawing an arch near the container top before flowing to the floor.

A doorway.

Shivering in the cold, she waited—fearing the worst, hoping for the best—as fire ate through the steel. With a scraping sound, the cut panel fell forward, banging as it hit the floor. Smoke billowed in. The acrid smell coated the back of her throat before the cloud cleared, giving her a clear view outside. Something moved and she caught a glimpse of purple.

"Bastian?" she whispered, her voice sounding as uncertain as she felt.

A huge man appeared in the doorway.

Myst's heart rate went into triple overtime. Not Bastian.

Obscured by shadow, the guy stood unmoving for a moment, then dipped his head and stepped into the container. She shuffled backwards, her focus fixed on his face... and the glowing amethyst eyes trained on her.

Oh, God. He wasn't a Nightfury.

"Myst Munroe," he said, his deep voice rolling on a thick Scottish accent.

Lovely under normal circumstances, but right now? She didn't like the sound of it. Or the fact he stared at her from beneath his black brows. It wasn't a good sign, and as he walked toward her, casting long shadows on the steel walls, Myst wanted to scream. She swallowed instead, trying not to shiver, keeping her gaze on his face. No way she was looking lower. The guy didn't have a stitch on. Even his feet were bare.

His eyes narrowed. "You're the nurse."

Her bottom lip trembling, she nodded. "W-who are you?"

"Forge." He stopped a foot away and sank to his haunches, bringing himself to her level. "You knew my Caroline."

Her mouth opened then closed. She shook her head, searched his expression, trying to guess his game. The amethyst stare that met hers was steady: no guile or subterfuge. She saw the pain in him, heard it in his voice as he'd said Caroline's name. His honesty prompted hers. She went with it, instinct warning that lying to him was a dangerous game.

"Caroline was my friend. I was there when she died." Unable to hold them back, tears filled her eyes. "I tried so hard to save her, but she was...I couldn't...I'm so sorry."

He studied her, his face an expressionless mask. "Bastian didn't kill her, did he?"

"No." The pressure banding her chest tightened another notch. "I called for help. Bastian got wind of the nine-one-one call and came, but...it was too late."

Reaching out, Forge grabbed her wrists. She gasped, the startled sound coming out as she jumped and pulled away. He tugged her back and, running his thumb over the zip tie, melted the plastic. As it fell away without burning her skin, he drew the cuff off her wrists and tossed it over his shoulder.

She murmured a thank you and, flexing her hands, worked the blood back into her fingertips.

He shrugged off the gratitude and gestured with his hand. "Give me your feet. You're coming with me."

"Promise not to hurt me?" Shifting onto her bottom, she presented him with her ankles.

"You have two choices, female." After freeing her feet, he paused, his hand hovering above her legs. "Take me to my son—"

"Gregor." Her eyes narrowed on him, his interest in Caroline making sense. And as the puzzle pieces slid into place, Myst finally understood the reason her friend stopped answering her calls and making appointments. Her patient had known about Dragonkind through Forge and had been trying to protect the father of her child.

"—or stay here and face Ivar." When she hesitated, he said, "Better me than the Razorback breeding center, Myst."

Man, that didn't sound good. No way she wanted anywhere near a "breeding center." And sticking around for Ivar? Forget it. She'd take her chances with Forge and hope like hell he looked the other way long enough for her to escape.

"I'll go with you."

He nodded and reached out. His big hands settled on her upper arms, and she tensed, curled her hands into fists, prepared to defend herself. But he didn't make a wrong move, just lifted and set her on her feet. Pain screamed up her legs, taking her knees out. As the numbing pins and needles spread, she moaned and crumpled sideways.

Forge caught her.

Without effort, he swung her into his arms and headed for the door he'd burned into steel. "Keep your head down. It's nasty out there."

Cradled in his arms, Myst frowned. He wasn't like Ivar or his scary first in command. Forge didn't have a cruel streak. Nor was he indifferent. He was...something else.

Not a Nightfury, exactly, but his vibe read as protective...
like Bastian's.

She glanced up at his face as he carried her out of the
container. "Are you sure you're a Razorback?"

His amethyst eyes shimmering in the dark, he stared
down at her. Time slid sideways, and one moment ticked
into the next before he looked away, refusing to answer. His
silence deepened the mystery, and Myst started to wonder.
Was he a good guy? A bad one? Somewhere in between?

She didn't know. And now was not the time to solve the
puzzle.

Forge was ramping up and, as his pace went from quick
to mach four in five seconds flat, all she could do was hold
on. And pray. There were dragons overhead. She caught
a glimpse of a wing over Forge's shoulder. Heard a roar.
Smelled the brimstone as a fireball streaked across the night
sky and hoped like hell Bastian sensed she was on the move.

Chapter Thirty-five

Cold air rushed over Bastian's scales as warm dragon blood flowed between his talons. With a twist, he retracted his claws and dropped the Razorback like a bad habit. The rogue plummeted toward the ground, his body disintegrating in midair. Twisting into a spiral, ash blew into Bastian's face, anointing him with the remnants of the dead as he attacked another.

So close. He was so close now.

He could smell the alluring scent of his female's skin. Her energy lit him up, and he zeroed in, all his focus on a single shipping container. Orange with the number six-seven-one on its side, it stood in the third row from the right.

Dead. Ahead.

Myst was barely one hundred yards below him.

On a flyby, he slashed a yellow dragon with his razor-sharp tail. He ignored the shriek and tangled with a second Razorback. The kill took seconds. A quick twist, a hard snap, and the enemy folded: broken bone knifing through scales, spine split wide open, the metallic scent of blood perfuming the air. Taking out another rogue, Bastian scanned the aerial firefight for his warriors.

All good. He spotted them, each one kicking ass without taking names.

Wings spread wide, he sliced around a mega-crane, coming in from the back end. If he could get low enough, he'd slip through the enemy front. From there, he'd have a straight shot at Myst.

He snapped another enemy neck, the kill efficient, his technique brutal. Without watching the decapitated Razorback fall, he pinged his warriors, giving them a heads-up. *"I'm going in."*

"Make it fast," Rikar said, breathing hard.

Venom chimed in, *"Thick as fucking flies out here. Grab her and get out."*

Dipping low, he gave the f-bomb a workout. Retreat wasn't in his playbook. He added another page, ignoring the hit to his pride. *"Rikar, cover me."*

"Roger that." The crackling of ice came through mind-speak as Rikar unleashed his frosty side on the enemy. *"Coming in on your right flank."*

Registering his first in command's presence, Bastian rotated, spinning up and over. He needed the most direct route…a fast in and out. The snatch and grab would secure his female and protect his back, allowing him to get them both out in one piece. He lined up his approach and—

Bastian's scales prickled, picking up a powerful vibe. *"Shit…Wick!"*

His warrior growled in answer.

"Deep Purple's here," he snarled, tracking him…realizing the male was too close to Myst.

"On it."

Fury replaced the blood in Bastian's veins. He flew fast, tracking low over rows of shipping containers. The bastard had his female and was moving fast. He scanned each alleyway, his night vision picking up trace energy. Seconds ticked past, cranking him tighter, making his scales feel too small for his skin. He needed to find them before Deep Purple left the—

Bingo.

Jesus, the male was in human form, running with Myst in his arms. Not wasting a moment, Bastian dove, coming in fast and furious, claws wide open. The rogue glanced over his shoulder. With a curse, he dropped Myst and shifted. Dark purple scales flashed in the low light. Baring his fangs, the Razorback curled his talons around the top of the container. Bastian let him climb, wanting a clear shot without jeopardizing his female.

One, Mississippi. Two, Mississippi. Three, Mississippi...four.

Bastian exhaled, drawing deep from his core.

The electro-pulse shot from his throat, hammering the male in the chest. Deep Purple cartwheeled, smashing into a crane beside the loading dock. Metal groaned as the structure snapped, raining steel down on the Razorback's head. Locked and loaded, Wick banked hard overhead. The rogue flailed, spiked tail arching as he struggled to get up. His warrior pulled the trigger. The three-pronged Taser nailed the enemy dragon in the side, pumping him full of electricity.

As Deep Purple went spastic, Bastian arched his wings and set down fast. He slid sideways, claws tearing holes in the steel container top, and shouted, "Myst!"

Sitting on the ground, she looked up at him. He saw the relief in her gaze—felt it fill his own chest—a second before her focus shifted over his shoulder. "Bastian...watch out!"

Her scream made him twist sideways. As he flipped, sharp claws raked his side. Blood welled along his ribcage, and he caught a flash of red scales. The spikes on the enemy tail missed him by an inch, and upside down—still halfway through his spin—Bastian lashed out. His paw connected with a crunch. The rogue pinwheeled, spinning like a top, and he got a good look at his attacker.

Ivar. The pink-eyed SOB had come out to play.

Primal need and brutal aggression ripped through Bastian. He'd waited for this moment forever. Had dreamed of coming face-to-face with Ivar. Wanted to rip him apart. Make him bleed. Watch him suffer. But an equal and opposite compulsion vied for airtime, turning him away from his thirst for vengeance. His female was on the ground, vulnerable and alone. Yeah, he craved Ivar's blood, but the need to protect his female was stronger.

Myst came first. No matter what.

But he couldn't get to her now. Not with Ivar catching air and his XO attacking his flank from the north. The best he could do was hold the line, keep himself between the rogue dragons and her. Yeah, that and call for backup.

"Rikar!" Baring his fangs, he launched himself at Ivar. *"I need you."*

"Thirty seconds."

"Make it fifteen."

Ten would be better, but his best friend was busy. He caught the sight line out of the corner of his eye. Frosty side deployed, ice shards were flying and Razorbacks dropping like flies.

With a quick turn, he sideswiped his nemesis. The prick roared, and Bastian smiled, baring his teeth in satisfaction. Ivar came at him again. He countered, unwrapping an uppercut beneath the asshole's chin. As the red SOB's head snapped back, Lothair snarled and attacked, making a grab for the horns on Bastian's head. He jerked out of the strike zone, keeping his skull intact, awareness shimmering through him. What the hell was Ivar's XO doing? Usually a dragon attacked head-on, never going for a glancing blow.

And Lothair's flyby? Yeah, there was all kinds of wrong with that attempt.

Whipping his tail, he kept Ivar at bay and searched the sky for the black scales. Lothair had dipped low, but...

There he was, rising fast with a harness in his claws. And snarled in the loops? Bricks of plastic explosives. Jesus. The rogues didn't know how to fight fair. They were trying to blow his head off. Bastian's eye narrowed. Fat chance of that. No way would he allow the rogue to get that close.

"Heads up, boys...C-four," he said, sending the info out through mind-speak.

Wick answered, *"Where?"*

"In Lothair's paw."

"Asshole." Coming around the crane boom, Rikar zeroed in on the black SOB.

With the cavalry in sight, Bastian rolled right, giving his friend a clear shot. As he disengaged, Rikar growled, sending ice crystals out in a foggy wave. Visibility went from good to rat-shit awful. Using the frigid cloud cover, Bastian pulled into a tight turn. He had one shot. Just one chance to hammer Ivar. The male would adjust quickly, and when he did? His plan to grab Myst would go from difficult to FUBARed in a heartbeat.

Lost in the icy swirl, Ivar roared for his XO. Bastian showed no quarter, coming in hard, striking with precision. The red fucker pinwheeled, spinning into the cold mist. And Bastian made his break.

Without slowing, he flew over the shipping containers. "Myst!"

"Here...Bastian, I'm right here!"

His heart shuddered as he spotted her thirty yards ahead. She was on her feet—thank God—and running down the alleyway toward him. He landed hard, pushed the containers out, widening the corridor. All sound ceased and time slowed as he reached for her. Seconds felt like hours, stretching out, and Bastian started to pray. He sensed Ivar closing in behind him...knew he was vulnerable on the ground, but he couldn't leave her.

Not now. Not ever.

The world returned to him, speeding into reality the instant his front paw curled around her. Ignoring her gasp, he hoisted her onto his back. She slid home, straddling his shoulders.

"Hang on, *bellmia*." Leaping into the sky, he mind-spoke to the others, *"Got her. Get out."*

A roar came from behind him.

Rikar cursed. *"B...hard right."*

Without hesitation, he shifted into the tight turn. Scrambling to hold on, Myst clutched at his horns as the Razorback leader circled behind him. With a hiss, Ivar exhaled. Poisonous gas and toxic fumes ignited, shooting pink flames from between Ivar's fangs. Bastian tunneled into a spiral. Myst screamed, losing her grip, plummeting toward the ground.

"Bastian!" Eyes wide with fear, in a freefall, she reached for him.

Wings stretched to capacity, he dove, straining hard to grab her. He caught her on the upswing, cutting her scream short, plucking her out of thin air. Ivar roared. Pink flame streaked past his wing tip, singing his scales as Rikar swooped in. He came in like an avenging angel. White wings spread, he hung motionless a moment, poised above the spikes on Bastian's back and unleashed hell.

The temperature dropped into single digits. A whistling sound hit the airwaves as eight-inch ice daggers sliced through the gloom. Cradling his female close, Bastian ducked and flew under his best friend's tail. No way he wanted to get in the way of Rikar and his arsenal.

Ivar sucked wind, tried to compensate, drawing up short to avoid the icy knives. But it was too late. The deadly shards struck, thrusting through his red scales. As the Razorback leader shrieked and lost altitude, Lothair rose.

Wings spread, black scales gleaming, he launched himself from a twisted heap of steel, attacking from below. Little more than a green streak, Venom grabbed the SOB by the tail and, making like an Olympic shot-putter, spun. The C4 went flying, landing in the harbor with a splash. One. Two. Three rotations later, Venom let go, tossing the enemy male headfirst into an ocean freighter.

The metal-to-skull collision clanged, echoing off the water as Sloan flew in, a squadron of Razorbacks on his tail.

"Go. Go. Go," Bastian shouted, signaling their retreat.

Another night. The Razorbacks would be there to annihilate tomorrow night. The rogues always were, but he only had one female. And as he cradled her—leaving twisted steel and the enemy behind, flying faster than he ever had before—Bastian didn't give a damn about vengeance or Dragonkind.

All he cared about was Myst. To hell with his pride.

The wind pulled at Myst's hair, blowing the tangled mess around her head. It seemed strange, but she wasn't cold. Bastian was all around her: beneath her in flight, cocooning her from the autumn chill with his magic.

Thank God.

She needed him more than she wanted to breathe, and as clouds rose in the dark sky, she pressed her cheek to his warm scales and struggled not to cry. But the fight was a downhill one. She couldn't forget. The scrapes and bruises reminded her. The awful scents and sounds stayed with her. And pink eyes flashed in her mind's eye.

Nightmares. She had a feeling she was in for some terrible ones.

Squeezing her eyes closed, she battled the shakes, clamping down on emotion, desperate to stay strong. But the internal cyclone hit her like a sidewinder, sent her over the edge, cracking her wide open. She choked on silent tears, the droplets rolling like twin streams down her cheeks.

How could she have been so stupid?

She'd fought Bastian every step of the way. Had run scared instead of standing strong. The "if onlys" were a litany she couldn't ignore. Or forgive herself for. Because of her, the Port of Seattle was a mess and Angela Keen was probably dead.

Another case of "if onlys" rolled through her head. Goddamn it. "B-Bastian?"

"What, *bellmia*?" As smooth as his glide, his voice surrounded her in a warm curl.

"Do you think Rikar will find her?"

He didn't say anything for a moment, and his silence told her all she needed to know. The chances that Angela had made it out of the shipyard were slim.

"Rikar's the best tracker we have, Myst." He banked in a slow tilt, changing his flight path. She caught a glimpse of forest below before he leveled out. "If she's out there, he'll find her."

His *if* didn't comfort her, and she nestled into him, needing to get as close as humanly possible. Strange, she knew. A week ago she hadn't known dragons existed. Now, she couldn't get enough of one. "I'm so sorry."

"Shh, *bellmia*." Crisscrossing the night sky, Bastian took them over the edge of the tree line. The landscape dropped off fast, falling over a cliff, moving from the skeletal outlines of evergreens into nothingness. She heard the rush of the river before she saw the midnight ribbon below them. "We're almost home."

The shaking got worse, launching her into full body tremors. "I didn't m-mean for anyone to g-get hurt."

"I know." His soft tone reached out in a soothing wave, stroking her, gifting her with understanding she didn't deserve. "Hold on tight, baby. We're headed into the waterfall."

Her throat closed up tight as Bastian flew around the river bend. It would've been easy to blame the quick shift in flight for the pressure banding her chest. But Myst was done lying to herself. She was to blame. All the denial, her fear and refusal to accept the truth about Bastian had created a ripple effect. And as much as she wanted to, she couldn't take any of it back.

Now she must own her part in this night's pain.

No matter how terrible the consequences.

Her mind kicked up all kinds of awful things, presenting worst-case scenarios. Maybe the Nightfuries would point the finger: hate her, blame her, reject her out of hand. A quick mind-scrub and a boot to the ass was all they'd need to toss her out of Black Diamond. But the worst thought—the one that made her truly afraid?

Maybe Bastian didn't want her anymore.

Cool mist landed on her bare arms. The wet brush was light, a barely there sensation that made her glance up. Rumbling with majesty, the waterfall came into view. Falling like a curtain, the cascade rippled blue and white in the moonlight. Without slowing, Bastian flew straight at it. She sucked in a breath and tucked her head, hanging on tight as he sliced through the living wall of water. The cold splash made her jerk, soaking her to the skin. Darkness descended, enclosing them in damp, musty air.

A glow appeared at the head of the tunnel.

Myst released the breath she'd been holding, welcoming the light as Bastian flew beneath the magical globes. The second he touched down on the LZ, he shifted, becoming the man she knew. Loved. Needed more than anyone in the world.

With a sob, she lunged at him. He caught her in his arms, settling on the stone floor, pulling her into his lap, wrapping her in his warmth. Unable to look at him, she burrowed into his body, breathed him in, soothing herself with his strength and familiar scent.

Murmuring, he gave her a gentle squeeze. "It's all right, Myst. I've got you."

His voice washed in like the tide. Deep and warm, it eroded the earth underpinning her emotional stability. With a crack, she split wide open, and pain hit her like a tidal wave. Needing a lifeline, she hugged him tighter. "Oh, my God. Oh, my God. I'm so sorry. It's my fault."

"Shh, love. It's not your fault." Stroking her spine, he cupped the nape of her neck. "You're safe now. Relax for me, Myst. Look at me. I need to make sure you're all right."

Unable to let go of him, she shook her head.

He kept caressing her, each pass gentler than the last. "Where are you hurt?"

"I'm okay."

"No...you're not. Look at me, *bellmia*," he said, coaxing her to raise her head.

Shivering hard, she obeyed, unlocking her arms from his shoulders. Free of her death grip, he palmed her waist and lifted, setting her astride him. His green eyes met hers, and she sobbed, raising her hand to cup his face. With a murmur, he turned his mouth to her skin and pressed a kiss to the center of her palm.

"Bastian...I'm—"

"Don't apologize." He frowned, brushing the wet strands away from her temple. A muscle jumped in his jaw, and he growled, "Jesus. The bastard. He hit you."

"I made him mad," she said. "He wanted my energy. I wouldn't give him any."

Surprise flared in Bastian's eyes.

"I figured out how to control the current...the Meridian...and block him."

"My beautiful female." His eyes crinkled at the corners, filling with so much warmth Myst wanted to cry. "Have I told you how extraordinary you are?"

"A time or two," she whispered, accepting his praise before leaning in. Her mouth brushed his, settling softly against his lips. "I'm sorry I ran away from you, Bastian. Dumbest thing I've ever done."

"I won't argue." His lips curved against hers before he withdrew and his expression went from teasing to serious. "I handled it badly, Myst. I didn't mean to scare you, but I... shit. I've never done this before."

"What?"

"Fallen in love."

And there it was...just what she needed to hear. Unable to hold them back, tears filled her eyes, then tipped over her bottom lashes, and rolled down her cheeks. As Bastian brushed each one away, she said, "God, I'm such an idiot. How could I not have known that I love you?"

His mouth parted, breath hitching on a quick intake of air. *"Bellmia..."*

"I do, you know." She held his gaze, making sure he saw the conviction in hers. "I love you so much it hurts."

"I don't want it to hurt."

"Too bad. It is what it is, but..." she trailed off letting her words hang in the silent vastness of the cavern. "If you ever lie to me again—"

"I won't."

"—or get me pregnant without my permission, the next time around...I'll skin you alive."

"Deal." His mouth curved, spreading into a slow, wide smile. Shifting her a little, he hooked his arm beneath her legs and, gathering her up, pushed to his feet. As he turned and walked toward the magical entrance, he dipped his head to kiss her softly. "No more secrets, *bellmia*. We're in this together."

"Together." Kissing him back, she pushed her fingers through his hair, playing with the softness at the nape of his neck.

Nipping her gently, he licked her bottom lip, gifting her with his taste one teasing flick at a time. "Every step of the way."

Yeah, that sounded good. Better than good. Fantastic.

And as he carried her over the threshold toward the lair's clinic, Myst knew she was bound for an adventure. The future lay stretched out in front of them, unproven ground, uncertain in every way but one. Love transformed the landscape, offering shelter from the harshness of the storm.

Home. Yeah, she had finally come home.

Excerpt from *Fury of Ice*

Chapter One

The globes swayed, bobbing like jellyfish against the cavern's ceiling as Rikar flew beneath them. White scales gleamed in the low light, throwing starbursts of iridescent color across stalagmites and uneven stone walls. He didn't notice the rainbow. Didn't hear his claws scrape granite or the water rolling off his wing tips go splat on the LZ's floor. His focus was absolute. Only one thing mattered.

He was going to kill the male. Open him up like a can of sardines. All while making him sing like a canary.

Lucky for him, he didn't have far to go.

The rogue was chained seven stories beneath Black Diamond, the home he shared with the other Nightfury dragons. Convenient? Not really. Nothing about tonight even approached it. The battle—the whole retrieve and retreat routine—had FUBAR written all over it. Yeah, a total catastrophe from beginning to end. The only good thing about it? Bastian had his female back...had pulled her from enemy claws in the nick of time.

He should be happy about that. Throwing high fives with his fellow warriors and yakking it up, telling war stories, reliving the action over Tequila shots and lime wedges. But that was a definite no-can-do. Not tonight. Not when another female was missing.

Right. *Missing.*

Wishful fucking thinking.

Rikar's stomach fisted up hard. The Razorbacks had taken her. He knew it like he was standing there, four paws planted on stone, horns on his head tingling, anguish pumping through his veins with every beat of his heart. Now she was in the hands of his enemy, at the mercy of Ivar, leader of the rogues, a psychopath without an off switch.

With a growl, he tucked his wings and stepped over the beat-to-shit Honda in the middle of the LZ, trying not to think about what the bastards were doing to her. But...God help him. He couldn't turn his brain off. Couldn't breathe without his imagination firing up, planting terrible images in his mind's eye.

Christ, he needed to get her back. Had to locate the Razorback lair and pull her free before...

Rikar swallowed the burn at the back of his throat. What a total mind fuck. The need. The obsession. The pain.

He'd only met the female once. One freaking time. Had spent a couple of hours getting his ass kicked by her in a friendly game of pool. Okay, so he was lying. He'd done a little more than that. But he refused to think about the feeding...or how good she had tasted. Rikar shook his head, and water flew as he tried to forget. His behavior. Her acceptance. The fact that his frosty side wanted more, another go-round with a female who drew pure power from the Meridian. From the energy source that fed Dragonkind.

Which made him...what? A sicko? A male without honor or conscience? Yeah, without a doubt. The female he didn't want to remember, but couldn't forget, was missing. Was probably in hell right now, suffering at the hands of a

Razorback, and what was he doing? Dreaming of her in ways he shouldn't be.

Angela Keen. She of the gorgeous energy and hazel eyes. God, he wanted her back. He wanted her safe. He wanted the clock to spin in the opposite direction and undo the last three hours. Maybe then, he could've prevented his enemies from taking her at all.

Angela.

Her name whispered through his mind: over and over, again and again. A shiver rolled through him, rattling the spikes along his spine as he pictured her face. With a violent swipe, he tried to erase it the way his buddy, Sloan, deleted info from computer hard drives. But memory was a tricky thing: hard to control, impossible to ignore. And as the bastard got busy planting images inside his head, he accepted the truth. He wished he'd stayed with her that night, taken all she offered, and given more in return.

Which was just plain wrong. In every way that mattered.

Wind rushed in from the tunnel mouth, kicking up dust and the smell of damp earth. A second later, green scales flashed in his periphery. Rikar shifted, moving from dragon to human form, and got the hell out of Venom's way as the big male set down. Poised on his back paws, his buddy wing-flapped, sending water flying and air rushing, making the light globes bump into their neighbors seventy-five feet above their heads.

Rikar conjured his clothes. Leather settled against his skin, feeling like home as he stomped one of his shitkickers and headed for the entrance into the lair. He glanced over his shoulder at his friend. "You coming?"

"Hell, yeah." Scales undulating over thick muscle, Venom indulged in another total body shake. Man, with e like that, the male looked more like a dog than a dragon. "No way I'm missing the show."

Show. Right. More like a beat down with death the end game.

Under normal circumstances, it would've bothered him that Venom knew what he was thinking. Not tonight. Rikar didn't give a shit. Transparency was the least of his problems. A female was involved. So, yeah. The Razorback would hurt until he gave up the goods. End of story.

Halfway across the cavern, he heard Venom shift and move in behind him. The sound of their footfalls became one, echoing together, two males moving in unison toward one purpose. Answers. Rikar wanted them. And like the upstanding male that he was, Venom would back him up.

Good thing, too. The next hour would get messy...in more ways than one.

About the Author

Image © Julie Daniluk

As the only girl on all-guys hockey teams from age six through her college years, Coreene Callahan knows a thing or two about tough guys and loves to write about them. Call it kismet. Call it payback after years of locker room talk and ice rink antics. But whatever you call it, the action better be heart stopping, the magic electric, and the story wicked good fun.

After graduating with honors in psychology and working as an interior designer, Callahan finally succumbed to her overactive imagination and returned to her first love: writing. And when she's not writing, she is dreaming of magical worlds full of dragon-shifters, elite assassins, and romance that's too hot to handle. Callahan currently lives in Canada with her family and her writing buddy, a fun-loving golden retriever.